THE SLAVE

Andrew Sanger is a freelance travel journalist who has lived
and worked in several countries. He has contributed to a wide
range of British national newspapers and magazines, and for
ten years edited French Railways' travel magazine. He is the
author of more than thirty popular guidebooks, mainly to
France, Ireland, the Canary Islands and Israel. In recent years
Andrew Sanger has lived in north-west London, the setting
both for his first novel, *The J-Word* (2009) and for *The Slave,*
his second novel. For more about Andrew Sanger, see his
website, www.andrewsanger.com.

The Slave

Andrew Sanger

FOCUS BOOKS
London, England
www.focus-books.co.uk

© Andrew Sanger 2013
ISBN: 978-09558201-1-3
Published by Focus Books
Paperback edition 2013

•

For Geraldine Dunham
Thank you, Gerry.

•

Acknowledgments

For information, thank you to
Paul Jessop, Mary Novakovich, Tania Rizov, Alex Scutelnic,
and others who asked not to be named.

For help with editing and translation, thank you to
Michèle Faram, Joshua Sanger and Andrei Yusfin.

•

And he that stealeth a man, and selleth him,
or if he be found in his hand,
he shall surely be put to death.

Exodus XXI, 16

•

You have among you many a purchased slave,
Which, like your asses and your dogs and mules,
You use in abject and in slavish parts,
Because you bought them: shall I say to you,
Let them be free, marry them to your heirs?
Why sweat they under burthens? let their beds
Be made as soft as yours and let their palates
Be season'd with such viands? You will answer
'The slaves are ours.'

The Merchant of Venice, W. Shakespeare
[Act 4, Scene 1]

•

In the UK, if you know or suspect that a person is being
kept as a slave, call Crimestoppers on 0800 555 111.
Callers' anonymity is guaranteed.

•

1

Men's voices, far away. It's hot, and the air terribly stuffy. She aches, as if she has hurt herself somehow. Where is she, what day is it, what does she have to do today? She breathes faster and hears her heartbeat, strangely audible as she realises that she cannot remember any of these things. She wants to go back to sleep. She is very uncomfortable. Extremely hot.

She moves to push the blankets away, but there do not seem to be any. She notices that she is dressed, and even has shoes on. Has she fallen asleep in her clothes? She must have been drunk! She wants to stretch her legs but her foot touches something hard. She tries to understand. Certainly she is not in her own bed. There is noise and vibration.

Alarmed, she opens her eyes, but it's as if they are still closed. She sees such complete darkness that it is not black. Instead a dense, dark grey encloses her like something physical. In it, as she stares, she detects colour, pulsating dots, tiny, shimmering patches, vague geometric forms moving. There is no edge or line to show any solid object. No hint of light from beneath a door or from a window. Is it the middle of the night? But even at night, there is usually a little light. She reaches for her face. Her arm is painful and heavy. She feels her eyelids with her fingertips. Her eyes are definitely open. Yet she can't see her fingers. Then she remembers something.

Waking in complete darkness is puzzling only for an instant, then frightening. Then terrifying. Now Liliana realises she is inside a moving vehicle. She feels sick with fear. She tries to remember what came before this moment. It is hard to think clearly. She met her brother. Her brother and some friends of his. There were drinks. She went with them in a car. She became drowsy and slept. They helped her to another car. He was on his phone. She reaches out slowly, feeling cautiously with her fingertips. There is rough fabric. It seems she is lying on a mattress. Without covers. She runs a hand over her chest, her stomach. Everything is done up properly. Thank goodness for that, at least! But her pockets – they are empty. There is nothing in them at all. Her money, her phone, her identification card, they have gone. She touches around the edge of the mattress. The floor is bare metal. This much she can feel in the dark. She sits up. The ceiling is a few centimetres above her head.

The movement stops. The engine is switched off. Perhaps they have arrived somewhere. The men's voices come closer. She waits.

And suddenly in front of her a door swings open. Now with a shock she sees everything clearly: she is on a dirty mattress in something like a metal box, in the back of a van. There are lights and an empty space like a sports field outside, and next to the van, she sees a high brick wall. A man with a shaved head holds the door and looks at her expressionlessly. He turns and speaks to someone she cannot see in a language she does not know.

* * *

With furious energy, Neil cycles between lines of traffic. On his headphones an alto saxophone cries plaintive screams. It's hard to say whether Neil is thinking aloud... or merely thinking. *Another weird thing about people, is how they get bent out of shape.* The cool air of an August morning blows on his face and stings his eyes pleasantly. *Like honeysuckle or a climbing rose, everyone grows to fit the frame they're on. There's no escape from that.*

He pushes hard and fast on the black tarmac, whole body muscled taut. At such moments Neil feels himself and his bike a single creature, as sharp and free as a swift darting above southern rooftops.

Back in north London, Bernard stirs in his bed. The warmth of his wife's body is close to him under the duvet. He runs a hand over the curve of her hips. Daylight beckons gently at the edges of the curtains. His eyelids flicker. Thoughts of justice and injustice pass through his mind, the battle that dominates his life. There are urgent tasks to be done. Even before his eyes are open, Bernard Kassin returns to the struggle, calculating how best to advance each cause. His preoccupation with justice is not good for his blood pressure.

A big robbery trial takes up much of Bernard's energy and most of his time. Other cases, too, crowd clamouring into his waking moments, this day and every day, statements, evidence, affidavits, client conferences, expert witnesses, prosecution papers, defence arguments, briefing counsel, court appearances.

Then there are all the cares of his little neighbourhood and its people: grievances and nuisances that pester him like gnats. Street lamps not working, broken pavements not replaced, park gates left open all night, noisy parties at number 27, those wretched offices in Blenheim Road. He will deal with them.

Ceaseless planning applications must be opposed, that have been put in by hungry developers for whom streets of houses are mere investment property. Worst of all is the comprehensive indifference of the salary-men at the council, untouched by all the wrongs which it is within their power to address. Intolerable, unbearable, unjust! It irks him that he has wasted so many hours in battle with the council. Only small things, he knows. The world is built of small things, and he is impelled to do what he can.

Then sometimes Bernard can do nothing more for anyone. In those hours he closes the door of his room, sighs deeply in solitude, and turns to his writing – his book of essays. They too are about justice.

This morning, though, his mood is good. He must press on! An email. A letter. He'll be in court later. There will be no time this evening. Better to start now. Perhaps he can get something done before breakfast.

In another Golders Green bedroom, if a room with a bed in it must be called a bedroom, Liliana at last lies down, defeated, exhausted and far beyond despair. Yet she knows this is just the start of her agonies. She dare not contemplate them. There will be pain, severe pain. She is frightened.

Once upon a time, Liliana would say a prayer before sleeping. But that was... she doesn't know when. She shuts her eyes. Her mind is aflame with images, lights, sounds, uncertainties. When this disaster began, how it happened, how she came to be here, she can't piece together. From one room to another, passed from hand to hand. Men, a van. A van with a locked cage inside it. In a sports field, during the night, different men. Four penetrated her savagely until she bled, roared with laughter when she pleaded with them. There is raw, torn soreness, she is defiled, hurting, maybe injured. Today they brought her to this place. Or was that yesterday? It is light again, so surely another night has passed. It means nothing any more. There are no days, only time. Not that she knows what time it is, nor what day. Nor where she is – this house.

Liliana does not bother to pray. God already knows about her and does not care. There will be no divine intervention. Probably God is on their side.

Instead she wonders how she and everything can be brought to an end. She cannot kill them; they are too big, too strong, quick and brutal as dogs, as hard as metal. If not them, then herself. She has been allowed three hours to sleep and must not waste them. She is tired enough to weep. Yet, fearfully, she glances around the room. Just a room with wallpaper and boarded windows. She is sick of rooms. Through the wall she hears men's voices. Men's voices are frightening. She closes her eyes again, but rest does not come. With her hands she presses her forehead, holds her eyelids shut, but still there is no rest.

This story is about three people in one quiet London neighbourhood. For the moment, Neil Chapman, Bernard Kassin and Liliana Petreanu know nothing of each other.

* * *

Neil swerved into Park Lane. Beside him, lofty frontages of red brick and white stone stared indifferently across the traffic, towards Hyde Park's tranquil greenery. In and out of the bus lane he skimmed deftly between sluggish double-deckers and hectic cars.

I don't want to be moulded and pulled and pushed. I don't want to be bent out of shape. I want to be alive and free. I want to wake up happy in the morning. But I wake up worried. Worried and angry – angry with myself, about Pamela.

Lights ahead turned amber, red as he approached. He continued through them without a pause. Despite the cold, he felt it would be a fine day. Thin cloud veiled pale blue. It might become hot later. He pictured girls in summer dresses. He pictured them sunbathing, buttons unbuttoned, zips unzipped, dresses undressed.

He damned himself for losing Pamela. Neil damned himself for all his misfortunes, especially that. Pam beside him, morning and night. To put his arms around her!

Passing the Dorchester's pale walls, Neil cut suddenly across six lanes of traffic to the other side of Park Lane. A taxi braked sharply to avoid him. Over the pavement and into Hyde Park. In the park, he rode fast, parallel to Knightsbridge.

Out of the park and down Sloane Street. Too late, he wouldn't make it to Critchlow's on time. He'd be five minutes late, and lose fifteen minutes' pay. And that bastard Sanina would have something to say about it.

The grandiose, immaculate Art Deco frontage of T. Critchlow & Sons, its perfect symmetrical lines, its elegantly curved glass, the opulent façade of blue and gold faïence, is set like a gaudy jewel among the blandly dignified designer stores of Sloane Street. Critchlow's uniformed commissionaires, with the demeanour of retired military men, wait ready to open its wide doors into a Byzantine emporium of marble pillars, mosaic floors, illuminated glass and polished bronze, of refinement, taste and quality.

Neil, though, does not glance at the front of the shop. He cycles at speed to the high red-brick wall at the rear of the building, and through a wrought iron gateway into Critchlow's dispatch yard. He pulls his time-card from the rack and slips it into the machine.

As expected, straight away "that bastard" called Neil into his office. Still wearing only shorts and singlet, Neil stood awkwardly, uncertain whether to affect a man-to-man equality, or to acknowledge his inferior position. On the other side of a desk, Critchlow's transport manager sat on a swivel chair. His heavy, hairless brow frowned. For a moment he remained ominously silent, head turned away as if distracted.

"Mr Chapman, why are you dressed like that?" He seemed to be speaking to the stacked sheets of paper on his desk, as if he could hardly bear even to look at Neil.

"Sorry, Mr Sanina, it's what I wear for cycling. I cycle to work."

There was a bizarre culture of old-fashioned formality between management and staff at T. Critchlow & Son. Neil rather liked it.

"You already know that Critchlow's drivers must wear the full company uniform while at work."

"That's right, sir, but – I only just arrived."

"My point is, Mr Chapman, you must arrive in good time to change."

Neil nodded as if in solemn contrition.

"Well, Mr Chapman, you have made a bad start."

"I'm sorry, Mr Sanina," said Neil. "I haven't worked out the best way to get here in the morning. I've moved into a new flat and I, well, I didn't realise the journey would take so long. I'm very sorry," he repeated.

The muscular face of Andrei Sanina, with tight mouth and small, enraged eyes, turned towards him. "You started work here yesterday, and both days – late. Not fair on colleagues, is it, Mr Chapman?" He spoke quietly.

Neil bowed his head and remained silent.

"Come on, Mr Chapman. I asked you a question. Is it fair on your colleagues?"

Neil was taken aback. The man was trying to humiliate him. "No, I suppose not, Mr Sanina."

I should just walk out. This is no different from being a kid bullied in the playground.

"You are not sure?" Andrei Sanina's voice had a constricted, foreign lilt that Neil found interesting. The vowels were all alike, flat, clipped. "Take it from me, Mr Chapman, it is *not* fair on your colleagues. And not fair on your employer. We pay you to start work by seven thirty. Solve this problem by tomorrow, Mr Chapman, or you will get the verbal warning."

Neil remained as still as a windless morning. There was no sign of annoyance. He couldn't remember how many warnings, verbal or written, employees might have without being sacked. He had an idea it was three. Best not to ask. Not on his second day.

"Sorry, Mr Sanina." He had lost his last job through utter stupidity. And what with the phoney references he had given... "I'll be on time tomorrow."

Sanina studied the young man on the other side of his desk. He had apologised profusely and politely and had not persisted with his excuses. Unassertive, unremarkable, deferential, correct, very calm. On the face of it, perfect for T. Critchlow & Son.

Yet Sanina detected a trace of something truculent and defiant. The politeness cloaked an insolence. Beneath the unrippled surface, something seethed. He also took note that Neil Chapman was muscular and well-built – lean and strong, tall and upright.

He saw a shine of sweat moistening the forehead and the bare limbs. Dark unkempt hair, cut short, pushed forward, gave the new driver a rough look, yet he thought Neil Chapman had an educated air. Though he had said almost nothing, he had seemed too articulate for a van driver somehow. There was even a hint of class hidden there.

Now Sanina looked furtively at Neil's eyes. They were shrewd and calculating. The brilliant blue was arresting, especially against his dark hair. Outwardly, he did not have the air of a troublemaker. There certainly *was* something in the voice. An undertone. One could sense that Mr Chapman was not quite the happy worker he should be.

Sanina appeared to be thinking things over. Neil felt curious about him, too. The transport manager seemed uneasy. Neil noted the man's huge shoulders and biceps flexing beneath the white cotton of his shirt. He looked more like a bouncer than a manager. Probably a weightlifter. A pathetic, narcissistic gym rat. Neil felt disdain for the vanity of such creatures. Yet Sanina was clearly not stupid.

He's come here from another country, learned English and landed himself a decent little job. Good for him. Bastard.

"Excuse me, but are you Spanish, Mr Sanina?" Neil suddenly burst out. A personal question might help him. "I mean, your family? Spanish name, right? Or is it Portuguese, maybe? Just wondering."

Sanina flushed slightly and looked angrier than before. "Romanian," he replied. "That's all, Mr Chapman. Go on, go back to your work. Put on your uniform. You'll go out on the City round today, with Mr Forrest. Come on, Mr Chapman! Don't waste any more time!"

Neil clenched his jaw. "Thank you, Mr Sanina."

Below the pavement of Sloane Street, where soon would click the high heels of pencil-skirted shoppers, the 'pickers' and 'packers' of Critchlow's Dispatch Room yelled conversation and banter.

Around the edges of the Dispatch Room – the men called it the 'Ring' – each delivery round had its own wire-mesh enclosure, which they called a 'cage'. Inside each cage, goods from mahogany tables to gold pens were being 'made up' – packed and wrapped – and their dispatch notes checked.

At the centre of the room was the Ring itself, a large wooden circle like an unmoving carousel, on which the dispatch men placed the packages ready for delivery, together with the paperwork. Drivers came to the carousel to take their packages, stacking them in trolleys and taking them up to the vans.

Like women around a village well, the Ring was where drivers and dispatch men met, loitered awhile and talked. Neil approached them uncertainly. A young man eyed Neil from one of the cages and slipped towards him, skinny and quick.

"Right? I'm Darren, right?" He shifted restlessly, throwing first one shoulder forward, then the other.

Neil looked suspiciously at a face boyish yet battered and pock-marked.

"Need anyfink, mate – any help, like – just ask for me. Know what I mean?" Darren's mouth was tight, the voice low and quiet.

In fact, Neil did not know what he meant. He was not sure what point Darren was making. He looked around awkwardly. "Where are the other fellers, the other drivers? D'you know a guy called Mr Forrest?"

"Canteen, innit?" suggested Darren with a jerk of the head. "Remember, mate – need anyfin'... or, you got anyfin' off the van, like. Off the round? A lot of these, like, fuckin' parcels and that... go astray, innit? They go missin', like. Bring it to me, right? Know what I mean? Give ya good price for it. Straight up."

Neil wanted to resist any temptation of that kind. He wanted to avoid any further trouble.

* * *

Neil knew, after just a few moments with Stan Forrest, that no one could be milder and gentler. Wiry, taciturn Stan was softly spoken, slow and careful, an old hand who would teach him – or learn him, as the men called it – a couple of Critchlow's rounds before Neil set out to do them on his own. The rounds were complicated, and some of Critchlow's customers had quirks that must be humoured.

He had an air of defeated decency and weary resignation. Stan's pale, freckled scalp was bald but for a few thin strands and a flaky patch of grey above each ear. The long face hung craggy and lined. His narrow lips were pulled into a stoical grimace. He struck Neil as a comic character from some dreadful old TV show – Dad's Army, perhaps. Wasn't there a Stan in that? But Stan Forrest was no comic. If he spoke at all, the Cockney voice was unhurried and serious. He gave sidelong, sceptical glances. One eyebrow rose slightly as if to say, *Who are you kidding?*

In any case, Neil and Stan spoke little while working. The van rattled and vibrated so noisily that it was hard to hear each other. The sound gave each man a privacy in which his mind could go its own way. In this solitude, Neil re-lived the moments when Pamela had told him to leave. Should he have said something different? Could he have saved himself? Had he been in the wrong? He was wrong enough to lose her. Shouldn't she have forgiven him? There's no 'should' about forgiving.

Stan pulled up alongside banks and office blocks, laconically directing Neil to take a parcel inside, throwing out useful information at the same time. "This one before that one. No exit at the end." He'd point: "Door on the right. Get a signature." Or, "Write on the docket what you done with it – 'Left on ledge as requested.' See?"

The docket, or dispatch note, torn off every package as it was delivered, showed what was inside: assorted extravagances in silk or linen, lace or leather, gold and silver, cufflinks, tie-pins and watches set with gems, and fountain pens, or diaries and notebooks, fine charcuterie and confiserie, men's clothes, and women's, from hats to shoes to lingerie.

Uniformed gatekeepers, each with a raised hand of greeting to Stan, slowly lifted barriers to allow the van to pass. Some deliveries were heavy: large boxes, and cases of whisky. Others were no more than a few dainties in a paper bag.

Into Fleet Street. "What's this place, then? Cathedral or something?"

"Can you read?" Stan asked bluntly.

At once Neil saw the Gothic lettering and gilded crest on the wall: *Royal Courts of Justice.*

"Give it to the security blokes."

Into St Martin's Le Grand, into Cheapside and Poultry. Again and again Stan pulled up at the kerb, simply pointed out a parcel, and gestured at the entrance to a building.

The private households were harder to find, along one-way lanes almost secretive, with warnings and no-parking lines and CCTV. Automatic gates opened into secluded, privileged little squares, blocks of luxury apartments hidden behind St Paul's Cathedral or on the Thames riverside.

Under crystal chandeliers in plush reception areas, Neil handed over the precious Critchlow's packages to concierges and porters. Then metal gates re-opened to expel them, and Stan navigated back into the glare of the larger universe: gigantesque global banks and corporations, phalanxes of their proud headquarters reaching the sky, steely Goliaths of international commerce.

Neil had never loved the City of London as much as now. As the van crept around tight corners and narrow turnings, he sensed vast destiny among the disorder. Long centuries of chaotic enterprise, tangled Dickensian stories, whispered among the smooth new geometry, and here and there a surviving scrap of ancient Rome, or a flinty medieval church with homely notice-board announcing Mass or Evensong.

He tried to remember if any film since the War had been set in the City of London. Not the East End, not the West End, or North London or the South Bank, but the City. He'd love to see it. Should it be in black and white, as befits Paris or Manhattan? No – in London, faded carmine brick, and pale Portland stone, and margins of soft greenery, are poignant, luminous in the muted brightness of clouded, changing skies. On the other hand, there's not much brick in the City. It's sheer white masonry and black iron, sheets of concrete and tinted glass, shining steel and dark marble.

He glanced up at narrow slivers of daylight shining between the tall buildings. "You got to learn all these little places," Stan cautioned. At Norton Folgate, Neil craned to take in the view of the Swiss Re Tower, the bulbous Gherkin whose form seemed to block the end of the street.

"What d'you think of it?" he asked Stan.

Stan glanced at him without a word. His expressionless contempt embraced both the question and the building, and, perhaps, all of the City's latest architectural conceits. Or, indeed, all novelty and modern life. At Shoreditch High Street, on every side rose a playschool of gargantuan triangles, slivers, immense curved glass frontages. Sudden expanses opened up, of sky and rooftops, where a site had been cleared in readiness for another new building.

Neil had almost fallen asleep, or been entirely lost in daydreams. He jerked back into wakefulness at the sound of Stan's voice, but did not hear what had been said. Stan was turning off Shoreditch High Street into a quiet side road with a cab rank and a church. Beside the parked taxis, the plate glass of a small café was opaque with condensation, threads of water trickling on the glass. They pulled up on a double yellow line and Stan turned off the engine. Neil looked forward keenly to a plateful of hot food.

The road pretended to have an air of tranquillity. Neil thought that he could hear birdsong mingled into the City's din.

"They make a good cup of tea," Stan jerked his chin in the direction of a tea-stall that Neil had not noticed, across the road. "And they always save me a cheesecake. They might have one for you, too, if you're lucky."

The cheesecake was a small pastry with a few shreds of coconut on top. Neil had expected a slice of cheesecake.

A tabloid newspaper propped on the steering wheel in front of him, Stan leaned back to smoke a cigarette. Ash gathered on his jacket and he brushed it off with a tired flick.

Neil sipped his tea. It was strangely intimate together, just the two of them.

"Is this a cheesecake, then? I thought..."

Stan shot him a withering glance but said nothing.

"You ever been in the caff?" Neil asked.

"Nah. Well, I been in. But I like a proper London cheesecake, see? Like this. They don't have it in the caff. Would you like to have a look at my paper?" he offered.

It was the Daily Mirror. Neil glanced through it quickly. A black teenager had been stabbed to death in London, the twentieth of the year. On the London Stock Exchange, shares had plunged by seven per cent in one week.

He found another snippet. "Seen this?" he read aloud, 'Labour to outlaw sex for sale'." Stan had not seen it. "Hey, listen – they're going to bring in a new law, make it illegal to pay for sex. They think they're going to stamp it out."

"What, sex? Or paying for it?" Stan tutted and pulled a face.

Neil snickered. "According to them, it works in Sweden. They reckon there's no prostitutes in Sweden."

"Must be a lot in Norway, then!" came Stan's sceptical response.

They laughed. But Neil felt uncomfortable, reading while Stan sat idly beside him. He soon tossed the paper onto the dashboard.

"See on the news about them Somali pirates?" he said instead. "They kidnapped these French sailors, right? OK, so these French commandos – right? – they went in there."

"Yeah, saw that," Stan nodded. "Only took 'em ten minutes."

Neil grinned. "Won't be so keen attacking French ships in future, will they – Somalis?"

"Wouldn't think the French had it in them, would you? French commandos! Sounds like a contradiction in terms."

Neil took a cautious bite at his pastry. It was sweet and plain, with a paper-thin layer of almond-flavoured paste in the middle. The coconut, if it was really coconut, had a pleasant, rough texture, but no taste. He put the remainder of the pastry into his mouth and swallowed it with a big gulp of tea.

Stan shot a questioning glance. "Like it – the cheesecake?"

Neil cocked his head a little as if undecided.

"You're an educated bloke, ain't yer?" Stan seemed almost to challenge him. "College. University?" He had been puzzled by his young companion from the start.

Neil shook his head emphatically. "No, I never went to uni. My sisters went. I wasn't good enough. I never went. I'm Mr

Average. Or Mr Below-Average."

Stan nodded. The phrase hung in the silence. Stan still felt there was something not quite right about Neil. The voice, or the accent, or something in his demeanour. He was like an actor playing a part. He was secretive, and too clever for this job.

"What did you get then? GCSEs?"

"Yeah," Neil laughed nervously. "Loads of *them*. And a couple of A-levels. French and Art. A-grade in both of them."

"Just for the record, I left school with nothing. Literally nothing. No General Certificate of Nothing." Stan pronounced it *stifkit*. "What work does your father do?" It was the age-old English definition of class.

"Teacher."

Stan nodded with tight-lipped satisfaction.

"Art. He was head of art in a private school. The Russell School, near Green Park."

Stan snorted as if slightly amused. "Well, that explains the old Art A-level, then, dunnit?" A puzzling thought occurred to him. "You never – did *you* go there – to the Russell School?"

"Yeah, well, I did as it happens. Kids of the staff got a cheap rate, see."

Stan opened the van door to shake the dregs of his tea onto the tarmac. "You went to the Russell School! Working as a blinking van driver, after an education like that! How old are you, son?"

"Thirty-one. But honest, I really *was* good at art. And French."

"Russell School! Thirty-one! And still no proper job! Dad's disappointed in you, for sure, son. Think about it: you could be a manager by now. You should be in Critchlow's head office, not a bloody driver."

"No way," Neil protested. He paused. "And I happen to know my dad's not disappointed in me. And he never helped me at A-level, neither. 'Cause he's dead."

Stan frowned. "I'm sorry, son. You should've said." He nodded slowly, thinking things over.

"It's OK," Neil said. "It was years ago. I was fourteen." He turned and looked away. Three African women in robes of flowing cotton, tie-dyed bright gold, brown and blue, strolled across the road with infinite ease. He listened intrigued as they passed his window, speaking some deep guttural language.

"How did your mum send you to the Russell School, then? What kind of job did *she* have?"

"They just let me stay there. It was a goodwill gesture. Dad was very popular." Neil wanted to get off the subject of his father. "What about you, then?" he asked. "Forgive me asking, but how old are you?"

"Tactful, ain't yer? You work it out. I been working at T. Critchlow & Son since the Coronation."

"The Coronation? You mean like, when the Queen come on the throne? When *was* that?"

"See?" Stan exclaimed. "The Queen's subjects don't even know when her Coronation was. 1953, it was. I bet you don't stand up when you hear the National Anthem. Probably don't even know the words."

"Well, I dunno. I don't remember the last time I heard it. Where can you hear it?"

Stan pressed his lips together. "Used to hear it all the time. Back when this was England and the people who lived here was English." Suddenly he opened the van door. "Just goin' for a Jimmy Riddle." He walked away towards Shoreditch High Street.

Neil watched cab drivers coming out of the café. They looked as if they had eaten well. In the wing mirror he saw Stan slowly returning with shambling, tired steps.

The old man settled back into the driving seat.

"Why didn't you retire when you got to sixty-five?" Neil asked.

Stan gave him an old-fashioned look. "Come on, mate. We got work to do. Let's crack on." He turned the ignition key and the diesel engine shook itself violently back to life.

Neil leaned back and stared out of the window. The van's metal racks and rear shutter rattled deafeningly as they drove over a stretch of road still made of cobblestones.

* * *

In a sitting room in Golders Green, two middle-aged women idly discussed affairs of the Kenilworth, Osborne and Blenheim Roads Residents' Association.

"This new chap," said Penny, shaking her head, "at 2 Blenheim Road. He's not the type for KOBRA."

After catching a glimpse of him a couple of times, she thought the new chap was likely to tell them to sling their hook. Nor was he the kind ever to come to a residents' meeting, nor would he ever ask for help himself, and nor was he likely to give a damn about the well-being of others.

"Oh, I like the look of the guy, speeding around on his bike," Lisa replied. She laughed rather lewdly. "*I'll* sit on his crossbar."

Penny pretended to be very slightly amused by this. In fact, she disliked Lisa's unbecoming humour.

"Is it too early for a drink?" Lisa wondered.

Penny said she had to get back. "Simon's expecting me," she said untruthfully. She thought it certainly was much too early for a drink, and that Lisa drank far too much, with her sauvignons and dry sherries and gin-and-tonics. She uncrossed her legs and toyed with a leather handbag as if to suggest imminent departure, but remained seated.

Although Lisa did not exactly like Penny, she revelled in the cosy intimacy of a womanly tête à tête with her. She did envy her rather cosmopolitan life, the journalist husband, the foreign trips, the almost impossible glamour of having "a little house" in the South of France (Penny's protests that it was very ordinary were taken to be false; no one would say such a thing if it were really true).

"KOBRA committee did agree, you know, to welcome new residents," Lisa reminded her. "I think it's nice to be welcomed when you move in to a new area, isn't it?"

Penny shook her head uncertainly. "Well – not everyone would like it." She, at least, would not. "Anyway, I don't think one of us girls should go," she declared. "I think it should be Bernard."

2

The morning service on weekdays appealed to Bernard. He went every Monday and Thursday. The drive to synagogue, in streets calm before the rush hour, gave him a poignant pleasure. In fine weather, he would walk there, from Kenilworth Road, into Osborne, along Blenheim.

Bernard felt something like wonder for Kenilworth, Osborne and Blenheim roads. All worlds contain smaller worlds, and each tiny world is vast to those within its sphere. He had gradually discovered that this small district, whose residents' association he had chaired for a decade, certainly contained nothing less than a whole world of human experience. Here were all physical and spiritual variety, all joy and grief.

Next door to native Saxons, or in flats above them, were Slavs and Norsemen, Latins and Chinese, and tribes of Africans, and those whose forefathers were slaves, and those whose forefathers sold them into slavery. In these three streets devout Muslims from Somalia and Pakistan and Arabia prayed and made their home, beside Hindus and Zoroastrians, and Jews religious and secular, Christians from Baptist to Catholic to Russian Orthodox, Quakers too and Unitarians, and Buddhists and followers of the way of Tao. Yes, a world indeed! Or at least, a London neighbourhood.

Heavy cloud swept across the sky. A few raindrops promised a downpour later. This morning, he made the journey by car. As usual, the other men were taciturn, reading quickly and quietly through the text. He wrapped the prayer shawl over his shoulders, placed the head tefillin on his brow, hastily wound the strap of the arm tefillin.

What could possibly make him want to attend this brief,

hurried ceremony? He was not even a believer. Yet Bernard did believe in the visceral pleasure of standing with his own people. The anachronistic rituals delighted him. Anyway, what's to believe, except that there's a God and he gave us commandments? And if it's not true, we can still keep the commandments.

At the end, the rabbi said a few words, mourners said kaddish one more time. It being the month of Elul, which comes before Rosh Hashanah, the shofar was blown, the eloquent, ancient clarion whose pensive notes instantly propelled Bernard into a mood of reflection.

He re-folded his shawl, unwound the leather strap from his arm and put his tefillin back into their velvet bag. The little group quickly dispersed, most to their work, where they would say nothing of days that begin not with a news programme but with a Torah reading.

Bernard himself travelled straight from synagogue to the Old Bailey. This morning the prosecution would be introducing additional evidence in the McDonal case. Bernard had a conference booked with counsel at nine o'clock. The trial would resume at ten.

He paused for coffee and toast at a sandwich bar beside St Paul's tube station. For a few moments he turned the pages of the Daily Telegraph, glancing over articles on the American presidential election.

From his briefcase Bernard took a folding umbrella. As he walked towards the court, the rain worsened. Puddles spread rapidly across the pavements. He raised the collar of his coat and quickened his pace, almost running through the court's low, arched entrance.

Putting together Tony McDonal's defence on a charge of armed robbery had been Bernard's main task for almost two years. After months of preparation, painful delays and preliminary hearings, the beefy McDonal had had a heart attack in court and been rushed away from the scene by ambulance. This year, Tony McDonal's trial began again, but in the meantime the prosecution had gathered new evidence.

Bernard joined his clerk behind McDonal's barrister. In the courtroom was a tranquil, intelligent atmosphere, in which professional lawyers understood one another. McDonal, sitting in the dock, struggled to stay awake during the soporific hours as the case against him was slowly presented and examined. Bernard saw the court as something like a workshop, where rights and wrongs were scrutinised with an eyeglass, and crafted as skilfully as silver filigree.

* * *

The gear cogs clatter quietly as Neil wheels his bike out of the house. The machine's polished precision, the poetic, mathematical accuracy of it, he adores. He grasps the narrow handlebar, and that sensation too he likes. The whole bike weighs nothing at all. Simple, strong, weightless.

He stands for one moment of calm. Dark clouds above the rooftops are shedding streaks of rain cool and refreshing on his skin. He looks up and down the street, Blenheim Road, its curve edged with trees. Just a few autumn colours have already appeared. In this grey light they seem especially bright. Birdsong fills the air, chirruping and chattering on every side. Magpies and blackbirds fly quickly, a male and a female together, between branches and rooftops, as if anxious to avoid a wetting.

Blenheim Road climbs a gentle slope. It's hardly prettier but no uglier than most ordinary London streets. Millions of people in the capital's thirty-two boroughs live in terraces no different, long lines of red brick under slate roofs. These, though, are of the meaner, plainer, two-storey style.

On one side of the road, most houses have been divided into poky little flats and bed-sitting-rooms. Behind their small back gardens rise the menacing blocks of a council estate in a poor state of repair. Yet over on the good side of the street, the houses have remained entire, with pleasant gardens backing onto larger, yet more pleasant gardens.

One street away, in Kenilworth Road, the houses are taller, wider, the ceilings higher, the finish more decorative. And in the other direction, detached and semi-detached homes continue for miles and more miles, as far as the distant Green Belt.

Every house has its small frontage, some neatly cultivated, others paved, with weeds pushing through the paving. All are disfigured by a clumsy assortment of plastic bins, blue, green, black, for waste and recycling.

Blenheim Road and Kenilworth Road, and Osborne Road which joins the two, were laid out on watery Middlesex fields more than one full century ago by a landowner who, day by day, contemplated the encroaching metropolis. The new Finchley Toll-Road had been opened; and streets of handsome new houses had appeared at St John's Wood and Swiss Cottage. He finally grasped the decision that had long been growing in his mind. Gangs of labourers were brought in to clear away his hay meadows, all his brick kilns, his laundries and small dairies. In their place – except for a couple of laundries that he thought might pay their way – he built an estate of modest homes for respectable artisan families, who were abandoning the city's squalor and moving to London's airy fringes.

Soon his estate was crowded about by others. Between Childs Hill and Cricklewood and Brent and Golders Green and Hendon and Hampstead and Camden and Kilburn, at last not a single field of pasture remained. Artisans have since become quite extinct, and Blenheim Road, after three generations as a working-class enclave, has been taken up by hard-pressed young professionals (in the better houses on one side of the road) and harder-pressed immigrants and low-income 'sharers' (in the houses converted into poky flats on the other side).

London's airy fringes have raced further into the countryside, the metropolis has entirely consumed Blenheim Road and Kenilworth Road, and Osborne Road, and there is no sign anywhere of brick kilns, hay ricks, laundries or dairies.

Neil raised a clattering metal shutter and stepped into the back of his van. Along the aluminium mesh racks he arranged parcels neatly, just as Stan had shown him, and put the dispatch notes – the dockets – in order. He was meticulous and careful. He wanted only to do his job correctly and feel the wages in his hand. He wanted nothing more than that from his job, except that he should be left alone. On the road, there was a curt, functional interaction between drivers that Neil viewed as the ideal of human communication.

Cash in his pocket and left in peace. Isn't that all he ever wanted? And some female company. The stormy weather gave way to a brighter, exhilarating sky. Clouds now torn to shreds scattered in every direction. Singing, talking to himself, in the happiness of solitude as he bowled along the washed tarmac, Neil's thoughts wandered freely. With a Royal crest, royal-blue livery and regal gold lettering, there seemed to be prestige even for the driver of such a van.

Since starting the Ascot round, Monday had become Neil's favourite day. Long hours alone, scudding through the traffic on the Great West Road, putting his foot down for a fast pace on the motorway, then slowly threading along country lanes between expensively groomed villages. With the street atlas of Surrey open beside him, he travelled between high hedges and paddocks and private parkland, calling at big houses with long driveways.

At most of them, he spoke only to women: housewives and housekeepers, maids, nannies, *au pairs*. On warm days, some answered the door not quite dressed, or in swimwear, or nightwear, dressing gowns or bathrobes, or even (only twice so far, but keenly counting) in underwear. Neil admired the peaceful, orderly world of the well-to-do. The crunch of gravel. Ring the bell. "Critchlow's." A smile. Sign here. Thank you. And often a tip. Then back into the driving seat, with one parcel less to think about. This was actually better than his old job.

Pamela was waiting at her flat when I got home that day. It started as an innocent, ordinary day. I went to work and had no idea what was in store. I really liked that job – delivering stationery to businesses in north London.

It was destined to be a special day for both of us. Specially bad. All the way home I wondered how to keep the news from her. I could, well, just not tell her. Keep it a secret. But she would be bound to find out I had lost the job by next Thursday evening – payday.

Trouble is, people don't really lose jobs, like losing a key or losing the way. If they are old, they retire. If they hate the work, or want something better, they resign. Which would not apply to me, because Pamela knew I was happy with it.

Or, they screw up and are sacked. Which would raise the question, Why were you sacked, Neil – what did you do wrong? And that's what I couldn't explain. Even to myself. I kept trying to justify myself – as if everyone else was wrong, and I was right. That didn't add up though. It was totally my fault. Taking unauthorised passengers in the van was a sacking offence, pure and simple. I knew that.

Or, of course, when the employer doesn't need them any more, a person can be made redundant through no fault of their own. Maybe Pam would believe that. Just say I was made redundant, and start looking for another job. And find one. And all this would go into the past. And everything would be all right.

Even as I reached the door and put the key in the lock and turned it, I still didn't know if I would try to kid Pamela that I had been made redundant.

Straight away when I walked in, something was already wrong. Instead of calling out 'Hi', she marched into the hallway and stood there, looking at me, as if daring me to speak. It was as though she already knew everything. But how much of everything? So that's why I decided to blurt it out. Make a clean breast of it – up to a point. But I didn't. I couldn't say a word because of the way she was looking at me.

Her eyes! It was just a reproachful look, hanging there all on its own. And almost a sneer, somehow, if eyes can sneer.

"Who's the girl?" She asked me straight off, without even saying hello.

"What girl?" I had been thinking to keep that part to myself. Because how the heck could she find out?

"Come on, Neil. I'm not stupid. I phoned the firm and I know all about it. Someone emailed them these not-very-nice photos and copied me in. Pictures of you and your friend. In your van. And on Hampstead Heath. Plus a little message in case the photos didn't make it clear what you were up to."

Fucking hell. She saw the pictures!

"I was going to tell you about it," I said, "but she persuaded me not to. Anyway, she's nothing. Nothing. I'm sorry. I am. I'm sorry, Pam. It was only..."

"A woman is not nothing." Pam was furious when she said that, but instead of shouting, she just talked normally.

That was twisting what I'd said, but maybe she was entitled to. "No, she's not nothing – her name is Anwen," I said, "She's actually nice, OK? She was at that party we went to, the one for all your old school friends. Her husband was..."

"Husband! Do I know him?" Pamela was even more annoyed when she heard that. "Don't tell me! Don't tell me about her husband, or her. Don't tell me her name!" For a moment she spread her fingers and grimaced with disgust, as if she had reached into a drain.

"No, Pam, Pam, what I meant, it was only sex."

"So now sex means nothing, and wrecking their marriage means nothing, but the lovely Anwen or whatever the fuck she calls herself is not nothing after all. Is that what you're saying? All right, Neil – you can have her. Feel free. Because you're not living here with me any more."

I was thinking she didn't mean it, or I could talk her round.

"I'm so very sorry, Pam. I was tempted, and I just went with it. I was stupid, OK? But I honestly, honestly, don't want to be with anyone but you, Pam. Look, I love you."

"Listen, mate," – how bitter and sad her voice – "I've heard it once too often. It's pathetic. I don't buy that 'love' crap from you. If this is your idea of love, I'll do without it."

"I said I'm sorry, Pam."

"Saying sorry doesn't mean shit. Look, I realised something – I *don't have to forgive you every time you say sorry. Right? It was you that said we were a team. But you don't play for the team, you just play for yourself. OK, you can have it your own way from now on. You've lost your job and you've lost your girlfriend. Now you can fuck off out of the flat, too. Make your own fucking way in the world."*

"Oh, come on, Pam ..."

"No, mate, really – I don't want a bloke that takes me for a mug. You promised it wouldn't happen again. You're not capable of keeping a promise, are you, Neil? I've put your stuff in bags, and your films and music and that. All neatly packed. Now call a cab and get the fuck out."

After being together more than three years. We had only just celebrated our anniversary with drinks and everything! My chest felt like a massive lump of lead. It was difficult to breathe, or to see clearly. I kept trying to apologise. She just wouldn't hear it.

"Neil, you poor loser," she said. I was pissed off by that. I didn't think it was fair. She didn't even sound angry, just sorry for me.

"Every time you have things nicely sorted out, you do something to screw it up. Neil – sorry, mate – I'm not going to live like that. I'm all grown up now and I want a proper man of my very own. I'm not trying to put you down, Neil, I'm really not. You're a nice feller and all that. But it's not enough. I'm not going to spend my life with someone that keeps screwing things up. A guy should know when he's onto a good thing, and try to hang onto it. If you don't do that – that's what we call a loser."

Worst of it is – I see now she's right. Three happy years. And the rest, all those good years we were going to have. I lost them. Threw them away.

He drove on gloomily. He turned on the radio to listen to the news. Three Islamists from London had been found guilty of planning to use liquid explosives to blow up passenger planes. From now on, airlines would not allow passengers to take liquids on board. More banks were going bust.

He turned it off again and drove in silence. Suddenly something like a paroxysm of regret landed a huge punch. It was a physical sensation, nearly a pain, like an airbag inside his chest. He thought he might be sick. He stopped the van and turned off the engine. Straight away there was no pain, only a terrible, tired loneliness. He put a hand over his eyes. They were moist, like tears. He held his breath tightly to prevent a sob bursting out. Maybe she *would* have him back. But no, Pamela surely wouldn't believe anything he said any more. He did not know if he had ever loved her, but he knew he had always loved being with her. They had had such fun, such good times together.

He could not bear to think how stupid he had been. All for the sake of a pointless little fling! He didn't even know Anwen, he wasn't even slightly interested in Anwen. Just because she wore a sexy dress at a party! He shook his head, willing it to be untrue. But it was true. That was the reason.

But she couldn't have loved me, could she? A woman that loved you would never ask you to leave.

"Pam, Pam." He was startled to hear himself say the words aloud. Anger flared in him. Why throw a guy out just because he has a fling with another woman? Is it really so important? And maybe, after all, Anwen... he still had Anwen's number in his mobile. He needed only to press it and... he imagined her Welsh voice, saw fanciful visions, Anwen in his new flat, in his bedroom, her shining hair of black silk. Or, no – surely more likely – maybe Pam would see reason if he gave *her* a call. He visualised a romantic reunion, a bottle of wine, ready forgiveness and simple, joyous lovemaking. He even asked himself if his *previous* girlfriend might be willing to take him back. She had moved since those days, and he had lost touch with her. He could Google her, search Facebook, Twitter, everywhere. He'd trace her somehow. Maybe she'd like to see him again. He tried to think clearly; none of his imaginings were possible. He told himself he was raving.

Following the edge of Windsor Great Park. A back road into Englefield Green. Virginia Water and Sunninghill. Gravel drives and fine double doors.

He rings a bell on a door marked 'Tradesmen'.

Comes the cry from within, "Who is it?"

Neil answers, "Critchlow delivery," and the door is opened at last.

Miss Delavingham is vast, ancient, spilling out of a blousy dress, hair half-held in place with beautiful combs. Something about her posture, and the set of her facial muscles, is unmistakeable: she has 'breeding'.

"Oh, hello Critchlow," she exclaims, eyeing Neil's uniform, reassuring herself. "Are you the new man? Your name?"

"Chapman, ma'am." For this is how Critchlow's teach their drivers to respond.

Neil has been warned about Miss D.'s procedure. "In here, in here." Flowers in the box room. Drinks on the trolley in the hall. Charcuterie and cheeses in the pantry. "What's that?" she flusters, "Is it my poultry? I'm expecting *three* ducks. Are there three? They go here on the table. What's that? Can you open it for me?"

Neil thinks she is going too far, but does everything she asks. He is obliging and polite. He toys with the idea of refusing. It would be the end of his job.

"Would you like a cup of coffee?" she asks finally. Neil is pleased, and feels as if all his labours have been rewarded, though he knows a cup of coffee costs nothing at all. He feels compensated not by the coffee, but by the offer.

He doesn't know if the correct response is to refuse. He says, "Please!" and is delighted when Miss D. also produces a tin of biscuits. "Help yourself," she says.

She does not ask him to sit, and he stands at a scrubbed-clean deal table as large as his entire kitchen. She lowers her own billowing hugeness into a creaking chair.

"You need a shave, young man," she remarks, eyeing him.

Neil is aghast at her impoliteness. "Sorry, ma'am," he replies meekly.

"Do you remember Mr Williams?" she asks.

"He's retired, hasn't he?"

"He delivered to us for thirty years," she says. "Always as

smart as a pin. Mr Billings was before him. Critchlow's is very different now, than it was all those years ago."

"Yes, one of the other drivers said that recently." Neil dips a biscuit into his coffee, wondering awkwardly if he is ill-mannered. It struck him that Miss D and Stan Forrest were strangely in agreement about things.

"It's not that there is anything *wrong* with Critchlow's," she explains, "at least, not compared with other shops. I will say, Critchlow's is the last proper department store left in London. All the rest are just a lot of concessions and noise. It's just that it used to be so much *better*. Why, nowadays, the assistants don't really care about one at all! Only the other day, well, Mr Chapman, I had three gormless young females on the other side of the counter, and not one of them moved a muscle to help me! Do you know what they were doing? Would you believe me if I told you that they were *talking* to each other? I stood *waiting* for some assistance. Certainly it was never like that. *Certainly* not, in the old days."

"They employ a lot of temporary staff, you see," Neil tries to explain.

"Oh! Offering excuses! That was *never* done! No one cares about anything any more!" Miss D. cries out, exasperated. "Ah, well," she muses, "those days are all gone. Quality. Integrity. High standards. All gone. A good deal of what's left in this country is just the reputation. The whole atmosphere of – ah – distinction. Sad."

"Well, um... thank you for the coffee. Very kind of you."

She struggles to lift herself out of the chair, but cannot make it. The strap of some huge silken undergarment falls across her upper arm. "Not at all. Goodbye."

An elderly gardener, bent over, staring at the waterlogged ground and about to pierce it with a fork, looks up in surprise as Neil comes out of the Tradesmen's door.

Neil nods. "All right, mate?"

He stares at Neil with fish-eyes, uncomprehending, as if from another age.

The minutes spent with Miss D. only added to Neil's wage packet. Whenever drivers finished their rounds before four o'clock, they were given a bonus; after five o'clock, they were paid overtime. There was no chance at all of getting back before four, so he settled in for a long day with as much overtime as looked plausible.

The only bad part of the Ascot round was the traffic heading back into London. Still, delays on the A30 or the Old Brompton Road put yet more pounds on his pay. He might as well arrive at seven or eight o'clock in the evening. What the heck – there was no one waiting for him at home.

* * *

Leaving the Old Bailey, Bernard threw back his shoulders and sighed deeply, glad to get out of doors. The weather had altogether changed. In the crowded street it had become pleasantly bright and breezy. He walked all the way to Trafalgar Square, a favourite place.

As always, he was thrilled by it; the majestic proportions, bold Nelson on his soaring column, guarded by ferocious black lions in alert repose, his face turned towards Westminster. Nelson's signal from HMS Victory rang in Bernard's thoughts: *England expects that every man will do his duty.*

Now, he thought sadly, there was no England, no duty and no men. And when invasion came again, there would be no victory. A great nostalgic patriotism stirred him. Yet he reflected too that the history which had made this vista was not his history. While Horatio Nelson raised England's flag over the defeated French, his own ancestors toiled in the medieval darkness of faraway Russia.

From Golders Green station, Bernard drove not to his own house but instead looked for a parking space near Hilda King's end-of-terrace, beside the Blenheim Road offices. Poor Hilda King, living right next to those damned offices! The offices were part of the menagerie of *bêtes noires* that preyed on his energies.

Universal House, proclaimed a cracked plastic sign screwed to the front of the little building.

On the offices' forecourt, rubbish lay on the ground beside an overflowing metal waste bin. It made Bernard feel nauseous just to see the mess. He felt his temper rising. He remembered his blood pressure. He must stay calm. He sat in the car for a moment before walking to Hilda's front door.

How large is an injustice? How can it be measured? Three ordinary English streets contain a multitude of wrongs so small that they cannot be seen at all from outside. Yet they are large enough to spoil lives. So it is throughout the land. People in the three streets came to Bernard. Some spoke bitterly and, it had happened, even with tears in their eyes. They sat on the sofa in his sitting room and asked for help in their struggles with officialdom. Hilda King was one of those, although she was too dignified to weep. For her problem was not the offices, but the council.

Bernard reached into his briefcase. "Mm – yuh, now. These new photos," he said, holding them out. "I followed the bin men on their round last Friday. Leaving the wheels unlocked is their usual practice."

Small and thin, wearing a modest, functional blue cardigan and brown skirt, at first sight Hilda King did not make an impressive figure. Her hair seemed frozen in place, a glacial pale grey. He wondered how she would come across in court. Probably quite well. Her plain and simple respectability rang true. An aggrieved determination tightened her lips. She was struggling to stay positive.

Hilda put the photographs down on a table. "Quite honestly, I wonder if it will make a bit of difference." She meant, that it wouldn't. "Would you like a cup of tea? I've made some nice cake."

"No, no, thank you!" Bernard held up a hand. "Mm – and, ah, I've drafted a letter," he said. "Make it easier for you." He handed her a sheet of paper and Hilda read.

It was addressed to the council's Insurance Department.

My car was damaged by a metal waste bin, property and

responsibility of the local authority, on 25 April. I reported it to you on the same day. My further letter of 19 May by recorded delivery enclosed photographs of the incident and details of an independent witness. I sent a quote for repair of the damage on 16 June. There has never been any response from you at all, she read.
...further action... County Court... issuing proceedings...

"And you are *sure* I won't have to pay costs and that if I lose? Because, well, I can't."

Bernard explained about Small Claims. "Each side pays their own costs. You won't have any at all."

"I don't know. They always try and get you, one way or another." Yet she sat down at the table and signed the letter. "What about that 'issuing proceedings', like it says here?"

"Oh, I've done all that, don't worry about it. We'll sort it out. It's only fifty pounds. Anyway, we'll get it back if you win."

Hilda smiled gently. "I get the feeling – don't you? – you know, bloody council, they'll never pay. Not to someone like me. Not in a million years. Even if the Court tells them. They just won't. Anyway the Court will back them up. You'll see."

Bernard had a different feeling. Hilda would get her money if it killed him.

* * *

Neil wheels the bike into the narrow hall and carefully props it to one side. He doesn't want to inconvenience his downstairs neighbours, since they are also his landlords. They seem friendly enough, within the limits of their English, but that fellow looks the type to have a savage temper. So does the wife, sometimes. The smell of their dinner cooking fills the hallway, always the same slightly unpleasant aroma of rich meaty stews.

He races up to his tiny, two-room flat. Straight into the kitchen-dining-sitting room, puts on music, turns it up loud. Sublime unearthly harmonies fill the flat. Neil listens for a moment, standing with eyes closed, lost in thought. He says aloud, "What a fucking idiot I am." He means, I might be living a good life somewhere, if I had made different choices.

For all his love of things French, Neil is content to empty a can into a saucepan for his evening meal. Besides, it's the cheapest way to eat. Nor does he mind taking the food straight from the pan, with just a fork or spoon and a piece of bread. That keeps cleaning-up to a minimum. Not that he bothers with that – his fork and spoon are unwashed since yesterday's dinner. In some ways, things are a whole lot simpler since Pam threw him out. He does not even lay a place at the table, though for a few minutes he does sit there, then gets up and walks around, eating from the pan.

Now he throws off all his clothes and steps into the cramped bathroom to shower. He stands naked in contemplative bliss as warm water streams over his muscles. Charlie Mingus plays exquisitely in the other room.

The doorbell rang and Neil cursed. *Fuck. Let it ring! No one knows me here anyway, so who could it be?* Yet when it rang again he stepped out of the shower and pressed the intercom. He heard a man's voice say "Association." Neil said, "What is it, a charity?" The man said no. "What then? A delivery?" The answer crackled, unclear.

"All right, I'll come down." Neil wrapped a small towel around his waist. He muttered irritably as he made his way down to the door.

There stood a short, slightly overweight middle-aged man with high, smoothly rounded forehead, dark eyebrows and heavy features. "Ah, mm – I'm *terribly* sorry!" exclaimed the man, somewhat horrified by the towel. A bluff, amiable character, he himself wore an expensive-looking raincoat open over a dark suit. Greying hair, trimmed close to the scalp, surrounded a bald area. In the domed head and curved nose Neil fleetingly perceived something aquiline. Much too smart to be working door-to-door. The man smiled painfully.

Neil was puzzled. He frowned. "Yeah, what is it?"

"Ah, my name's Bernard – Bernard Kassin. I live round the corner." He ran a hand nervously across his temples. He was uncertain whether a handshake would be in order, and decided against. The chap's towel might fall off.

"Yeah?" Neil repeated brusquely.

A guy comes to the door, says he's your neighbour. Straight off, that could be a lie. He wants something. Is he going to talk religion? Try to sell something? Con me into signing up to a different phone company?

"Mm – yuh. I'm the chairman of the local residents' association. It's called KOBRA. Should I come back another time?" He politely ignored Neil's wet, naked torso.

"No," Neil answered irritably. He did not want to be disturbed a second time. Just the type, he thought, to be chairman of a residents' association. The very picture of censorious respectability, although the name 'cobra' struck a surprisingly menacing note.

Neil imagined a body akin to Neighbourhood Watch, Boy Scouts or the Women's Institute, all of which he assumed to be composed entirely of pompous, interfering, puritanical do-gooders. The bloke had a posh accent. He reminded Neil of that raddled old aristocrat on the Ascot round today, Miss de What's-her-name. She spoke like this – a bit. This fellow wasn't as posh as her, though. Nowhere near.

"Don't bother, mate. Really," Neil advised him. "It's not my thing."

A frown appeared on Bernard Kassin's face. "*What* isn't your thing?"

"Sorry, I'm not interested, thanks. Anyway," Neil said curtly, "I'm only renting."

"Renting makes no difference to us." Bernard struggled to keep a friendly smile. He knew he ought to stop and leave this young chap alone, a poor fellow protected by nothing but a damp towel.

Neil glared impatiently and moved to close the door. He didn't want to be so rude as to actually slam it in the fellow's face. "Just forget it."

Bernard judged that he should drop the subject and leave. "Nice music, by the way. Charlie Mingus, yes? Who's that on sax?" Neil's CD played loudly upstairs.

Astonished, Neil pulled the door open again and looked the man all over as if to reassess him. Nothing had changed. "On sax? That's Booker Ervin."

"I'm not really into bop like this. I don't like fusion, either, or any of that, you know, that avant-garde sound. But still, Mingus... and Booker Ervin, he's brilliant too."

Neil gazed. Someone was *talking* to him – about jazz! Nor could Neil stop himself from responding. His shower was ruined now anyway. "Don't like bebop, what *do* you like?"

Bernard chuckled. "*Proper* jazz! New Orleans. Trad," he replied. "You know what I like? A big band. And real jazzmen. Bix Beiderbecke, Louis Armstrong, Duke Ellington. And Swing. Benny Goodman. Fats Waller. You'd better go in," he warned, "you'll catch pneumonia standing there. Mm – yuh, I have a big collection. Of records, obviously, not digital stuff. Anyway – I'm sorry to have wasted your time."

Neil frowned in mock disgust. "Swing? That's just pop music. And you're into Louis Armstrong – but like Mingus as well?" He grinned quizzically. "How is that possible?"

Bernard Kassin laughed. "Mm, well, you know, I'm not a Catholic but I have catholic tastes! I do like *some* modern stuff. Dave Brubeck. I'll make time to hear Dizzy Gillespie. And Parker, of course – Bird. Hard bop, soul jazz type of thing, is about as modern as I can take. Don't stand there in the cold like that!"

Neil was almost dismayed to feel a sort of affection for this crusty, dreadful old gent. "You like Bird? I have a lot of Bird! And Miles Davis. Not so keen on those big bands. That's not really jazz."

"Yes, well, we can argue about that," Bernard responded genially. "Give them another listen – come round, I'll play you some."

Neil nodded, astonished by the invitation. "I can't stand here and talk. I'm freezing.

Bernard nodded. "Course you are! You should go in. I hope you're not annoying your neighbours with this music. It's far too loud."

"What, Mr and Mrs Viktor, you mean? Nah, they don't mind.

Well, they haven't said anything."

"Mm – ah, well, better ask them," Bernard suggested. "Very good people, very kind. Hungarian refugees you know, from the 1956 Uprising," he said. "On a short fuse, though. Always calling the police about kids from the flats. Police aren't interested, of course. So! What else've you got?"

"Ton of stuff. Every note ever recorded by John Coltrane. Look, I can't stand here. Come up, have a look. Or a listen."

He opened the front door wide and Bernard stepped inside. "Sorry, the place is a bloody tip. No, really, it's gross. I'll get dressed." He hoped there was nothing lying around that Bernard shouldn't see. Porn or dope.

3

Risky. Stupid. Critchlow's van, Critchlow's uniform, way off the round. He hurried forward urgently. The show might have started already.

Hackney Road was shabby, fronted with rows of tired old craft shops, wholesalers and workshops no bigger than a front room, one-man furniture makers, shop-fitters, scruffy import businesses, long terraces of crumbling red-brick façades ready to be swept away. Neil wondered, though, where they would go, all these sweat-shops and mean shoe-string businesses on the edge of the City of London. No, they cannot be swept away: they are needed just where they are.

Finally he saw The Maypole on a corner ahead. His lips were dry. Outside the pub, a hand-painted sign offered "striptea's".

Facing it, a housing estate loomed, edged with razor wire. An incendiary ethnic mix of louts stood together around entrances and doorways, some staring silently. One group stood apart, muscular young black toughs in bandanas. Neil did not want to leave his van unattended in such a place. There was no choice. His stomach clenched tight with excitement and his heart raced. He hurried and fumbled clumsily, slammed the van door and locked it, fearful of missing even a minute more. He pushed open a swing door into the pub.

The bar room was dark, crowded, sweaty; the music too loud, pounding on speakers that hummed and crackled. His ears hurt. The staff would go deaf, working here. Everything vibrated to the beat. The cramped space was tightly packed with men; black and white, young and old, in suits, in overalls, gazing. On a small wooden platform, under a dazzling spotlight, a slender young woman gyrated and thrust to the pulsing sound. In front of her, dozens of men sitting on upright wooden chairs leaned forward intently. Standing behind the chairs, a crowd jostled for position, edging as close as possible. There was an atmosphere of no-nonsense violence in the air.

He had missed a lot of the act. This is no local housewife, Neil thought. She's professional. So why is she in this crummy place? She even remembers to smile, sweetly playful and seductive. Long swirling red hair in loose waves, flat waist, lovely breasts. What he wouldn't give to touch them! By now she wore only stockings, a pink satin miniskirt with a fringe, and a tight velvet ribbon around her neck. Legs opened to give men the view they craved. The room was small enough that Neil could almost have reached out and touched with his fingertips. In the intoxicating darkness, at last he did not have to avert his gaze. His thoughts eagerly slid over her, exploring, lingering.

The show was free, so Neil knew he had to buy a drink or be asked to leave. Behind the bar, too, were bare-breasted women, shapeless lasses who, he felt, were just ordinary bar staff: it was unreasonable that they had to work undressed like this, in a place like this, in this dim light, putting up with this painful noise. Why work here? Was the pay so good? He ordered a pint and quickly turned back to the show. A beer mug, crammed with notes and coins, was held out towards him by a big man with a shining scalp. "For the dancer." He dropped in a couple of one-pound coins. A shake of the shaved head showed that it wasn't generous enough; he gave another two coins.

At the climax of her act the woman, naked but for the velvet choker, rhythmically squirted a thick white liquid onto herself in time with the steady thump of the bass. Suddenly the music stopped, the girl jumped up and gave a pretty wave as she ran from the stage. The lights came on, and Neil stood with his pint, breathless, slightly stunned.

He sipped slowly, tense, wired, ears still ringing from the noise. This was suddenly nothing but a tawdry, old-fashioned East End pub. It made him feel that he and all his desires were seedy. His excitement, in such a place, felt like something he needed to wash off, or wash out of himself. At the bar, the chubby servers were pulling on tee-shirts, being handed banknotes and leaving. Suddenly he understood why they do the job. Cash in hand for an hour's work. In the middle of the day. Kids at school, husbands at work. Anxiously he remembered that he was being paid too – to deliver parcels in the City. He looked at his watch. Still plenty of time. If he lost this job, though, at least he wouldn't have to discuss the reason with Pamela. He went to the bar and asked for a cheese sandwich to take away.

Outside in the daylight, the bandana youths had gone. His gleaming royal blue van with its golden crest seemed outlandishly elegant. Yet, in this surly, truculent street, it remained intact! In the driver's seat he leaned his head into his hands. He blew out a great sigh, as if exhausted. As he looked up, men streamed from the pub, alone or in small groups, heading in all directions, until the crowd died away. Finally a young woman slipped from the door. She wore blue jeans, a denim jacket and white plimsolls and carried a pale canvas shoulder bag. It was the hair he recognised. Bouncing loose red curls trailing over her shoulders. Funny, she seemed so unglamorous now, an art student maybe – but too old for that. An art teacher, then. He hadn't noticed before how old she was; probably his own age, maybe more.

He watched as she crossed the road and walked fast along the pavement, quick, alert, with a kind of delicacy, cat-like, looking at nothing until she reached a bus stop. It offended him that she, this unusual, beautiful creature, had to stand among such squalor, waiting for a bus. He felt sorry for her. Besides, surely it was dangerous? One of the men who had seen her might get ideas.

Slowly he peeled the cling-film from his sandwich. The bread was damp and unappetising. He prised the thin slices apart and looked inside: hardly any cheese. He bit into it and chewed without pleasure. Stan's tea-stall was much better. But then, there was no stripper at the tea-stall. His gaze rested often on the young woman at the bus stop. A small crowd had gathered there now. There was no semblance of a queue. It was somehow wretched, he felt, to jump around like a rag doll in front of a bunch of leering guys, and take off her clothes to amuse us, then to stand neglected in the street waiting to return home.

Swallowing the last clammy piece of bread, he started the engine and moved forward. The van's rumbling, clattering sounds were reassuring. Without any thought, he drew up beside her and called through the open window. "How far you going? Give you a lift."

She did not turn to look.

"That was a nice show. You were good. I'll drive you somewhere if you like. It's not a problem."

Her eyes flicked warily in his direction, noted the clean van with classy livery and the neat uniform. A guy like this would have a lot to lose if he tried anything.

"Up to you," he said. "Just wanted to help."

Something in the voice said he was harmless. She knew the type: impetuous, generous, basically decent. She had plenty of experience of what men will or won't or might do. And she very much *didn't* want to wait for the bus.

She took two small steps in his direction for a closer look. He submitted to her scrutiny. He had a kind, intelligent face. She recognised the suppressed agitation; of course, he had just seen her show. But she could tell if a man liked women and would be no trouble. He really looked OK. Besides, in one pocket she had her little embroidery scissors, a very feminine possession as sharp as a heron's beak, that had proved effective whenever needed.

"Are you allowed to take riders?" He had not expected an American accent.

"No, but that's *my* problem. Sacking offence."

She shook her head. "So please don't take me. Anyway it's too far. I'm going a long way," she said. "'Cross the river. It's kind of you, but a bus'll be along soon, hopefully."

"Well, it's up to you," he said again, but added, "Come on, I'll drop you somewhere."

She opened the door and stepped up. "Just take me to City Road. It's an easy bus from there."

The door slammed. Neil stole glances as she settled into the seat. He must calm himself and not do anything foolish. "Where you actually going?"

"You know Denmark Hill? Down that way."

The accent was something he couldn't place. She sounded like Sally Field, playing Forrest's mom in *Forrest Gump*. Or, no, more like Hattie McDaniel playing the black servant, Mammy, in *Gone With The Wind*. Even though she was white. Not servant, of course – Mammy was a slave.

"Denmark Hill," he pondered, "let's see now. I don't know anything much, south of the river. Where is it?" Neil said. But he had already set off, turning away from Hackney Road. He would take a route through Whitechapel down to Tower Bridge. So long as he wasn't seen by another driver, or anyone from Critchlow's, it didn't matter which way he went.

"How come you don't have sat-nav?"

"That's not the way they do it at this firm. You're supposed to learn the round, and remember all the customers."

"That's good, I guess. What about Coldharbour Lane? You know that?" she asked.

"Nope," he replied again, "we don't deliver down there. Heard of it, obviously."

She laughed. "OK, what *do* you know? Do you know Brixton?"

"Mm, yeah. Well, I went to a couple of gigs at the Brixton Academy. Don't remember how I got there. Don't remember how I got home."

She smiled white teeth and shook her red hair. He said, "Don't worry, I've got an A to Z."

"OK, head to Elephant and Castle. Then due south a couple of miles or so."

He grimaced. "I should've just taken you to City Road."

"It's not too late to change your mind."

"Nah, just kidding."

They passed a succession of tatty, low-rise blocks and ragged patches of soiled grass. At first Neil's passenger gazed tiredly out of the window. This worn-out eastern backwash of the City seemed to him – imagining it through her eyes – a formless chaos, crumbling old brickwork and cheap concrete slabs, viaducts and sidings, mean workshops, off-putting take-aways, disintegrating houses. Most of the people seemed to be down-at-heel immigrants.

As they crossed Whitechapel Road, pressing crowds in a multitude of diverse robes, black with white scarves, pale blue, thin white cottons, moved slowly beside market stalls. He turned right into Cable Street and left towards Tower Bridge. And suddenly they were back in the world of dazzling white stone cladding and black glass and men in grey suits.

She craned to look as they reached the ornate bridge, turning back to take in the massive walls of the Tower. "Tower of London," Neil explained.

"Yah, I know. I came here a few times. I do love this place, the old Tower and all that shit." Her tone was almost grudging. A few small clouds flew over the river: it was the best day for weeks. "This whole fucking city. I love it." As they edged forward in the traffic, she sighed deeply. "London, England! Being here makes me feel rich somehow. Know what I mean? It really does. If my folks could see me now, they'd spit."

He smiled at the phrase. She was gazing across the parapet of the bridge. The battleship HMS Belfast was moored majestically in mid-stream. In the distance, the arc of the London Eye skimmed the sky.

"That's City Hall." Neil pointed at a misshapen glass ovoid next to the water. "They call it the glass gonad. Or the mayor's bollock. You can see why, can't you? Our new mayor is up there," he said. "He can see this van right now. Mayor Boris."

The girl dutifully followed his gesture. "That thing? City Hall? Is that what that is? Mayor's bollock!" She laughed freely. "Boris? He the guy with the hair?"

"That's the guy." He might have to explain, back at the yard, why the round had taken so long. Or – a better idea – he could just leave the rest of the parcels on the van for tomorrow's round. No one would ever know, probably. No one looked in the vans overnight.

It was sheer unexpected joy to have such a girl beside him. Any girl would be a delight, but this one had done a show for him. She had an easy, decadent, seductive quality that some women just do have. She gave it out like a perfume. Something in the posture, the angle of her head. Something about the uncontrollable mass of hair. The way her fingers reached up to fiddle with it. She was beguiling in every loose-limbed movement. The shoulders, the hips, the crossing of the legs, the hang of the wrist. She was trying to remain reserved and distant, but something about her was too alive. She was coquettish, devil-may-care. She couldn't help it.

With a bench seat in front, things would have been too intimate. Sitting out of reach in a passenger seat on the other side of the gear lever, her presence simply decorated the van like a bouquet of flowers. In the midst of Neil's hurried, fretful mood, it seemed an orchestra had struck up, playing Mozart, and glorious, joyous choirs burst into song, even though his ears were still ringing with the bump-and-grind disco beat. Her femaleness improved everything.

On the road, Neil did not waste time. He quickly passed lines of slow traffic and slipped back in at the front. He was quick to see an empty lane ahead or a faster way through. The van was too noisy to speak normally, but he said loudly, "Are you a student? I thought you might be at art college or something."

Amused, she shook her head. "I'm post-grad. And not art." She too had to raise her voice. "I'm doing a Master's in London."

"A what?" Neil wondered if he had misheard.

"An MA degree? Sociology and Psychology," she said. "I'm doing this" – she jerked her head as if back towards the pub – "to put myself through school."

He laughed. "Yeah, I *thought* you were a cut above the average stripper.

"Oh yeah? Is there such a thing as an average stripper? What do you know about it? Have you made a study of striptease?"

"Well, I've done my very best," he smirked.

His passenger was unamused. "Well, I *have* studied it. And if you want to know, I'm totally sicked out by some of the stuff. My dissertation is on Gender Studies. Erotic dancing. I have to write 20,000 words. My title is *Gender and Entertainment: Metaphors of Power and Disempowerment.*"

Neil chuckled at this. "You're having me on!"

"I'm *what*?"

"You're shitting me. Kidding me."

"No," she protested indignantly. "What's so funny? I've been researching it for years."

He smiled wickedly and shook his head. "Hey, I'm Neil. What's your name?"

"Goldilocks."

"Really?"

"Oh, come on," she mocked, "do you think my name is *really* Goldilocks? That's my stage name."

"What's your real name? What shall I call you?"

"Don't call me at all."

"I told you *my* name. I'm Neil, OK? Don't be unfriendly."

"Call me Goldilocks. Goldie for short, if you like. Or Locks."

"OK, OK. I'm sorry if I said the wrong thing, or something. Hey, does it hurt your ears, the music in that pub?"

She shrugged. "Not really."

"Why do you live so far away? How long does it take, on the bus?"

She frowned. "Hours and hours. Over an hour, anyway. Plus there's some walking, and the waiting. I allow two hours to get there, worrying about being late. Yeah, I need something closer to home. But my problem is... I don't *wanna* do this close to home." Neil nodded several times to show he understood. "I don't want neighbours – you know – guys – well, I don't want *any* neighbours to see it, women either."

"Why don't you get some other kind of work, near home. Waitressing, I don't know. Something you can tell the neighbours about, no sweat."

She shook her head. "No, it *is* worth it. I make more in four twenty-minute dances than a whole week of waiting tables."

"What about a bike?" he suggested. "Quicker than the bus."

"Like, a motorbike?"

"No, a cycle. A bicycle."

She shrieked with laughter. "*What?* Me, on a bicycle? All the way to Hackney?" She giggled again at the suggestion. "Anyway, riding a bike is so dangerous."

He loved her cowgirl drawl. And let-rip laughter. And fancy-dress hair. And the wide smile of perfect white teeth. He said, "I cycle everywhere. Six miles to work every morning. Six miles back at night. It's nothing. Not even a long ride."

She glanced in his direction. "Yeah? That's why you look like an athlete." He liked the way she said that, 'a-ther-leet'. "What you say your name was again?"

"Neil."

"You got a wife, Neil? Girlfriend?"

He shook his head and asked. "You married?"

"Yep."

He took time to digest this. "Doesn't your husband mind... you know, mind his wife doing that kind of work?"

She hardened her expression. "Huh, yes and no. It's a long story, too long to tell." They sat unspeaking.

Suddenly he noticed something harsh and bitter, moving just below the surface of her features. Perhaps it was determination. Maybe it was anger.

"Where you from?" he asked.

"The U.S." she said. "U.S.A." Then, as if he might not have heard of it, "America?"

"Yeah, I know – but I mean, like New York, Texas, where?"

"I'm from Alaska."

"Really?"

"No, not really," she laughed at him. "You really think I'm from Alaska? Is that what I sound like, to you?"

"No – I dunno. I thought maybe people in Alaska..."

"Alaska!" She carried on snorting at his mistake. "No sir, I'm a genuine Southern country girl." Abruptly, she became calm and pensive. "If you want to know, I'm from Kentucky," she said tersely. "One hour west of the Mississippi River. Two and half hours from Nashville, Tennessee. 'Bout three hours from Memphis, Tennessee. You musta heard of Memphis. Both my parents came from there. Is that what you want to know? Why would you want to know *that*?"

He did not know where Kentucky was, or Tennessee, and understood her point. None of it made any difference. She was from somewhere, and had a story too long to tell.

She carried on talking in a quieter voice. He slowed to hear her more clearly. "We lived out in the middle of nowhere. My folks ran a gas station out on the highway. That's where we lived. Right at the gas station, in a couple rooms above it, and a kind of shack at the back. I don't never even want to go near the place ever again. I dunno why I should tell you all about it. It's all personal stuff, private."

"What's your real name?"

"Joy-Belle."

"Really?"

She turned and grinned. "Yeah, I know! Sounds like a stage name too, don't it?" Outside, crowds thronged Coldharbour Lane. The word *Murder* caught his eye, across a yellow and blue police signboard on the pavement. *We are appealing for witnesses.*

She directed him into a street of terraced houses just like his own. Except that this street was not curved, not on a slope and had fewer trees. It was uglier. The houses, though, were more attractive, because they all had porches. He stopped where she pointed.

"We made good time," she said, "didn't we?" It had been less than twenty minutes. "I might still be waitin' at a bus stop in Hackney." She turned to him with a pretty smile and swung the van door open.

"OK?" he said.

"Cool. Wanna come in?" Her eyes were gazing straight at his.

"You asking me in?"

"Yeah, I like you. I want to say thanks. You know, for the ride."

His heart raced. "Just say 'thanks for the ride.' That'll be fine. I said there were no strings."

"Come in. I have another way of saying thanks. I don't mind a few strings."

Fearing a trick, or a trap, Neil locked the van and followed her into the flat. It was calm and quiet inside, restful with smooth, creamy, magnolia-coloured walls, and rugs of rough undyed wool on a polished floor of pale wood.

She led him to an open-plan kitchen-dining room. Maybe she just meant she'd make him a coffee. "So nice, this place. Looks like just-decorated," he remarked uncertainly. His mouth was dry with nervousness. Was he about to get laid? Or was someone about to jump out of somewhere, maybe mug him.

She agreed. "I like it. Little bit expensive." She seemed perfectly at ease.

"How much?"

She told him her weekly rent and he whistled at how cheap it was. "I'm paying almost the same, for a crap place in north London. It's like, a little studio flat. Just two rooms."

"Yeah, well, maybe it's a better neighbourhood. Round here, it's scary to leave the house after dark."

"Joy," he began –

"Joy-Belle," she corrected him.

"Joy-Belle, where's your husband? Is he at work?"

She smiled. "Is that what's hanging you up? He doesn't live here. He's in L.A."

"Yeah? You're separated from your husband, then?"

"Yep, in a way. Temporary separation." She opened a door and led him into a bedroom. He wondered what was happening.

More pristine pale walls. Two canvas easy chairs, a wardrobe. Against one wall, a double bed. The furniture was all white, and all kit-style, maybe from Ikea. Slatted blinds covered the window. He approached them and peeked through. He looked across small gardens to the back of a row of houses. People moved around in some of the rooms, living their lives. Everyone he could see was black. He pictured being in a house where everyone was black, where he himself was black, and reflected that in the area where he lived now, almost everyone was white.

He turned back to the girl. Nonchalantly she pushed the door shut and turned to look at him, quizzically. What was the catch? He glanced around anxiously. "Come on, feller. Get me out of these things." Her manner was brisk, which somehow put him more at ease. "You want take your pants off, honey? If you like. It's up to you. Just a real, real quick one. A quickie, OK? Can you do it real quick?"

Even now Neil was afraid he had misunderstood. Was she inviting him to have sex? Would he be accused of rape, later? He felt that he was watching a film.

"Why you doing this?"

"You truly just wanted to help me. You brung me here an' never asked for nothin'. An' you're horny as a ram."

"Really no strings?"

"Just a couple of clips at the back."

A few minutes later he was driving back towards the City, while Joy-Belle sat in her kitchen and congratulated herself.

Neil laughed aloud. He marvelled. The street seemed cheerful. People were swinging their arms, smiling as they walked, children skipping happily, birds scooting nimbly from tree to tree, cars gliding merrily along the road. He heard calypso music somewhere, laughter and singing. He heard her southern accent, her coaxing, delicious compliments. His palms could still feel her smooth, shapely body. His fingertips remembered everything. In his chest and stomach a sensation of joyous relief, as if he had sprinted a one-mile race against all the world and won it by a mile.

It's like water. When there's plenty, you drink, drink, drink without a second thought. Even throw it away.

But go without for one day and you can't stop thinking about it. You start to imagine that cool liquid, clear in the glass, those cool fresh sips, splashing, sparkling drops, touching your dry tongue, your dry lips, your dry mouth, your dry throat.

But then! Suddenly a great gulp of soothing water, let it pour over your mouth and face. I was bathed in pure spring water and drank my fill from finest crystal. That bad thirst... for weeks. Can't even remember. Because when there is enough to drink, you

cannot remember. This very morning, it vanished into the past.
Before Goldilocks.

And then she had made her offer.

"Hey, feller." It made him smile to remember the matter-of-fact trailer-trash voice. "You take me to and from the Maypole pub, like today, fast and on time, and we do this – each and every time. Only a quickie, though, yeah? Just like this, OK? You cool with that?" She looked at him. "That's good value for me, if it is for you." Still she waited for an answer. "I do the show Tuesday an' Thursday, right? Two days a week." That was the offer. "Can you do it?"

"Do what?" He again began to fear a trap.

"Take me to Hackney Road and bring me back, real fast like you did today. Two days a week. Just until my old man gets back."

"Shit!" Neil realised he had not understood about the husband. "When will that be?"

"Couple of weeks, couple of months. Maybe never. Can you do it?"

"What about the deliveries? My job?"

"You find a way." She arched an eyebrow suggestively.

He thought – it could go wrong. Sometimes Stan would be sent out with him; or he might be taken off the round for a day. Sooner or later someone would see them and report him to Critchlow's. No point in explaining all that to her.

"All right," Neil replied, "it's a deal. If there's a problem, I could text you."

Joy-Belle smiled sweetly. "And like you said – no strings, OK?"

He punched the air. He began to sing, bursting into *What a Wonderful World*, la-la-ing where he couldn't remember the words, imitating Satchmo's growling, mellow voice, overflowing with contentment. A wonderful, wonderful world!

* * *

Bernard's desk stood beside a window at the top of the house, in what had once been the loft. He turned the chair to peer through the darkening glass, seeing an indistinct geometry of rooftops, and black treetops moving. A few lit-up windows, scattered illuminated rectangles, gave glimpses into neighbours' lives. Beyond lay a vast sweep of suburban London, glittering unknown land, tiny yellow streetlights drawn in parallel lines. Millions of homes, happy or unhappy.

A painful sympathy, rather like love, went out towards all who work, who struggle, who pay their bills, who try to do the right thing and who make sacrifices for their children's sake. At the same moment a bitterness burned in his blood, against all who oversaw a nation sinking into disorder, in which commerce had triumphed and community was trodden underfoot.

He turned back to his desk. His next task was to write a letter on behalf of KOBRA.

Dear – and he typed the name of a functionary.

Bernard was used to this sort of thing – letters to council officials, Members of Parliament, offices in Whitehall, Government departments, the police, the whole grim corps of officialdom. He regarded them all as traitors and cheats, guardians of the common good who care nothing for the common good, mutinous public servants who refuse to serve the public. All wallow in idleness, deceit, greed and venality. All have to be buttered up and flattered.

I would like to speak at the hearing on behalf of the Kenilworth, Osborne and Blenheim Roads Residents' Association.

We object, he continued.

Yes, indeed, he did object. A developer wanted retrospective planning permission for a shoddy side extension that had already been built and was already filled with tenants. He longed to write that the whole sorry structure ought to be demolished, the rubble swept away, the house restored to its former modest dignity and the developer deported to his own country for breaching British planning regulations. The tenants, too, should be deported. That was not going to happen.

He needed three sound reasons to object. Firstly, *Out of character.* Secondly… he pondered.

Secondly, *Exceeds permitted development.*
Thirdly...
Now he heard the doorbell, and hoped it was nothing.
Elizabeth would deal with it. A male voice spoke, that he
recognised but could not place. Bernard stood up and went to
the door of his room to listen.

* * *

After his shower that evening, relaxed and contented and in
celebratory spirits, Neil opened another bottle of beer and put
on the Cannonball Adderley Quintet. He turned up the volume
and rolled a large joint. He leaned back on cushions, inhaled
deeply, and closed his eyes in joy as saxophone notes went
shrieking and flying all over the room, exotic birds in a lush
fecund wilderness of piano and drums and whistling, clapping
and catcalls like a hot black swampy jungle of sound. The music
ended with a sudden reverberating silence and he lay on the
sofa. The room wheeled round, circulating his mind as slowly as
stars in the heavens.

Suddenly he sat up. He needed some air. He'd go somewhere,
he knew not where. Outside, the sky had become a rich evening
blue, as flawless and smooth as paint in a tin. Even the weather
had caught his mood, it seemed. There was not a cloud
anywhere. He smiled slightly, utterly stoned.

All along Blenheim Road, front room lights were on, curtains
and blinds not yet drawn. He glanced into each window. Figures
on sofas watched television, or gathered around tables. Family
life! He remembered sitting at tea with his sisters, Mum in the
kitchen, the house always haunted by the unmentioned ghost of
his father.

He saw how Blenheim Road was like two streets, slummy at
the top, button-down smart at the bottom. The change came
abruptly, about half way along, near a small office block. At the
end of Blenheim Road, a gateway opened into a park. *Osborne
Park*, read the sign. Double gates stood wide open. He stepped
through. Trees were darkly silhouetted against the blue velvet

dusk. Lights at a café on the far side of the park shone invitingly. He heard, and then saw, some youngsters gathered on the grass, boys and girls, cigarette ends glowing intermittently, like fireflies. They quietened and ignored him as he passed.

It turned out that the café was closed. Its doors were locked, though a dozen men stood inside, drinking from paper cups and bottles, laughing and talking loudly in some foreign language that he did not recognise. East Europeans, by the look of them. He tried the handle, but they made no move to let him in. Maybe it was a private party.

He left the park to stroll along Osborne Road and into Kenilworth, parallel to Blenheim. The houses here were much bigger, with space in front for a car as well as a garden. Dazzling security lights clicked on suspiciously as he passed each one.

Suddenly Neil remembered something, and walked back. Yes, this was where that bloke lived, the feller from last night – Bernard. He said his house was on this corner.

Neil stood and looked it over. Luxuriant plants in half-a-dozen majestic glazed pots stood either side of a large porch. Two cars stood where part of the front garden had been laid with fine old paving. A small lawn, weedless and trimmed, looked as immaculate as an architect's impression. Neat flowerbeds decorated the perimeter. A pretty little ornamental tree was swathed in delicate red leaves, Neil wondered what you have to do to get enough money for something like this. Last night, they had only talked about jazz. He hadn't asked Bernard what he did for a living. The curtains were drawn across a bright front room window.

Impulsively, Neil found himself stepping into the porch. He pressed the bell and heard its ring, then footsteps approaching. It struck him that he had forgotten why he was standing there. As the door opened, he realised he would have to ask Bernard something, about music, about jazz.

"Yes?" Elizabeth forced a faint smile and struggled to sound amiable. Her voice was crisp, clear and cool; the accent, educated and middle class.

"Uh – is Bernard in?" he replied sheepishly. "Is it a bad time to call?" Jeez, he felt smashed. He assumed this was Bernard's wife and certainly she was about the same age. She was trim, and wore a pale shirt and dark trousers. She held an apron and some oven gloves in her hand. The effect was all at once casual, expensive, modest, homely and very reserved.

Her face, framed by straight hair, nicely cut and nearly grey, and with old-fashioned tortoiseshell glasses, struck him as severe and unwelcoming. What did they do under the sheets, he wondered, the jovial Bernard and this prim, prissy schoolmarm? And he considered, as men sometimes do, that there was no accounting for other men's tastes.

Elizabeth shook her head. "I'm sorry. He's very busy." She spoke brusquely despite herself. "I can give him a message."

Neil was glad to hear this, as he didn't really want to see Bernard. "It's not important. Tell him Neil called. 2 Blenheim Road."

"Neil," Elizabeth repeated, as if determined not to forget. "All right, Neil. I'll tell him. Does he know your phone number?"

Bernard called out, "Liz, I'll come down. Hello, Neil. Come on in – I'll be one minute."

Elizabeth, astonished, opened the door wider to let Neil step inside.

"Hello Bernard," Neil said breezily, "just wondering if you have Louis Armstrong singing *Wonderful World*." Of course, that would be just Bernard's type of thing.

"Ah – yuh, that's one of mine. Wouldn't have thought it was *your* cup of tea, though."

"D'you mind if I have a listen? I've been wanting to hear it all afternoon. I can't remember the words and it's driving me crazy!"

Elizabeth caught Bernard's eye questioningly. Bernard too was puzzled. "Well, I am busy, very busy, you know. Very. I'm right in the middle of something. I really can't stop now. But come in, come in. You want to borrow it, you mean? Can't really lend it to you, sorry – much too valuable. It's the original recording." He led the way along the hall. "If you only want to hear the one track," he queried, "can't you buy it on iTunes for 79 pence, or something? Or even watch it being performed on YouTube?"

Neil now realised horribly that he most certainly should not have come. It was outrageous. It was embarrassing. He had met Bernard for the first time only yesterday and now he was dropping in like an old friend. He felt himself an idiot. He must sober up.

"Um, yeah, actually," he feebly sought some better motive, "what I really wanted, was to ask you... about the Residents' Association. What it does... and stuff. I'd like to, er..." he tried to clear his head and make sense. He stopped short of saying he would join it. "Y'know, I thought maybe I'd... you know, I'd like to... if there's anything... like, to help. Sometimes. Not all the time. Yeah?"

He glanced around and exclaimed "Sheesh!" The sitting room struck him as extraordinarily elegant. It was bright, as bright as a sunlit holiday island. Maybe it was because he was stoned, but everything had the sheen and plumpness of considerable expense, from rich, ivory-coloured walls and framed paintings, to polished oak furniture, the glittering chandelier and thick-pile circular oriental rug. This was so much smarter than a lot of places on the Ascot round. Incredible that it was just around the corner from his own crummy little flat.

Neil wondered if Bernard and his wife had deliveries from Critchlow's. Hadn't Stan said he came here on the Hampstead round?

"Ah!" cried Bernard, "You are a good citizen after all! I knew it! Neil, can I ask, are you all right? Is there anything wrong? You don't seem yourself. Please do sit down."

"No, I'm..." Neil heard his voice echoing in his head. "I'm tired, yeah. A bit tired. Had a tiring day. And, um, I was just passing, so... anyway. And I thought, oh, you know... but I'm... Well, I'll go now and leave you in peace. We can talk about KOBRA another day, yeah?"

"No, no! You're here now! Sit down, sit down! Let's talk about KOBRA for a couple of minutes. Well, we have all sorts of issues going on in the neighbourhood." Bernard paused to flick through a huge collection of vinyl LP albums on tall shelves, muttering "Wonderful world, wonderful world. These records! They should be put in some sort of order."

Neil looked around at the sofas and armchairs, but did not sit. He feared he would never get up again if once he sat down on all that upholstery, among those cushions.

"Hey, is that an old radiogram?" He stared at a piece of fine mahogany furniture, with two enormous built-in speakers, standing in an alcove.

"Yah, yah. Lovely, isn't it? 1937 GEC. I need it to play my 78s."

Against another wall stood a splendid upright piano, massive and polished. "Do you play the piano?" Neil asked.

"No," said Bernard. "It's my wife's. It was her mother's. My daughter, Ruth, can play very well."

Inside a cabinet with glass doors, Neil noticed a silver candelabra and other curious silverware arranged beside leather-bound books embossed with gilt. He stepped forward for a closer look.

"What's that writing?" he asked.

Bernard turned and laughed awkwardly. "Oh, that. It's Hebrew. We're Jewish." Better to bite the bullet straight away. This fellow Neil was probably an 'anti-Zionist', as they call the old affliction nowadays. Looked like a Guardian reader. Probably went on that Gaza march with one of those placards, *We are all Hamas now*. One day, they would all be blown sky-high by their Islamist friends. But what can you do? Carry on regardless.

"Ah, yeah, right," Neil mumbled. "I'd like to ask you about that. I mean – um, I'd like to know more about it."

"Really, would you?" Bernard raised his eyebrows as if sceptical. "Well, we'll go out for a bagel sometime and talk religion." He laughed again quietly. "Now, where was I?"

Neil tried to remember, but Bernard had already resumed his thread.

"Ah, yes. A lot of issues. People suffering in our neighbourhood. *Minor* crime, that's what they call it. Little things like mugging, burglary, vandalising cars, harassing old people, theft. That wretched café in Osborne Park! Of course, the park gates are never locked at night! Supposed to be."

"Yeah, um, I saw the café," Neil said. "Looks nice. What's wrong with it?"

Bernard shook his head, "It's OK in the daytime, I suppose. Anyone can go in and have a coffee. In the evening they lock the door and it's like a club for – well, we don't quite know what they are – Kosovans, I think, or Albanians, something like that. Guy that runs it was some sort of commando in the Yugoslavia war. Doesn't speak much English. They haven't got a licence, but they're boozing in there all hours. They throw down litter. They make a racket. They drive cars into the park, which is not allowed."

"Really?" Neil quite liked the sound of it. "Do the police know?"

"No police round here any more. Just these Safer Neighbourhood bods, strolling around chatting to each other like kids on a date."

Neil could not share Bernard's concerns. He had never liked the police anyway. There had been one or two scrapes in earlier years. He had seen the inside of police cells. These objections to the café struck him as trivial.

"Found that record?" he asked.

Bernard did not seem to have heard. "Yup. So much for 'Safer Neighbourhoods.' Safer neighbourhoods! That's all eyewash. People round here don't even bother to report it when they are mugged or burgled or even assaulted," he exclaimed indignantly. "Everyone thinks they just have to put up with it. That no one will protect them. And they're right."

He said he was busy. Now he can't stop pouring out his soul. Fellow's got a major bee in his bonnet. A whole hive of them.

"I expect that's true, yeah?" Neil looked for the words. "But listen, you don't wanna end up spitting tacks about everything. After all, no one obeys all of the laws all of the time."

"That's for sure! 'Twas ever thus! But the situation now is – more and more laws, more and more gimmicks, while descending into utter lawlessness." He pressed his lips together as if it were all intolerable.

Neil shook his head doubtfully. "You know what," he warned frankly, "you'll give yourself a blooming heart attack if you care this much about every little thing."

"Mm – yuh, well, no doubt," Bernard admitted. "Trying to make the world a better place, you know. And isn't that what you want, too? Don't we all?"

Neil held up a calming hand to stop him, "But I mean, wars, disasters, banks going bust all over the place, and you're more bothered about, well, litter and stuff – see what I mean?"

"No, no, no," Bernard shook his head furiously. "You are so wrong! Small injustices lead to larger ones. Society is a myriad of tiny things, a mosaic. You can't solve the massive problems. You can't help everyone. So just do your best for people you *can* help. If you want to make the world a better place, start with your own street. Do your bit!" He clenched his fist for emphasis and said it again. "*Do – your – bit!*"

Neil laughed and wondered how to respond. Somehow he rather admired the older man's ludicrous strength of feeling. Bernard turned back to his music collection. "Now, where is this *Wonderful World*?" He held up an LP. "Ah! Here it is! See this, Neil? The original recording. Released in 1968."

Neil sensed that Bernard had known all along where the record was.

Now that he heard the words, he discovered they had nothing to do with what had happened to him today. But Satchmo's rough breath was wild honey, dripping sweet, the sound of happiness itself.

Neither of them spoke till the last note. Neil opened his eyes.

"Neil," Bernard ventured, "I must get on now. What about Sunday? Are you free? D'you want to come for tea, or something?" Surprised, Neil said he would. Bernard promised, "We'll really *talk* about jazz. So few people can say a sensible word on the subject. Bring a stack of your best music. We'll compare notes."

* * *

At about half-past two, Neil began the walk home from Camden. It took him most of an hour. He liked walking at night. This was the darkest, quietest hour when human life seems at its most subdued. His thoughts returned constantly not to the stripper Joy-Belle, but to Limor.

That was her name, the girl at the Latin bar in Camden Lock, where he had ended up after leaving Bernard's. And that's all he knew. No, he did know a few other things about her. She was some kind of therapist, a "naturopath", she had called it. Best of all, she was a cyclist like him – went everywhere by bike. And loved dancing. He pictured her cycling beside him in some heavenly, sun-dappled countryside.

"Didn't ride here tonight, did you?"

"Why not?"

"That must look pretty. You, in that dress, on a bike," he said.

She pursed her lips in amused disapproval of such brazen compliments. "Anyway, I did not cycle here. I walked."

The walls were bare brick, the ceiling vaulted like railway arches, the floor bare wooden boards painted black. Trumpet and saxophone played raucous, loud and up-tempo. Neil didn't know what kind of music it was – some kind of samba or salsa or merengue. It thrilled him that older couples were dancing. They seemed shockingly provocative for people of their age.

At the bar he had sipped at a cold liquid, sweet and fiery, from a glass sprouting greenery and lime. He watched as two women self-consciously began to dance together. They noticed his good-humoured scrutiny. The short-haired one caught his eye as if sharing his amusement. Suddenly she approached and he heard, or felt, her voice on his cheek. "I see you love tango, but you don't ask anyone to dance."

He returned her smiles. "I would love to dance, but I can't tango. I can buy you a drink, though."

She did not want a drink. Smiles still wide. "You must learn," she said. "I am learning." He liked her accent.

"You're learning tango? Where?"

"At a class, of course! In Swiss Cottage."

"Well, d'you want to teach me a little bit? Now?" He nodded towards the dance floor. "Tell me what to do."

She smoothed her dress and ran a hand over her hair. "All right."

They stood and faced each other. She showed him where to put his hands.

"Where are you from – what country?"

"Where do you think?" she challenged him.

"I don't think you are from anywhere in South America. Or Spain. Not anywhere European. Or Asia. Or Africa. You are not Australian, obviously. You are not from anywhere."

"You are nearly right," she said. The 'r' was guttural, as in French, but she could not be French.

He shook his head. "Where then?"

"I will tell you if we ever meet again," she said, but they did not make any arrangement.

The gates of Osborne Park were still standing open. The park café was shuttered and quiet, the last Kosovan commando gone home. The gang of kids had gone too. A city sky of orange luminosity intensified the park's empty blackness, its menacing calm. Alone in the dark like this, Neil often had an impulse to do something wild and stupid, and that mood rose in him now. He knew the cathartic pleasure of destruction. Something antisocial and illegal. It was the feeling of not being watched.

Yet he discovered, absurdly, that he did not wish to do anything that might upset Bernard.

In Blenheim Road, even the murmur of distant traffic had ceased. His heels made a clear, sharp sound on the pavement. At every house, lights were out and curtains covered the windows.

* * *

And Liliana Petreanu? Still in her room, awake, with the light on.

4

*t*ango *"swiss cottage" london.* Two hundred and thirty-seven thousand, five hundred and sixty results in one eighth of a second. Nine seconds later, Google had told Neil exactly where and when to see Limor again: Saturday evening at The Primrose in Adelaide Road.

Concrete steps outside led down to a shabby basement underneath the pub. A heavy door with reinforced glass opened into a cold, empty room, large and bleak. Neil looked around for something related to tango, but saw nothing.

There were just three people inside, men, all of them middle-aged. Two at the far end were setting out chairs and a folding table. A reedy, nervous type by the door collected fees. Cash only.

"This the right place – tango class?"

The man assured him that it was, adding that the beginners' class would be first, then the intermediate, then the milonga.

"What's a milonga?"

"Just a dance. Where everyone can join in."

"Am I too early?"

"Not really. Starts in ten minutes," was his high-pitched, cheery answer. "You a beginner? Don't worry, there'll be more people. We don't have many beginners. Most come just for the milonga. Have a seat." He gestured to the far end of the hall.

He was right. The first were arriving, as far removed as possible from Neil's expectations. More than half were men, few were young, most were lumpish and graceless. It was difficult to see what had drawn them here. Worse, Limor was not among them. As rattling fan heaters began to blunt the chill in the hall, the arrivals draped their jackets and coats over chairs or in corners. Not one wore the sharp suits and stylish dresses and gleaming leather shoes he had imagined. Neil had put on his white shirt and black trousers. He felt out of place.

With a clap of the hands, two teachers – a man and a woman – called the beginners to the centre of the floor. This small number were shown how to shift the weight from one leg to the other, how to lead and how to follow, how a man should place his hands – on the lady's back, gentlemen, and *never* anywhere lower down than the small of the back! – and how a woman can anticipate what the man wants her to do.

Neil was teamed with a jolly, clumsy partner, her face artlessly made up. A tango began to play from tinny speakers on an old portable hi-fi system.

"Ladies, be sensitive – don't wait to be pushed – you should be able to follow him even if he wasn't holding you! Try it!" They worked at that for a few moments, a curiously meditative tango for the chaste, dancing without touching. The woman teacher took Neil aside to correct him. "Step out! Stride, stride, gentlemen, take bold steps! Don't be timid! She will go where you lead!"

People arriving for the intermediate class, Neil noticed, were better dressed than the beginners; more serious about tango, presumably. With a shock he now saw Limor, taking off her coat. She wore the same clinging wrap-around red dress as at the bar in Camden. She must be freezing! She was joined by a tall, slender middle-aged man, elegant and interesting in a close-fitting black suit, with long grey hair tightly tied back in a black velvet band.

Neil felt that he could not compete with such a man. As he practised different steps with ill-matched fellow students, he glanced often at Limor. He tried to catch her eye, but she was engrossed in conversation with her companion. When they looked up, she did not seem to notice him.

At last a clap brought the agonising lesson to a halt. As the classes changed places, Neil greeted Limor with a friendly "Hi!" She gave "Hi" in return, as if uncertain who he was. He felt himself a fool.

Now real tango began to play, raw and old-fashioned, lilting, sensuous tones that aroused unnamed emotions and invited movement. The intermediates, Neil saw, were far ahead of the beginners. He was entranced by the sensuous elegance of those who had mastered the steps. The women were being shown how to twist a leg around that of the man. The men were shown how to use slight, subtle movements to make the woman follow side steps. Most seemed familiar with these moves already. Limor's friend was annoyingly good. As the lesson progressed, she was paired with several other men. Inwardly Neil raged against them all. He followed every line of her body as she moved around the floor.

As the milonga started, excitement rippled through the crowd. Chairs were pushed back. The volume rose. New people were arriving, some in just the kind of outfits Neil had hoped to see. Women pulled strappy, high-heeled tango shoes from their bags. Almost everyone in the room walked smiling onto the dance floor, some hand in hand. Limor was still with her companion. A few of the beginners stayed in their seats, determined at this stage only to watch, not dance. Most students had come as couples, and began to put their arms around each other and move to the tango beat. Neil knew no one – not even Limor remembered who he was – but nor did he want to hang back. A girl from the beginners' group stood shyly wondering whether to venture onto the floor.

"Shall we?" he said to her.

They began by doing as they had been shown in class, shifting their weight from one foot to another until they were in tune with the rhythm and with each other. Neil's right hand rested on the small of her back, her breasts close to him. He stepped forward, she stepped back, and soon they were, tentatively, dancing the tango.

"Take bigger steps," she suggested.

"'Stride, stride, gentlemen!'" he replied. They laughed crazily at their efforts. He felt that he was making love to this unknown woman. There were many mistakes, quickly put right. They congratulated each other as the first piece finished, and parted. Another man stepped forward to try his luck or his dancing skills with her.

Neil looked around and saw his chance. "Hey, Limor! I took your advice! I'm learning to tango!" he said brightly. He could have kicked himself: why else would he be at the class, if not to learn the tango?

She smiled indulgently. "So now you ask me to dance, Neil, yes?"

"You remember my name!" He took her hand. "I have a lot to learn. This is my first lesson."

"No – your second. I gave you a lesson at the Club Latin."

"Yes! But I haven't made much progress since then."

"Now I give you lesson number three: put your right hand *around* your partner, not on the back. Your left hand – stretch much further out. Make closer communication. Intimacy."

Music started for the second dance, and he did as she had said, drawing her close. He would barely begin a movement before Limor felt it and followed, stepping where he wished her to step.

"Did you cycle here?" He was just making conversation.

"No," she looked at him quizzically, "it's a nice walk. You came here by bicycle?"

"Yup. And you were going to tell me – what country are you from?"

"You can't guess?"

Neil had not guessed, so she told him.

"Oh! Never occurred to me. Were you in the army?"

"Yes, of course. I was a sergeant."

"Wow! You don't look like a sergeant. You don't look like a military man at all."

"That is a rather stupid remark. I shall ignore it. Try to say something intelligent."

"OK." He did not want to lose her, nor argue. Nor sound stupid. He said simply, "Did you like being in the army?"

"Also rather stupid. Army is not about liking. Please – don't talk about that now. You dance beautifully," she said. "Now you must add more steps, more variation."

Her left arm rested lightly on his shoulder, the other reached out so she could hold his hand.

She had not seen, let alone touched, such a strong, upright, vigorous man since leaving Israel. And his eyes! That blue! What a lovely colour. She would like simply to gaze at it. There is no hidden emotion in that blue, no history, no soulful inner world. Only clear light, as bright and perfect as a summer's day.

"Make a sideways to the right. That is easy – a basic step. Then your feet together. Now with the left. Very good."

"Your friend, your partner – is he Israeli? "

"What friend? Step again. That's it, good."

"Tall bloke, with a pony tail?" Neil explained.

"He is not a friend. Just someone in the tango class. An Englishman. Another anti-Semite. Oh –you were jealous!"

Neil laughed. "I don't know."

"Anyway, he's gay," she said.

"I wasn't jealous, but I am *so* glad to hear he's gay!" Neil mocked himself happily.

Limor said, "I like to dance with him because – lesson number four – there is *no* reason to have always 'man leading and woman following'. Sometimes we dance the other way. Why not? Why leaders and followers, in politics, in the bedroom – or in dance?"

"Well, fair enough," was Neil's comment. "Now I'm wondering," he asked, "how come you live in England? Do you have an English boyfriend?"

She laughed. "Ah! You wonder!"

"Well?"

She did not reply. It suddenly struck Limor that this man really desired her. There was an intensity about him. Was it something in the breathing? He looked at her with unwavering concentration.

"Now right foot towards the left," she said. "No, to the left. Cross over."

"Towards the left? I'm not sure of that one," he replied.

"Just take a step, a big step. Yes! Now feet together. Big step out to the left with your left foot. I will tell you what to do."

Neil pushed his bike. Next to him, Limor walked thoughtfully. It was a while since he had felt this thrill, not quite touching, uncertain where it might lead, wondering if she had the same thoughts.

Perhaps not, for she remarked blandly, "It's cold tonight."

"Yeah. Nice evening though."

Primrose Hill rose beside them, dark but for a few low Victorian streetlamps illuminating the line of a path. "Shall we go up?" he suggested.

"Yes, I would like to," she answered simply. "I do not go there at night. On my own."

"I think it's safe enough, isn't it? Primrose Hill?"

"I don't know. Who knows what a man is thinking when he sees a woman on her own?" she said. The words excited him.

They walked up the path. To either side, black trees were silhouetted against the night sky, as if waiting patiently for day to return. At first a pair of red lights high on the Post Office Tower rose above the crest of the hill, then Limor gasped as the whole view opened onto the broad, silvery band which was central London. At the top, Neil leaned his bike on the orientation panel and stood beside her.

"It's wonderful," she whispered. "I did not know. And I live so close! Look – the London Eye!"

The Eye's luminous three-quarters arc curved open beside the proudly upright Post Office Tower. Neil pointed out some other landmarks. The dark foreground below them, the other side of the hill, was marbled with oval pools of yellow light cast by footpath lamps.

"Beautiful, isn't it?" he said quietly. "Did you see the moon?" They turned and looked up at a bright, gibbous moon.

"Let's dance a little more," he said, and moved his hand around her. She gave a wry smile.

"This is exactly why," she said softly, "I don't come up Primrose Hill in the dark."

He stepped forward, she back, and in silence they did dance, he in his thick jacket, she in her overcoat, surrounded by darkness but for the moon and the shining city. Neil remembered vivid scenes from a film, *Assassination Tango*, and felt himself in the shoes of the calm, deadly hit-man who loves dance – and women.

Limor abandoned herself to the mood Neil spun around her. She knew she would never forget this moment, even if she never saw Neil again after tonight. She was tempted to give this man what he wanted. The tenderness of his touch pleased her. She would like to experience him; feel the vitality of this alert, muscular creature.

In the morning, Neil, naked, luxuriated in Limor's clean white bedclothes, a duvet pulled half over his face. She wore a demure white cotton nightdress, neck-high and ankle length. With the cropped dark hair, he thought, it gave her a melodramatic, slightly unhinged appearance. She could have been some kind of weird nun. She had a look of Mia Farrow in *Rosemary's Baby*, but with shorter, darker hair and stronger features and… or – no, better – Jean Seberg in *St Joan*. Or Falconetti in the silent film *Passion of Joan of Arc*. Actually, there *was* something military about Sergeant Limor. Or militant.

She smiled sheepishly, bemused and a little taken aback, in the sensible light of day, to find him there.

"Boker tov, haver. Ma shlomha?" she said.

"Mm… boker tov, haver. Ma shlomha," he repeated.

"No – *ma shlomeh* to a woman. *Ma shlomha* to a man," she said.

"Means?"

"It means 'How are you'. *Boker tov* is good morning. *Haver* means friend. I am *havera*; that is the feminine."

"Good. Tov. Limor gave me my first tango lesson, and now, my first Hebrew lesson. I'd like to learn more. I like languages. I collect alphabets. How do you say 'breakfast'?"

Bacon and eggs, a pile of buttered toast and a big pot of tea, would be perfect. Limor struck him as the croissant and coffee type, though. He'd settle for that, happily.

"Aruhat boker. It means 'morning meal'. You remember boker tov?"

"My mum was a linguist. I think it runs in the family."

Limor suggested home-made rye bread and mint tea.

He pulled a face. "Got any ordinary bread – and coffee?" he asked.

"You don't need coffee, Neil. That is poison," was her reply. "It dehydrates the body. That's not what you need when you wake up!"

"Or tea, then. *Proper* tea, I mean. Nice cup of tea in the morning."

"I have some green tea. Green tea from China is rich in antioxidant polyphenols that clear your body of free radicals."

"Oh, delicious!" he mocked her gently. "Though I have a soft spot for free radicals, personally."

"I have some *decaffeinated* tea somewhere, maybe, I think," she offered, "but it is very old."

"Oh, great. Let's go out for breakfast," he suggested. "There's nice places around here."

She frowned. "*Not* nice places, you mean. We will have rye bread and mint tea. Ze tov me'od – it's very good. If it will be not enough for you, I have home-made cottage cheese and some tomatoes."

Neil grimaced like a gargoyle until Limor laughed out loud.

"Ze tov me'od," he repeated.

* * *

In the Kassin household, Bernard was the first out of bed each day. To him fell the task of making Sunday breakfast. He laid the table with plates of egg-fried bread and maple syrup and steaming jugs of hot milk and dark, strong coffee. It was a labour of love, for nothing in the world gave him such joy as to be at leisure with his family. Elizabeth lay against pillows enjoying the pleasant sounds of her husband singing downstairs, and the pleasant aromas that rose temptingly to the bedroom.

Bernard considered that the goyish day of rest had many

advantages over Shabbat. On Saturday he put on a suit and tie just as on working days. In synagogue he had to make small talk with friends, colleagues and neighbours and perhaps would be called up to make a blessing on the Torah scroll. Sunday, he liked to imagine, was when he would be able to indulge in a morning of utter relaxation. He pictured himself lounging half the day in his dressing gown, feet on the sofa, jazz quietly playing, as he turned the pages of a broadsheet newspaper, uncritically reading whatever caught his eye.

Indeed the Sunday paper was delivered to the door and Bernard contentedly carried it to the sofa. Its bulky, luxurious superfluity of unwanted sections conjured up the gorgeous self-indulgence of the day.

Islamist bombs rock Delhi, announced the headline. *30 dead, 90 injured by explosions in busy market. Bomb defused at children's park[1].* On the other side of the page he saw *Lehman bankrupt, Merrill Lynch sold to Bank of America.*

They tried to blow up a children's park! He felt it had been a mistake to read the paper. In any case, Sunday was always irreparably marred by countless irritations. The curious calm of the day as he remembered it, the sound of space, stillness and emptiness, a haunting peal of far-away bells, all commerce halted, had vanished forever. Bernard's Sunday lacked the poignant sense, for which he painfully longed, of an orderly, civilised nation in repose.

After no more than half an hour of the news section, he took his coffee upstairs to get on with some work. In truth, he felt better that way. A short spell of gardening, or a walk on the Heath, a stroll and a little shopping in Hampstead, remained possibilities for the afternoon.

"I've got to do something on poor Hilda King's case," Bernard told Elizabeth as he threw down the paper and made his way out of the room. "Remember the bin that hit her car? She finally had a response."

"At last! Will they pay her for the damage?"

---

[1] 13 September 2008.

"No! Trouble is," he said, "the letter wasn't from the council. It's from their solicitors. Not the council's own legal department. This blasted council of ours, how they mock and despise the residents! They've employed a top City firm to fight Hilda King. You know Huxters? It's them."

"Good God! Wasting such money on something like this! A couple of hours of Huxters' fees would pay to repair her car!"

"They've scared the wits out of her. Asked her to draw plans, and calculate the speed the bin was moving, that sort of thing."

"How *can* she? All this aggravation, at her age! What does she do now?" asked Elizabeth.

"Oh, nothing. *I'll* do it. I'll just have to answer their questions and draw their plans. And they want photos! Of course, I'll also send *them* some questions to answer. I'll win this for Hilda."

"Oh, Bernard! Oh, and that chap – is he really coming for tea?"

Bernard said he expected Neil at about four o'clock.

"Well, I don't think I approve," she said.

"Don't approve!" Bernard smiled, puzzled. "Of Neil?"

"There's something about him."

Bernard shook his head. "Is there? What sort of thing?"

"I don't know. I think he's trouble."

"*Do* you?" Bernard pondered. "Trouble? Well, I can't refuse to see a fellow on that sort of basis," he said at last. "I rather like him. Tell you something – he has a real knowledge of jazz."

After lunch, Bernard spent some happy moments choosing music to play for Neil. He would teach the young fellow to love big bands! Ease him into it gradually. An appetising smell of baking rose through the house. Elizabeth was making fresh scones. And her scones were a marvel!

Suddenly Elizabeth's voice called sharply, "Bernard, could you come for a minute?"

She and Ruth were in the midst of a tense confrontation. "Daddy –" Ruth tried to get in first, but Elizabeth spoke up: "What do you think of how Ruth is dressed?"

Bernard quickly cast an eye over the form of his daughter in cropped top and a brief, low-slung skirt that seemed to have been trimmed with a pair of shears. "Well, what do you think?" his wife challenged him. "Her going out dressed like that?"

"What?" Ruth responded petulantly. "Is there a dress code for going out into the street? Formal attire?"

"Just look at you!" Elizabeth said. "What do you think you look like?" Then immediately, "God, I'm sorry to put it that way! I sound just like my mother! It's only that I don't want you to be hurt. Can't you say something, Bernard?"

Ruth replied sharply, "So grandma used to say it to *you*, did she? And how were *you* dressed, Mummy? That was the Swinging Sixties, wasn't it? Miniskirt, was it?"

"Look, Ruth, darling," Elizabeth pleaded, "you know what I mean. People can see your *underwear*. And there's not much of *that*."

"Oh God, Mum – *please*!" her daughter exclaimed with disgust. "I'm going to be with *friends*. Are you thinking one of my friends would rape me? Which one do you think it would be?"

"It's not your friends I'm worried about!" Elizabeth protested. "I don't know *who* you are going to see. Or more to the point, I don't know who is going to see *you*. Come on, Bernard, for goodness' sake, what do *you* think?"

"You don't know *what* you are saying," Ruth shot back. "You are always *so unreasonable*. Always! This is actually *modest* compared to the other girls! They think I'm some kind of prude, because of you."

Bernard wanted to support his wife without opposing his daughter. Nodding sagely, at last he spoke. "Mm – look, Ruthie, it's like this. You're nearly eighteen," he said in a quiet voice. In his own mind he sounded insufferably pompous. He tried without success to change his tone, now smiling a little falsely as he went on, "What Mummy says is absolutely true. Don't you see that it can be dangerous for an attractive young woman to make a temptation of herself?" He regretted the word at once, but pressed on. "You won't just be seen by your friends, but by all sorts of other people too. By everyone. It's risky. You don't know what men are like."

Ruth tutted with exasperation. "Well, that's *their* problem!"

she retorted angrily. "*You're* a man, Daddy – what are *you* like?"

How could he explain? Bernard tried to remain calm. "Ruth, I understand how..." The phone rang and instinctively he stopped to listen as the answering machine picked it up.

"Bernard? It's Neil," they heard the message being recorded, "about this afternoon. Can we leave it? Would you mind? Do it another time?"

Ruth took the opportunity to flee in fury from the room. The front door slammed. Aghast, Elizabeth followed close behind, picking up her car keys as she ran into the street, calling, "Ruth, Ruth! Please, darling! I'll give you a lift!"

Alone, Bernard wondered if he could smell burning. "The scones!" But they were ruined. He turned off the oven and dropped miserably onto a chair. His disappointment with the day was complete.

✳ ✳ ✳

Neil spent that Sunday with Limor. Already he knew that it could not last long with her. Still, he hoped they could enjoy one happy day together. He asked if she would like to go out somewhere. There is an understanding among men and women in their thirties, of the pleasure they can give each other, the joy of a fleeting, false intimacy.

"Well, there *is* something. I want to see the Hammershøi exhibition at the Royal Academy."

Surprised, Neil said he would like that. "Is the Royal Academy open on Sunday?"

Open all day, she said. First, though, would he like a ride up to Hampstead Heath?

"Where's your bicycle helmet, Neil?" she asked. "Did you leave it behind last night?"

He admitted he did not own one.

"I have a spare," she insisted.

Neil still in the white shirt and smart black trousers of the tango class, and now with Limor's pink helmet poised absurdly on his head, they started out companionably, riding one beside the other. He glanced often at Limor's rather severe, purposeful face, but she did not return his gaze. She pedalled lost in Hebrew thoughts.

From Primrose Hill they rode to South End Green and followed the paths up steep Parliament Hill. Pausing among kite-flyers at the breezy summit, he pointed out the elegant dome of St Paul's Cathedral, even at this distance radiating a sort of serenity from the very centre of London's vast disorder.

Across airy meadows of long grass they climbed at last to Whitestone Pond, at the top of Hampstead and the top of London. Next to the pond's half-moon of shallow water, encircled by traffic, they rested and talked.

"We're nearly at my flat," Neil said, and he pointed in the direction of Golders Green. "Come and visit me one day." He knew that she never would.

Beside them rose a tall white flagpole flying the red cross of England.

"Who raises that flag, and who takes it down?" Limor wondered.

Neil did not know.

"What does it mean that there's a red sword in one corner?"

"Funny, I didn't notice." He stared up, surprised. Sure enough, in the top left quadrant a slender sword pointed upwards. "Hey, yes, I know what that is." He had seen this emblem, flanked by two ferocious winged creatures with red pointed tongues, several times every day on the City round. "That's the flag of the City of London."

She said Tel Aviv had a flag too. "It shows a lighthouse by the sea, and some words from the Bible. *I shall build you and you shall be built.* From the Prophets, of course."

"You don't look like a Bible-reading girl. Tell me your life story, Miss."

She laughed slightly. "What to say? I am Dr Limor Shalit –"

"Or Sergeant Limor Shalit," he interrupted.

"Yes. A doctor and a sergeant, but not really a Miss. I married to someone, and then I unmarried from him. First I studied at Tel Aviv University. Medicine. And music. I was interested in natural remedies and physical fitness. In my post-graduate studies, I began to look at the mental effects of dance. That is why I am learning a new dance now."

"Not 'cause it's sexy and nice?"

"No!" Limor shook her head. "Sexy and nice?" she shrugged, "That is why it makes good therapy. You know, after trauma and so on. Human closeness, embrace and rhythm is good for the mind. Of course I like to dance. But I am more interested in therapy – not dancing. At London University I make important research into the effects of dancing on the brain. Not the mind – the brain. The students, professors too, they tell the world to boycott this work. Lucky for me, and maybe for the world, no one takes any notice of them. And I work on therapy especially for women. Women's health is a special interest for me. I have my own practice here, private dance therapy for women. I volunteer also, one day every week, to help women in a clinic." She turned to Neil and smiled grimly. "Well! It's a good story?"

"Tov me od," he agreed. "What made you choose London?"

"London is good for medical science. Anyway, now I am British! I can work here, live here. I vote who will be in the British Government."

"How did you get to be British? Was your husband British?"

She shook her head again, "No problem. I lived here five years already! Anyone who lives here five years can be British."

"Anyone? I didn't know that," he said. "And in the army, were you a medic?"

"I was not a medic – it was before my studies. After national service, I stayed in the army. I was in an armoured brigade."

"Wow. You mean – like, tanks? So you've driven a tank?" The astonished question sounded childish in his own ears.

He could not read her expression; it looked slightly contemptuous. "You think I could be a sergeant in the tank corps without driving tanks? Why, you think a woman can't drive a tank? You think women can't fight? In Lebanon, I fought for my country. I expect to fight again. And every year, I do my *miluim*, reserve duty."

"But you're British! Would you fight like that for Britain?"

"Ah! Not a stupid question," she acknowledged. "But the real question is, Mr Englishman, will *you* fight for Britain? No, you will not."

"Come on," he said, "give me a kiss. Let's ride."

She laughed ruefully and kissed his cheek. Side by side, they cycled back over the Heath down to the Hampstead ponds. This was the very place – awful to think of it now – where he used to meet Anwen. That had all started with a dance, too.

He sat beside Limor on a bench. They watched as a pair of dignified swans glided effortlessly. Squealing gulls ganged mob-handed on pieces of bread tossed by Sunday strollers. Hesitant pigeons pecked nervously at whatever scraps fell on dry land.

"Now is your turn," said Limor. "Tell me about Mr Neil Chapman."

He shook his head. "I am not a sergeant, not even a private," he said. "I am a civilian, a member of the public. I am a van driver, and I am," he did not know how to put it, "well, I am nothing special."

She smiled gently. "Never married?"

"Will you marry me?"

"OK," she said.

"Want some lunch?" he asked. "Lots of nice pubs round here. The Heath Gate is good. Do terrific Sunday lunch. Roast beef, Yorkshire pud, the works – you know."

"No, I *don't* know what is Sunday lunch. Or Yorkshire pud. And I am vegetarian."

"Fair enough," said Neil dryly. "They do a veggie version. Nut roast, roast potatoes, all the trimmings. *And* Yorkshire pudding."

"No, it's not good to eat so much."

How can a person become British if they don't even know about Sunday lunch? Never heard of Yorkshire pudding? They need to know all our great British things, like leaves on the line, wrong kind of snow, bonfire night, bangers and mash, poll tax riots, sink estates, sod's law, the Blitz, The Duke of Edinburgh, Auld Lang Syne, Essex Girls, August Bank Holiday, Pancake Day, no rhyme nor reason and a cock and bull story.

They ate salad at an organic café she knew. Neil confessed he didn't want to cycle to the Royal Academy. "Let's go by tube," he suggested, "then if we want a drink afterwards..."

Limor rejected the idea. "A drink! You mean, alcohol?" She was puzzled. "Why should we want a drink of alcohol? You drink too much! It will weaken you, make you ill, maybe kill you."

"Kill me! I don't think a pint – "

"Anyway, the tube is unhealthy."

"Bus, then."

"London buses pollute the air! This is why you ride a bicycle, no? Green and healthy life. You care about the environment? The climate change?"

"No, I don't," he retorted. "I just like to ride a bike, that's all."

Limor was exasperated. "Well! You are *selfish!*"

"So what? S'pose human beings are wiped out. There'll be new species, won't there? Think about it! Anyway, I'm not that bothered about seeing Vilhelm Hammershøi, either. Let's just go back and have sex."

Limor pulled a face. She would have liked to stand her ground, but this man had such frankness and charm about him. Besides, he was actually familiar with Hamershøi! Clearly Neil was not the Everyman he claimed to be. She would not say goodbye to him just yet. Not until this day had come to its end.

* * *

Joy-Belle opened the door and stepped into the street as the van approached; she must have seen it through the window. Up till now she had always worn the same denim jacket and white plimsolls, and carried the same canvas shoulder bag, but today, he saw, instead of jeans, she was wearing a pretty, Fifties-style calf-length patterned skirt.

She did not return his friendly smile, saying nothing more than Hiya and Thanks. She could be surly sometimes. He drove fast, which as usual made the van too noisy for conversation. Anyway it was clear she had nothing to say. Outside the Maypole in Hackney Road, Joy-Belle simply opened the door and stepped out of the van. She said only, "One-thirty, OK?"

As always on a Tuesday, now, Neil had no time for a lunch break. He was waiting outside the pub as Joy-Belle finished her show.

"How did it go?" he smiled.

She shrugged and shook her head. She looked tired, maybe depressed. "OK."

"What's up?"

She tutted. "I said it was OK."

"Something on your mind?"

She turned and gave him a withering look. "I *said* it was OK."

Neil judged that he should not annoy her in case anything went wrong with their arrangement. He took the usual route through Whitechapel. She gazed blankly out of the window.

As they crossed Tower Bridge, he spoke again. "Why'd you say it would make your family spit to see you here? With envy or what?"

"Ah, fuck them," she replied.

He turned and looked the other way for a moment, downriver. A majestic clouded sky spread wide over the empty expanse of once-busy docks. The Thames took a sweeping bend.

"Where are they, your family?" he asked. "In – what was the name of it? Kansas?"

"Kansas? Not Kansas!" she answered irritably. "Kentucky. It's Kentucky, right? Jeez. Kansas is nowhere near Kentucky. Anyway, most of my folks're in Tennessee. I told you that."

Neil acknowledged his mistake. When he glanced at Joy-Belle, she seemed preoccupied, maybe musing about the past. They had moved off the bridge into South London.

"Anyway, there's nothing and no one for me in any of those places," she said. "My parents are dead now, thank God. Both of them. Mom died years ago. My two brothers... I don't know where they fetched up, and I don't want to know. They can go to hell as far as I care. They probably both as bad as Pa by now." She stared ahead at the cars. "Screwin' their own daughters," she muttered angrily.

"*What* did you say?"

"Yep, that's how it was. It's a whole long story, mister. Don't go there."

"What are you telling me? Your father... "

She nodded briefly. "It's not quite as bad as you prob'ly think. Bad enough, but you know, funny thing, Pa was the nicest, kindest man. Better'n most. Didn' exactly *force* himself on me. Well, not too much. Only when he wanted to."

"Jesus Christ." Neil looked her over. She was sitting there beside him, as relaxed and comfortable as before in her skirt, legs crossed at the ankle. There was something incorrigibly provocative about her. As she spoke, she flicked her head to shift the red curls from her face.

"Hey, mind the traffic, mister. Watch the road."

"What happened? Did your dad..."

"I don't really blame anyone, you know. When Mom died, I was the only female thing for a hun'erd miles. Almost her last words to me, right there in the clinic, was *Take care of Pa*. I was kind of mixed up about that. I wanted to show I could take over from her, make her proud of me if she was looking down from Heaven or wherever. I thought she was saying she *wanted* me to do that. She used to talk about it sometimes. I knew that was one of the things she did for him, like fix his dinner.

"He was a wild man, a fighter, a drinker, but there was something so awful sad about 'im. 'Specially after she died. He had a heart of gold in 'im. I ain't kiddin', they were real fond of each other. It was true love.

"And, ah, I *look* a lot like her, so – know what I mean? He never used to beat up on any of us much, like a lot of men do. Sometimes he hit out, you know, bust a few heads. Mom'd whup 'im right back sometimes. She used to come off worst, of course." She laughed at the memory. "We were all scared as hell of the guy, but we all kind of loved him, too. Pitied him, I s'pose. I never thought nothing about it. Everyone I knew was like that. I don't know as it was all that unusual, what happened. Anyway, I wasn't a kid. I was goin' on fifteen when she died, an' I guess I was a sexy little thing. That's when it started to get bad. I split a couple of years later... why did I start telling you this?"

Neil looked at her in horror. "Your dad knew it was wrong." Then he scoffed at his feeble word, "*Wrong!* It was more than *wrong* – it's unbelievable. You were fifteen! *You* might have been mixed up about it, but *he* knew what he was doing! What about your brothers? Didn't they stand up for you? Didn't they help you?"

She guffawed. "Them? No! They were nearly just as bad like him. Hey, that's enough turning over all that shit. 'S in the past. I practic'lly forgot about it. Fuck 'em. Anyway, it was just horseplay. Teenage brothers and sisters do get up to horseplay, don't they? Only *they* played and I was the horse." She laughed loudly again. "I'm sorry I was snappy with you before," she said. "What was your name again?"

"Neil." It dismayed him that she could have forgotten.

"Well, I'm sorry I was snappy, Neil," she repeated, "You're a good, kind man." She pronounced it *kaand*. "You have any brothers and sisters? Any sisters that you used to make suck you off?" She shrieked with laughter.

Neil reflected that it was the first time she had asked him anything about himself. "Yeah, I've got two older sisters, and no, we never did anything like that. As far as I know, Dad didn't fuck them, and we didn't live in a gas station or a shack. We lived in a nice little house in a nice little street. No one hit anyone. We were all happy until he died. Is that what's on your mind today? Or are you thinking about your dissertation on – what was it, gender studies?"

Suddenly she was calm again. "You *are* a real good guy. You're right, there's something on my mind today. It's not about my folks, or my course, or the show. It's nothing about you, but it's gonna affect you, because our little set-up maybe is about to end. But the reason ain't nobody's business. It's private."

"What, then?"

"It's private. You don't want to know. It's about my – well, his name is Winston. That's my old man. My husband."

"Yeah?" He thought Winston was an unusual name. Perhaps the guy was named after Winston Churchill.

"About his parole. He reached parole eligibility. He had his first hearing last week. He's findin' out this afternoon. But when there's like, eight hours of time difference – well, that makes a heck of a long of a wait for a phone call. It's only six in the morning there right now. You realise that?"

"OK, so," it took a few seconds for Neil to understand. He stopped talking and tried to think what she meant, "is Winston in prison?"

"You got it."

"In America?"

"That's where he is, honey. M.C.J."

"Uh?"

"M.C.J. You know?"

He shook his head.

"Biggest fuckin' jail in the whole fuckin' world, and you ain't never even fuckin' heard of it! Men's Central Jail in Los Angeles? That's been his home for four whole years. One of the worst hell-holes in America. Four years and ten days, to be precise. He was parole eligible at four years. Likely he won't get parole anyways. But he has a lot of good time credit and we're hopeful. That's all I can say."

"Jesus Christ. You're counting the days; *of course* you are. What did he... I mean, well, why is he in prison?"

He comes up for parole after four years. So the total sentence is much more than that. What could it be except something heavy?

"OK, that part *is* private. We agreed no strings. You just drive me home, no more questions. Only thing, honey, that you need to know: *if* he gets parole, he'll be coming here, and long before he does, I want to clear away *every little thing* that he wouldn't like. You know, one thing he wouldn't like, is *you*. My plan is, wipe the whole slate clean and start over again, like brand new, when Winston arrives. That'll be the end of the strip show. I'll be in school, a student, an' Winston'll find some straight job. We'll be fine upstanding citizens. That's our dream."

"Is it a secret, then, the striptease – Winston doesn't know?"

"He knows and he doesn't know. He knows what I'm like, but he doesn't want to hear the details. I promised him I would never go back to bein' a hooker. And you want my opinion 'bout that? It's a hooker that *you* need, Neil. Why all the hassle drivin' me around? Why pay for it by *drivin'*? Just be like normal guys and pay with cash."

Neil shook his head. "It's not for me. I don't think I'd enjoy it with a girl in that situation."

"You so sweet! You *would* enjoy it, honey. The girls, they just want you to have a nice time, go away happy. That way you likely might want to come back for more, right? That's good business for them."

They had reached the junction of Denmark Hill and Coldharbour Lane. In a few minutes they would arrive at her door. Neil decided to keep off the subject of her husband. He wanted Joy-Belle to be in the mood for sex. He could ask how the show went. No, he had already tried that. Stupidly, he found himself saying, "Are you really married to him? I mean, you're not just living together?"

"What's that supposed to mean? How can we live together if he's in jail?"

Neil turned by the hospital and looked for a parking place near her house.

"I dunno," he shrugged apologetically, "lots of people do live together, right? That's all I was asking. I lived with my ex for three years." He realised he should not have said three years. It was thoughtless; even before he had met Pamela, her guy was already in prison.

"That's cool for you. But me and Winston are legally wed," she retorted sharply.

"Why would he come over here? Why don't *you* go back to America? If he's paroled, I mean."

"Man, you are dumb sometimes. Why d'you think I came to college *here*? Because Winston is a Brit, that's why! Yeah, this is his home turf. Non-US-citizens is mostly deported when they released. So if we're lucky, he'll be coming home. If we ain't lucky, he won't."

Oh, great. Just about to go into her bedroom, and we're chatting about how she and Winston are joined together in holy matrimony. She's thinking how much she loves him, and hoping he

gets parole and looking forward to being with him. She'll
probably just say let's forget it for today – come back next week.
By which time, the guy will be here and that will be the end of
Goldilocks.

He had not understood that Joy-Belle cared nothing about
being in the mood and was always prepared to carry out her
side of the bargain. In the bedroom, her eyes were suddenly
twinkling as if with delight. He noticed how easily she did that.
She smiled coyly and invited him to take a peek under her dress
and then slip it off.

Everything was deliciously pleasing. Fifteen minutes later
Joy-Belle was already standing in the shower and Neil was back
in the driving seat. He sat a few moments in dreamy, mellow
contentment before turning the key.

That was Tuesday. On Thursday morning, his mobile phone
bleeped: a text message.
Not 2day. NO more rides. Winston paroled. Tnx 4 yr hlp. Plz no ph
or contct. U a swEt guy. Gud luk. Goldilox.

That afternoon, Neil finished the City round early and took a
walk inside the store. It happened to be the first occasion when
he would be entitled to benefit from the Critchlow's staff
discount. He had in mind to buy a parting gift for Joy-Belle, or
maybe something for Limor. He wandered among hand-made
chocolates and fine wines, among sumptuous furs and opulent
evening gowns, shining diamonds and pearls on dark velvet,
and the cleverest, flimsiest lingerie.

It struck him at last that to buy either of the two a gift would
be inappropriate. Joy-Belle had said not to contact her, while
Limor was just a one-night stand. He thought about buying
something for his mother. Maybe for Christmas, or her birthday.
She had no wish to be given anything. She was past all that. She
wouldn't understand.

He left the store. Even with the discount, Critchlow's was too
expensive to buy something for himself.

And on Friday evening – what sort of things does a healthy young man do, single, on his own, at a loose end, with time to kill and a whole weekend ahead? He was determined to fight the urge to get stoned and savour some porn. Nor did he want to go out and pathetically try to pick someone up, or get drunk in some place where he didn't know anyone. If he were still with Pamela, what would they do tonight?

He had a whole library of music and movies. He should sort out his life. Splitting up with Pamela had thrown everything out of balance. He had hardly seen anyone since. Not that he wanted to see anyone. Nor did he want to discuss anything.

One cool beer. For the first time since they broke up, Neil went onto Facebook to see what Pamela was up to. But her page was now Private and she had unfriended him. Anyway, not many of his own Facebook friends were friends at all. He read what they had posted on their walls, their status and comments. Everything was upbeat. It was all irrelevant and trivial. He couldn't simply message them his troubles or suggest a drink together this weekend.

He and Pamela mainly knew people who had been *her* friends, not his. His had been a load of deadbeats. He had been glad when she took him away from them.

Even the few who had known him before Pamela, who were properly his own friends rather than hers, would think it pathetic if he suggested getting together. They'd know it meant he was bored and lonely. They'd realise that was because he'd split up with Pamela. They knew it was all his fault. They were in couples now, while he had reverted to on-the-pull mode.

He must get out, be with other people, anyone. He put an Indian ready-meal into the microwave, and ate it with most of a bottle of Sainsbury's House Red. After his meal, he rolled a joint and listened to some music, nice and mellow – it was an album by Courtney Pine. He browsed his film collection for something suitably frivolous and sexy. Nothing seemed right. He turned on the television and flicked through the channels, switching stations until he felt he was watching them all at once. He was irritated; he wanted something.

A copy of the local newspaper – delivered free to every house in the neighbourhood – lay on the floor. He turned the pages to see what was happening in the area tonight. There might be a brilliant band playing in Golders Green or Hampstead while he sat here wondering what to do!

If not, he could go to Camden, or into the West End. He wasn't too tired to dance. That Latin Bar was good. He might pick someone up. He'd like to put his arms round a woman. It would be weird, though, if he saw Limor there again. He could try some other place.

It was a crying shame, losing Joy-Belle. He pictured crowded pubs, dance clubs and strip joints. *God, I have got to get my rocks off.* He remembered going out dancing with Pamela. He missed that. He thought of a milonga, elegantly suggestive tango steps, holding Limor in her red dress.

Everything in the local paper was second-rate. There was no mention of anything good in Golders Green or Hampstead. On the last pages, under the heading Personal Services, were sleazy ads for 'escorts', 'massage' and 'relief', each with its titillating little picture. He tried to imagine the reality, wondered how it would be.

Paradise til 2am. Friendly Girls. New Faces Welcome. 7 Days – 24 Hours.

A busty blonde in white underwear. Looks good.

Honey Pot. New Faces Welcome. Til 3am.

A sultry girl with big lips and dishevelled blonde hair.

Pandora. New Faces Welcome. To 7am.

Pandora? Not good. Except she was the first woman. And of course, for her box.

Sweet Dreams. Girls waiting. New Faces Welcome. Big choice of girls. Girls for you. Luxurious. Girls. Until 6am.

Joy-Belle had recommended him to do it. They want to please you, she said. He looked at the time. Past eleven o'clock already! Well, he had all night to think about it.

So trashy. What poor mug would fall for this? That's the real shame of it.

Save the money. Spend it on a jazz gig somewhere.

People might find out. A call can be traced. A record kept.

Trouble is, I don't know how much it costs. Or how to choose between them.

It's all lies and cheating. You can't ask anyone for advice.

Why even bother? I'd hate it anyway.

5

No knock, suddenly the door opens. A man walks into the room. An instinct makes her look up at the face, maybe to assess the danger. Behind him comes the woman, as old as her mother, who checks he is happy with what he sees. Liliana is always on edge. Jumpy and afraid. She smiles in his direction.

The wallpaper is a pale colour, nearly white, with an embossed pattern of shapes that could be plumes, like peacocks' tails. Liliana often looks at the wallpaper, trying to find some meaning in the pattern. The ceiling is not quite flat and you can see the outline of the plasterboard panels, which have been papered over with lining paper. If you look carefully you can see the round tops of the screws or nails that attach the panels to the ceiling. She wonders if it is not plasterboard, but just hardboard. She often looks at it, as she is lying on the bed, and thinks about that. Sometimes she counts the number of nails around each panel, and tries to find some connection between the numbers.

This one is about the same age as her father. He's a little more portly. His hair is short and was brushed a few hours ago. He looks nervous and perhaps a little angry. She reaches out her hands towards his hands, invitingly. Be nice, be welcoming. This is what the woman told her to do. The man nods. He is happy with what he sees and steps towards her. The door closes behind him.

There's a window, but it's mostly covered by shutters. She isn't tall enough to see over the shutters, even standing on the chair. She can see the tops of trees, though, and the roofs of other houses. Lying on the bed, too, in daylight hours she can see twigs at the top of a tree, and clouds, and birds flying past, and aeroplanes passing slowly across a few inches of sky. At night, she sees dark shapes against an eerie background of orange streetlight.

He is wearing dark trousers with a crease, lace-up shoes that need a polish, an ordinary shirt with a collar and, over it, a thin woollen sweater. She smiles in a friendly way. He says something, but of course, she cannot understand. She grins and speaks to him in her own language. He laughs and says something more, but once again, she has no idea what he is saying. His words are not English. Most of them do try to speak to her in English. She cannot speak that language either. Maybe it is better for them if she cannot speak.

On a bedside cabinet she has a bowl for washing and a jug of water, together with a pile of towels. There's a large mirror; not the kind that you hang up in a bedroom, but the kind which is screwed to the wall, like a big bathroom mirror. She stares into it sometimes, and tries to see herself in the face which stares back. That face, she thinks, must once have been pretty. The lips are nice, and the nose, too. The skin is getting a weird colour, a faint blue under the surface. Doesn't matter anyway.

The eyes remind her of herself, a little. The hazel green, anyway, is the colour of her own eyes. She sometimes examines the flecks of dark brown in the green. The long honey-blonde hair is hers. She remembers brushing that hair so carefully, once! When she was a little girl, she used to sit on the edge of her bed and brush, brush, brush, as her mother told her to do. Sometimes, and these were the loveliest moments of all, her mother would brush it for her.

She smiles faintly at such recollections, and the face in the mirror smiles faintly too. She does still brush it, but not for so long nor so carefully, nor with her own hairbrush, nor in front of her own mirror, and not sitting on the edge of her bed with mother in the next room. Sometimes she whispers to the image in the mirror, and it whispers to her: "Lili?"

She wonders what to expect of him. Anything is possible. Sometimes her stomach becomes tight with the fear of a beating. When the fear is bad, she wants to go to the toilet. Then she realises she must not think about it, just be like a pillow or a piece of cloth, and her stomach relaxes and the fear becomes less. There is not often a beating or anything violent, and when there is, really very little pain. She is resolved to do what is asked rather than suffer the consequences of displeasing them.

"You like?" she says. Afterwards they clean up and go quickly. She wipes herself with a cloth and water from the bowl.

When she has spare time, when there are no men, she sometimes stands near the window, even though she can't see out, just for the sense of space, and to hear the traffic. She no longer dreams of seeing the world outside. Things have gone far beyond that point. The outside is not a place, but a memory, and it is not *this* outside, but another one, for she does not know what is outside this place, or where it is.

That she will kill herself is the one fixed truth and her only comfort. Somehow, and soon – but she cannot find the energy to think how it might be done. She recoils from the idea of slashing her skin. Anyway there is nothing sharp enough in the room.

He stands still and stares at her quietly. It could almost be him, her father, but smarter dressed than he ever was. She recognises the expression – many of them have it. The face is grotesque with wonder, yearning, fear and anger. He approaches her.

Those in the daylight hours often seem in the grip of a hysteria, a delirium of desire, almost mad with a frenzied need to touch, to hold, to look at her. A lot of them like to look, look, look. They stare intently between her legs or at her breasts. They part her legs for a better view. In the night, they are often drunk. Others are quick, don't look, say nothing and are gone, and she like a used paper handkerchief. His hands look strong, but smooth. Her father's hands had skin as tough as leather gloves. This man is a little too old to be really muscular. Just as her brother is now stronger than her father. If he hits her, or manhandles her, it will hurt, but won't be as bad as some.

He is talking, glancing at her occasionally as if she understood, and now unbuckles his belt. Sometimes they want to hit you, or hurt you in strange ways – pull and twist parts of you, squeeze till you want to scream, push, slap, press with their hands, with their knuckles, sometimes bite. She does not know what to expect. Some are tender, almost loving. Some like to kiss and cuddle and pretend you are their girlfriend. Some like to do both: cuddle you, then hurt you.

She remains calm on the bed, smiling. He speaks a little more in his language. She flinches as suddenly his hand lunges towards her. But he only wants to touch her nightdress, which is the sum of all her possessions. His touch is not violent: he almost caresses the transparent nylon. He keeps talking, sometimes glancing at her for a response. She can only smile.

They are watching her. They are listening. Through the mirror. Or somehow. She does not know for certain if they are or not, but why take a chance? So she always keeps smiling. They see everything that takes place in the room. She flinches again, as suddenly he lunges forward once more, now to touch her face, a little more roughly.

Sometimes the nervous ones do become more violent after a few moments. She has a panic button to press if someone tries to punch her hard, or cut her with a knife. She has used it; what happens is, the men burst in and prevent it. He strokes her face, then her hair, his touch is still gentle, but might change at any time.

His hands now return to his trousers and he undoes the top button. He gestures that she should kneel down and take off his trousers. She unzips them and pulls them down. Most of them wear boxers. Some have no underwear, especially if they are wearing jogging pants. This one is wearing old-fashioned Yfronts, again like her father. You can tell a lot by the underwear. What sort of thing he will do. For example, if it is dirty.

He pulls down his underpants just a little so that his genitals drop down in front of her face. He grabs her hand and places it on his penis. It is slightly enlarged. It is not too revolting, though she can smell the rancid, greasy odour that men sometimes make. He is really quite a clean man, compared to some. With some of them, the smell and the taste is so bad that even before they put it in your mouth it makes you gag. Then they put it in. She knows what he wants her to do, and she does it.

She watches tensely, braced for any change of mood. The man almost grimaces with pleasure. Now he pulls her up, pushes her onto the mattress and parts her legs with one hand. He is talking, perhaps to himself. She smiles. She does whatever they wish rather than risk the punishments.

She has observed that some of the screws or nails that attach the panels to the ceiling have been plastered over, others have not. The ceiling was not well plastered, she tells herself. That is why you can see the outline of the panels. She often thinks about this. Or she counts the pattern of plumes on the wallpaper.

Being hungry is the worst part. Always feeling hungry. Nothing to eat unless they are happy with you.

She remembers walking on Armenească Street with her brother, Sergiu. It was a nice early-summer day, the trees along the roadside green and full. They passed the entrance to the Piaţa Centrală. They had argued again earlier but now suddenly they were getting on all right. Sergiu had said how angry the family still were about her boyfriend. He said it was wrong how she was carrying on with Pavel. And they didn't like Pavel being in Noua Dreaptă,[1] whom they called Nazi thugs.

The stupid thing was that most of them actually shared Pavel's opinion of Jews and homosexuals. Sergiu was even insulting about the Noua Dreaptă members' uniform. He made

---

[1] Militant Romanian and Moldovan antisemitic nationalist organisation.

fun of it, and said all the family were ashamed of her, and she guessed that was true. It wasn't right to make fun of Pavel's uniform. They were so ignorant, so backward. She had had the same rows with her parents, but they had nothing intelligent to say about this or anything else.

The family were fed up with her and she was fed up with them. They were against her living in Chișinău at all. She had virtually stopped having anything to do with them, they were so completely unreasonable and their views so primitive. It was beyond them to understand that she would have a career one day – and they would all eventually reap a reward from having a clever daughter who had escaped the rural life. It hurt her, though, that she could not be happy with her own family. It seemed unnatural.

Only Sergiu could she talk to sometimes, but even he just asked her again and again what was the point of this internship or training or whatever it was, when instead she could be working in a real job to pay her way and help feed the family and get on with finding a good husband. Sergiu said what she was doing wasn't training at all. He called it slave labour. "They are taking advantage of you, Lili! You are too stupid to realise!" But that discussion was over now. She told him she would train as a computer programmer and was not going to give it up for them or anyone.

"You'll see, I will get something good abroad, in the West, and send more money than you can imagine," she had told them. "You will be able to live in a proper house." It was her ambition to live in Brussels or Paris or some such place.

"At this rate, we will all be dead by then," Sergiu replied once, "probably of hunger." It annoyed her that Sergiu had never believed in her ideas. Nothing works out the way people plan it, he used to say.

This afternoon, though, for some reason he was friendly and solicitous. He wanted to meet to tell her something important, and it was urgent.

"Lili, I have found a job in the West. Yes, it's true. I found something wonderful. A wonderful opportunity for you, too, and for all of us. Here's your chance to show if you are serious about helping the family." He was acting as if none of their disagreements had ever occurred. "By the way, I want to show you a shop you'll like, where all the clothes are white," he said. "Dresses and everything – all white cotton and linen. You'll love it. You could try something on, maybe. It would suit you. You will need nice clothes to wear in the West."

Of course, she knew the shop already, but had never been inside. It was for wealthy women. Certainly it would suit her. She was tall and slim, and as good-looking as anyone, she thought. She hoped to afford such things one day.

"What opportunity?" she asked. Liliana tried not to sound too sceptical. Sergiu always said she was negative about everything.

"I know someone. His friend works for a Moldovan company in the West, and they want more Moldovans to work for them. I am going there for a job as a warehouse manager. He said they need temporary staff to help them with their computers. I already said you would do it. They pay Western wages, give training and teach English as well. Why don't we go together? It would be better, being together, in a foreign country."

"In the West? Where in the West?"

He paused as if uncertain whether to answer. "It's in England."

"England? Where in England?" She knew she actually did sound sceptical. On the other hand, he was right, it would be ideal. The job sounded almost too good to be true. It was no secret, though, that such jobs really did exist in the West. "Why did you say I would do it? Without even asking me?"

"Look, I don't remember everything he said. I had to give him an answer. They needed a quick answer. Why do you doubt me? Why do you doubt everything? The two of us could travel together, look after each other. And we could send money home and solve all their problems. If you come with me, and leave Pavel out of it, mother and father will be so happy. They will be pleased with you."

"England is far away. You can't – we can't – afford to go to England."

"We'll be driving there. We won't spend any money, except for petrol. It will all be worth it when we arrive, you'll see."

"What will they pay me?"

"It will be hundreds of dollars."

"Hundreds of dollars! For how long?"

"Hundreds of dollars – *every week*!" Sergiu laughed and clapped. Suddenly he grabbed her hand, "Come on, Lili! Be a proper sister! A proper daughter!" With these words, he pulled her into a side turning. It was a narrow, crowded street, lined with busy little stores. "Let's go this way." This was not the best route to the white shop, but no doubt he had his reasons. She would not argue. She thought maybe everything was going to be all right with Sergiu from now on. He seemed so nice today. Yet somehow he was acting strangely. He was never this friendly to her, even at the best of times. His suggestion that they live together sounded far-fetched. Still, it would be good to prove to the family that I.T. skills were worth money.

"When are you leaving, for this job?"

"This evening. In one hour."

It sounded impossible. Either madly impulsive or something fishy. "This evening! Today? You are leaving today? In an hour from now? Why is it so sudden? Have you said goodbye to mother and father?"

"Yes! Of course I have said goodbye. Come with me, Lili! What is there to lose?"

He was right about that. There was nothing to lose by leaving Moldova, except Pavel. Maybe he could come too? She wondered about luggage. "I need time to think it over. And to pack. What's the hurry? I want to ask Pavel what he thinks. Don't I need a passport and exit paper, and what about visas? And I would have to explain to –"

He frowned angrily. "Always making objections!" he snapped. "Just write to Pavel and tell him! I have taken care of the papers. Tell him you will soon be back, or that he can join you in England. No, you don't need visas. I have some new papers for you. Just give me your Moldovan ID, that's enough for now. Why worry about packing? Anyway, we can't take luggage. We have to travel light. And we have to leave straight away – there is no choice."

"Why, Sergiu?" She implored him to be honest with her. "Why is there no choice? Tell me, Sergiu, tell me the reason."

"Look, it's obvious. I don't want to explain it all, Lili. We know someone who will help us with the formalities. You know, the visas, the border. We knew it would be short notice. There is no point in discussing it. It may seem strange, but we are travelling first to Hungary. We have a friend there who will show us a way into Austria. Then it's easy. Italy, France, England – and that's all. I have put your name on the paper for leaving the country – "

"Why did you? Without asking me? This all sounds illegal, Sergiu. Are you allowed to do this?"

"That's taken care of – I said, we know somebody. Come on, be brave, Lili! Take a chance! Do it for Mum and Dad! And it will be great for you, too, your career. It's not really such a great crime to cross a border, is it? Anyway, Moldova is going to join the European Union in a few years. Then we'll be able to go to the West whenever we want, so what's the difference?"

As they walked, they bumped into some friends of his. In retrospect, they seemed to be expecting him. Straight away, everyone had a soft drink. She cannot understand where they were, she cannot remember a café in that street. Was it perhaps in a store? They really did go to the white dress shop, but Sergiu only talked quietly with the owner in a back room, and she felt too drowsy to look at anything. She often tries to recollect exactly what happened. It's hard to remember why she began to pass out from fatigue so soon afterwards, or how it happened that she found herself joining them on the journey.

This one is a big, strong young man, almost hairless. The woman shows him in. There's a kind of dog like that, she thinks: muscular and hairless. From Mexico, she seems to recall. It has an X in the name.

He looks as hard as nails and she fears the worst. She smiles. He does not bother to respond. When he speaks, it is in Russian, so Liliana could talk with him. But they are listening. The only thing she wants to say is, *Help me*. He is quick and determined, again like a dog. He rubs his penis with his own hand in front of her face, until it is ready, and thrusts it into her mouth.

He pushes so forcefully that she cannot breathe or swallow. She might be able to talk to him afterwards, when he has finished with her. She visualises herself uttering the words, *Pomogit emnye – Help me* – and telling him she is not doing this of her own free will. He might let them know downstairs, or might simply ask them if it is true, and there will be severe punishment.

She has been punished before. Like torture. The beatings with the plastic cable, and the other things that she cannot think about, the pins and the burns. On the other hand, he might believe her and go to the police.

And the police might come. The men would pay them to go away and the police would go away, and nothing would happen. Except that if they ever found out that the police had come because of her, the punishment would be much, much worse than anything before.

Liliana does not know how long ago they brought her here. Hundreds of men have ejaculated into her or onto her, slapped her or kissed her.

She has developed an annoying habit of pressing her teeth together until her jaw hurts, and biting the sides of her tongue until it is raw. She wishes she could stop doing that! She has made her tongue sore.

When men kiss her, they might taste her blood, which they might not like, so they might complain, and she might be punished. But when they kiss her, it sometimes makes her almost retch, so they might complain anyway. Especially the ones whose spit has liquor and cigarettes and vomit.

Now he is talking to her, to himself, just filthy nonsense. He takes it out of her mouth and climbs onto her. Of course, if she asked a man for help, he might not believe her at all. Or, he won't go to the police because probably he is a criminal himself.

He takes it out of her again and back in the mouth. She hates the taste but is past caring about that. He takes it out and spins her round – oh no, he wants to do it in the rear. He grips her in a frenzy. She grits her teeth together against the pain.

The most likely, and the worst, if she said anything, is that he would mention it downstairs. He is getting faster and writhing wildly. Now he comes out and climbs on top again. He presses it savagely against her face.

The man is in a silent rage of arousal. She hopes he won't try to push it into her eye socket or something. He seems mad enough. She thinks of holidays as a child, before she fell out with her family. They went by train to her aunt's village. Anyway, he doesn't know or care about her and does not want to hear. He would simply complain about her. That is the most likely.

A man is shown into the room. He has red hair, cut short. He is too young even to shave. There is a terrible scar. He is grizzled, a grandfather. She has never seen such black skin in her life. She smiles. Tissues, a wet towel. Outside, the streetlights have come on and shine on the tops of the trees. The sky is a sort of turquoise colour. A man is shown into the room. She smiles. She rubs him, tugs and caresses it, and puts the thing in her mouth, but nothing happens. He leaves angrily, humiliated. A man is being shown into the room, by one of the other girls. He asked for her specially. She glances at the faces. She is terribly tired, and longs to sleep. She smiles. She will be able to sleep in the morning. Unless they don't let her. He talks, she smiles. He does it onto her stomach. She wipes it up with tissues, then with a damp towel.

Hideous face and body massed with monstrous spots and swellings; he wants her to confront his deformity, love him in spite of it, thrusts her face hard into his tumours. She smiles, holds his hand. Say it, say "I love you." A giant, gigantic head near the ceiling, penis terrifyingly large, the rubbery hardness like a truncheon. It is painful. A salty, stale smell.

She is tired, and needs to sleep. She is terribly sore between the legs. The skin is raw. This one is young and strong. She smiles. He looks at her and says a few words in English. She smiles and reaches out her hands. He stares at the bed, the washing bowl, the stack of towels, the ceiling, the floor, the walls and the window and at her face. He is nervous. She smiles and nods. He is talking very quietly. Most of it she can't make out, but she does recognise "Do you speak English?"

She knows the question, and the answer – a shake of the head and a little laugh.

He is asking more questions and she gives the same answer. She is afraid of his nervousness, in case it turns to violence. He is a nuisance because he won't just get on with it. If he tries to communicate with her, she may end up being punished. Without a word she takes his hand and places it on her body. She moves to undo his jeans, but he stops her and begins to undress himself.

He has the same expression that so many of them do have. She smiles. He takes off his tee-shirt and jeans, pulls off his underwear and runs both hands gently all over her body, everywhere, appreciatively, like a sculptor admiring his work. Nothing to be afraid of. Perhaps.

Suddenly he picks her right up off the floor and holds her up so that her breasts are at his eye level. He presses his face into her breasts as if her body emanates some drug to which he is addicted. It makes her feel like a toy, a doll, and she tells herself that that is exactly what she is. Her former belief that she was a human being was the illusion that a doll might have in a storybook.

He says something and smiles warmly at her. He must be a fool, if he thinks she would be interested in him or want to talk with him.

She studies the arrangement of plumes in the wallpaper, and counts the nails in the ceiling.

When he has finished with her, he seems unhappy. Some of them do seem unhappy, and that is a danger to her. He quickly pulls on his clothes. He is asking her a question. "Italiana?

Polska?" he says. "Russka? Shqip? Hrvatska? Magyar? Ellenika?"

She tries to wake up. She cannot rouse herself to full consciousness. It's the hunger and the pills, as well as just being too tired to think properly. All these words, she realises, are different nationalities. By "Russka" he means Russkaya. This man is educated. He is a linguist. He is interested in things. Maybe he can help. She has been told not to tell anyone about herself, her name, her nationality, her background, her family or anything about herself. She can say "Hello", say "No English", say "I love you", say "My name is Valentina" – for Valentina is the name she has been told to give. She can say, "Cost extra", say "You like", "Yes" and "No."

"Ha! Ha! Russka! Russki!" she laughs. Then she pulls his ear to her mouth and whispers, "Ne Russkaya – Moldoveancă," then, seeing that he did not understand, "Român, Român, Românesc."

He still does not know what she is saying. Now, from his jacket he takes a ballpoint pen. He feels in his pockets and finds a small slip of paper.

Nothing like this has happened before. She holds the paper between them in the hope that it cannot be seen and writes ten Russian letters. She reads them aloud, "Ya lyublyu tibya!" He repeats it. "Ya lyublyu tibya!" She nods and translates, "I love you." If they hear her saying this, it will be all right. She has almost forgotten what it feels like to write.

With a warning expression and a shake of the head, the finger on her lips makes clear that the next message is private and not to be said aloud. Hastily she writes some other words, tears them from the rest and pushes the scrap deep into his jeans pocket. Puzzled, he nods and thanks her and leaves the room, shutting the door behind him. Liliana hopes that if they ask what she wrote, he will show only Я люблю тебя – *I love you.*

* * *

Neil had thrown down the newspaper and decided against such idiocy. He had even started to get ready for bed. Then he went back to the paper, picked it up again and – quickly, before he could change his mind – almost nonchalantly dialled one of the numbers. Straight away, a woman answered. She had a thick foreign accent, East European. Neil realised that she didn't know him, couldn't trace him and he could say anything he wanted to her with impunity. It was fine. He took a deep breath.

"How much?" he asked quietly. He had some idea that there would be different prices for different pleasures that he might want to indulge.

Instead she said simply, "Forty pounds, thirty minutes. Nice clean, pretty girl. Guarantee satisfaction," as if reading aloud from her advertisement.

Ignorant of the usual prices, he balked at the sum.

You really have got to be desperate to pay that much for it!

"OK. Where is it?" he asked. This too might stop him. He almost hoped it would be in some place impossible to reach without a car. Watford, maybe. Walthamstow. Weybridge. Walton-on-Thames.

She told him it was in Golders Green. For a moment he tried to comprehend what she was saying. He should look for a house behind a tall hedge on the corner of Finchley Road and Heath Avenue. Heath Avenue? Heath Avenue was as respectable as it gets. And it was just around the corner! To walk there would take little more than five minutes. Two minutes by bike. He was astonished, and thrilled, and curious to see what kind of place this was, that he had passed so many times without noticing.

First he had to get the money. Maybe as he rode to the bank's ATM, the mood would pass and he would come to his senses. Neil did not want to disturb his downstairs neighbours at this time of night. He was careful to be quiet as he took the bike outside. He freewheeled to the bottom of Blenheim Road and through the unlocked gates into Osborne Park, past the café – where, like last time, he could see people drinking inside even though it was closed. He cycled to Golders Green Road, drew out the cash and turned down Finchley Road. The mood had not passed. His heart pounded with anticipation. In his stomach was a grip of eagerness.

Just as the woman had said, the house stood on the corner of Heath Avenue, large, detached, red-brick, two storeys, but with dormer windows in the roof. A tall, unkempt hedge partly hid it from view. The garden gate had been replaced by a high piece of rough board, but next to the board was an entryphone, which, Neil now considered, was an unusual place to put an entryphone. On it, a tiny lens eyed all visitors. His finger paused nervously; he pressed the button. The board gate unlocked automatically.

The garden had become what his mother called 'a jungle'. Weeds sprouted from a broken path. All the windows seemed to be boarded up – inside, not outside. *Funny place*, he thought. *Must be worth something, a big house like this. Strange to let it go to ruin.* But then, he had never done this before and did not know what to expect. Perhaps they were all like this. He wondered where to leave the bike so it wouldn't be stolen, and wheeled it round to the side of the building. It should be safe there. Besides, he noticed, there were security cameras scanning each wall.

As he approached the door, his muscles tensed and his mouth became painfully dry. Now he felt his genitals shrinking with anxiety. He would not be able to do anything. Gingerly, he pushed at the door and it clicked open. His desire had vanished. He should stop now and save the money.

It could have been the carpeted front hallway of any ordinary house, except for a security camera on the ceiling viewing everyone going in and out, and a few armchairs arranged near a blank screen and DVD machine. A sour-faced middle-aged woman, dyed blonde hair elaborately wrapped around her head, sat on an ordinary dining chair behind an ordinary office desk at the foot of the stairs. She smiled tightly. "Hi. Nice to see you. Forty pounds for thirty minutes," she said without ceremony.

"I phoned…" he said stupidly. Of course, he realised, she knew that.

She pushed some photos towards him. Six pretty girls in their underwear. It wasn't obvious what she intended. He glanced at her questioningly. "What one you like?" she explained. "You must pay now." Forestalling any questions that he might be too shy to ask, she added, "You can anything, what you want, mouth, spank, anything. You can two girls if you like. Anything."

He ran his tongue over his lips nervously, taken aback by the offer. They were all attractive, happy, smiling girls, nicely made up. They looked like professional lingerie models. "Are they all free straight away?" He gave her the two twenty-pound notes he had brought specially.

Without an answer she stood up and beckoned that he should follow her up the stairs. A row of doors opened onto the first-floor landing, as in any ordinary large family house. The woman pointed at one of them, "Bathroom, toilet."

By chance, one of the doors opened wide as he passed. A man stood in the doorway for a second, a tall, well-built young man with a crewcut, in white tee shirt and grey track-pants. He seemed to have been interrupted in the middle of laughing at some joke. Still grinning broadly, he nodded briefly at Neil and at the woman; she returned the greeting. Neil glanced through the open door into the room.

He drew breath sharply. He saw two other men there. One, head shaved into strange patterns, wore a shirt but was naked from the waist down. The line of a tattoo twisted across his cheek and neck, disappeared under his shirt collar, and reappeared on his legs. The other, rosy complexioned as if drunk, was fully dressed in a track suit, with the pants pulled to his thighs.

Tanned, robust and in high spirits, they stood either side of a padded low table – it was a massage bed. Both men were holding their erect penises. On the bed between them, a young woman was stretched out naked, half propped on one elbow. Neil noticed rich mahogany-brown hair and brown pubic hair. The tattooed man pointed his penis at her face.

Neil thought she was timidly smiling as if sharing their amusement. At that moment, she noticed the open door and looked straight into Neil's intrusive eye. Then he knew for sure that her amusement was terror, the smile forced and frightened.

In the next instant Neil had passed the room and was continuing along the corridor. The tall young man stepped out, shut the door and went into the toilet. Neil wondered if the three men were sharing the cost, or had to pay forty pounds each, or was it, perhaps, a special rate, say sixty pounds the lot. Somehow, he felt that it was one of the most upsetting things he had ever seen.

Neil was shown into a small, sparsely furnished bedroom. A girl, a woman, say about twenty years old, sat quietly on the edge of a bed that was covered with a sheet, no blankets.

The older woman closed the door and at last Neil was alone with a girl whose time he had bought.

Neil knew, of course, about human trafficking, and the trade in women. He wondered if what he had just seen was anything to do with that. But this girl stood up and welcomed him with a smile, reaching out her hands. She did not seem scared and her smile did not seem especially forced. Rather, everything about her was artificial, automatic and lifeless. *Why would it be otherwise?* he reasoned, *It's only a job.* She wore nothing but a short transparent nightdress. Beneath it, she seemed frail, thin, half-starved. The air had a familiar, unpleasant bedroom odour, emissions, secretions, perspiration and air-freshener.

It was hard to believe he was standing here in this repellent place with another human being. That both of them had been so reduced! He would like to open the window but, when he pulled the curtains aside, it was almost completely covered by wooden shutters which were screwed together and could not be opened. If it were him, he would want to be able to open the window. It would depress him to spend more than a few minutes in this room. Well, he had paid to spend thirty minutes in here, with this smiling, willing companion.

Joy-Belle had assured him that such girls only want to please, because that was, as she had put it, "good business." He frankly could not believe that the wretched young woman reaching out to him was in any kind of business. She must be an employee. Despite the phoney smile, she looked tired and unhappy and slightly stoned. Her room was little more than a white box. Still, he had stayed in hotel rooms that were no better.

Next to the bed stood a chair and a table with a basin and some towels. His gaze fell on a waste-basket filled with used tissues. Other men's tissues! That's *not* good business. She could at least clean up between clients, make each one feel special. He knew it was all a pretence, but she should try to give you the illusion.

It was an interesting, pleasant sensation, knowing that she would do whatever he wanted. She did seem very subdued and pliant. He could tell that she would not resist anything. She would not have the strength to object.

"Do you speak English?"

She shook her head and giggled at the question. Her response struck him as unnatural and practised. Her thin body, though, behind the veil of her nightdress, was utterly natural and real, intoxicatingly within reach. She smiled as if to say, *What are you waiting for?* Gently she took his hand in hers, and placed it on her breast. That heat came flowing back as all his anxiety subsided and confidence returned.

"You know what I'd really like? I'd like to take you somewhere nice for a drink, have a talk and listen to some music and relax, then have sex."

Of course! That's all available too, you idiot. But not with this girl and not for forty quid.

"Well," he smiled at his foolishness, "you don't speak English, and we're stuck in here, and I'm broke, so that's off the agenda."

The girl smiled dumbly, giggled without amusement and started to undo his belt. She seemed quite keen, somehow. This surely meant that he really was free to do as he wanted. He ran his hands over her. What joy! An exuberant delight made him lift her up in his hands. She was so young, light, unresisting.

"Blimey! That picture of you downstairs – you've lost a lot of weight since then! Are you on a diet or something? You look hungry. You need feeding!" He grinned, then realised that she had understood not a word. "Parlez français?" he ventured, but no, her reaction to French was the same as to English.

They lay on the bed. In a strange way he could almost imagine it was Pamela. Though she was nothing like her. He reached down – he would try to give her some pleasure too; it was the least he could do – but she pulled his hand away and urged him to continue. Of course, he reasoned, because pleasure did not come into it; this was simply a job. Perhaps she even had a boyfriend, a lover.

Afterwards, free of desire, concerns filled his mind. She had been like an automaton, so entirely unresponsive that he suspected she might even have fallen asleep. He wondered if she was drugged.

Who, after all, is this person? An unknown, anonymous girl. Something is wrong with her. This is no Joy-Belle!

As he pulled on his clothes, he tried to ask where she was from, just guessing at the feminine forms. "Italiana? Polska? Russka? Shqip? Hrvatska? Magyar? Ellenika?"

She whispered something in his ear, but he did not recognise the language. He gave her a scrap of paper and she wrote something in Russian characters but then, in English, said she loved him. Perhaps she could speak English after all. Loved him! How absurd. He didn't want that! Surreptitiously she tore the paper, wrote a second note and shoved it deep into his pocket.

Neil left the room and went downstairs. A young man in blue overalls was standing there. The woman glanced up, "Good?"

He nodded, "Good, yeah. Thank you."

She led the other man up to take his place.

Definitely not worth forty pounds, unless you couldn't go another day without it. Anyway, he had done it. He had visited a prostitute. That was a barrier broken. He felt both proud and ashamed.

Afterwards, Neil rode slowly home, thoughtful, the air fresh on his face. Voices were shouting not far away, and laughter, dance beats echoing around the London night. A party! Someone had something to celebrate. He cycled past Bernard and Elizabeth's house, where every window was in darkness, and wondered whether Bernard was lying awake in bed grumbling about the noise.

In fact, as Neil passed, the two of them were still sleeping comfortably one beside the other, as yet undisturbed. They had gone to bed early so that Bernard would not be "too tired." After their lovemaking, Bernard, exhausted and satisfied, took his pill for high blood pressure and his other pill for high cholesterol. He fell into deep sleep even as Elizabeth kissed him goodnight.

It is said – some would prefer it to be so – that couples are never as happy together as they appear. Between men and women, we are told, there can be only at best an uneasy understanding. Some like to consider male and female as creations of the devil, enemies, oppressor and oppressed, worker and drone, master and slave, giver and taker. Love, as dreamed of everywhere, seems to exist only in imagination, or in a wedding dress, or in telephoto snapshots of fleeting celebrity romance.

However, all that is false. Between men and women up and down every street, in every land, and always, there is calm and profound devotion. Behind closed doors they have helped each other in their work, and at leisure have enjoyed one another's companionship, and caused children to be born, and cared for them together, and have known the nearest thing to happiness that ever may be found.

* * *

Neil brought some CDs he had burned of his favourite tracks, and a few others he thought Bernard might appreciate. Bernard had done something similar, selecting tapes, vinyl records and even some precious old 78s. He welcomed Neil into the sitting room with delight.

"You know Archie Shepp?" asked Neil at once. "Got something you should hear."

Bernard rubbed his hands in glee at the prospect of several hours of good listening.

Neil wondered if Bernard could see anything different about him after his experiences during the night. Going to a prostitute wasn't something he would ever be able to mention. He could not contemplate what Bernard would think of him! Suddenly Neil felt that it had all been horribly squalid and a little nightmarish, akin to sleeping in the street or begging strangers for coins or searching for food in garbage bins. It wasn't even laughable, just embarrassing and pitiful.

"Now, let's see," Bernard said, "first things first – tea or coffee?"

"You wouldn't happen to have a cold drink, would you?"

"Juice?"

"Haven't got a beer, by any chance?"

Bernard grinned. "I have – but it's not ideal with Elizabeth's scones. Have one, they're good."

Neil smiled. "Cup of tea for me, please. And a scone, if I may."

"We'll open a bottle of wine later," Bernard assured him. "We've got the house to ourselves. Liz and Ruth have gone out. Right, who do you think this is? Here's a clue: we're in the 1920s."

"No mistake about that!" Neil laughed, and shook his head to the music, tapped his feet. "Haven't heard Jelly Roll for ages."

"Have you heard Mike Dawson's band play this?"

"Who?"

"Seven-piece band, 1950s. Sort of thing I grew up on, listening to BBC Jazz Club."

"No, but I'll play *you* something," Neil said, "composed – incredibly – at *exactly* the same time. But it's like another era! I love this. Ornette Coleman. *Lonely Woman*."

Bernard closed his eyes and moved as if he too did indeed love the tangled, wandering sounds of Coleman's fluent saxophone. "People call the Twenties the Jazz Age," he mused, "but the real golden era of jazz was the Sixties. Modern stuff, free jazz and trad revival all at the same moment. Stan Getz, Charlie Parker, Miles Davis, John Coltrane, Buddy Rich. And music like this. Ah! A great time!"

"You actually remember it!" said Neil enviously. "I wasn't even born."

"Not even born! How strange! There was jazz everywhere,

then," Bernard told him.

"OK if I turn this up just a notch?"

"No, no, leave the volume as it is," Bernard replied. "You weren't at that noisy party last night, were you?"

Neil laughed. "No. Did they disturb you?" He remembered hearing a party after leaving the girl last night.

"They did! Woke me around two in the morning! I know which house it was. Number 87. They put speakers in the garden and danced outside. At this time of year! I phoned our rotten council's noise nuisance people, but they didn't send anyone. That's what always happens. I called the police, too, and they told me it was for the council to deal with. And *that's* what always happens, too. Neither of them want to do anything about anything."

Neil shook his head. "Oh, I wouldn't bother complaining. No, really, I mean it's not as if they do it every night. After all, you know," he tried to sound wise and tolerant, "it's just people having a good time. A bit of fun."

At this, anger flared in Bernard. He could not stop it. "You know something, Neil? I really don't give a damn about people wanting to have a good time!"

Neil looked up at him, startled by the sharp edge in his tone.

"What I care about," Bernard said with force, "is *ordinary* times, not good times. People who want a quiet life, a working couple with children trying to sleep, an old woman or an old man alone in their house, and all the poor souls with problems and the decent citizens whose peace is being disturbed." He jabbed a finger. "While *you*," he cried, "you stick up for the selfish antisocial bastards who are *having fun* and *just want a good time*. I say they can go *hang*."

Neil reddened under the onslaught. He did not know if he was expected to argue his point. Then he understood that Bernard was doing no more than speak his mind. The attack wasn't personal. "People aren't all saints," he replied calmly. It seemed to suggest that Bernard had the temerity to claim he was one.

Bernard paused at this. "True," he admitted sadly, "but at least they could try not to be totally selfish. Neil, look, I'm not against anyone enjoying life," he explained, "but not if it causes suffering to another person. That's the key to it all."

Inwardly, Neil squirmed. It was almost as if Bernard *knew* what had happened last night, what he had done and where he had been.

"That's my view, anyway," said Bernard with finality. "If having a good time means harming someone else, well, just don't. I'm writing a book about these issues."

Neil nodded. "Yep. You said."

"I'm writing about the old idea of the commons – you know, the common people, common law, common land, the common weal, the common good. All that!" Bernard smiled. His annoyance had evaporated. He spoke eagerly. "And, you know, fairness, and this character called the 'reasonable man' in common law."

"Has it got a name yet, your book?"

"Mm – yuh. I've decided to call it *Return to Common Sense*."

Neil appeared to approve the name, but had a few suggestions of his own. "What about common criminals, common as muck, and the common cold?" he asked mischievously.

"Of course! I'll make a point of including those," Bernard chuckled. "Have a listen to this. This is my real treasure. An original 1930s recording of Sidney Bechet on soprano sax."

* * *

Liliana started her three hours of rest. She sat exhausted on the bed. Outside her shutters, the morning was cool, pleasant, the sky a milky blue, full of promise. Neil dressed more warmly for the ride to work. Bernard put up the collar of his overcoat and walked to synagogue.

As soon as Neil arrived at Critchlow's yard, "that bastard Sanina" called him into the office.

Neil stood silently in front of the transport manager's desk.

"Well, Mr Chapman," said Sanina at last, "a lady living in Whitechapel would like a regular Critchlow's delivery. What do you think about that?"

Clearly Sanina had found him out and was playing some sort of game with him. "Well, I don't know, it's a matter for you, Mr Sanina. Don't see why not. I mean, it could go out on the Friday deliveries, couldn't it?"

"No, you see, the customer says there is *already* a regular Critchlow's driver in the area, on Tuesday and Thursday. One of our vans goes right past her door."

Sanina stared at the blue eyes. He watched Neil's face carefully, but it remained impassive and gave nothing away.

How ironic! Just when his arrangement with Joy-Belle has finished, someone has reported him. The last thing he needed now was to get the sack. Neil wondered if Sanina was slowly working his way to revealing that the driver had a woman in the van.

Of course, he could not absolutely deny passing through that district, in case the customer had taken his number. Or, he could take a chance.

He replied simply, "That's funny. Which round is that on, then?"

Sanina suppressed a grin at Neil's audacity. "Mr Chapman, I think you know that it is not on any of our rounds. Whitechapel isn't really the sort of area where Critchlow's – if you see what I mean."

"Forgive my ignorance, I'm sorry, but where exactly *is* Whitechapel? I'm not sure if I've ever been there."

Now Sanina knew that Neil was playing a game with *him*, and again he grinned slightly.

"Come, come, Mr Chapman – you are a Londoner, aren't you? Whitechapel is in the East End of London. It is next to the City of London, where you deliver on Tuesdays and Thursdays."

"Oh, yes – but I do the City on Wednesdays too. So this van she sees, does it pass on Wednesdays, too?" He wished he hadn't said that. It was tantamount to admitting it was him. He quickly added, "Or on any other day?"

"No, it doesn't," Sanina replied. "And here's another strange thing. One of the warehousemen has suggested a possible explanation."

Neil suspected that he meant the little crook Darren. Or could it be the guy who told him about the Maypole striptease?

"OK, so what's the explanation?" Neil asked innocently.

Sanina paused. If he went any further with the accusation, he would have to give Neil Chapman a final warning. He did not want to get rid of this young man. He was a good, quiet worker. Several customers had said they liked him. In particular, one of the most valuable customers on the Ascot round, Miss Delavingham, had said how helpful and polite he was. That was worth something.

"So – you know nothing about this mystery Critchlow's van?"

Neil shook his head. "No, sorry I can't help, Mr Sanina." It looked as though he was in the clear, for the moment.

"Thank you, Mr Chapman," Sanina said abruptly. "That's all. Get changed and carry on with your work."

"Excuse me, Mr Sanina," Neil ventured cautiously. "Could you help me with something?" From his pocket he produced a scrap of paper.

Sanina looked at him frostily. "What's sort of thing, Mr Chapman?"

"It's this. You said you were Romanian. Do you read Russian?"

Sanina glared.

"Only, I've been wondering what this says." He passed Liliana Petreanu's note to Andrei Sanina.

With a single glance at the words, Sanina said, "Mr Chapman, I don't have time for this. Are you trying to be funny with me?"

"No, Mr Sanina, I honestly don't know what it says. And, well, I was worried it might be important."

Sanina snorted. He raised his eyebrows and held the scrap contemptuously. "It says, *I – love – you*." He handed it back.

Neil half-smiled, then frowned as if struggling to understand. "Does it? It really says that? So – "

Sanina was puzzled by the response.

"So, I hope you don't mind, Mr Sanina, but – " he reached into his pocket and unfolded the other scrap. "There's another one. This one is not in Russian." He passed it across the desk.

Sanina began to read and glanced at Neil sharply. He looked down at the paper again. He read the note slowly, then re-read it. He turned the paper over to look at the other side, but as Neil knew, there was nothing more written there.

He seemed uncertain how to translate the words.

"Mr Chapman," he said, "where did you get this? If the question is not too – " He stopped. "Or maybe it is another joke?"

"A girl gave it to me," Neil replied. "Is it Romanian?"

There was no answer. Sanina held the paper in one hand, and flicked it thoughtfully with the fingers of the other hand. He gazed at it again with pursed lips. Neil waited, wondering what to say.

"Yes, it is Romanian," Sanina said at last. He looked up, his expression altered. "Mr Chapman, now I ask you a favour – don't come to me about this. We will carry on with our work. I cannot do anything for you."

"I don't understand. What does it – ?" There was a slight smile of embarrassment on Neil's lips. He wondered if the girl had perhaps written something obscene.

In his flat voice, Sanina read aloud. Neil thought the words sounded a little like Italian. "*Sunt un prizonier, nu o curvă. Bărbaţii sunt periculoşi, ei ucid. Vă rog să mă ajutaţi.* I am a prisoner, not a whore. The men are dangerous, they will kill. Please help."

6

Terrible screams woke him; a woman or a child. Shadowy figures inside a kind of hotel or house or guesthouse. Two young women scratch at one other with fingernails. A little girl cowers, desperate to please, smiling ingratiatingly. She smiles ever more widely, full of fear, until she is all smiles, nothing but smiles. In horrible metamorphosis, the young women are old women. The girl is fighting another girl, a mirror image. It is herself. Both of her are screaming for help. And all the time, everywhere, wriggling on the floor, on the bed, onto their bodies, are hundreds of strange, nauseating creatures – enormous, oozing, flesh-coloured slugs, with curious D-shaped heads that turn into fists. The little girl is seized and dragged away, smiling, flailing, grabbing. She is locked alone in one of the rooms. Screams rise to a crescendo that fills Neil's mind.

It's only a dream, only a dream, only a dream; he wakes sweating and lies in the bed trying to remember. Well, the meaning is ridiculously easy to understand. He already knows he has been disturbed by his visit to that house. It's got to be about the plight of women from generation to generation. And those disgusting creatures everywhere – they look just like penises. So obvious! But there were no children in the house. Well, dreams don't have to make sense. You can ignore them.

He really mustn't let himself become so upset. Anyway, the screams were probably nothing more than a whistling sound in his nose, or something. He is annoyed, though. He paid forty pounds and ended up with nightmares!

He reaches for the clock: three thirty-two. With eyes firmly shut he resolves to go back to sleep. Images from the dream spring back to life. He opens his eyes once more and stares into the darkness.

Oh, yes, *now* he can see why there were children in the dream. It wasn't only about women. It's because of the way he treated that girl. He hears the word in his mind as shrill as a bell – *girl*. And he *did* treat her like a child, even lifting her up! He cringes at the memory.

Don't beat yourself up about it! Millions of blokes are paying for sex all the time! Pretty sad, isn't it, when men who want to get laid are reduced to paying? Well, men have been paying for it, in all sorts of ways, all over the world, all through history. Sad? It's the human condition. The male condition. The female condition.

Only thing is, though, I didn't pay her.

I paid someone else.

"Help me!" she wrote.

Locked in a room! At the mercy of...

What's the point of having nightmares?

If there's a problem, don't stress out – just find a solution. Action, not anxiety.

"Help me!" on a piece of paper.

Suddenly Neil threw the duvet away from himself and sat up in the darkness, struggling with his thoughts until he experienced something like pain. He wondered if he was mentally unbalanced, as images and imaginings, questions and answers, went around and around his mind repeatedly, like the jangle of a hated pop song, vicious circles without end, overlapping and interlocking.

Why had she not written her name in the note? She had not said her name and he had not asked. Who exactly were the 'dangerous' men who would kill? Was any of her plight his fault? Suppose she had not written the note? Shouldn't he just pretend she had not written it?

And always he heard Bernard's tiresome injunction, "*Do your bit!*"

Neil looked at himself and found that he was *not* doing his bit. What had he done since his visit to her room last Saturday night? Nothing at all.

Two days without making any effort to help! But how *could* he help?

He'd like to talk it over with a friend, but there was no friend close enough that he could admit what had happened. He could hardly think of anyone in whom he had ever confided – except maybe Pamela. He knew how she would have reacted, scornfully pitying his weakness.

Pamela had called him a loser, and she was right.

Absurdly, he longed to discuss it with Bernard. His reaction too could be guessed. Somewhere in his exhausted thoughts he heard Bernard's voice, robustly condemning him.

Neil couldn't deny that he liked Bernard, stuffy old git though he was, with his posh accent. He sort of admired the guy. He had a bloody good jazz collection. Inexplicably, it was almost upsetting to think he wouldn't measure up for Bernard's approval.

Last night Neil had cycled to the house again just to look at the place. From across the road, the upper floor and red-tiled roof could be seen above the tall, unkempt privet hedge. And even as he stood there in the dark, every few minutes a man pushed open the rough board gate, and another left. At the side, concealed by the hedge, Neil saw a driveway, it too closed behind high boards. He paused for a while and looked up at the windows. He saw light above each of the shutters that covered the glass inside. Behind each of these windows, a woman was being raped.

He gazed at an upstairs room and tried to visualise escaping from it. He could not see how it would be done. Maybe just unscrew the window shutters and jump out? Maybe let yourself down with the bedsheets? A ridiculous idea. Especially with security cameras scanning the walls.

Which window was hers? He tried to work it out, but remained uncertain. He imagined her at that very moment. Was there a man in the room right now? What was he doing to her?

How could this pass unnoticed on a main road? Didn't the neighbours realise what was going on? But on one side there was no neighbour because the house stood on a corner, while the neighbour on its other side was a nursing home, busy with its work.

"I'm not against anyone enjoying life, but not if it causes suffering to another person." Bernard's voice resounded in his mind, admonishing, castigating, urging him to go to the police.

Neil had already thought about that. Tell the police? How could he possibly tell the police? He could not go to the police, when he was the very one who had committed an offence. Hadn't they just made it illegal to pay for sex with women trapped as Liliana was trapped?

Suppose he went to the police and told them what he had seen and done in that house. He would be arrested on the spot, and likely end up in prison!

And didn't the new law say that ignorance was no defence? He was sure it did.

Ignorance no defence! "You are under arrest for crimes unknown."

If he didn't tell anyone, no one would ever find out. Because as Bernard had said, the police don't go looking for crime. They simply wait to be told. If nobody tells them anything, they don't know anything.

So if you paid for sex with a girl who was a prisoner, you don't tell the police.

Maybe he could call the police anonymously? He could just give them the address. They'd have to break the gateway down. They wouldn't be let in simply by pressing the buzzer. No, the police don't work like that.

What, go to a house, just on someone's say-so? No way.

Obviously the police can't simply break in – not without hard information. What's the accusation? Where are the witnesses, the evidence? They'd have to get a warrant from a magistrate. They need names, facts, people who will make a statement and go to court.

Most likely the only provable crime was that everyone inside the house was an illegal immigrant. For that matter, they might all be perfectly legal immigrants... from Slavonistan and Baltasia and Eurabia and God knows where.

Think it through: suppose he *could* persuade the police to go to the house. What would they find? A brothel. The girls whose pictures he had been shown would end up in police custody. They'd be questioned. Detained. Shouted at. Disbelieved. Treated with contempt. Abused. And they'd *still* be prisoners. They might go to jail. Perhaps for immigration offences.

Or, they'd be kept for months, even years, in a detention centre waiting to give evidence against their captors, and then, wait again to be deported. Or suppose a girl couldn't give evidence? Was too scared? Then what? Contempt of court?

And if she were deported - back to what? Fears ran rapidly around his mind. Had the girl been kidnapped in her own country? It was complicated.

He looked at the clock. Three forty-one. He won't be able to sleep any more tonight.

At last the alarm clock bleeped. Neil discovered that he had gone back to sleep after all. He was lying naked on top of the duvet. He forced himself to wake, and walked to the tiny bathroom to splash cold water onto his face.

* * *

The first glimmer of morning seeps into the strip of sky above the shutter. The orange glow of a London night slowly fades to pale, fragile blue. By this time of night, or day, Liliana is always literally faint with hunger and exhaustion. Smiling makes her face ache, too. Soon, she will have her meal and the three longed-for hours of rest and solitude and sleep. In her three hours, awake or asleep, the lonely darkness descends and wraps her in its cool embrace. She could almost kiss the person – woman or man – who came into the room with her plate of food and her pills.

Liliana does not think. At least, she tries not to. Yet the thoughts and daydreams coil around her. When she was a little girl, she saw a man in another village who cried out the same phrases again and again as he walked on the road. He was mad. She half-remembers that he shouted, "They cheated me! They cheated me!" Now, she feels that a tormented spirit like that lives inside her own body, always returning to the same aggrieved, miserable debate. In her mind, she calmly tells the villagers, and her teachers and her parents, and the authorities, what has happened, endlessly searching for words to explain the enormity done to her. But they never care.

As she eats, she wonders, what happened about her promised job in England? What of Sergiu, what of Pavel? Is Sergiu in the same plight as herself? Do the family know what has happened? How could they? They might not even realise she wasn't at home, because she had more or less given up contacting them.

Her theory is that Yids must be behind all this. Clever, crooked Yids. Not that the men here are Jews, or the old woman! God forbid! No, they are probably Russian. Though who knows? You can never tell with Yids. Maybe these are Yids in disguise. Thinking about it, in fact they don't seem like true Russians at all. They speak to her in Russian. Maybe they are Serbs, or something. What is sure is they must be working for the Jews. How else to explain what has happened? It's the only logical explanation.

Perhaps we should forgive Liliana her ravings. Or perhaps not. Like her body, her thoughts too were locked in, pacing, circling endlessly, reworking her obsessions and misunderstandings.

She felt sorry now, to have fallen out with the family. What else do you have, if not family? Well, of course, you have your friends. Once – she remembered it as if years, not weeks, had passed – she shared a nice little flat in Chişinău and went out with friends and even had a boyfriend all of her very own.

Some people criticised her choice of boyfriend, too. Pavel wasn't so bad. There was a deep, manly goodness in him. Everyone disapproved of him just because he supported Noua Dreaptă. What was it to do with them, anyway! He loved his country; what's wrong with that?

They did agree with Pavel that she should give up her work. Her hope had been that she would land a better job, eventually. The firm that was training her said she should look upon her work for them as an investment. They told her she was very bright, and obviously she knew that was true.

Of course, Pavel said, all the best jobs in Moldova had been taken by Yids. He said the Government had made it a crime even to criticise Jews. Everything was done to protect them. She would be better off leaving Moldova altogether. Her boss said if she was willing to work for him with not much pay, like an intern, she would soon learn enough to leave the country and find a better job in the West.

That happy, innocent person no longer seemed like her. She would never be that person again, if she ever had been. The West, the West, her great dream. Well, now she was in the West! As far as she knew, she was in the capital of England. She will never be able to return home, and doesn't want to. She couldn't face them, after what has happened. How will she ever be able to send a letter to Pavel, now? She has no paper, no pen, is not allowed to write and there is nothing she would tell him. She feels sick just thinking of the words – to describe what has happened.

She did write something, though, didn't she, for one of the men who came to her? She half-remembered that he spoke many languages. He was obviously clever. He kept looking around the room at everything, as sly and devious as a Jew. Maybe he would discover a way to read her note. She should have written Pavel's address and phone number! She hated herself for not thinking of it quickly enough. Poor Pavel does not even know why she left. It grieves her that she did not say goodbye to him.

All of that is finished. Pavel would not want her back, after what has happened. What she has become. It would not fit with Noua Dreaptă's image. No man would want her now. And she would not want any man, either. No, not even Pavel! She has seen men for what they are! Revolting animals, panting and grasping, coating her with their foul breath and sweat and saliva and their stinking, spurting slime. She will never be able to clean it all off as long she lives. She is sickened by them. She doesn't want another man to touch her, ever again. Or come near her. She doesn't even want to see another one. Not even in the distance. She knows that more of them wait outside the door, eager to crawl over her. No, she does not want to be with Pavel any more, nor any man at all, and not with her family, nor anyone else, nor alone.

* * *

Cycling through the traffic, trying to unravel his tangled thoughts, it seemed to Neil that he would free that girl, one way or another, whatever it took. He was certain. It had been his destiny to visit her, and it was his destiny to help her. She had written in her note that the men would kill. Presumably she meant it quite literally; if he tried to free her, that's what they would do. So how could he possibly take them on? With his bare hands? Alone? There was no way he could do this without some kind of weapon. The very idea of a weapon seemed alien and inconceivable. He had never used any kind of weapon in his life. Yes, he needed a weapon. Not a gun, obviously. But not a knife. He could not push a knife into another person's flesh. So, a gun, then.

He was just fantasising! He could not be serious. Did he really think that he, Neil Chapman, would confront violent armed criminals? With a gun! It was laughably improbable. He could not handle a gun and had no idea where to get one. He ought to pull himself together and forget such madness! Guns were just for movies, for fiction.

Yet how difficult could it be? No, guns were not a fiction. Every day newspapers reported the proliferation of firearms in London. Black teenagers were being shot dead by other black teenagers all the time. Or was that just media hype? Kids on bicycles, little tyrants ruling tower-block council estates, ride around with automatic pistols to defend their concrete turf. So it said in all the papers. Maybe he had to go into a black neighbourhood to find a weapon.

*Suppose I get hurt? After all, they will probably have guns too.
She said they would kill. So what? Everyone has to die sometime.
At least I can say, I tried to do the right thing.*

Thinking back to his reckless early years, it came into Neil's
mind that, in fact, in those days he did know someone who could
get hold of a gun. He tried to remember the man. Not a friend;
just a guy they had dealt with, a professional criminal. Big,
stocky bloke, overweight but muscular. Yes – Ernie was his
name. Ernie. Or Eddie. The surname might have been Dawkins
or Dawson. Eddie Dawson. That was far, far back in the
grimmest part of Neil's youth. He recoiled from any return to
that period. Anyway, all those people he used to know would
have forgotten him by now, if they were still alive.

Neil mused on those bad days. After leaving school, he had
drifted aimlessly for a while. Wheelers and dealers and...
skivers, dodgers, squatters, scroungers and... thieves. And
beyond the edge of that world, harder men, insensitive men,
violent men. Eddie was one of them. They used to meet up in the
Blind Beggar in Whitechapel Road, in the East End. They were
coarse and loud, not really his type at all. Oh, his poor mother,
how his mother had suffered and despaired because of him. It
had been a free and easy life.

A girl had taken him away from all that. Put him in her flat
and made a normal human being out of him. Then, he had met
Pamela, fallen in love and got a proper job. Though come to
think of it, he had never really lost the feeling that he was just
drifting.

Eddie Dawson used to have a car workshop off the Mile End
Road somewhere. Neil wondered if he was still there. Eddie
would be able to find him a gun.

Neil ranged the City deliveries neatly on the van's metal shelves,
struggling to order his thoughts. Step by step, he worked once
more through the night's arguments and, unhappily, came to the
same conclusion: the police would not break into the house on
the strength of an anonymous tip-off; even if they did, the girls

would not be freed. The police could not act without witnesses and statements.

As he finished loading the van, he noticed that sneaky young fellow Darren from the Dispatch Room approaching. Darren's narrow lips grimaced tightly in greeting.

"How ya goin', all right?" Darren's speech was clipped and somehow menacing. His narrow eyes darted around. His endless shifting about irritated Neil. Why couldn't the bloke stand still for a minute?

"All right," replied Neil. Maybe Darren knew where to get a gun.

"Uh, y'know – you, like, I was finkin', funny you ent come up with nuffin' yet, yeah?"

Neil was puzzled. "Like what?"

"Sumfin' we can use, innit, yeah? A drop-off." Darren peered with interest into Neil's van. "You get a good drink out of it. Percentage, yeah? Don't worry about that. Know what I mean?" He threw his right shoulder forward.

"Never promised I would, mate. Anyway, nothing's come up," said Neil.

Darren wrinkled his brow. "Trouble is, mate, you got to like, make sure it does come up."

"Or what?"

"Or we put yer on a different round," answered Darren quietly. "Fuckin' simple as that, yeah? Fuckin' let someone else have the fuckin' City who knows how to fuckin' use it. Yeah? And you've like, got the Ascot, yeah? Two fuckin' top rounds and fuckin' nuffink to fuckin' show for it. See what I mean? Be fair. Do you know what I mean? Then, like, we can just like fuckin' make life hard for you, yeah? Which we don't want to."

Neil would have liked to ask Stan how best to deal with this. Stan would know how to see Darren off. Men were loading their vans, but Stan did not seem to be among them. Maybe he was down in the Ring, or in the canteen. He would have to manage without Stan's advice for the moment. And what would Bernard Kassin do, with all his talk of law and order? Snitch to that bastard Sanina? It sounded as though Sanina was in on it, too.

How else could Darren put anyone on a different round?

"How do you do that, then?" Neil replied sceptically. "Can you get me any round I want? Are you the boss here?"

Darren snorted with slight amusement. "I know what you're finkin'. You're like, you fink the rounds is all down to that cunt Sanina, yeah? Don't ya?" His lips twisted. "All right. See what fuckin' round you're on tomorrow, mate, and fuckin' figure it out, yeah? Know what I mean?"

Neil's flesh chilled. Clearly Darren was not bluffing.

Yet, stupidly, Neil found himself retorting, "Tell you what, mate. You can stuff it up your arse, all right? If I lose either of my rounds, I know who to blame and what to do about it."

Darren grinned. "Don't fuckin' be like that," he said. "No need to get nasty, yeah? Better you play along, mate, yeah? Everyone else does. Know what I mean? You still new here, innit? So maybe you just not... well, I'm tellin' you, that's how it works." His voice affected a great reasonableness. "Like, any fuckin' little fing will do, yeah? But you got to let us have *sumfin'*, see? Or, you know."

Neil spoke slowly, "Tell you what I'll do for you, mate." He paused as if pondering a generous offer. "Sweet fuck all. All right?"

Darren glanced up, wondering whether to be amused by this bold, naïve outburst. He held his surprise in check. For in Neil's expressionless face and blue eyes he saw something strange – an icy, savage madness, and a kind of violent fear. It brought a caged animal to mind. He didn't know what – a wolf, a leopard. Neil's gaze held him. The yard and the vans became faint and distant.

"OK, mate – only jokin'," Darren said quietly. "No one wants to change your fuckin' round. No one wants to change nuffin'. I'm only sayin', *if* you fuckin' get us summink, it'a be nice. No pressure. 'S up to you, yeah? Like, your choice, yeah? Know what I mean?"

Neil ignored him and turned back to the van. He pulled down the back shutter and locked it. He was ready to head into the City. He went to wash his hands and face before leaving. He noticed that Darren had already gone.

Suddenly it occurred to Neil that he might have been able to do a deal with Darren: a gun in exchange for parcels off the van.

* * *

While Neil faced Darren, and Liliana desperately tried to take her rest, Bernard made coffee and toast and listened to the *Today* programme.

"Shame you can't come!" he said breezily to Elizabeth. "We need a few residents, otherwise it looks as if people don't care. But how *can* people go, when it's during the working day? Let's hope *somebody* turns up."

For this morning, Bernard would be attending a planning appeal at the Town Hall.

"Yes, well, maybe residents actually *don't* care," said she. He was not surprised by her tone. Elizabeth often took a jaundiced view of his efforts on behalf of the local community.

He looked at the clock and drank his coffee. "I suppose I'd better get ready," he said at last.

It was another bright, agreeable morning, under a milky sky. From the heights of the Brent Cross flyover, he looked down onto the North Circular Road where stationary traffic waited in long parallel lines. How many cars were idling there? It was like one of those funfair games – how many beans in the jar? He would guess thousands; no, he did not have any idea.

Giving up valuable working time to defend his neighbours' interests galled him sometimes. They did not even know! They did not want to know. And as Elizabeth said, nor would they care. Yet he well understood how they felt: days follow one another and life goes on; there's no sense in running to meet trouble; if everyone minded their own business the world would be a better place.

Better not to think about that. Bernard Kassin took a large view of what was possible and what was not; whether an effort was worthwhile, or not. He had decided that KOBRA was worthwhile. It was right to protect one's own community, because community was the foundation of all things. Besides, by making the neighbourhood more pleasant, he and his family could enjoy it the more. Of course, it also protected the value of his family home. And in any case, he really did feel upset about the injustices suffered by the people around him, and wanted to help.

Bernard had a sharp sense, too, of what was a priority, and what could wait. He took his briefcase from the car and walked briskly to the Town Hall. The Town Hall, inspired in an era of civic pride, thrilled him. Its white-pillared portico, Renaissance flourishes, fantastical mock-medieval touches! Inside, dark panelling and crests, portraits of aldermen long dead. At the same time, it displeased him, charged as it was with the secret fraternity of officialdom, its pomposity and self-importance.

A notice, pinned to a board, pointed towards the broad stone stairs: *Planning Appeal – Public Hearing. 1st Floor.*

Bernard's heart sank. The large wood-panelled chamber echoed with emptiness. No one else had arrived. No one at all.

Long tables divided the room into two. On one side, were chairs for the parties to the case, and for the Planning Inspector himself, representing the Government (and, thereby, Her Majesty).

On the other side, were rows of chairs for the great public, whose voice must necessarily be heard at a public hearing – with the Planning Inspector's permission. However, the rows of chairs for the public stood empty.

Bernard admired the wood panelling. He chose a chair near the front, and took a folder of papers from his briefcase. A group of voices, noisy in laughter and conversation, could be heard approaching along the corridor. At last four men and a woman in jolly mood pushed open the door into the chamber and went towards the seats set aside for parties to the case – the appellant and the council.

The appellant was the property owner and developer Mr Kemi Açgözlülük. He was appealing for permission to build flats that were already built, and indeed were already occupied.

Of Mr Açgözlülük, it was not possible to say anything much, since he was not present, other than that Bernard was already familiar with his depredations in Golders Green. He was a serial builder of cheap flats without planning permission.

In his stead sat his fleshy and smiling agent, Mr Alvin Palwin, spilling comfortably out of a black double-breasted suit and wearing a black kippah on longish, swept-back hair. Beside him, the young, pretty and nervous counsel instructed by Mr Palwin, Miss Wanda Sickert-Hart, sat demure in grey skirt and jacket.

Opposite them sat Mr Pip Littleman, planning officer representing the council, respectable in a simple grey business suit sparkling with dandruff.

And at a right-angle to these parties, sat the Planning Inspector who would judge the case, Mr Tim Kann, calm, correct and upright, immaculate in tailored worsted, waiting for the exact moment when the proceedings were due to begin.

Bernard's days and years were much taken up with such encounters.

During the delay, quiet, good-humoured banter continued between "Pip" and "Alvin". Bernard was troubled. He had seen this, in court, on numerous occasions: professionals engaged in a harmless amusement, the stakes measured in human happiness, in imprisonment or ruin – for their clients. This morning, the game was "Planning Law", and the stakes were neighbourhoods, homes and the peaceful enjoyment of ordinary life. Such trophies would be won or lost in word play between congenial rivals Mr Palwin and Mr Littleman, under the friendly adjudication of Mr Kann.

To Bernard's surprise, two other local residents arrived, nodded a greeting to him and sat at some distance. It made a sorry sight, Bernard thought, for a public hearing.

At ten o'clock precisely, the calm voice of Mr Kann summarised the issues. Mr Açgözlülük had purchased a house on the corner of Blenheim and Osborne roads; he had greatly enlarged it without permission and without conforming to building regulations; finally, he had applied for retrospective planning consent. The council's planning officers had recommended councillors sitting on the planning sub-committee to approve his request; but, under pressure from local people, they had refused to do so. So it was that the council refused to grant permission to Mr Açgözlülük. Today Mr Açgözlülük was appealing against their decision.

In turn, prim Tim Kann called upon hesitant Wanda Sickert-Hart and confident Alvin Palwin to put the case for Kemi Açgözlülük. He turned then to Pip Littleman for a faltering, unconvincing defence of the council's decision and a keen willingness to be over-ruled. At last he invited an impassioned and eloquent Bernard Kassin to say his piece on behalf of the troublesome local people.

It was over by twelve-thirty. In bitter mood Bernard drove to Golders Green station. The hearing had not gone well for the residents of Blenheim and Osborne roads. At a little café beside Temple tube station, Bernard sat sadly with a bowl of soup and leafed through the Daily Telegraph. The American Democratic presidential candidate Barack Obama, he read, had a lead of 2.5 per cent. The Republican candidate, John McCain, was a "good kisser", according to a Brazilian model with whom he spent a week when he was a young man, fifty years ago.

* * *

A turn into a dark lane, across the road from Saint Paul's Cathedral, leads to another lane hardly wider than the van itself.

The address on the docket is a small block of maisonettes. There's no concierge, no reception or hall; the entrance opens straight onto the roadway. Neil presses a button and leans his ear to the entryphone, but it remains silent. He pushes gently on the front door, but it's locked. Perhaps he could leave the package with a neighbour. He presses all the bells, but none replies. He pictures all the flats utterly deserted. Next door is a neat, old-fashioned barber's shop, the sort of place Stan would go. That is closed too. Why is everything around here closed on a weekday morning? Where is everybody?

He ponders the size and shape of the parcel, and weighs it in his hand. It's almost a foot square, an inch or so thick, surprisingly heavy. He visualises some kind of ornament, onyx or quartz or carved ebony.

Darren said everyone was doing it. Neil slides back into the van, puts the undelivered package on the passenger seat and continues with his round.

He has been daydreaming about going back to the Maypole pub to see if a new stripper has replaced Joy-Belle. He idly reviews his memories of her. Now all of that pleasure belongs to Winston alone! Winston is a lucky man!

No, of course, Neil remembers, Winston is not a lucky man. And of course – Winston probably knows exactly how to get hold of a gun. Maybe even carries one. Trouble is, he'd probably turn it on Neil if ever they met.

Neil doesn't drive to the Maypole, though. Instead, he parks near Stan's tea stall and carefully prises open the undelivered package. It turns out to be a kind of coffee-table-book in a box. A beautiful book of photographs, with a set of CDs fitted inside, called *The Jazz Age*. What amazing luck! He leafs through it carefully, lingering over black and white portraits of pre-War jazz musicians: Benny Goodman, Artie Shaw, Fats Waller, Hoagy Carmichael and a dozen more.

No way would he hand this over to that creep Darren. Neil slips the docket into his pocket. He could still change his mind; he could deliver the thing another day. If no one notices it's missing, well, it would make a great gift for Bernard Kassin!

Every day, each van starts out from Critchlow's yard loaded with about one hundred deliveries; the drivers call them 'drops'. So good does the driver's memory become, that if asked about a drop that went missing, or was damaged, or wrongly delivered, he can always remember it. This time, though, he had better forget. With luck, everyone else would forget it too.

And what will I say to that bastard Sanina when he asks? Left it with a neighbour? Left it at the barber's shop? No. No explanation at all. Nothing. I don't remember the place, the docket, the parcel or anything. What can they prove?

Next delivery is in Leadenhall Street. Another in St Mary Axe. Something in Sugar Bakers Court, in Great St Helens, and in Undershaft, weaving from one ancient lane to another between modern buildings, along intricate one-ways and down no-entries. He follows narrow Mitre Street to an office block in Aldgate. Here Neil looks east, makes a decision and turns sharply.

The diesel engine roared as he drove briskly towards Stepney, cutting in and out of the lanes of traffic. He did not remember the name of Eddie's street, but felt sure he would recognise it as he went from one landmark to the next.

It turned out, though, that many landmarks had vanished or changed. He did not think he had seen the East London Mosque before, with its slender minaret. Scores of men had gathered on the street in front of the London Muslim Centre. Hundreds of green and white awnings and tarpaulins covered lines of market stalls. Dozens of overflowing purple garbage bins were pushed to the edge of the kerb. The pavements were densely crowded, almost everyone in Muslim dress.

When he reached the Blind Beggar pub, Neil knew he was close to Eddie's territory. He began to feel anxious, remembering the big man's unnerving combination of affability and menace. Inwardly he rehearsed what he would say and what Eddie might say to him. In the event, none of it was said.

And there it was, Calcutta Street. Slowly he drove past oily little garages and workshops crammed into the brick arches below a railway line. Oddly, most of the faces inside were white. One of the lock-ups seemed to have been squatted by East Europeans who had made it their home. At last he saw Eddie's archway. Security lights and cameras focused on its metal sliding door, which stood open on this fine afternoon. Just inside, a skinny young man sat idly on an upturned crate, holding a mug of tea. Neil came to a stop beside him.

"A'right, mate? Lookin' for a bloke I used to know. Eddie. This was his place."

"Nah," retorted the young man with a shake of the head,

perfectly amiably. He had an accent Neil recognised, Greek Cypriot. "Don't fink so, mate."

Neil frowned. "Eddie," he repeated. "Eddie Dawson. Or Dawkins, yeah? It definitely was here. I remember him sitting right there, where you are now. On that same crate. Drinking tea. He used to like a cup of tea. I think it was out of that same cup you're holding now. So it would be funny if you never knew him."

"Yeah, all right," the young man half laughed. "Who wants 'im?"

"I want to ask him a favour. It's confidential, yeah? Business. Straight up."

"Only he don't never show up round here no more. He hangs about up West now."

"Where exactly?"

"You know – Soho, Piccadilly and that."

"Where can I find him, then?"

"Try the Trophy."

"What's that? Is that a pub?"

"Yeah, London Trophy. Off Jermyn Street."

Neil thanked him and turned back to the van.

"Hey – by the way, mate," came the young man's parting word. "Not Dawson. Dawkins."

Neil returned the way he had come, hurrying along Mile End Road and Whitechapel Road, to Victoria Embankment and back towards Critchlow's. He clocked off at five and cycled the short distance from Knightsbridge to Piccadilly. Slowly he wheeled the bike along Jermyn Street, turning his eyes from one side to the other, until he caught sight of the little pub, hidden in a secretive, narrow alley that he had never noticed before.

The London Trophy was utterly charming and old-fashioned, its lacquered and gilded wooden exterior framed by a couple of Victorian brass lamps. The frosted windows were richly etched and patterned. On the pavement outside, big, ebullient men in expensive-looking suits and ties, each one holding a pint glass of yellow beer, were crowded together, laughing and braying.

Among them, a few women in dresses and pearls clasped smaller glasses and matched the men laugh for laugh.

Inside, an oval bar of dark wood dispensed 'real ales' from a row of ornate beer pumps. Above was an inlaid ceiling and elaborate plasterwork. Dozens of built-in mirrors, each of them polished and silvery, reflected the grey daylight. On the far side of the bar, tables and chairs were set out on bare floorboards dark with age and, around the back of the room, high-backed snugs and private corners and alcoves disappeared into the distance. The whole pub was noisy with talk.

Chalked onto a blackboard, the menu for *Today's Dinner* was pea and ham soup, roast beef (premium Scottish) and roast potatoes with market vegetables, finest Stilton with a glass of port, and College Pudding with egg custard. There was no choice at all and the tariff was twenty-five pounds.

Neil wondered if he had ever seen such a perfect meal. But even that sum was far beyond Neil's means. Anyway, his money had to go towards the cost of a gun. Not that he could think of eating or drinking until he had done what he came here to do.

He nodded to a tall, lean young man busy behind the bar, who promptly asked, "Hi, what would you like?"

"Looking for a feller called Eddie. He's a regular here. D'you know him?"

The barman glanced at his watch. "'Bout ten minutes," he replied briskly. "That's his table." He nodded in the direction of a table standing alone at the back. Indeed, Neil could see a note on it, "Reserved".

"Come every night, then, does he?" Neil queried.

The barman looked up, startled by such inquisitiveness. "Yeah. Six till seven every evening. You know, to meet his..." He shook his head as if lost for a word.

Neil shook his head too. Whom did Eddie meet here? Girlfriends, an ex-wife, drinking companions, partners in crime?

"...associates," the barman concluded.

He's aged! Just another big man in an expensive suit. Something about Eddie's face, though, was less showy, less full of himself, than the others. It looked cool, unsentimental and calculating. His posture was heavy and slightly round-shouldered. The hair, a little too long, flicked over the tops of the ears. Some in the crowd greeted him, and he responded warmly with a false smile, a tight little laugh or a quick handshake.

"Eddie Dawkins? I was hoping to find you."

He gave a quizzical nod as if in greeting. An eye took in the young man's physique, his intensely blue eyes, tee-shirt and jeans, battered old rucksack and generally unprosperous mien.

Neil felt embarrassed and somehow ashamed of himself under the older man's scrutiny. He coughed nervously. "D'you remember me? It's going back a bit. More than ten years. I met you a few times. My name's Neil."

Eddie remained as silent as if there were nothing he could ever want in life that Neil could possibly provide. He reached the bar and stood patiently while the barman filled a pint glass.

"I was wondering if I could ask you something. A bit of a favour," continued Neil. "Here, let me buy you a drink," gesturing as the barman pushed Eddie's glass across. "I'll get that." He reached into his pocket.

The barman caught Neil's eye and slowly shook his head, as if warning him of something.

"No ya fuckin' won't, pal," Eddie picked up his glass and sipped from the rim. "I prefer to pay for me own drinks." He had a sudden, irritated frown. "'Ow d'you know me?"

"I saw you over in Stepney. About something I was doing in those days. I'd like to –"

Now Eddie studied him disconcertingly. "What was the something?"

Neil drew in his breath. "I don't even want to think about it. I've moved on."

"Yeah, well, so have I." He squinted and pursed his lips. "Yes," he said thoughtfully, "I do remember ya. What I remember most is that fuckin' mate of yours, Lee."

"Yeah – Lee, that's right. He went to prison. He never was a mate of mine, by the way. Actually, he's dead now. Overdose, or something." Neil paused nervously, then quickly went on,

"Eddie, if you don't mind, I was wondering if I could ask you something."

"Let's sit down," said the older man. Unhurried, he moved to his table. "Your mate Lee tried to blag me out of some money. He tried to con me. Was you in on that? I reckon you was."

"No, no, no! No, I wasn't. I don't even know the thing you're talking about. He wasn't a mate of mine. Really he wasn't. I never even really knew the bloke."

"Yes, ya fuckin' did. Well, I'm glad to hear he's dead, if that's true. Yeah, well," he sighed. "Water under the bridge."

Neil thought to strike a friendlier note. "You given up the motors? I went over to Stepney to find you."

"Did ya?" Eddie raised his eyebrows cryptically. "Wouldn't say I gave it up, exactly."

This did not invite further questions, but Neil pressed on. "Your gaff over this way now?"

"I only come here to see my broker," replied Eddie.

"Broker?"

"Stockbroker, to discuss my investments," Eddie said sharply. "Look, why have you come here? What do you want? Sell something – or buy?"

"Buy, actually."

"Go on then," said Eddie, questioningly.

Neil lowered his voice. "I was wondering where to get hold of a gun. I thought you would know."

"You?" Eddie smirked. "Want a shooter? What, you the hard man now?" He let out a throaty laugh that ended in a smoker's cough. "So you *have* moved on then! Look, mate, why don't ya just pop into William Evans, round the corner? Gun and rifle makers to the top brass. Best quality."

"No, I'm serious. I really need to help someone who's in big trouble."

"You'll be in fuckin' big trouble if you don't hop it, son. I can't help ya. Anyway, you can't afford it. Got three hundred quid on ya?"

"No, really, I can pay. I came because I thought you were the right guy." In fact, Neil had not considered where he could find that much money. He had assumed guns were cheaper than that, since even children were carrying them.

"No ya never, ya cunt. You came 'cause you don't know no one else, that's why." Eddie uttered this insulting truth with a cheerful grin. "Look, jokin' aside, look at it my way – last thing I need is some hopeless fuckin' amateur wanderin' round London blastin' away with a fuckin' shooter that he got from a geezer called Eddie fuckin' Dawkins. See what I mean?"

"No, really," Neil insisted. "This is actually a life and death thing. No exaggeration." He wondered if he should tell Eddie about the girl and her note.

"Clear off," Eddie replied, "'fore I call the police." Unexpectedly he roared with laughter at this, and Neil wondered if he was supposed to laugh too. "'Ere," and Eddie's tone abruptly became amiably conspiratorial, "if you're looking for the real thing, I'll give ya one tip. Don't buy one, just borrow. Go up to Manchester, that's the place. If ya don't want to leave London, go across the river. Don't assume nothink and don't trust no-one."

That was at least four tips, but Neil did not argue with him. None of them were any use.

He unchained the bike and pushed it along Jermyn Street, staring into shop windows. Men's outfitters displayed hats and shoes, even shirts, costing more than a gun. In Regents Street he rode weary and despondent among buses and taxis. He resolved to just get on with life. Forget his foolish visit to that girl. Put the whole miserable experience behind him. Yet as he rode home, annoyingly, the foolish visit did not leave his thoughts.

* * *

From Marylebone Magistrates Court, Bernard returned to his office. He dictated some letters and made his way to the tube station. At Golders Green he picked up the car and drove home.

"Such a depressing day," he announced.

Elizabeth put her arms around him and kissed his lips. They

sat together at the kitchen table and sipped dry sherry as he gave her an account of the morning's hearing at the Town Hall.

"No one turned up. Apart from me, there were two other residents and ninety-seven empty chairs. The council withdrew their objections. It was an absolute bombshell."

"Really! Withdrew completely? Why?"

"The developer offered a more generous Section 106 if he was given planning permission, and that was that. The Inspector advised the council to accept. How can that be right?"[1]

Elizabeth nodded, "I wonder why they even opted for a public hearing?"

"Especially as it makes no difference what the public think! It's so wrong that an unelected official can overrule elected councillors! Well, you know my views!"

Elizabeth did know his views, and recognised his bitterness and anger. She advised him to take a walk round the park while she made dinner. They both knew she was referring to the doctor's urgent instruction that Bernard should avoid stress and take more exercise.

"I'll walk up to Sandy Heath and back," he agreed.

Elizabeth assured him there was no hurry. "You've got at least an hour. Go a bit further."

Bernard marched briskly, looking about him, trying to arrive at a happier state of mind. It was, after all, a pleasant neighbourhood. People tried hard to make a good life. He struggled with his mood. In this last hour of daylight, the weather had improved. He peered into a blue sky, cut across by the vapour trails of passing planes. A perfect evening! Foolish swallows, leaving too soon!

To his surprise, just as he turned the corner into Heath Avenue, there stood that chap Neil Chapman, leaning on his bicycle and apparently gazing intently at something on the other side of the road.

"Hello, hello! What can you see?" was Bernard's greeting. Neil jumped. Did Bernard know what he was looking at? "Going this

---

[1] Section 106 permits developers to offer a financial contribution to the local authority as part of a planning application.

way? Want to walk to the Heath with me?"

Neil preferred to be on his own and declined the friendly offer. "But Bernard," he said. "There *is* something I want to ask you about."

"About jazz?"

"No, much more important than that."

Bernard turned his head. "Fire away then."

Neil did not know what words to use. "There's some really, *really* bad things happening right around here," he ventured.

With tight lips, Bernard nodded with concern. He waited patiently to hear what troubled the young man.

"I mean, seriously bad stuff," Neil said at last. He wondered if he dared mention Liliana. No, this was not a discussion he could have with anyone.

"Yes, absolutely there is," Bernard agreed emphatically. "I know about it. Things that are illegal. The authorities have stopped caring."

Bernard had in mind the whole bubbling cauldron of wrongs suffered by ordinary people, the derelictions of public servants, the delinquency of the police, the crimes and corruption of officialdom, a catalogue of degrading irritations, encompassing everything from fraudulent Members of Parliament to park gates left unlocked, streetlights not working, accumulations of litter, nuisance from the Blenheim Road offices, damage to Hilda King's car, burglaries, muggings, vandalism and, of course, flawed planning applications granted if developers pay enough.

"What can we do about it?" Neil asked urgently.

"Mm – yuh, well, I *am* doing everything I can, you know," Bernard answered. "Sometimes you just do whatever is possible. It's not always easy. The way I feel is – every moment in which you do nothing to help is a moment in which you are complicit in the crime."

Complicit in the crime! Neil struggled to shoulder this new burden.

Bernard asked breezily, "I say, want to help me with some leafleting later this week?"

Neil hesitated, but could not bring himself to refuse. Besides, it could be a chance to talk. On reflection, he knew he would never be able to give Bernard the stolen jazz book. "Call me about it."

"Good chap! You're a good person. I knew you were."

Neil was uncomfortable with such praise. He felt Bernard had been deceived.

"Some people are human. Humane," Bernard insisted. "With others, there's nothing there. Not a glimmer. Well," he raised a hand in farewell and turned to carry on with his walk, "take care."

As promised, Bernard strode up to Sandy Heath and into Hampstead Garden Suburb. The prosperous roads made a veritable arboretum of fascinating specimens, a Kew of colourful, tended gardens. There are things, he reflected, beautiful things, in which one can take refuge for a moment. How delightful this time of year! Bernard was a man who lived not in Nature but in Society. A well-kept park or garden, or a tree-lined street, made him think of property, social order and law. Even on holiday, even in the Sahara or in Alpine peaks, he saw not landscape but the families who live in it.

Nevertheless, a walk always soothed him. In the gardens, overblown herbaceous borders were bursting with fleshy, fading summer blooms. Red berries clustered thickly on spiky shrubs and bushes, and low sunlight picked out brilliant leaves. High rowan branches were turning to copper. Some trees were as pretty as candy, speckles of orange and lemon among pistachio green. One bright yellow-clad birch seemed spotlit, the star of the show.

In places the roadway was marbled all across with brown and gold, and the pavement as crunchy as gravel underfoot with beechnuts and hard little acorns. Horse-chestnuts newly burst from their green shells shone like polished mahogany, while others were ground to fine white flour by the wheels of passing cars.

7

eed ur advice its urgent. So much easier to text than speak! But that would not work this time. Neil tried to think what would happen if she said yes, and then again, if she said no.

"You shouldn' a called me. I'm serious. Didn' I say 'don't call'?"

"No, it's life and death. Listen, I went – "

"Life an' death! What the fuck is that?" Joy-Belle replied sharply. "Don't care if it is, hun. You must learn to get along without me now. Forget all about me. I mean it."

"Look, I went to a girl, like you said. But this girl – she was a prisoner, a slave. I'm going out of my mind. You know about this stuff, don't you?"

"Jeez, nor *do* I! Don't land that shit on me!"

"You said you were studying it, the sex industry, gender and stuff. You said –"

"No, honey, I'm tellin' you, *don't* call me. 'F you have problems, what about you phone the police?"

He explained. "I can't go to them, can I? Because look, I committed a serious crime just by seeing her, didn't I? That's the law now. Anyway they wouldn't help, would they – the police? I have an idea what to do, but I need to talk to someone about it. Is Winston there? I'd like to speak to him."

"No, no, no!" she answered. "You don't speak to Winston! What do you mean, slave? Like, to do chores? Or to have sex?"

"Listen. This girl, this woman, not a sex worker. Locked in a room, right?" Neil told her. "She's foreign, can't speak English. Guys come in and do what they want. I mean, like, *anything* they want. They don't pay her. Not a penny. They pay her owners, right? See what I mean? And she *asked* me to help her."

It was just like old times, slipping away from the City round, crossing the river and heading down Coldharbour Lane. He rang the doorbell.

"Winston?"

Somehow, the last thing Neil expected was that Winston would be black. He didn't expect, either, that he would be so much older than Joy-Belle. His hair was greying and closely cut, in its natural tight curls. He was above average height, and dressed with some style in a crisp, white cotton shirt, baggy pale blue jeans and white brogues.

His sturdy neck and shoulders, broad chest and wide, taut biceps made it clear he was a fitness enthusiast, which Neil usually considered a sign of contemptible vanity. Yet this man had a modest, retiring demeanour. He looked subdued, tired and restrained, as if his energies were muted. Curiously, Neil envied him.

The two shook hands.

"Joy-Belle not here?"

"She's at college." He spoke quietly, the voice deep and pleasing.

They went into the familiar rooms. Neil burst out, "I need some advice. It's something heavy. Did she tell you?"

"Uh-huh." Winston frowned. "This thing – human trafficking, right? That's what it is, yeah? It's too big a thing for me, man. Or for anyone. You ain't gonna do it, you can't take them on. You don't look – no disrespect, man – but compared to these guys, you just a babe in arms. Tell the police and have done with it." His accent was hard to follow, oddly not American nor English nor West Indian.

"It's not about taking on the whole thing. It's about freeing just one person. What did Joy-Belle tell you about this girl?"

"Only that she's a prisoner and a," Winston faltered for the briefest instant, "a slave. Two things I wouldn't want to be."

"Me neither," said Neil.

Winston gestured to the table and chairs, and the two men sat. Neil could see the bedroom door. He must not let Winston know he had been in there. He should have agreed a story with Joy-Belle. And straight away, Winston posed the awkward question.

"How d'you know Goldi?"

Neil did not want to give away any secrets, but he calculated it would be better to tell him the truth. "Goldi? I thought her name was Joy-Belle," he answered.

"Yeah!" Winston laughed, low and warm, as if to himself. "Everyone calls her Goldi."

Puzzled and nervous, Neil accepted the explanation. "I saw her do a strip show, and drove her home afterwards."

"Cool." Winston nodded slowly. "That was nice of you. In that van? You drove her here, just you alone with Goldi, in that van, after seeing her strip?"

"Yeah."

Winston pressed his lips together. "OK," he said quietly, "where d'you see her strip?"

Clearly Joy-Belle had told him nothing. Neil replied evasively, "In a pub over in Hackney somewhere. It was a lunchtime thing. I stopped there for a sandwich. Then, like, afterwards I saw her in the street just waiting at a bus stop. That didn't look right to me, you know what I mean? So I felt I'd better drive her home."

Winston frowned. He seemed about to ask something else, then changed his mind. Suddenly he stood. "You got time for a cup of tea?" He put the kettle on and set out two cups. "You Brits like a cup of tea, right? Actually, I'm a Brit myself." He laughed at the idea.

"Yeah, I know that. Joy-Belle – I mean, Goldi," – Neil wondered if Winston was kidding about the name – "she talked about you. She said she loves you. She told me you were in prison. She said you'd been there four years."

"She *told* you that? She said she *loves* me?" Again the thoughtful frown. "When did she tell you all this stuff? You musta seen her again, right, after that first time?"

"Well, yeah, I did see her a couple of times. I wanted to make sure she was OK. Man, that must've been something big, to put you inside for that long."

Winston carefully dropped a tea bag in each cup. When he turned and stared, the frank gaze was as unsettling as a baby's. "Little bit indiscreet of Goldi to discuss me being in jail, yeah? And of *you*, to mention it. But now you *have* mentioned it."

"Don't tell me about it, that's cool."

"Nothing to tell," answered Winston. "You call it something big. It didn't feel like such a massive thing to me. You know, I went about my business. I was careless, someone got hurt. The one thing about it, he had it coming. No regrets about that. The only bad thing was the next four years."

"What was it like?"

"Crowded, is what it was. Yeah, as crowded as hell," Winston stopped moving and seemed locked in thought. "Fighting," he said. "Beatings. Fours years of fist fights an' knife fights an' abuse an' insanity. Fighting to keep your bunk to yourself. Or even have a bunk. Guys gang-rapin' each other. Extort the weak ones to suck 'em off an' give 'em food an' money," he shook his head. "Rats an' roaches an' toilet overflow on the floor. Dark in there, too, no daylight. Don't believe me, do ya? No, it is unbelievable. A lot of guys, it's too much for 'em. They don't make it. Specially if they're innocent."

"Fuck."

"Anyway, it's in the past. Gotta move forward, move forward. I'm living a new life now, back with Goldi, model citizen."

"You working?"

"Well, truth is, nothin' jus' now. I'm looking. I used to be in close protection, but they took away my licence."

"Close protection? Isn't that – you're a bodyguard or something?"

"Yeah, sometimes a bodyguard, or sometimes, well, you know, we did whatever was needed. Could be security at a rock concert, or a visiting VIP, surveillance, anything."

"And you can't do it with a criminal record?"

"You can't do it without a licence." He turned back to the kettle, poured the boiling water. "Some people get to keep their licence. It depends." He gave a long sigh. "I used to enjoy it. And good pay. I don't know when I'll be able to do that again. Ten, twenty years. By then, I'll be too old for the work. And out of date; you have to keep up to date with the law, in close protection. You want milk? Sugar?"

Neil thought Winston already seemed too old. "How d'you get a job in America? Was that legal?"

Winston explained that during his teenage years, his father had moved to Chicago, so he too had the right to live and work there.

"And can you vote? Be cool, won't it, if America gets a black president?"

"Yeah, everyone sees it like that. Funny, when a guy is half white, he's black. That's all wrong, a wrong attitude," Winston replied quietly. "I ain't denyin', it *is* good to see a black man coming out ahead. But deep down, Obama ain't *black* black. I mean, he may be African and he may be American, but the way I see it, that don't make him African-American. To my mind, an African ain't a *nigger*. When they get themselves a candidate whose ancestors was *slaves,* on a Southern plantation pickin' cotton, that a be *the* turning point. I would a liked to see Condaleeza Rice run for president. First black president, first woman president. And from Alabama. And a Republican."

Neil made no response at all. Winston laughed and shook his head, "You don't know *what* I am talking about! Do you?"

"Yeah, yeah, I do, I do," Neil asserted. "Well, maybe it will happen one day. But slavery, slavery, listen, there's more to it than picking cotton. It's not about that any more. This girl – "

"Yeah, well," Winston took a deep breath and sighed, "a lot of people are slaves to one thing or another. We have hang-ups. We can't stop doing stupid things, and we *know* it's stupid. I known a lot of girls become, like, the plaything of some guy. I seen it many times. And some of them even *want* to be."

"No, listen. I know all about that crap," Neil said impatiently. "This is different. I'm talking about a girl who is locked in her room." Neil was afraid that he sounded too earnest. It would put Winston off.

"I understand," Winston murmured. "She's been kidnapped, or..."

"She was traded, bought and sold, maybe swapped for something. There are men there who think she's their *property*."

"Well, that's her problem. Not ours. Yeah, I'd like to help, but you know, I'm on parole. Any trouble and I'll be back inside. I have to avoid that."

"So, you've got a probation officer? You have to check in at the police station every day, every month, or something?" Neil was exasperated.

"Huh, that's the theory," Winston answered. "Fact is, I never actually seen my probation officer. And police don't seem to know I exist. I'd like to keep it that way."

"OK," Neil paused, "but if you know where I can get a gun – "

Winston smiled, amused and suprised. "A gun! Is that what you have in mind? You gonna take on the human trafficking business with your gun?"

"I'm serious."

Winston laughed as if to himself, gently, slapped his leg, shook his head. "Did I just say I was a peaceful citizen? And want to keep my nose clean? Did I mention I'm on parole? Did I just say that?"

He put the cups of tea on the table.

Neil pursed his lips. "I don't know who else to ask," he said.

"You ever use a gun?" Winston looked at him as if he were a child.

Neil shook his head and bit his lip.

"Ever use a knife? Cut someone deep? You ever drawn someone's blood, seen it running out?"

Neil shook his head with disgust.

"OK, you ever even hit anyone? With an iron bar? A baseball bat? A hammer, maybe? Anything?"

"Fuck no! No, I haven't. No."

"Well, with your fists, then?"

"Yeah, yeah, of course. As a kid, a few times. Not too many."

"I don't mean as a kid. Man, you don't know *what* you are doing. You don't know *this*: when you shoot another person it makes you sick. Yeah, literally throw up. It fucks your head. You think about their Mom and Dad. You can't sleep. Yeah, really.

You might even cry your eyes out thinkin' what you done. Unless you are an animal. Which I can see you're not."

Neil said nothing at all for a while, but then he argued, "What about soldiers? Are they animals?"

"No, no," Winston conceded with a shrug, "but I do wonder about it, you know, the effect on them. And, uh, Neil, did you ever hear about the law of unintended consequences?"

"Yeah. Meaning what?"

"Just sayin'. Whenever anyone shoots someone, there's a *lot* of consequences. Mostly bad ones."

The two of them sat in silence, sipping their tea. Both men were pensive.

At last Winston said, "And suppose you get her out – then what? Where you gonna take her? You have to plan it through. You planned it through?"

"No, well," Neil shrugged and shook his head dismissively. Winston was making everything unnecessarily complicated. "Probably haven't planned every detail. I'm just going to get her out of there. I'll take her wherever she wants to go."

Winston shook his head as if pondering Neil's folly. "She won't fucking *know*, man. She'll be petrified with fear that they will catch her again. She'll be as disoriented as crazy. Need a doctor, too. She might be a junkie. She probably don't know a soul she can trust in the whole world. She won't trust you. Why should she?"

"Listen, it's better than leaving her where she is." Neil tutted with exasperation. "All right, I'll take her to my place. We'll work it out from there. Hey, I'll show you something."

From his pocket he took Liliana's note.

Winston watched as he unfolded it. "What does it say?" he asked.

"It's Romanian. It says, I am a prisoner, not a whore. The men will kill. Please help."

Winston leaned back in his chair wearily. He seemed profoundly tired.

"No need to buy a gun, you know. Just borrow. Or rent. Then, if you don't use it, there's less to pay."

"Look, can you help?"

Winston tightened his lips. "Only because it's a slave," his deep voice, already quiet, became almost inaudible, "only because of that."

* * *

Bernard clutched Neil's hand warmly. He seemed in jovial spirits.

Neil was less so. All week he had waited edgily for Winston's call. He rushed the deliveries on Wednesday. On Thursday, all drivers were instructed that, starting next week, winter uniform must be worn. It seemed absurd – September had brought the best days of the year – but there was no arguing with Critchlow's timetable.

The light summer outfit, a suit of fine blue cotton serge, was wonderfully comfortable. Although Neil had not yet worn the darker blue, army-style, woollen uniform of winter, he did not look forward to the change. It seemed a melancholy portent. Another Christmas was coming, and he was achieving nothing.

On Friday evening he went to the Earl Cadogan after work for a couple of rounds with some of the other lads. Quite simply, he did not want to become too isolated from them. For once, he joined in the banter, laughed at wisecracks and agreed with every damning comment about that bastard Sanina. Yet he could not connect. He wondered how many had ever paid for sex. Just a few, or all of them? Or was he the only one? Some of these blokes *must* have been to prostitutes – by the law of averages. Some had surely seen lapdances and sex shows of different kinds. Most guys do like to watch a striptease. No doubt some had weird tastes. You never knew what other guys were into, and you never asked. Most of it is innocent, harmless stuff that women will play along with for a man they like. Some of it is more sinister.

As for himself, by Friday evening he had had reached the stage where his eyes ran tenderly over every well-shaped woman. But he could hardly look at porn with an easy mind any more; disconcertingly, he found himself studying the women's faces for signs of distress.

Now a guy was telling a joke about an English hooker, a Welsh hooker and a Scottish hooker. Something about the Union Jack. Neil laughed and downed his beer.

By Sunday, when he met Bernard to help with his leafleting, a full five days had passed without any word. Maybe Winston couldn't get the gun after all, or had changed his mind.

"What fantastic weather, eh? What a wonderful Indian Summer we've had this year!" exclaimed Bernard cheerfully. It was a balmy day, in that turn of the season when the caressing September air can be exquisite, neither cool nor warm.

"We'll do the Kilnmeadows council estate, shall we?"

"Is it rough?" Neil asked.

"Well, can be," Bernard nodded, "but most of the people are very decent."

He handed Neil a sheet of folded glossy paper. "This leaflet is what we're delivering. Have a read. It's something KOBRA has signed up to."

As Bernard drove the short distance, Neil looked it over: *Community Help and Action Volunteers – CHAVS.* A photograph showed surly young men standing on a corner.

"What is this?" He read the first few words aloud, "*Don't just stand there – do something!*" A second picture showed the men at a meeting, and a third, apparently repairing something in a garden under the beaming smiles of a grateful grandmother.

This will never work, thought Neil. *Guys like this hate anything organised.*

Bernard clicked the radio on. Scotland Yard had foiled an attempt by Islamists to kill a publisher. A building society had been nationalised as the financial crisis worsened. A Muslim warehouseman was suing Tesco's for asking him to carry cases of alcohol. The Taliban claimed responsibility for shooting a policewoman in Afghanistan, pointing out that they had given fair warning that women must not join the police.

They pulled up outside a shabby block of flats. Neil gazed out at a long building, six storeys high, with the strange name Kilnmeadows and the words Hendon Borough Council 1955 embossed in stone over the main entrance.

He thought it actually did look rough. "I can see these flats from my bedroom window," he said, "but I never thought I'd come over here."

Wouldn't mind betting there's some guns in this place. Knives, for sure. Prostitutes, too, maybe. Imprisoned women? Hopefully not.

Bernard had dressed as informally as he knew how, in sports jacket and old chino trousers, a rather attractive casual shirt and suede shoes. To Neil's eye he looked ridiculously well-to-do. He himself was dressed in his usual hooded top, tee-shirt, jeans and trainers. Bernard opened the boot of his car and each of them took a large shoulder bag of leaflets. Neil urged Bernard to give him more. It was plain to see that he could carry three or even four times as much.

The council flats seemed securely locked, but Bernard knew – so did every burglar, presumably – that the door would open automatically if they simply pressed a button marked *Tradesmen*. It led them into a bleak tiled hallway regularly doused in cleaning fluids, Neil guessed from the smell. Concrete stairs led to concrete landings lined with narrow fibreboard doors, and out onto concrete balconies where more front doors stood closely together. Without ceremony, the two men began pushing leaflets through corroded little letter flaps.

"CHAVs is a scheme we put together," Bernard explained as they worked. "KOBRA and other residents' associations in the borough. It'll be a task force of volunteers willing to take on essential jobs that the authorities are failing to do."

"Wow, direct action! Vigilantes, even. I'm really surprised at you. Clever, though, the name!"

"No, no, no, not vigilantes! God forbid! But where the authorities are failing, it's right for the people to tackle the job themselves."

It was curiously quiet as they made their way up the steps. Neil commented that it felt eerie. Hundreds of tenants – he assumed – lived in the block, but they saw no one. *Were* there slaves here, after all? Was one of these flats a prison just like that girl's? Did men who used her live here? No one would ever know. As they passed the front doors sometimes voices could be heard within.

"I think they stay indoors because there's nowhere else to go," Bernard speculated. "Or maybe they haven't got up yet."

"What sort of thing you reckon these CHAVs are going to do, then?" Neil quizzed him. "Helping old dears cross the road? Clearing up litter?"

Bernard heard the note of mockery, but ignored it. "Yes, yes, of course! They could do that. Painting over graffiti, sweeping the streets, that type of thing. We could all muck in. Why not? Another idea is for local people to collect evidence to bring prosecutions."

Neil was startled by this. "So, like, do-gooders snooping on each other?"

"Snooping? You could call it that," Bernard nodded. "But not on each other, Neil, obviously. On criminals. On anti-social elements, like the Blenheim Road businesses that cause such a nuisance to residents. And lazy council employees skiving at our expense! Killing time till they draw their ruddy pensions!" They walked along a corridor lined with front doors, putting a leaflet into each letterbox. "One thing CHAVs could do is lock and unlock the park gates at the right times, with our own padlocks and keys. Let's see what happens when the council try to stop us. We'll get the local press onto it."

Neil laughed aloud, his voice resounding in the stairwell. "Blimey! That *is* direct action. *That* won't go down well with the park café commandos, will it? Be careful! I expect they have some sort of, you know, *understanding* with council staff, that the park won't be locked."

"If they do, so much the better. Something seems to prevent the council from dealing with that blasted café."

"What do you reckon, then – they getting a kickback?"

"Exactly the sort of thing we could try to find out. I hope if CHAV groups catch on, they could become a force to reckon with," Bernard said. "I don't see it as snooping or do-gooders. I see it as community trying to defend itself. I'm a great believer in community. Community is a human instinct. People are nothing if not members of a group."

"No, you're wrong – not everyone's a joiner. I'm not," Neil commented. "I never wanted to be counted part of anything."

"What, no family, no friends, no workmates, nothing?" Bernard looked at him, perhaps disbelieving, or perhaps troubled by the reply.

Neil himself was surprised by the remark. Surely he had some sense of belonging to a family, at least? He barely knew his cousins or aunts and uncles. His sisters were remote from him. And even with the medication, his depressed mother lived more and more in her own locked world of distant, troubled visions. Dad was dead. It occurred to him that they could go, as a family, to Dad's grave. But then, he was the only one who would want to make such a visit.

"That doesn't sound good!" Bernard exclaimed. "Well, at least you're part of a neighbourhood. Look at you, you're a KOBRA volunteer now!"

Neil certainly did not feel that he was any such thing.

Some flats had tried to prettify themselves with a leafy potted plant beside the front door, although it had usually been vandalised. Others had metal bars to protect themselves from neighbours. Some had colourful leaflets glued to the door, praising Jesus: *My debt has been cleared, my sins have been washed away.* Some had stickers with Arabic script. Outside one, a worn doormat parodied the traditional *Welcome* with the words *Fuck Off.*

Then, as he pushed the leaflet through one of the doors, it swung open abruptly. A man stood in pyjamas, indignant. Neil could not judge from which part of the world he came. South-east Asia, Indonesia perhaps. Somehow he had made his way to this place in a faraway land. Inside, the flat seemed unfurnished; there were children playing, women's voices. He reached out to take the paper from Neil's hand.

"Council?" he asked.

"No."

"Mister, you look! I am" – now suddenly the man was shouting loudly – "*not satisfied!*" His fury echoed around the tiled walls, the concrete stairwell. "This *no good!* We want *different one!* We want *bigger!* We want *more!* We want *better!* Tell council." He jabbed a finger.

"Look, I'm not *from* the council, all right, mate?" Neil retorted, but the door was already slamming. "Why pick on me!" he grumbled.

Bernard's mood had changed. His face was grim, and for a while he said no more. As they trudged up and down the stairways and balconies, Bernard opened his heart to Neil.

He was driven, he admitted sadly, not by altruism or compassion for others, but by anger and fear. Anger about injustice, fear of tyranny. "I hate the way good people feel unable to live decent lives in peace. I am scared for all of us."

"Are you? And 'tyranny' is," Neil queried seriously, "what, exactly? Police state, fascism, military coup?"

"No, no, no," Bernard replied. "Bureaucracy. Officialdom. Everyone with authority over the citizen. They should all be accountable directly to the man in the street. Chief constables, directors of children's services, planning officers, should all have to stand for election – and re-election. Not a job for life, but a job where you bloody well get chucked out if local residents aren't happy with you. That would improve people's lives overnight."

While Bernard raged, Neil's phone interjected a brief sound. He glanced down at a text from Joy-Belle's number: *2day Albert G8 BatterC Park 5pm prompt w £70.*

He shrugged. "I dunno. People wouldn't vote, would they? They don't vote now, do they? *I* don't. I'm not into politics." They trudged to the next storey. "What a dump, this place. They should put in lifts."

Bernard stopped on the stairs and gently held Neil's arm. "Lifts? You think they should provide lifts? Who? Who should provide them? Neil, that's money taken from ordinary working families. You say you're not into politics. Putting lifts in here is politics."

With Bernard's fatherly hand on his arm like that, Neil longed to talk frankly to him. Not as neighbours, but as... he didn't know what it was he wanted. As one man to another, one human being to another. He would have liked just to tell him about that wretched girl locked in her room.

But opening up is easy when you have nothing shameful to tell. Although, perhaps, even Bernard... you never knew for sure. They continued their climb to the next landing.

"I've been into quite a few of these flats," Bernard went on, "and a lot of them are nice inside, comfortable. People everywhere try to make a good home, don't they? Don't forget, there are children here who will do well at school, go to university, and move on to somewhere better. *That's* politics. Oh, and talking of that, did I tell you that I'm involved in starting a new political party?"

"You're not, are you?" Neil shook his head. "God, Bernard, you should ease off. Something's going to blow, one day."

"Mm – yuh, the Federation of Residents' Associations is going to put up election candidates. Yes! We'll put *residents'* interests first. Not wages, nor profits, not workers, not business. Residents!" He frowned quite furiously. "People talk about the economy as if it were all that matters, but that's back to front! *Citizens*, families in their own homes, should be top of our concerns. That's who I believe in!"

"Best of British luck, mate." Neil shook his head. "Anyway, residents *are* workers, aren't they? Well, some of 'em. And business pays their wages. So it *is* all about the economy."

"Bah!" Bernard cried out. "Home is more important than business." Neil looked up, surprised by the sudden flare of temper. But he saw only sadness in the older man's face. "Don't get me wrong," added Bernard irritably, "I'm all in favour of enterprise. But, trouble is, commerce has no conscience."

"You're a bloody socialist, on the quiet, aren't you?" Neil teased him.

"I am not!" Bernard protested vehemently. "Socialists,

capitalists – between them, look at the dog's breakfast they've made. Let's get on – there's another block to do, after this."

Neil looked again at his phone. "I'm running out of time. This is taking longer than I thought."

"Time! Time! Time is running out! In no time at all there will be no time at all!" Bernard said.

* * *

Online, Neil saw that the route to Battersea was much the same as going to work, so he knew it should only take half an hour at most. Better, though, to allow an hour or so than risk any delays on the way.

First he needed Winston's cash. He cycled to the ATM in Golders Green. The receipt showed his account was now overdrawn. He knew he was a bloody fool. As he came back through Osborne Park, a few boys were kicking a ball. Outside the café, Bernard's bête noir, families were gathered cheerfully around tables and chairs in the sun. It made a pleasing scene that should delight anyone. Neil thought that he might as well eat here as anywhere. Bernard had said it was not the daytime which bothered him, but what went on at night.

He dismounted and ventured inside. A group of men, big and shaven-headed, crowded together at one table; behind the counter, another idly tidied cups and glasses and interjected comments into their conversation. They talked in a language that he did not know. Neil asked for a coffee and a sandwich and went out to a table in the open air, sitting there until it was time to go to Battersea.

As usual Neil rode fast down West End Lane, without a pause through the smiling tourists on the Beatles' famous pedestrian crossing in Abbey Road, into Lisson Grove and Seymour Place, to Marble Arch. Curiously there was almost as much traffic as on a weekday morning. All the way he tried to visualise the meeting with Winston, but could not. He did not know what to expect. The police might be waiting there to arrest both of them.

He wasn't even sure that Winston would have the gun.

Perhaps at this stage he simply wanted the money. He cut through Hyde Park to Sloane Street, lined with Versace, Dior, Vuitton, Hermès, Bulgari, Chanel... and, grandest of them all, the blue and gold Art Deco façade of T.Critchlow & Sons. Today he cycled quickly past with only the slightest glance, around Sloane Square, into Kings Road.

Although it was Sunday, everything in Kings Road seemed to be open. All was pleasant. The pavements were crowded. Neil had time to kill, and slowly made his way along the narrow, busy road. On the lampposts, hanging baskets of trailing geraniums, tired but still colourful, were a little revived by the autumn sunshine. Drinkers and diners sat at tables outside pubs. To either side people strolled lazily, jackets and cardigans draped over arms or shoulders, as they enjoyed a glorious afternoon.

He turned left towards the Embankment and crossed the rushing Thames on Albert Bridge, flimsiest and prettiest of London's bridges. Already he could see the treetops of Battersea Park, there on the other side. A light breeze blew along the river.

Reaching the south bank, he cycled beside the park. Ahead, a big pub stood wrapped around a corner. Facing it, set back from the street, a grand semi-circle of stone and wrought iron was inscribed with the words Albert Gate. He was more than an hour early.

This is a really uncool place to meet. There's a stack of people around. Security cameras looking this way. Everyone at the pub can see me too. They'll all say, yeah, there was a guy on a bike by the park entrance.

Neil cycled through the gateway. He noticed that a camera surveyed the car park inside. Anxious not to attract attention, he dismounted as soon as he saw the *No Cycling* sign. He walked the bike along leafy paths among trees and flowerbeds and wide grassy lawns. The air was as pleasant as it can ever be. Dogs trotted beside their owners, young couples pushed pushchairs, laughing children held coloured ice-cream cones. Two attractive runners passed, pretty with pony-tails and enticing in clinging lycra. He tried to imagine Liliana running here with a friend. She couldn't possibly run, she was too frail and worn out. Did she have any friends?

In the distance, the four white chimneys of Battersea Power Station looked like the funnels of a vast cruise ship. On the grass, families sat contentedly together, some picnicking. Dads and children and dogs played while women rested or talked or laid out plates of food. Neil thought he had been here once with his own father. Hadn't he been brought here as a child, to Battersea Funfair; hadn't they too run on the grass together? There did not seem to be a funfair here now. He tried to imagine Liliana enjoying a picnic. That would be ridiculous: she needed therapy, not a picnic. And what about the other girls in the house? Why only rescue one, and not the others? He remembered what Bernard had said, don't agonise about everyone who is suffering in the world – just help those you can help. *Do your bit.*

Old people in brilliant whites played bowls on a bright lime-green lawn as flat as a billiard table. One of the players was on crutches. Is there another sport, Neil asked himself, that you can play on crutches? And now he passed a boating lake where men and women, in love or half in love, pretended at a Venetian romance. It was a joyful sight. This, surely, was the good, decent world Bernard desperately wanted to protect. No, on reflection, Bernard knew life was more complicated than that.

Neil turned to take a path towards the river. He was surprised to find a Buddhist temple, placed incongruously by the Thames waterside. A notice explained pompously that it was the Peace Pagoda. A couple stood puzzling at its gilded statues and curling roofs. Neil stopped on a wide riverside walkway to look over the embankment wall. Below, the olive-brown waters lapped at an expanse of sludge and gravel. On the far side of the river, the dignified redbrick mansion blocks of Chelsea Embankment hid among tall plane trees, traffic passing to and fro in front of them like electric toys.

As he passed the time idly, seagulls squawked, yachts tacked against the breeze, a little swarm of kayaks dashed by. Suddenly half a dozen large black birds with long necks appeared and circled above him – they were cormorants, but Neil did not recognise them. He thought them sinister, and, sceptic though he was, wondered anxiously what they augured. He knew, of course, that the answer was, nothing. He called them Nazguls.

Unhurried, he made his way back to Albert Gate. Straight away he saw a pair of headlights flash. The car was parked on the other side of the road, a little way up from the pub. Neil swung back onto the bike and rode over.

"Jeez, man. Look at you. You didn't come here on that thing?" Winston pulled a face. "Why didn't you drive? Parking is no problem on a Sunday."

"I haven't got a car," answered Neil. "Anyway, bike is better. You can go anywhere. You're not held up by traffic. You're free. You don't have a number. There's no record of you on a bike."

"You think you gonna ride home like that, wearing a pistol for all to see?

"So you've got it, then?" Neil replied.

"Talk in the car."

Neil had seen scores of old films in which people used revolvers. In vivid memory, James Cagney, George Raft, Humphrey Bogart, Edward G. Robinson appeared in turn before him, metamorphosing into Al Pacino, Russell Crowe and many more. He had seen plenty of thrillers in which high-powered guns were used. He could visualise a revolver. He could visualise something black or 'gun metal' grey. He could visualise a shoot-out in black-and-white.

All fictional characters, he noticed, even the most respectable, seem strangely familiar with firearms. Neil knew that in the real world, most decent people expect to go their whole lives without ever touching a gun, maybe without even seeing one.

Neil knew that shooting is a favourite pastime of the landed gentry. He knew that they like to crack a sportsmanlike shot at a frightened pheasant. He knew that a starting pistol can be made to fire real bullets. He knew criminals use ordinary shotguns with the barrel sawn off. He knew the police have the latest automatic weapons. He knew that gangsters have guns, bank robbers have guns, even kids on council estates have guns.

But there was a lot he did not know. He did not know what types of guns such people use, or even what type of guns exist. He did not know how big they are, or how small, or how heavy or how light. He did not know how they feel in the hand, or how they look up close. He did not know how they affect the mind.

Winston rummaged under some sports gear in a battered holdall and pulled out a plastic carrier bag. He opened it up gingerly to allow a peek inside. At the bottom, Neil was startled to see, lay a leather holster containing a pistol, along with a couple of unidentifiable metal objects, one black, the other shiny steel.

"A holster! I wasn't expecting a holster."

Winston looked on wryly as Neil carefully slipped the gun out of its sheath and touched it tenderly, smiling with wonder.

The pistol was black and dark blue, cold to touch, solid metal, about eight and a half inches long and weighed more than he expected, two or three pounds. It had a pleasing, smooth, precise feel, a piece of expert machine-tooling to delight any engineer. There was a kind of beauty to it, and a kind of insanity.

Neil remembered that in films, police use a short gun like this, something that fits in the palm, and has a barrel more rectangular than circular.

"That's a top-quality handgun," Winston said quietly. "That's a 9mm Beretta semi-automatic, 92F model. It's the US Government version. It's the business. It's not a joke. Anyone who knows firearms is gonna back off when they see that, OK?"

Neil calmed himself and nodded solemnly. "What's that in there?" He meant, the other two pieces of metal in the bag.

Winston casually took them out of the carrier bag. "Well, this here is the clip – you know, the ammunition – and this thing is the silencer. Now, Neil, number one priority, for Christ's sake, *never* forget to keep the weapon totally out of sight. Get it home quick and keep it well hid. If anyone sees it, police sirens a start blaring. They'll be on their way to take you out. Helicopters, everything."

Neil nodded wryly and let Winston talk.

"Now, you understand about the money? Seventy pound is you return the weapon unused, right? Fire the damn thing, and you pay another hunner'n fifty. If you don't give it back at all, that's another three hundred pound you owe. They want payin' even if you dead. It's me they'll come to, not you. They don't know 'bout you. By rights you ought to leave me a deposit. But I know you ain't got it. My advice is, scare people all you like, but don't pull the trigger."

"But I *am* planning to use it," Neil said directly.

"Man, you don't even know how."

"Show me how."

Winston chuckled softly. "OK, let's walk in the park and shoot something," he said. Neil glanced up with a smile, "That's a joke, right? There are too many people," but Winston said he knew a place. He added, "The one clip is included in the price. There's eighteen rounds in the clip."

"So I can... fire it eighteen times?"

"Exactly. But whether it's once, or eighteen times, that'll cost you the same. See?"

Winston led the way. They took a small side gate into the park, close to the bridge, and walked away from the path into a rough, overgrown area. "There's no cameras along here", he explained. They were concealed by bushes.

"What if someone sees us?" said Neil.

"They'll think we're gay and won't look."

Winston showed Neil how to push the pin to insert the magazine, and remove it, how to work the safety catch and how to aim. He showed him how to attach the silencer, and fixed it in place.

"Stand four-square and keep perfectly still," he said. "Hold the piece out in front so you can aim right, and to take the kick – you know, man, like, the recoil. Now, if it feels too heavy, don't get macho – jus' take the piece in both hands. Hopefully, you'll have time to use the sights, right? Line up the sights with your target. Remember to keep perfectly still! Don't get the shakes, man!

Pull *gently* on the trigger. Keep it smooth and clean and steady."

He glanced to either side and suggested Neil take his first shot at a nearby tree. Neil said "Won't people hear?"

Winston shook his head, "No. Well, yes. One or two of them will say, 'What was that?' Then they won't think about it. Just one shot is OK."

Suddenly Neil decided against pulling the trigger. Maybe it would work, after all, just to let the men see the gun. That way he could save a hundred and fifty pounds.

After the scornful remarks about riding home wearing a gun for all to see, Neil explained he had expected to put everything in the rucksack. Discovering that Neil had a sweatshirt in the bag, now Winston advised him to wear the holster and put the sweatshirt on over it.

Neil objected. "Just put everything in the rucksack. It'll be fine like that."

"No, someone could steal the bag," Winston said. "I always prefer to wear a weapon on my body. A shoulder holster's better than the hip or a leg strap. To my mind, that is the best way to carry. Discreet. And remember, man, 'til you're ready to use the thing, *always* keep it hid."

"I might want to use it for some reason, you know, something might –"

"No, no, no," Winston was emphatic. "You think you can just pull out a gun and use it 'for some reason'?"

"No, but what about if I see, I dunno, a bank robbery or a mugging? Or a girl being raped? You're not saying I should walk past? Why should I help the one girl and not the other one?"

Winston acknowledged that would be a curious dilemma. "Look, if you want to deal with it, OK – but do it *without* the weapon," he insisted. "It happened to me, you know," he said. "One night I saw a young guy hassling this poor broken-down old drunk, an' I stepped up to stop it. I didn't show him no weapon, but he just stopped. But you know, second thought, while you carryin', leave it alone. Don't intervene. Walk on by – just this once."

Step by step, Neil put the clip into the gun, the silencer in his pocket, strapped the holster under his arm, slipped the Beretta into place and zipped the sweatshirt over it. Patiently, sometimes shaking his head as if in disbelief, Winston watched these careful preparations.

As Neil bent to unlock the bicycle, the holster came into view. Winston roughly grabbed him and pulled the sweatshirt zip higher. "I said keep it hid! You *must* keep it *completely* out of sight, no matter what."

At last Neil was ready for the ride home. Winston got into his car and opened the window. He said, "Oh, here's another tip: don't kill anybody. Aim away from the chest, OK? Or head. If you kill someone, you get to keep the gun – or throw it away, that's up to you. What you *don't* do is bring it back to me! Just send me the three hundred in cash. Jeez, I mus' be crazy to let you do this. You don't know *what* you are up against. Don't speak to no one, man. Promise me! *No one*. No matter how good-lookin' she is."

Neil smiled. Things, he felt, were moving in the right direction. He promised he would ride straight home and say nothing to anyone.

Winston did not expect to see Neil again. Hardly above a whisper, he wished him "all the luck in the world." There was a shake of the head, as if to say, the poor, naïve blue-eyed bastard will end up dead for sure.

Neil walked through Battersea Park towards Chelsea Bridge, pushing his bike briskly along the riverside path. The weight and bulk beneath his arm could not be ignored. Somehow it heightened a feeling of being alone in the world. He rather liked that.

At first he glanced anxiously to see if the shape of the holster could be seen by passers-by. They clearly did not find anything unusual about his appearance. He avoided making eye-contact, instead turning to gaze at the Thames.

The tide had risen. The river surged deep and cloudy, swirling, splashing grey against the embankment wall. Flotsam formed trails of matted weeds and splintered wood and polystyrene, abandoned plastic bottles and cups, scraps of paper and dead leaves.

8

Precious, perishable merchandise in the back of the van must be swiftly delivered. At this time on a Sunday afternoon, traffic is light and the journey fast along the Thames Embankment.

"Ndegjove diçka? [Hear something?]" The driver frowns.

In the passenger seat his colleague listens intently, then shakes his head. "Asgjë – ende. [Nothing – yet.]"

They resemble each other as closely as cousins, these two men. Both are in their late twenties, with dark, lean, strong features and thick dark hair cut short. The eyes are deep and passionate. One man chats. He is voluble. He comments on the traffic, observes that it's a nice evening, mentions idly that his family are still toiling on the farm. He explains to his companion, not for the first time, that the farm is way up in the hills above Silovë, close to the border of both Kosova and Macedonia. No explanation is needed, because his companion is from the same place and the same clan and shares the same history. Yet once again he recalls the icy lakes and high meadows, the green valleys and rugged, wild mountains of northern Albania. Wistfully he says that the weather is so lovely back home at this time of year. The other, his passenger, says nothing, gazing blankly ahead.

Near Blackfriars Bridge the van angles away from the river, continues on empty Queen Victoria Street, left into Friday Street, round the back of St Paul's Cathedral into New Change, and up the deserted canyon of office buildings which is Aldersgate. At the end of the Beech Street tunnel, the driver U-turns into a residents' car park beneath the Barbican estate.

Only the passenger gets out of the van. He walks to an

entrance, pushes a buzzer to unlock the door. Up a flight of stairs, a receptionist nods with recognition and waves him through. He takes the lift to the thirtieth floor and strolls to one of the apartments. The door is already standing open, waiting for him.

In the lounge, his boss leans back comfortably in an easy chair with friends all around, several glamorously dressed young women among them. Sharply fragrant cigarette smoke spirals in the warm air. Windows on two sides look towards the Gherkin and the dome of St Paul's Cathedral and, glinting in a rosy sunset, the glass bracelet of the London Eye.

Oriental rugs cover the floor, and in the centre of the room is a round table inlaid with ivory. On it, a handgun lies among vodka and raki bottles empty and half empty. Perhaps the women are not so much friends as companions. The man neither knows nor cares. He has come only for instructions, and is also hoping for a tip. He stands by a window and waits. Far below, tiny figures are strolling or sitting at tables and chairs on the terrace of the Barbican Arts Centre.

His boss makes a few jokes at his expense. The girls giggle nervously, the men guffaw. The man is slightly embarrassed to be laughed at, but only slightly. He asks where to take the "valuables" and is given his instructions in a single word – Osman. Now his boss pulls a handful of banknotes from a pocket and ostentatiously draws out two fifties. "Thanks, Nazim. One for you, one for Leka."

Nazim's father would not have seen that much money in a whole month, back home, even with all the cross-border rackets. Nazim would like the life that his boss has, but still, he's not complaining.

Leka again made small talk to his unresponsive companion as he drove from the Barbican to King's Cross, skirted Camden Town, climbed the long hill into Hampstead and sped down into Golders Green. It was getting dark.

"Tani? [Now?]" Leka jerked his head towards the back of the van.

Nazim looked at his watch. "Po, zgjohen [Yes, waking]."

Just beyond a grandiose red-brick synagogue, they saw the narrow footpath into Osborne Park. Along it they cautiously drove towards the park café. Inside, lights shone invitingly, and – though the shutters were half closed – several men were gathered, holding bottles and watching a sports game on a large television screen. Beyond the café, darkness obscured the big square park, though a little light remained in the sky. A final majestic sweep of peach-coloured cloud drifted behind Brent Cross.

They pulled up under a lamp at the windowless rear of the building. Two men, big and crop-headed, waited to meet the van. Their round, sturdy features, ghostly in the lamplight, nodded in terse greeting, "Leka. Nazim."

"Osman. Zlatan," came the response. In English, Leka amiably asked the men if they were well.

"Poluchil tovar? [Got the goods?]" Osman addressed them in Russian.

"No problem," Nazim replied in English, then reverted to Russian.

Leka caught the words 'moldavskoya bryunetka' and 'ukrainskaya blondinka' and guessed at the meaning – something like *We have a dark Moldovan and a blonde Ukrainian.*

Although the two pairs of men met from time to time for this transaction, they had no language in which to conduct it. All except Nazim had learned English, although so badly that often they were not mutually intelligible. Nazim felt that his English was improving – he sometimes half-understood what was being said. He and Leka both knew a few words of Italian, and the other two a few words of German. Nazim spoke a clumsy Russian, as did Osman.

Nazim also had a good knowledge of Osman's own language, Serbian – or 'Bosnian' as Osman preferred to call it – but would not speak it. Nazim had spent a couple of teenage years with a hard-bitten irregular unit dealing harshly with Serb police and villagers in Kosova, and picked up the hated tongue in the process. He knew that Osman had been with a militia there at the same time, but did not know the details, and did not want to know. It was not something to discuss, especially not with a Bosnian.

However, the lack of a common language did not matter to the men. They did not even notice it. Their business was short and simple. Leka and Zlatan listened as Nazim and Osman talked.

"Ukrainian? Never no Ukrainian before."

"Dragan got a new source."

"Uh, but we like Moldovan. Clients like Moldovan."

"Look at Ukrainian. Strong, healthy, good." He made the hourglass shape with his hands. "Pretty. Age fourteen. Same price."

"Blonde?" Zlatan interjected.

"Da, blondinka," Leka confirmed. He ran over the details again, in English. "Moldovan not blonde. We can only dark Moldovan now. You can, um –" but he did not know the word – "ngjyros flokët – to change hair colour. And Moldovan older – twenty-five. We bring Ukrainian for, uh, to see if you like."

"She is fourteen? You are sure?"

"Yes." Switching to Russian again, he offered, "Try her, if you like."

"New?"

"Fresh, both. Ukrainian, very nice," said Leka.

"Fresh," Osman asked, "but broken in?"

Leka did not understand. Osman repeated his question in Russian, looking at Nazim for translation.

Nazim shrugged. "They are ready."

Osman looked puzzled. "How long you had them?"

"Ukraine to Italy couple of days ago," Nazim explained. "Moldovan we pick up in London last week. We see her in Paris, always alone. She came to London by train, on her own. They don't speak not much English. Speaking Russian," he added.

"Good, good. Another thing," Osman glanced at Zlatan, who nodded his agreement, "we have something to sell. Do you remember a piece name Liliana?"

"I remember. Problems? You try her yourself. You like her," replied Nazim.

"She's good," Osman acknowledged. "But she wants a change. We paid eighteen hundred. So, half price? Nine hundred pounds off new girl, in exchange?"

Nazim turned to Leka and translated for him – "They want to sell Liliana back to us. Half price."

Leka frowned and jerked his head back with an emphatic *tsk*. "Too much," he answered in English, with a gentle, regretful smile.

"She's in good shape."

Zlatan added a few words. "Africans would like her. A pretty blonde. But we don't know any Africans."

"But," Nazim protested, "what price can we get for something after two months hard use? Everyone prefers fresh material to work with. Even Africans."

"Hard use? What are you saying?" retorted Osman, holding back his distaste for these ignorant, uncouth, backward, arrogant, godless Albanian peasants. "Good food, plenty of sleep, nice room, friendship, everything. They love it with us. Liliana is a lovely girl. Very willing. No trouble. In good shape, ready for a lot more work."

"You made your Liliana money back in one week," said Nazim, suppressing his own contempt for these treacherous, untrustworthy Bosniaks, not a proper nation of people at all, and speaking the heathenish language of the Serbs. Bosniaks might be Muslim, but who cared about that? They are Slavs. He wouldn't be surprised if they had helped Christian Serbs massacre Kosovans. Anything was possible with such polluted mongrel blood in their veins. "It's not for me to say; I'll talk to the boss. He will make you an offer. What about these?" He jerked his head towards the van.

"Let's look at them," replied Osman.

Leka unlocked the rear of the van and swung the door open.

Osman peered inside.

A girl and a young woman, both fully dressed, lay on dirty mattresses. Still waking from a long stupor, they sat up dazed and confused, staring in fear as the light burst in on their unaccustomed eyes. Osman raised a finger to his lips to show that they must not make any sound.

He turned away and spoke in his own language.

"Hej, Zlata, pogledajte na ovoj – Hey, Zlatan, look at this. The blonde is only a child. Not fourteen at all. More like twelve. I don't think we want the little girl. But the dark one, old enough to be her mother. And fucking lovely! I'm going to try her out, OK? Just a quick one. Wait for me, I'll only be a couple of minutes. We'll tell them she's not much good, too old, and get a better price. Maybe get Liliana off our hands in part exchange. Give these Albanian peasants a drink from the café."

Nazim, standing beside him, remained expressionless. He understood every word.

* * *

Even before Neil left Battersea Park, a genial old man greeted him in passing, "Warm enough for you?" Despite his promise to say nothing to anyone, Neil realised that he could not avoid some good-humoured response. "Not bad for the time of year," he said.

Further along the river path, two giggling little boys gleefully threw a tennis ball in his direction. He tossed it back. They called out a remark, and he called back with a little wave.

He rode across the river on Chelsea Bridge, and into the terraces, squares and gardens of Belgravia, cycling parallel to Sloane Street. To avoid people or any kind of encounter or mishap, he planned a peaceful journey through the parks – Hyde Park, Regents Park, Primrose Hill, Hampstead Heath. Between the parks, he would use quiet residential streets. He knew them all in this area, so close to Critchlow's, and equally well closer to home. There was little traffic. He rode briskly but attentively. Repeatedly his hand moved to the zip of his sweatshirt. The pistol and its holster had to be kept covered. Nervously he pulled the zip up high.

Between creamy Georgian façades in privileged streets of

Bayswater and Marylebone, he zig-zagged towards Regent's Park. Across the park's empty greensward, London Zoo provided a distinctive landmark, its huge aviary and Bear Mountain rising in the distance. Of course, he was not going to the zoo; he skirted its fences. Inside, groups of children gawped at the imprisoned beasts.

He would like to free them, too, the endlessly pacing lions and wolves, the despondent elephants and maddened orang-utans, and give them all a first-class ticket home.

Sometimes, though, animals in the zoo don't want to go home. Their minds are used to captivity. They can't live in freedom any more. Like honeysuckle on a frame.

He told himself that he could murder a cup of tea. He touched the zip of his sweatshirt; it was still pulled to the top. Along the footpaths of Primrose Hill, soft white lamplight was coming on. Men and women strolled in the balmy dusk, joggers ran, dogs chased balls, children played in the playground as evening drew long shadows across the grass. A little crowd gathered on the hill's summit, where he had kissed Limor, to watch the sun cast its western beams across the city. When was that, the tango class, the dance in the dark? His one night and one day with Limor? She seemed a long, long time ago. Again he checked that the gun was concealed. Warily he left the park and cycled along a quiet road towards Hampstead Heath.

Yet, somehow, despite his caution, just here a reckless van sped out of a junction and forced him against the kerb. Neil had to jump from the bike. Impulsively he banged van's window, gestured and yelled "Moron!" at the driver. The van squealed to a stop.

Behind the wheel sat a skinny ginger youth with a wispy pencil moustache and a narrow soulpatch beard, who coolly opened his window and spat a gobbet of phlegm in his direction. Excellently aimed and delivered, the spit landed squarely on Neil's face and began to drip down. Though he admired the man's skill, Neil felt crushingly humiliated. With fingers and thumb he made a masturbation gesture, but it seemed too feeble a response.

The driver threw open the door. "What ya fecken problem?" he said. The accent was Irish, of a sort. It was clear enough that, skinny or not, the youth had no fear of a confrontation.

Neil had hardly finished saying, "Fucking gobbing at me – arsehole", when the van driver yelled back, "Feck off or a give ya a feckin' back'ander cross ya feckin' mowf," and was already jumping from his seat into the roadway.

Braced for a fight, the familiar meditative calm settled on Neil, an inner stillness as his anger was corralled. Straight away, he knew it was trouble. His heart did not race; instead, his mind quickened, calculating. This van driver looked stupid and vicious. There was no way to reason with such a face, such body language. What had seemed skinny now looked like lean, wiry muscle. He was the type who might even use a knife. Neil visualised the edge of sharp metal, his running blood, his cut flesh.

Contemptuously he shoved the young man away and took a step towards him. He heard the astonished intake of breath. And now Neil was astonished, as the young man began to apologise, almost bowing as he begged for forgiveness, abasing himself to the point of producing a filthy handkerchief from his pocket and attempting to wipe the saliva from Neil's cheek.

Reluctantly accepting this distasteful apology, Neil rode away puzzled. What had caused such a complete change of heart?

A few minutes later, he noticed his sweatshirt had unzipped a little. The pistol and its holster were uncovered and plain to see. Hastily he pulled the zip up high.

Up to that instant, it had not occurred to him that he could have shot the guy, or at least threatened to shoot him. He knew only that he must keep the pistol out of sight. He considered the gun a treasured burden to be protected at all costs. Into his mind came wide-screen scenes of Frodo, the Ring Bearer, beset by evil orcs and black riders and crazed companions. He had misunderstood the power of what he carried. The sight of it caused terror. Only then did he grasp that soon he himself must wear the Ring, pull the trigger.

Perhaps the van driver would tell the police. *Mad cunt on a fecken bike, fretten me wid a fecken gun. I never done nuttin to im, honest. I just, like, run for me life.*

He rode fast across the Heath. At the same time, he damned himself for reacting as he did. He shouldn't have banged the van window, shouldn't have yelled. Because there were more important matters to deal with.

Music and laughter, sunshine and sea. Good, simple life. A good, simple place. There is no such life and no such place. Only this. This life, this city.

A police helicopter slowly circled above, its thudding blades shaking the air. Were they looking for an armed cyclist? Or maybe a burglar escaping with his haul, or a gang of muggers on the loose, or couples having sex on the Heath? But it flew off lazily.

On a table, the Beretta looked absurd. He washed his face vigorously to remove all trace of the spittle which had landed there. He tucked the pistol under his duvet. He would sleep with it beside him in the bed.

He wanted to get on with the task straight away, just rush into that wretched house and free her. Any delay chafed. Strangely, into his mind came the journeys with Mum to and from the hospital when Dad was dying, and later, when Mum herself was sectioned. He touched a hundred miles an hour once, on the Seven Sisters Road, trying to get to Mum in one of her suicidal crises. He felt now as he had then. Stress and urgency pleased him. He liked it when nothing else mattered.

Every space in the flat that normally had a mundane purpose – a kitchen, a bedroom – seemed to lose its everyday function. All now became one single place dedicated to waiting.

How would he tell the girl what was going on? Into Google Translate he typed *Let's get out of here. Follow me*. The Romanian came out as six words, which he carefully wrote down in large letters, complete with accents and cedillas. The grammar was probably all wrong but it would have to do. He clicked *Listen* and heard an electronic voice repeat the words. At least he must remember how to say the last two, "Follow me", which sounded like *urmátsi-muh*.

Standing in his kitchen, he drank milk from a carton and picked at the remains of a ready meal in a saucepan.

Tomorrow – he declared himself an idiot for still not having a workable plan – he would go and free the girl. It was the Ascot round tomorrow, so he would have plenty of time. Either way, he would go in there and change the situation.

Then what? Would life carry on as normal, after that? No, he could not imagine anything at all after that. He had an intuition, or a premonition, that everything would go wrong and he would die in the attempt. He could see himself laid out in the coffin. Who would come to his funeral? Not a soul. His sisters would say they were too busy. His mother would not be well enough to come. Anyway, what funeral? No one would pay for him to have a funeral. Which wouldn't make any difference to him.

Tomorrow he was going to shoot some people. The woman at the desk. Those three men he had glimpsed through a door. Anyone that tried to stop him. Pull the trigger. He could fire the gun eighteen times. Of course, they would shoot back. Even the woman at the desk might be armed, for all he knew.

He wondered if he ought instead to stop now. It was not too late simply to call the police anonymously. He could then tell himself he had done his bit. No, he would not be able to live with such a thing on his conscience.

He sat on the sofa and watched *The Spy Who Came In From The Cold*. Richard Burton plays a clever spy who passes as a boozy, down-at-heel loner. At the end he gives his life to save a girl. Just a coincidence, that. Neil opened a bottle of beer and put on The Modern Jazz Quartet. Intricate sounds lifted him like the swell of an ocean. Neil listened without thought.

* * *

Bernard Kassin was not a believer, and nor did he care if others had a faith he lacked. He did not concern himself with faith at all. When compelled to give an opinion on matters of religion,

Bernard argued for the prosecution rather than the defence. Ladies and gentlemen of the jury, there is *no* Book of Life. It has *not* been decided who shall live and who shall die. Repentance makes *no* difference to the harsh decree, nor to anything. Good and bad alike prosper or suffer this year and every year, all live and all die. There is no justice in this life or the next.

Yet somehow he thrilled to the stirring liturgy of the High Holy Days and their portentous mood. How he would have preferred it to be so, that our deeds be judged, weighed in the balance and our fate duly inscribed in the columns of some awful ledger, a Book of Life. If only it could be a little bit half-true.

Bernard considered himself "up with the lark" (not that Bernard would recognise a lark by either sight or sound), except that there were no larks in Golders Green, only the arias of blackbirds and the squabbling of harsh magpies. The streets, the synagogue, the very air seemed charged with anticipation. Today, after the psalm at the end of the service, the shofar remained silent, for it is never sounded on this final day before Rosh Hashanah.

While Bernard recited the morning prayers, Neil cycled to work. In his rucksack today were a tee-shirt and cotton trousers for Liliana. As soon as he arrived at Critchlow's yard, things began to go wrong. He had forgotten that on this very day, the van drivers were to be given their winter uniforms. Instead of loading-up and making an early start to Ascot as he had expected, Neil waited with the other men to be sent down to the Ring for a dark blue woollen blouson, trousers and cap.

Neil's plan, such as it was, went no further than this: finish the Ascot deliveries as quickly as he could. On the way back, drive to the house where the girl was kept captive and pay forty pounds to go to her room like any client. Bring her out of the room, take her quickly down the stairs and into the street, pointing the gun at anyone who stood in his way (and even shoot them if necessary, though not in the head or chest). Take the girl to his flat, return the van to Critchlow's and cycle home as usual. Then he would feed the girl, let her rest, help her get in touch with friends and family, and do whatever she asked.

He already knew the whole madcap scheme was utterly ridiculous. It was foolish, idiotic. Unfortunately, long hours of thought, while cycling and driving, during the day and at night, had refused to offer him anything better. He would do as much of it as he could and, for the rest, deal with problems as they arose. Of course, it might succeed.

Ten minutes later, as he dressed, he realised that he could not possibly take the gun with him to work. *What on earth was I thinking?* He decided to leave the thing at home, under the duvet. He would return home to collect it before driving to free the girl.

As he rode his bike through the morning traffic, Neil visualised himself going into the house, visualised the girl's desperate eagerness to escape, visualised men standing aside in horror at the sight of the gun, just as the van driver had done yesterday. His mind turned at last to imagining what would become of the girl tomorrow, and the next day and the next. Suppose he managed to rescue her today. Then what? Tomorrow he'd have to go to work as usual, and where would she be? In his room? For how long?

Well, the plan is crazy. Do it anyway.

The rough cloth of the winter uniform scraped his legs like a nail brush, while the short, tight jacket was stiffly uncomfortable and too warm. It all looked rather like something soldiers wore in the Second World War. Several grumbled about swapping the cool summer cotton for something so stifling and heavy on a day like this.

"Mr Chapman!" It was that bastard Sanina. "I see you've got rather a lot to do on the Ascot round."

"Yes, Mr Sanina."

Disastrously, Sanina now said it was too late to deliver the whole Ascot round today. He told him to work only until four o'clock, and return to the yard for five. He would go out to Ascot again tomorrow.

"But that means I won't get any overtime, Mr Sanina."

"No, that's right, Mr Chapman. Overtime isn't a human right, you know! It's compensation for having to work late. Lucky for you, today you don't have to work late."

"I would prefer to try to finish Ascot in one day, even if it means working late," he said.

Sanina looked annoyed. "No, Mr Chapman. I said I want to see you back here at five o'clock."

That is a bloody nuisance. Bastard.

Neil rolled out of the yard, and turned his van into Cromwell Road. As he drove towards the M4, he realised what to do. Quite simply, Sanina was right: the Ascot round *could* wait until tomorrow.

* * *

Liliana does not bother to smile any more. She does not care if she is punished. Nor if she eats, or sleeps. She does not care if she is watched, or if the face in the mirror was ever hers. Anyway she sees no face at all now, simply a few unconnected fragments.

Men's voices. Pain is still pain, but it is the only thing that she can call hers alone. Enduring the pain is her secret treasure, her life, her self, her small island of calm, hidden within the twisting, turning agonies of mind and body.

She presses her teeth together until it hurts, and bites into her tongue to make it bleed. Liliana does not think: she has no thoughts, no memories. She only dreams, in dreams that are less than a dream yet as vivid as a hallucination. Tired, she sleeps awake, sees herself as a kind of vessel, something being carved, sculpted, an object worked. She is a tool, an implement, something of use.

This room is not a room. It is a country. She sees a field, a vineyard, a hillside, a village, a group of men, men working the earth, men digging deep into soil, into dirt, filth, rot, decay, fungus, fibres... A soft piece of woven fabric, light and delicate, cast onto a bed. Cloth, rag, paper, tissue. She is a knitted toy soaked in semen. Semen drips out of her mouth, her hair, her eyes, her anus, slides down her legs. "Smile, damn you!"

It cannot be said that Neil did nothing at all on the Ascot round today, though he did not actually get as far as Ascot. He made just a couple of deliveries close to the M4 exit, and followed a country route between ploughed fields and the playing fields of Eton. He made his way quickly to Miss Delavingham's. Getting rid of all her parcels of food and wine and flowers would make the van seem much emptier.

"Who is it?"

"Critchlow, ma'am," and the door was opened, as always, by the vastness of Miss Delavingham herself, struggling to maintain a dignified comportment as her dress and her hair-combs threatened to abandon her.

"Hello, Chapman! Have you brought my venison?"

"Yes, ma'am."

"My port?"

"Yes, ma'am."

"My pumpkins?"

"Yes, ma'am. For Halloween, are they?" He assumed she must be buying them before the rush, since Halloween was still a month away.

"For what d'you say?"

"Halloween, ma'am. The pumpkins. You know, to make..."

"Oh, I see! All Hallows' Eve! Jack o' Lanterns, you mean? Certainly not! We are not Americans! Thank God for it, eh? *Bonfires* are our way of driving away demons. Remember, remember, the fifth of November! Put them on the table over there, would you? Pumpkins are for eating! For roasting! Baking, sautéing, purées, delicious soup, you know, pies, puddings. Pumpkin season! Excellent, in season, pumpkin."

And now suddenly he did have a plan. Miss D had illuminated his mind. After coffee and biscuits at her scrubbed kitchen table, Neil thanked her politely.

He drove briskly back onto the M4. It took forty minutes to

reach the North Circular Road. There, the traffic became creakingly slow. He had allowed plenty of time. As he drove, or sat waiting in stationary lines, he tried to think. He would go to his flat. He would strap on the holster. He would wear the gun under his jacket. What about the silencer? It made the gun less manoeuvrable. He would take it in his pocket.

It was an odd, disorienting feeling, returning home while still at work. Hearing an unaccustomed sound, his Hungarian landlady looked out from the downstairs flat. "You home early?" After more than fifty years in Britain, her English remained heavy with accent.

"Hi, Mrs Viktor. Yah, just came to get something. Forgot something."

The men must not see his van, with 'Critchlow's' written on the side. He drove it around the block and pulled into Sainsbury's car park.

Neil sat there, wondering how he and the girl would get away from the house. Not on foot, of course. Did it really matter so much if the men saw the van, and knew where he worked? Or could it be done by taxi instead? He watched people coming and going with their trolleys and their shopping bags. Then he noticed cameras scanning the scene. He could not park here either, except to get some shopping.

With sudden resolve he climbed out of the van. There were things he needed. Sainsbury's wouldn't sell them. He crossed the road and went into a hardware store run by an Indian couple, a bazaar of plastic, a cornucopia of curiously outdated products, of unfamiliar cheap brands. Among the shelves of old-style light bulbs, camping stoves, dish cloths, clothes pegs and key tags he found what he wanted. He returned to the supermarket and made a few purchases there, too. Bread, bananas, milk, a newspaper...

At the store's exit, Neil noticed a wall phone with a sign above it. *Customer Freephone*, it said, *Just pick up the phone to book your cab.* Amazed, he did pick up the phone.

"Don't come to the shop," he said. "Can you collect me on the corner of Finchley Road and Heath Avenue?"

"OK. To go where?"

"Just a short trip in Golders Green. Finchley Road."

"Minimum fare five pounds, all right? What name?"

"You'll see me standing there."

"OK. With you in ten minutes."

He moved his van to a quiet street behind the car park and slipped coins into a meter, enough for an hour. There were no cameras here. All was ready now: his money, his gun, the paper with Romanian words and, in the rucksack, everything he needed. He hoped he hadn't forgotten anything. Without hurry, he made his way to the house on foot. As the minicab pulled up outside, Neil stepped forward.

"Sorry, could you wait for me? I have to see someone. I'll be five or ten minutes. Don't go away, will you?"

The driver, a sweating, weighty Bengali or Pakistani slouched wearily in his seat, nodded agreement without a word.

9

As he spoke into the entryphone and pushed open the sheet of rough board, he remembered the CCTV. Embroidered in gold above his breast pocket were the words *T. Critchlow & Sons.* He had meant to cover that up! He had forgotten. The van was hidden from view, but they need only look at his uniform to know where he worked. He could not take the woollen jacket off now, because underneath it the Beretta rested in its holster, clip in place, ready to be fired. Instead he pulled the strap of his rucksack across his chest, hoping that would be enough to hide the logo from the cameras.

Nothing had changed inside the house. The same woman sat at the same desk. Her hair was wound around her head in the same sculpted style. As before, she barely looked in his direction, smiling without a trace of pleasantness. "Hi, nice to see you again. Forty pounds for thirty minutes," she said bluntly. "All girls busy now. Wait please, not too long. They want to see you very much."

This time, though, someone else was ahead of him. A man, with silver and turquoise jewellery in his earlobe, and a pony-tail of grey pulled tightly across a patch of bald scalp, was slumped in an armchair, staring at pictures in a magazine. Next to the chairs, the DVD player showed a blank screen. The atmosphere was as joyless as an airport departure gate.

If the cab driver became impatient and left without him, that would be a catastrophe. The only escape then would be to shoot people and run for it.

Just like last time, she showed him six photographs. Neil flushed with panic. He looked and looked, but Liliana was not among them. "What has happened to her? Is she still here?" He insisted he wanted the same girl as before. "She is busy. Have another one," suggested the woman. "This one nice new girl, pretty."

Neil did not understand why he would choose another one, if all the girls were equally busy. He said again that he would wait for the same girl. The woman leaned forward to murmur quietly, "It is her time of the month." Neil repeated that he did not want any other girl.

The woman slid his four ten-pound notes across the table and put them in a drawer. Neil turned awkwardly, trying to cover the embroidered words on his blouson.

A frail, elderly fellow appeared from a downstairs doorway, using a stick to walk with difficulty. "Nice," he said meekly to the woman as he passed, "thank you." He sounded sincerely grateful, and Neil felt sorry for the old chap. The pony-tail man took his place and Neil waited alone.

Without explanation, the woman changed her mind and led him upstairs. Apparently Liliana was available after all. Again the woman gestured "bathroom, toilet." He said he would use it now, and she nodded indifferently, merely pointing at Liliana's room as she turned and walked away. He thanked her.

Behind the closed door of the bathroom, Neil opened one of the bottles he had just bought. Lighter fluid, solvents and spirits, fuels and accelerants, none of whose names he had ever seen before, but all of whose packaging bore the correct warning in a vivid red pictogram. Volatile. Flammable. Methanol, heptane, naphtha. He doused the floor.

How many minutes does it take for the emergency services to respond? Neil didn't know, but now he called 999.

At last, he had found a way to draw attention to this place.

Inside Liliana's little room, he recognised the slightly repellent acridity of sweat and air-fresher, the dirty white wallpaper and the large mirror. However, the girl herself struck him as terribly altered in little more than a week. Neil felt a sickening wave of regret that he had not acted more quickly.

"Hello," he said softly, sadly, "remember me?"

The change in her was not physical, although she seemed even thinner and more exhausted. Rather, she had suffered some more awful alteration. She had become a different person. Her face did not look the same. Her eyes, her expression. He could not tell what had happened to her. She did not smile, nor did she beckon him, simply standing there in her short nightdress which had ceased to tempt him. This time, she wore transparent panties underneath. Normally, he would like that. Now he just felt painfully sorry for her. She sat down on the bed and mechanically reached out a hand, as if without seeing him. Her jaw was clenched tightly shut.

"No, no, look." He tried to show her the message he had written in Romanian, "Follow me", but she did not raise her eyes.

From his bag, he took out his tee shirt and loose cotton trousers and tried to give them to her. "I know they're the wrong size," he said. He gestured and spoke more loudly. "Put them on." But she stared uncomprehendingly. He felt a fool. None of it would work. Again he urged her to cover herself. "At least the tee shirt." But she did not respond.

Now he heard an approaching siren.

He peered over the window shutters. The fire engine was already arriving. His plan was unravelling. He could not wait any longer. He shoved the clothes back into the rucksack.

Yet for a brief moment more, Neil stood as if paralysed, or in repose, listening to the siren. He had done nothing yet, and could leave now blamelessly, returning down the stairs and out of the building. An irrevocable decision was upon him.

Neil opened the door of her room, and looked out. From his bag he calmly took another bottle and turned the screw top, throwing the inflammable liquid freely along the corridor. He took his lighter and quickly the cheap carpet was aflame. He shut the door and let it burn. In the street, the siren became silent and the fire engine's flashing light shone as bright as a heartbeat through the curtains.

There remained not one moment more to be spent in

reflection or doubt. In sudden haste he pulled the curtains aside and freely poured liquid over them, and onto his newspaper, and splashed it around the floor. He looked around for something else. He pulled the soiled sheet from the bed, dousing it with fluid.

Liliana looked on as if dazed, trying to understand.

With his hand Neil tried to smash the strip of window above the shutters, but it would not break. He took the gun and hit the glass as hard as he could, shattering it with a shocking sound. Liliana stood amazed and backed away. He put the gun straight back into its holster, but Liliana had seen it. She seemed confused and deranged rather than scared. She ground her teeth, muttered, banged her fists together in anguish, pressed the sides of her head, contorted her face.

Grabbing the chair, Neil struck furiously at the broken glass. As the window gave way he pushed the bedsheet through the serrated edges and flared his lighter directly onto it.

In an instant, searing flame enveloped the sheet, inside and outside the window, and leapt onto the curtains. With a sighing sound the curtains flashed into burning heat and light which swept across the ceiling. Flames dripped down. Neil was amazed at their spattering, mercurial speed and heat.

At this moment he felt a real fear that he had made a mistake. They were in danger. The fire began to catch on the carpet and the mattress. Now at last Liliana did respond, screaming wildly and tensing her body until it shook.

Footsteps approached, then retreated. There were shouts. A smoke alarm began to shriek. Neil threw open the door of the room and cried out for help. He stepped back in shock. The fire was much hotter than he could bear. They had to get away at once. Liliana's nightdress – it might catch fire. Neil grabbed at her washing jug, and the dirty slops lying in a bowl, emptying the water over her towel, throwing it around her shoulders.

He ran back to the window where the bedsheet burned. There were firemen outside the house.

"Fire, fire! Up here!" he shouted at the top of his voice through the broken glass. This was no pretence. They might all be burned alive. "Jesus fucking Christ, we're on fire up here. Help us! Can you help? Can you help?"

One of the firemen pointed up at him and yelled something. Neil seized Liliana's hand and dragged her towards the door. She resisted. He had lost the scrap of paper with the words he had planned to say, but he remembered "Urmátsi-muh" – Follow me. She did not understand. Maybe it was his accent.

Outside the room, the landing was entirely in flames. A hot, oily smoke swirled in dark clouds, scorching every breath, and billowing up to the next floor. The bathroom door burst out with an explosion of burning light. Women and men, running half-dressed from the rooms, crying out urgently, pushed past each other frantically towards the stairs, almost falling down the steps. The deafening squeal of the alarm made it hard to think clearly.

Liliana seemed unable to move. Part of the carpet was on fire and she had no shoes. Neil cursed himself for forgetting to bring something for her feet. Half-lifting her, Neil forced her to the stairs. In the hallway below, firemen rushed into the house with a wide hose.

A fireman urged people towards the front door, calling "Get out, get outside quick, don't stop for anything!"

In the front hall, the woman at the desk refused to leave. The fire, after all, was upstairs, although flames were tumbling down from step to step. She made a grab for the drawer where she had put Neil's forty pounds, but the fireman picked her up in his arms and almost threw her out of the building. He had to bar her way as she fought to get back inside.

As she struggled viciously with him, a second fireman rushed forward to drag her away. Neil calculated that there was a brief opportunity to have his money back. He pulled Liliana to the abandoned desk and turned the key of the drawer. Astonished by what he saw, at once he began throwing thick wedges of banknotes into his bag. The rucksack was almost full when the fireman turned, shouting to leave all that and get out quickly. Neil shoved a last handful of loose notes into his pocket and pulled Liliana from the burning house.

He gasped with relief as they escaped the heat and noise. The weedy, overgrown garden was a mêlée as firemen instructed everyone, even if undressed, to go out into the street. A fireman argued with two big men who stood like a pair of marble kouroi each side of the open gate. It seemed that they would only let men leave, not women.

The firemen's crew manager was already phoning for instructions, "Something not right here. It's not domestic premises. Like some sort of dodgy hotel. Or more like, well, I don't know what."

Running hard, Neil pushed and tugged Liliana towards the gate. She pulled back in terror, but he did not let her go. The two men raised their arms to block his path, confused by the blue uniform. "You, sir, not her. Don't worry, we look after her."

Confused they might be, but thoroughly confident in their mass and muscle, sure that they would have no difficulty with anyone here. Neil recognised them: one was the laughing brute coming out of an open door on his first visit, the other had been inside the room, wearing a track suit. He had rarely seen men who appeared so unafraid of a fight.

With one hand Neil pulled the pistol from its holster and released the lever. He swung the gun from side to side, thrusting it towards one man and then the other, ready to pull the trigger.

Open-mouthed in outraged surprise and fear, the two seemed uncertain how to act. Shouting in a Slavic language, holding up their hands as if to calm him, or in supplication or surrender, they backed away rapidly. The fireman began shouting too, in English, for armed back-up.

Outside the gate, buses and cars passed innocently. The taxi was still there, the driver leaning out of his window to enjoy the spectacle of a house on fire and the escaping men hastily dressing. Other members of the public had stopped to watch from the other side of the road.

Now the bystanders gasped – some screamed – as a young man, wearing some sort of uniform and holding a gun in his right hand, pulled a reluctant, barefoot, skeletal young blonde in a transparent nightdress through the gate with his left hand. They ran towards a parked car.

There were shouts of alarm – "That feller's got a gun!" and "Anyone called the police?", "Look what she's wearin'!" and "Let's get out of here!" Mobile phones began calling 999.

Immediately behind them came another woman on her own, attractive, dark-haired, older, wearing only a bra and miniskirt. For many of the watchers, this was fun. A dozen camera phones recorded the sight.

Now a third woman, another blonde, ran from the gate, in nothing but underwear, followed by two men swinging slender metal rods, grabbing at the escaping girls, striking furiously at them, reaching out to hit their legs. The second woman was hurt, but kept running towards the car. The third woman fell to the ground.

Neil opened the rear door and pushed Liliana into the taxi. "Let's go, let's go!" he shouted. The second girl was pulling at his open door, trying to stop him closing it, trying to climb in after him. The driver shook his head emphatically, "No, no, no! What is happening here? Get out of taxi."

Neil yelled and pointed the gun at the distraught cab driver, "Drive, drive! I'm telling you to fucking drive. Don't mess about."

Even as the car moved sharply forward, the second girl managed to clamber through the door, crying in French, "Aidez-moi! Je vous en supplie. [Help me! I beg you!]" Tears began to pour down her cheeks. Neil grasped a desperate hand and pulled her onto the seat beside him.

He turned to see if the men had given chase. They were beating the third girl without restraint, swinging the steel hard against her thighs, hauling her across the pavement like a bag of trash towards the burning building. The police would soon arrive, he thought, and would find what they would find. But they would not find him. He had done all he could.

Two girls! It was bad enough being responsible for one. And hardly wearing anything! What now?

Liliana sat hunched beside him, her hands over her face.

On the other side, the dark-haired second girl gripped her hurt leg and sobbed. A thin red weal showed where the rod had struck.

"Where you want go?" shouted the frightened driver.

"Sainsbury's."

"Sainsbury's?" It was not a hundred yards from the house.

"Yeah, just drive round to the back of Sainbury's car park."

"This Sainsbury's just here? You sure? That's all?"

A voice crackled on the driver's radio. Neil said, "Yep – round the corner and into the car park. Don't answer that fucking phone." Without turning, only pointing his thumb towards her, he spoke to the second girl. "Votre jambe, ça fait mal? Elle est blessée? [Is your leg hurt? Is it injured?]"

"Ça fait mal; mais blessée, non [It hurts, but wounded, no]," she replied, breathing jerkily after her tears, "Les hommes là, ils m'ont violée. Et d'autres hommes, ils m'ont violée. [Those men, they raped me. And other men, they raped me.]"

"Oui, oui, je sais. [Yes, yes, I know.]"

"Vous êtes policier, vous? Ou soldat, ou quoi? [Are you a policeman, a soldier, or what?]"

"Non. Pourquoi? Comment ça, soldat? [No. Why 'soldier'?]"

"Votre uniforme. [Your uniform.]"

"Turn here, into the car park," he said to the driver. "When I say 'Stop', stop straight away, let us out, and drive off, all right? Don't wait, don't watch. Not for one second, all right? Don't use the radio. Don't phone anyone."

And to the girl, "Non, je n'suis rien. Juste un mec. [No, I'm nothing. Just a guy.]"

The driver nodded vigorously. Without looking away from the road, Neil pulled out some banknotes, thrusting them at the terrified man. "I'm sorry for the trouble. These girls, they were being held prisoner in that house."

He handed the tee-shirt to the second girl, wrapped the wet towel tighter around Liliana's shoulders, put the gun back into its holster.

"Three, two, one... Stop!"

The cab did leave very abruptly, speeding away as if Neil might change his mind and shoot after all. Liliana stood in the car park weak and confused. Neil held out the cotton trousers he had brought, and the other girl helped her put them on. Together they took Liliana's arms and walked. They did not hurry. It would have drawn attention to them. The second girl spoke in Romanian: "Cred că vrea să ne ajute. [I think he wants to help us.]" Liliana made no reply.

Sainsbury's customers strolling to and from the shop, pushing trolleys or carrying bags, took no notice of them. No one even glanced as they walked casually out of the car park to the Critchlow's van in the street behind.

As if trying to solve a Sudoku problem, the girl studied him more closely, scrutinised the uniform. "Bon alors, vous êtes... quoi? Chauffeur de camionnette? [So you are... what? A van driver?]"

Neil opened the door and urged them both into the passenger seat. "Do you speak English?" he asked.

He already knew that Liliana understood only a few words. The second girl answered, "Yes, I speak English – not very well. What are you doing, where are you taking us?" She was scared.

"Relax now," he said. "I'm going to help you. I'm taking you to my flat. It's nearby. You'll be safe there."

He grinned at the two women. He was jubilant. He wanted to hug them, share a bottle of champagne.

Of course, that would be ridiculous. Nor did they return his smile. Instead they looked at him in fear, suspiciously.

From the rucksack he pulled a bread roll and a carton of milk. He had thought it would be for one person only. "For you two. To share."

He peeked inside at the assorted banknotes he had taken. It was an immense quantity of money. Most of the notes were twenties, in bundles about half an inch thick. Each little bundle, he guessed, must be about a thousand pounds.

Neil turned the ignition, the van juddering noisily into life. As he pulled away, the second girl grabbed at the food and began to eat. Speaking French, she said, "We will *not* be safe there. You don't know *what* you are dealing with. They will catch us again, and kill you." In Romanian, she urged Liliana to eat.

He looked nervously out of the van window. It would be better not to be seen by anyone at all. A view clear down West Heath Drive showed fire engines and flashing blue lights. Instead he turned away to find a different route.

"No, they will not catch you," Neil said. "I'll help you get home, or whatever you want. What are your names?"

She gestured, "She is Liliana. I am Irène. You don't understand, Monsieur. We can't go home. We can't go anywhere. We have no money, no passports, no papers, not clothes, nothing. And Liliana is... I don't know, look at her. She's sick."

"Are you French? You don't sound it. And Liliana, is she Romanian?" he asked.

"I'm not French. I live in Paris. We are both from Moldova. Our language is Romanian. What are you going to do with us? I need a doctor." She began to cry again, but forced herself to stop.

"Is 'Irène' a Moldovan name?"

"I am not really Irène. I am Irina. In Paris, I call myself Irène."

He told her his own name and glanced at the clock. It was past four. He had to get rid of these girls now and take the van back to work. He wondered how long it would take to finish the Ascot round tomorrow.

"Why have you stopped? Where are we?" Irina asked sharply in French. She was suddenly alarmed.

He pointed out of the window. "This is where I live. It's just a tiny flat. I must leave you here for a while. I have work to do. I'll be back in a couple of hours."

He began to leaf through the dockets. Many were from the "Fashions" department. He spoke to Irina, "Hey, come and look at something."

In the back of the van he opened a sealed box. Inside, smart skirts and tops were neatly folded between layers of tissue paper. They rummaged through parcels, finding expensive, stylish clothes that – Irina said – might fit them.

"You are insane. What you have done? Are you giving us these things? You are going to be in big trouble."

Neil replied, "Just so long as my conscience is clear."

"You know, these men, such men get what they want. They are strong. They will hunt for you, and for us."

"Things could not be left as they were."

Across Irina's calf a bloody crimson stripe was darkening. With horror he thought of the third girl, beaten with metal rods. And the other women in the house! But the house was no more, surely, and the police must have arrived there by now, and taken them all into custody.

He had done it. The girl was free. Two of them! And all without a shot fired!

Neil did not realise how bad things were going to become. His problems were just beginning.

* * *

In fact, the police had not yet reached the house. By the time the armed response unit arrived, there was no one there. The fire brigade had sealed the entrance and put up a *Danger* sign. The reported 'person with a firearm' had gone, and so had everyone else. The police took the opportunity anyway to close Dunstan Road, Finchley Road and Heath Avenue, to give the impression of a force doing its job.

Meanwhile, the café in nearby Osborne Park locked its doors. The boss brought the shutter rattling down. Inside, the lights stayed on as five men and a woman, in grim mood, began a private meeting. They spoke in the Bosniak tongue.

"The CCTV. If the police..." one man warned.

Another said he had removed the CCTV hard drive and brought it with him. The others nodded, impressed. The woman commended him.

"And the safe?"

"Yes, I have that, too. I took it out straight away."

The men were Zlatan, Osman and the three Neil had seen at

the house. Some wore sleek grey suits and polished leather slip-on shoes; the others, jeans, trainers and hooded sweatshirts. The woman is she, the handsomely-coiffed, who not an hour before had taken Neil's forty pounds and led him upstairs to Liliana's room.

If the woman knows anything about the world, it is that men have a weakness and even the poorest of them will pay to satisfy it. From this she has made a reasonable living – and, after all, one has to live. One must be realistic.

As for the girls she purchased, well, they too are alive in this cat-eat-cat world. She has looked out for herself and her family, and those stupid girls should have done the same. They are attractive young things who thought they could manage on their own without family or husbands to protect them. They soon found out they were wrong. They learn a lesson. So be it. They are fools.

Sometimes she almost felt sorry for them. At other times, well, it rattled her that she housed and fed them at her own expense. The laundry bill was a nuisance, too, but she was prepared to look on that as a business outlay. When it came to food and rent, though, they ought really to pay her! She had a feeling these young women didn't realise how lucky they were – compared to some she knew about. Every evening she fed them! But the girls have no money, so, after all, one must be realistic.

What the woman dislikes most of all, is how the undercurrent of violence has grown to a torrent since they set up in England. A few slaps, a little bit of chastisement, such things are normal, even in the best families. No one has a problem with that. But the shootings, the vicious cruelties, the careful cutting and beating, these do weigh on her mind a little. She never wanted her own sons and nephews to end up doing things like that. Still, that's the profession she has chosen. And it does have advantages. One must be realistic.

Besides, she is proud of the boys. The truth is, she has always liked such men, big, strong men, men not afraid. Manly men who cannot be ruled. In her sons' faces she sees all that remains of her husband.

Before speaking she sits with lips pursed. The others look away restlessly, as if pained, waiting for her to say what they already know.

She summarises. Two girls, one of them brand new, and more than a whole day's takings, are missing. The house needs a lot of work before it can be used again. The police are probably there at this moment. They know nothing and will find nothing, because there are no girls there, and no clients, and no CCTV records. Anyway, the police are probably more interested in this Englishman with a gun.

One of the young men asked a question. "You say a whole day's takings. How much is that?" He tried to calculate the total, "Eighty pounds an hour, seven girls, twenty hours a day..."

The woman forestalled him. "The girls don't take two clients every hour, you know. Think about it before you speak. Sometimes they wait a whole hour without anyone, don't they? They are only turning about sixteen, seventeen a day each. And I am not giving Liliana so many. Nor the new girl, yet. I'm not sure how much," she dissembled, unwilling to reveal the truth.

She considered it better that none of them realise how many thousands of English pounds were gone. Unwisely, she had not put the takings in the safe for several days. She flushed slightly at the thought of such a loss. The girls could work harder for a while to make it up. Or perhaps a small increase in price would be feasible. Either way, it was still a big loss. On the other hand, what's a few days income? Perhaps they would even get a lot of it back, when they found the Englishman.

"I usually put the cash in the safe at eleven o'clock every day," she said, untruthfully, "but sometimes... well, today was busy, clients waiting, you know, and I..." She shrugged apologetically.

The men spoke up noisily. "Who would do this to us? It must be some trick of the Albanians. But why Liliana? No one would want something like that, no one would steal her, would they? What use is she?"

"Look," said the woman, "the Englishman who did this is nothing to do with the Albanians. This was his second visit. I think he wants her for himself."

The men were doubtful. "No, not as she is now. More likely he was sent by the Albanians. They brought us the new girl yesterday. Maybe they sold her to someone else too. Good scam, sell the same one to several buyers and just steal her back. And we offered them Liliana, too. Coincidence? So? You see?"

"No, anyone doing that would not last long. This Englishman, he wanted Liliana only, he said. Anyway," the woman pointed out, "the Albanians would never attack us like this. We are good customers. Have we annoyed them? Have we insulted them? Of course not. Zlatan, Osman, everything was all right when you picked up the new girl yesterday?"

Zlatan shrugged and grinned sheepishly, "If we insult them," he said, "it's in Bosnian."

"Of course you are joking. But don't joke. That lunatic Nazim speaks Bosnian as well as you."

Zlatan and Osman swallowed nervously. "No, he doesn't," Osman shook his head. "He speaks only Russian to us."

The woman insisted, "He understands everything you say, he hates Bosnians nearly as much as Serbs, and he is a dangerous man. Don't cross him. I don't want to lose any of you. He will kill you for an insult."

"Let's just ask them," was suggested. "Ask Dragan, ask everyone, if they stole our girls, and see what they say. Whoever has taken them, and our money, we must get everything back. Everything. In the meantime, we have other girls. They are all in the van. That's a waste of their time. We must put them back to work. We can get a house or a couple of flats somewhere, London, another city, any street, that doesn't matter. I think Slough is good, and Southampton. And Leeds. We should give them some water, by the way. They must be hot, crowded like that in the van. There's not much air in there."

The woman greatly approved his practical approach. She asked about the girl who was beaten and concluded that she too could safely be put to work. "It's a good lesson for the others."

A man slapped the table angrily. "Whoever did this must be punished. If they think they can treat us with contempt..."

The woman cautioned against haste. "They will be punished. We have the film. Let's look at this Englishman."

* * *

Neil had never driven the van back to Critchlow's yard so fast, nor cycled so fast on the return home. At every moment he felt dizzy and nauseous with the awareness of what he had done. The gun, still in the holster, rested now on top of his wardrobe in the bedroom, where he hoped the girls would not find it. A fortune in crumpled banknotes remained undisturbed in his rucksack at the back of the cupboard under the kitchen sink. The clip with eighteen unused cartridges was in his pocket.

He no longer wanted to celebrate. His elation was stained with lurid fears, and his mind seethed. The girls would need food tomorrow. They might need medicine. They might be afraid of men. They might not be safe in his flat. There might be retribution.

He would not return the gun to Winston just yet.

When he arrived, Irina sat hunched, seemingly exhausted and miserable, on the edge of his bed. She had washed her face, brushed her hair and put on a linen skirt taken from a Critchlow's parcel. It was not quite long enough to cover the now purple mark on her calf. The shirt she wore, he noticed, was his own. She looked up at him anxiously, bit her lip.

Liliana slept beside her, face down as if to smother herself in the pillow.

He spoke very tenderly. "Are you all right?"

Irina replied, "Yes."

"Has she slept all the time?"

"We drank some milk and ate some yoghurt. Liliana has some sort of problem swallowing, I didn't know. She found the kitchen knives and tried to... uh, put it," now she simply gestured, a violent stabbing motion, "into her neck. I had to... it was almost a fight. I brought her in here and she fell asleep, like that. Deeply asleep. She doesn't trust me, or anyone. She thinks you and I, we two, are preparing something bad for her. I think she'll cut herself. She can't be left alone."

Neil had not thought of that possibility. He suggested they take it in turns to sit with her.

"She needs help," Irina said. "She's very ill."

"Ill?"

"Perturbée." She twisted a hand beside her head.

He paused. "I hope you had something else to eat, not just milk and yoghurt."

She shook her head and shrugged.

"And your bruise! It looks worse. I'll get you something for it. Does it hurt?"

"Don't worry," she replied wearily, her eyes bloodshot and wet. "I can see you properly now, without the uniform," she said. "Yes, juste un mec [just a guy]." She looked away. "What happened? I can't understand. I came to London... why did they... how did they know I existed? And what is happening now? I wish I had never heard of London. Why are you helping me, Monsieur? What are you going to do with us?"

"Nothing. You can leave any time you want."

"And go where? I need rest. I was raped!" She sounded incredulous. "Not once, but many times. Not just raped. I had disgusting things done to me, that I can't tell you about. I can't say the words. Just to think it makes me feel sick." She held her head with both hands. "I am not brave. I never said I was brave. But now I know what a coward I am. Pain is a terrible thing, what it makes you do. I discovered that I will do anything at all, no matter what, to avoid it."

Neil wished he could at least lay a hand on her shoulder. She needed to be held in the arms of another human being, a sister, a daughter, a mother, a friend. Perhaps, though, she could sense his compassion. "Yes, I know. I know what happened," he said, "I'm sorry."

"Do you think we can call a doctor, at least for Lili?"

"Yes, let me think about that. Most doctors only speak English. To see a doctor you have to be registered. To get registered, you need ID and you must be a UK resident, I think. No, of course – you can always see a doctor privately. We could make an appointment."

"What about a hospital?" she suggested.

He tried to imagine what would happen there. "Yeah, we could get a taxi to the Royal Free. That's the nearest hospital. You wait for hours, though. Literally hours. In a crowded room of metal seats. You might have some drunk next to you, swearing and stinking. Do you think Liliana can manage that, the way she is now? If there's any charge, I can pay."

"And I was robbed, you know," Irina added, as though she had not heard him. "All my money, papers, everything, is gone. I must tell the police, or someone."

"We can talk about that later."

"But really, even what they did to me... it's absolutely *nothing* compared to some of the others. I think men like the look of Liliana. She was raped by hundreds of them, dozens every day, all day, one after another."

"I know."

"Ugh! They are monsters, animals. It was horrible. They were repellent. I can't tell you. Another thing I hated," she spoke more slowly, "it sounds ridiculous, but I am... well, you will say I am over-sensitive, or *bourgeoise*. I'm not tough. I'm not stoical. I can't bear... I need tranquil space, solitude, time to think, somewhere to call my own."

She shook her head unhappily. Tears began to wet her eyes. She flicked them away with a fingertip as they emerged. "I wish I were at home. I need beautiful things, music and art, and time to think, and books to read, and my own life again."

"I do understand," said Neil. "I'll try to make things right for you again. What music do you like? Tell me your favourite artists."

She shrugged hopelessly, almost writhed. "Oh, I can't think about that now. I like Cézanne, Van Gogh, Gauguin. I like ballet. Prokofiev. Stravinsky. I don't want to talk about it. You know, for days they simply kept me in the back of a little van! They drove me from place to place. It was cold and filthy and dark. Men raped me in there! Do you hear what I'm saying? These creatures would intrude on me at any time."

He nodded. She looked intelligent and pained. There was a natural diffidence. He saw the gentle timidity there.

"Would you like to phone someone? Talk to someone at home? "

"No, no, never. How can I ever tell anyone? I don't want to burden them with it. I don't want them to think of me like that. Always they would make it part of their picture of me. No, I am sick with shame. It must be a secret, with no one."

"Except Lili?" he suggested. "She knows what you went through." And Irina nodded unhappily.

Neil sat down on the floor, at her feet. "Would you prefer me to call you Irène or Irina?"

"Oh, I don't care."

"Do you, did you, have a job in Moldova?"

She paused as if shocked by the recollection. "I am a university lecturer in French in Moldova."

"That's why your French is so good."

"Yours is perfect," she said, "I've never heard... how did you..." She abandoned her question and grasped her head in both hands. "I was, I still am, on a research sabbatical in Paris. I came to London as a tourist! Two men were waiting for me at the station, as if they expected me. They made me go with them. That was a few days ago. Then they brought me to that house, it must have been yesterday. My God, I want my passport back! I could simply return to Paris and forget all this. No one need ever know."

Tears began to flow again, tracing down her cheeks. It grieved Neil that he could not comfort her. He dared not touch her, after what she had suffered at men's hands. Suddenly Irina frowned in puzzlement. Something had come into her mind. "Liliana – how do you know her? From Moldova? Where did you first meet her? How did you know she was in that house?"

Neil pressed his lips together.

"When I said I had been raped, you said you knew about it. How *could* you know?"

He remained silent, searching for a response.

"Oh God, please tell me you weren't one of them, one of the –"

Neil wondered whether to simply admit the truth. But Irina had guessed. "So you – yourself – have raped Liliana."

At the sound of her name Liliana stirred restlessly. She awoke and sat up, stared around, seeing nothing, talking agitatedly as if in a dream. Her face was red, sweating. Irina rested a hand on her and spoke softly in their own language, "Sh... calmează-te..." Liliana flinched at the words and clenched her fists, but soon lay down again with eyes closed.

"We must speak more quietly, let her rest as long as she wants," said Neil.

Liliana muttered, afraid. Irina caressed her hand gently.

"I didn't know," he said. "I didn't think it was rape. I wouldn't rape anyone. She smiled at me. I paid money. I thought it was just a deal between us. Two adults. A man and a woman."

"She *smiled* at you? Idiot!" Irina's eyes showed fury. "*Didn't know?* That does not excuse you! You think it's about money? You pay, so you think you can do anything. You are one of *those* men! This whole rotten business is because of men like you! And your pathetic little pleasures."

"I didn't go for pleasure. I went for sex. Sex isn't about pleasure. And it's not a little thing."

She sneered with derision. "Not a pleasure! What then, a pain?"

Neil wanted to tell her, *art is a pleasure, music is a pleasure, an afternoon walk is a pleasure, a well decorated room is a pleasure. This isn't about pleasure.* But he said only, "It's too complicated. I can't explain."

"I am leaving. I can't stay here with a rapist. And I'm taking Liliana with me. I don't trust you."

"Rapist! If that's what you want to call me. Leave, if you want to. It's up to you. I've done what I set out to do. I don't need to discuss it."

"Now I understand! You were only trying to make your conscience clear. But it's not so simple, is it, conscience?" Even in anger, her eyes were wet with misery.

"Christ," Neil muttered, "look, I don't want to argue with you."

He tried again. "Maybe you think love, the embrace of a lover, intimacy, that's all pleasure," he said. "But it can become, I don't know the right word, something urgent, une angoisse, une faim. Not only for me; I'm sure most men do feel this, don't they? Or maybe you think it's not true of any man that *you* know?"

"Oh! It's an anguish! A hunger!" she mocked him. "Vous exagérez, Monsieur. Embracing a woman gives a man pleasure, tout simplement. I've seen the horrible joy on their faces. Not to mention dribbling and groaning with ecstasy. Enough to make me sick."

"No, you're right, you're right," he willingly agreed, "that's what I'm telling you. It's something *more* than pleasure. Like with an addiction, or obsession."

"I see that with *you* it's an obsession," she said scornfully. "Maybe you should try to control yourself?"

"That's what monks and priests have been trying to do for hundreds of years, isn't it? So far, they haven't had much success."

"They are weak and selfish, like you."

"Yes, I'm sure they are. And of course the whole thing of, what do we call it? The thrill. Setting eyes on, you know, someone attractive."

"And wanting to punish and humiliate her!"

He shook his head dismissively. "Of course not! To hold her in your arms." He could not possibly tell her the whole truth, about the raw physical side of it, not that he knew how to describe it. "And don't *most* women feel they have to be, *must* be, attractive?"

"What?" Irina gritted her teeth in fury. "Now women deserve to be raped for being attractive? Is that it?"

"Of course not! But it's a good thing to be, right? Beautiful, pretty? Desirable? All very nice. Makes the world go round. But there's something else going on – much, much more. Something in the blood. Yes, literally. When it gets you bad. Like something has dug its bite into your flesh and you can't shake it off."

"I don't want to hear your mad ideas! This is about rape! Don't you understand? Liliana was *raped* – by you. Now you say it's *her* fault, for being attractive."

"I don't say that! When I went into Liliana's room, it wasn't for anything unkind or to hurt anyone. I was just glad she was willing. To solve a problem."

All the way through this little discussion, Irina looked on with contempt, enraged, clicking her tongue with irritation whenever Neil spoke. At his final words she almost retched in disgust. "Solve your problem? And for *that* you think women should be used and tortured. *Your* problem?" – as she raised her voice, Neil shushed her with a finger to his lips. He gestured towards Liliana, sleeping on the bed. – "You think it's *you* that has a problem?" she hissed. "Are you looking for sympathy?"

"No, no, no," he protested, "Irina, I'm trying to talk to you seriously about why things happened the way they did, the way they do."

"You are trying to excuse yourself. Don't bother."

"Well, all right, if that's what you want. You think the clients are animals? So I'm an animal. We are all animals. So what? That's how it is."

"How childish you are!" Irina looked at him angrily. "Of course, we are all animals. What a stupid thing to say! I don't mean an animal *physically*, moron. I mean an animal *morally*. No, not even an animal! Does a dog have something on its conscience when it rapes a bitch? No, this is something worse than any animal: a creature that *can* restrain its desires, but insists on indulging them. Bastard!"

Neil was annoyed with himself for arguing with her. He had started out intending to give only help and kindness. He stood up and made to leave the room. "I'm going to cook some dinner for you. I don't want to talk about it."

"No, obviously you don't," she exclaimed bitterly. "You can't defend yourself and your apologies mean nothing. You are guilty of the crime of rape. Don't cook anything for me – I don't want to touch your food."

Neil turned towards her sharply. Despite himself, the limit of his exasperation had been reached. He stood immobile. Irina studied his features, illegible and impassive. The blue gaze scared her, as if eyes alone could cause harm.

"Hey, Irina," he said very quietly, "I don't defend myself. I don't have to. I don't bother to make apologies. Why should I? And I don't have to help you, either. *I don't have to do anything at all.*" He did not raise his voice for emphasis; rather, he lowered it. "You want me to feel guilty? I don't."

"A human being would feel guilty."

He shook his head very slightly. "Agreeing a price – that *is* human. Everyone wants to buy, everyone has something to sell. Something they can offer. It's good, it's civilised. But Liliana *wasn't* selling anything. She was *being* sold. *That's* the crime here. She was not at liberty. That's all I care about. Anyway," and his eyes turned away, "she asked me for help. I couldn't refuse."

"Liliana *asked* you? I don't believe that. How could she?"

Neil moved back towards the door. "She wrote it on a piece of paper," he assured her.

"*Non!*" Irina shook her head emphatically. "She did not. Not in French nor English. Do you speak Russian? Moldovan? No. We had no pen or paper. That was another cruel thing I hated about the place."

"Well, now she's free. She can leave, and so can you. And if you think I'm a rapist and a liar, the sooner you leave, the better. That's all."

Irina glared. "I must remember," she said grudgingly, "what you have saved me from. My God, what would have happened to me? Did *you* start the fire? Was that you? You are completely insane! If you wanted to help the girls, that was incredibly stupid," she raised her voice, and glanced anxiously at Liliana, who seemed now to be half awake, yet quite unaware of them. Immediately quieter again, Irina hissed, "You might have killed us! Maybe some of the girls *have* been hurt. Did you think of that?" She shook her head, confused and angry. "Where *is* that awful place, that house? Is it far away? I still don't really know what has happened today. Anyway, Lili can't stay here with you. That's obvious."

"Look, I'm going to make some food now. How hungry are you? Would you like roast chicken? Or just soup and bread?

There's wine, if you want some. I haven't got any wine glasses, though, just ordinary. Or there's beer. And Irina, would you like a pen and some paper?"

* * *

At nightfall, Elizabeth struck a match and held it to the first candle, and then to the second. As the two flames took hold, she put a hand over her eyes and pronounced the quiet blessing to begin a new day and a new year.

On the white damask tablecloth were set out loaves of challah under a white cloth, beside a bowl of honey and a plate covered with thin slices of apple. Sweet wine filled the silver kiddush cup.

"Shana tova, l'shana tova!" Embraces were exchanged amid a flurry of kisses. "Hag sameah!" and "Good yomtov!" To a good year, happy festival, good holy-day!

At first all gathered in the sitting room, expectant and cheerful. The older folk brought satisfyingly old-fashioned voices into the house, and a few Yiddish words like echoes from the past. Whatever their usual habit, tonight all the men wore kippot.[1] Even Ruth had dressed elegantly.

Bernard stood and held up the decorated silver goblet of dark wine. Silence fell and he began to chant the singsong blessing for the first night of Rosh Hashanah.

"Amain," they cried in unison. Each of them took a sip of the sugary liquid, and all together recited the Shehchianu, which marks the progress of life, the passing of the years, "*shehehianu, v'kimanu, v'higianu, laz'man ha-zeh.*" He who kept us alive to bring us to this season.

Now the blessing for challah, and every one took a piece torn from the fresh, soft bread – eaten not with the usual sprinkle of salt on this day, but sticky with a lick of sharply sweet honey.

Each picked up a slice of apple, heard its blessing and, with another amen, touched the fruit into the dish of honey before

---

[1] Skullcaps [Hebrew].

eating. Second and third slices were dipped, as Elizabeth and Ruth laid out the first course of the meal.

They ate, and there was voluble, good-humoured talk, sometimes comfortable agreement, sometimes mutual exasperation, as conversation encompassed all the hopes and fears of the day, crime, al-Qaeda, Israel, the bank crisis, the American presidential elections.

"Did you see the house that was on fire, near Sainsbury's?" Ruth asked.

"I heard sirens," came a reply. Someone mentioned that he had seen smoke in the air. There had been a smell of burning.

"I didn't actually see the fire, but I saw fire engines and everything," said Ruth.

"Oh dear! I hope no one was hurt!"

Exclamations of delight greeted every course. Wine was sipped in tiny quantities and food enjoyed in generous portion.

And the talk ran to books and plays and films, to work and holidays, tales of success and failure, of joy and of grief, the progress of grown-up children in their chosen careers, and reminiscences of childhoods long ago, in London, in Cape Town, in Vienna, Łódź, Vilna and Bucharest.

10

They all have something weird: this one wants to see a woman burn, burn, burn. He wants to do something to me, set fire to my sheets and throw me into the flames. You never know what a man will want of you. On you, in you, everywhere, make you crawl, lie down, stand up, kneel, smack you, use you. Open you right up and climb inside.

I can press the button and the men will come and stop him. Except there is no button here. Those brutes, bad as they were, did look after me. They protected me, brought my food and pills. I'll show these two I can stand their fire and pain.

The woman is sly. She makes out that she is Moldovan, but she does not look or sound like any Moldovan I ever saw. A Jewess! Lots of them do look just like that, with wavy hair like that, and those eyes. She has a Jewish forehead, too. You can always tell a Jewess from the eyebrows, as well.

The two of them scheme together, hissing in low voices, eyes darting, planning, plotting something evil, un-Christian and foreign, whispering in Jewish. What are they talking about together?

I am not frightened. Why should I be? Pain, pain, so what? I am dead already. I don't even think about them. I think about nothing.

The woman tries to win my confidence. The woman has a sick mind. The woman – but it's Irina! She seems to be on their side now.

* * *

Neil stood in his untidy living room with head bowed, relieved to be alone. He felt achingly tired, and his eyes sore. He weighed the pistol in his hand, uncertain what to do with it. Like Irina, he wondered if he could please just go back to the life he had before. He gazed at the dark metal as if it were an oracle holding visions. He had feared retribution. Now though, he wondered how there could possibly be any retribution. After all, no one knew who he was or where he had taken the girls.

Still, he had better keep the gun by him. He tried it in his pocket; it was too big, and felt awkward. For the moment, he stuck it under his belt, at the back, where it could not be seen.

Quietly and slowly he pulled the cushions off the sofa and set them out as a makeshift mattress on the floor. He had not yet lain down on them when a horrifying sound tore through the silence.

That must have woken the whole neighbourhood.

For one second he thought it could be the dream again. This time, though, he knew he was awake and the screams were real, and had come from his bedroom.

Liliana cowered by the bedroom window, apparently terrified of what she could see outside, while Irina held her, struggling to put her arms around her. The more she tried, the more Liliana fought. She did not want to be held or comforted.

"No, leave her," Neil said. He looked out of the window to see what had alarmed Liliana, but the garden was still and dark. Beyond the back wall, the council flats rose into an orange night sky. Liliana crouched on the floor, panting, hugging herself in terror. Neil thought it looked like a panic attack.

"What can we do?" Irina cried out anxiously. "Call an ambulance! You have some – comment on dit – somnifères, pillules, tranquillisants, sédatifs?"

"No, she'll be all right." From his jeans pocket Neil took a torn scrap of paper. He squatted down in front of Liliana.

"Do you remember this?" he said tenderly, in English. He unfolded the scrap and held it up for her to read the words written there.

She stared nonplussed by the sight, then plunged frowning

into agitated thoughts, then became calm and looked up at him. Softly she began to weep.

"Yes," she murmured. "Îmi amintesc de tine. Îmi amintesc de ochii tăi."

She took the note from him and held it with wonder.

"What did she say?" Neil asked Irina.

But before she could answer, the doorbell rang and a wild pounding shook the front door.

Even Liliana seemed startled. Irina cringed at the sound. Neil grasped the metal stuck in the back of his belt and approached the door warily. To his astonishment, there stood his elderly landlady, enclosed in a long, pink candlewick dressing gown buttoned to the neck. She wrung her hands fretfully.

He let go of the gun handle. "Oh, er... hello Mrs Viktor," said Neil meekly, "Is it the noise? I'm sorry about that."

Her husband came clumsily behind, with choleric red face. Perhaps his wife had gone to bed before him, since he was wearing blue work trousers and check shirt; or perhaps he had taken the time to dress while she rushed ahead in her gown. Such things passed through Neil's mind. He keenly wanted to avoid annoying either of them. The man had a slightly uncontrolled, even unhinged quality. It didn't help that he had crazily unkempt eyebrows. Bernard had warned he was on a short fuse.

"I'm so sorry," Neil began again.

"What is screaming? Huh?" demanded the man.

The wife turned to her husband and spoke to him earnestly in Hungarian, She placed both her hands on his chest to restrain him. Ignoring her, the man continued forward to the very door of the flat and right through it, making Neil step backwards.

Neil perceived in this bulky Hungarian, what he had not noticed before in their occasional brief encounters in the hallway, a vast capacity for action. Despite his age, he was vigorous. Close up, the face was old and careworn, the eyes sorrowful. The grey hair was still thick, and slicked back from a forehead deeply lined.

Bernard had told him the Viktors were refugees from the Hungarian Uprising, and now, before he replied, Neil ran through a myriad of thoughts. His landlord had grown up in another land with another history. If he had ever hoped to live a good life there, that hope had been abandoned. Instead he struggled to make the best of things in a poky flat among Englishmen who knew nothing at all about the Hungarian Uprising – as Neil himself knew nothing about it.

"There are two girls, two women, here," Neil forestalled him, "who need help."

The landlord's heavy brow rose in surprise. "What kind of help?" His voice was deep and grainy, the schoolroom English ponderous, laboured and slow, and even more than his wife he preserved all the intonation and accent of his mother tongue.

"Maybe a doctor," Neil answered. "They're in trouble, really big trouble. They are hiding from some people. They're frightened. I'm sorry about the noise."

"From whom do they hide?"

Neil hesitated. "Dangerous people." He sensed the Hungarian's own plain-speaking honesty. "Russian criminals," he admitted.

Neil did not say this to deceive them. He believed that the people from whom he had rescued Liliana and Irina were indeed Russian. Both women had said the men spoke Russian.

His landlady breathed in sharply, shocked at the words.

"It's true, this? Russians? Russian bandits?" demanded Mr Viktor.

Neil doubtfully confirmed that definition.

"These ladies must leave now," was his immediate reply. "Or it's not safe for us – for me and my wife."

For a moment Neil was tempted to refuse. He said, "But I can't take them anywhere. I haven't got a car. Anyway, they aren't well enough."

The landlord insisted that they must leave. If necessary, he would drive them in his own car. "Where to take them? Do you know any doctor?" And when Neil shook his head, he carried on, "We don't want screaming here. I will take them to hospital. We must go now! Come on, come on."

Without enthusiasm, Neil agreed. "I was wondering... will they need ID, do you know, at the hospital?"

"No! Of course, no!" The landlord was emphatic, almost shouting. "They don't need no ID, no money, no nothing."

"We'll be downstairs in two minutes," Neil replied.

Somehow he had to prepare the two women for a night of waiting in Accident and Emergency, alongside the coarse and violent men who populate such places. Afterwards he would have to find somewhere else for them to stay, maybe a hotel.

He found Liliana sitting quietly on the bed. Irina held the scrap of paper in her hand.

"Why didn't you show me this note before?" she demanded. "You made me say you were a liar. Yes, I see it's true, she did ask you for help."

"What did Liliana say to me, just now?"

"Nothing. Only that she remembers your eyes."

"Irina, I'm sorry, but you can't stay here after all," Neil told her. "I have to find somewhere else."

* * *

For the two women, Neil imagined, it was just another strange man taking them somewh   .

"László," the man barked, holding out his hand to them, "László Viktor."

"Really? Like in the film?" smiled Neil. "You know the film, *Casablanca*? One of the characters..."

The Hungarian's huge eyebrows descended to his nose. "I never been to Casablanca," he interrupted. "Anyway, Viktor is my middle name. My family name is Szilágyi, but the English are scared to say it. And what is your name, young man? I forget."

This was forgivable, since the Hungarian had nothing to do with his upstairs tenant, leaving all such matters to his wife. Until now, the two men had hardly seen each other.

Grasping the steering wheel vigorously as though wrestling

with it, Neil's landlord urged his battered little hatchback towards the Royal Free Hospital. The engine roared as it climbed.

All of them were anxious and silent. Neil cleared his throat and ventured, "Um, Mr Viktor, by the way, I've been meaning to ask you, does my music bother you – not too loud?"

"What music? My hearing is not so good now. Screams, I can hear."

Neil was uncertain if that was a sort of joke. After another pause, he asked awkwardly, "So, uh, you, like, lived in England since the Hungarian Uprising, right?"

"Ah, so you know about it? That's why I don't like Russians. Yes, a long time ago. Lifetime! I was twenty-one years old," László sighed. "I graduated that summer, as an engineer. They were proud of me, my good mother, my good father. I remember it well. By the end of October I was fighting in a militia. At Christmas, I had to leave my country behind. The only thing that worries me now," again he sighed deeply, "I did not bid adieu to my dear parents. Twenty-one years old, and I did not kiss them farewell! Later I tried to send my parents a message on Radio Free Europe, but probably they never heard it. I never found out. Ah well!"

Neil had not imagined that this bluff, unpolished man could be a graduate. He put it to him that he must have been homesick, over the years.

"Yes and no!" László declared. "I am always Hungarian, but the Hungary I am sick for, it never existed. It was a dream. You know, there are Hungarians in London. Plenty. Thousands. Nice Hungarian restaurants, too. We have many Hungarian friends. We belong to the Hungarian Cultural Centre, and Hampstead Hungarian Society. We go for Hungarian folk dancing. And Hungarian chess club. Everyone knows everyone. We even have our own Hungarian patisserie in Hampstead!"

Neil would have to abandon his view, so recently formed, that the poor couple must be lonely and pining for their homeland. "And couldn't you go back?" he asked.

"Back where?" asked László. "Oh, to Hungary? No! Or yes! We

been back! First time, in 1993. That's when I learned my parents were murdered by the Reds. We went again two years ago, for the fiftieth anniversary."

"Sorry, fiftieth anniversary what of?"

"Of our failed Revolution. But skinheads ruined our celebration. My country is very divided." He shook his head sadly and lowered his voice. "These girls, in the back, who are they? They stay quiet. Not Russians, I hope."

"Well, I don't know, exactly." Neil did not want to say more; Moldova, as part of the Soviet Union, might be encompassed by László's animus for all things Russian. "They don't speak much English," he said. He leaned closer and murmured, "They have been raped." The Hungarian was horrified and exclaimed that he would do anything to help.

The dense woodland of West Heath lay beside them, obscure in the dark. László turned up the steep hill to Whitestone Pond.

One happy day, not long ago, Neil reflected, he had cycled to this very spot with his tango dancer, Limor. The two of them had liked hilltops, apparently! On the first night, they held each other at the top of Primrose Hill and danced close. The next day, they had pointed out the dome of St Paul's Cathedral from the top of Parliament Hill. Then, side by side under trees and along paths, they rode their bikes up to this shallow semi-circle of water at the top of Hampstead Heath.

Tonight, the pond's black water gloomily reflected shimmering streetlights and headlights.

Limor had asked him about the tall flagpole by the pond. He turned now and could just see it in the dark. The flag of the City of London was still raised there, moving slightly. Bad luck or something, isn't it, he wondered, to fly a flag at night? Seems an ominous, menacing symbol.

Right here he and Limor had lingered, talking together. He grinned ruefully as he recalled the ridiculous pink cycle helmet she had insisted he wear!

Know a doctor? Until this moment he had thought of her only as a sergeant in the Israeli army and a tango dancer in a sexy dress. He remembered now, she had said she was interested only in therapy, not dance. Oddly, Neil had completely forgotten that he did indeed know a doctor. She even ran a clinic for women.

* * *

Limor's dark street of stucco façades seemed bathed in contented prosperity, each door freshly painted, the cool autumn night perfumed with the airs of liberal intelligentsia. Good jobs all! Good salaries, good taste, *bien-pensants* and everyone with accomplishments to be proud of! Music from one of the apartments faintly penetrated the tranquillity. Someone was having a party. Neil could picture the civilised young professional people, the casually attired middle-class folk who would be attending it, wine glasses in hand.

It had passed midnight but Limor's lights were on. Neil ran up the steps while László and the two women waited in the car. Liliana peered out at him anxiously as he pressed the entryphone.

At last someone answered. As the voice crackled, music sounded loud in the background – so the noise was coming from *her* flat.

"Hello? Yes?" Then, "Ken? Mi zeh?"

"Limor?" he said. "Shalom. Ze Neil. Ma shlomeh?"

He could not understand the answer.

"It's Neil," he repeated. "Remember the tango lesson?"

"I remember only you don't like Hammershøi. What are you doing here, Neil? Are you drunk?" In truth, she remembered much else, a muscled, upright physique, cold eyes of clear blue, a moonlit dance and the most romantic moments she had ever experienced.

"Limor, listen. It's extremely important. I want to ask you a very big favour. Not for me. For two women who need help urgently."

"Send them to my clinic. If I can help, I will help. If I can't, I can't."

"This is much more important than that. It's an emergency.

They've been beaten and raped."

"What? It's noisy here."

He raised his voice.

She sounded puzzled rather than concerned. "Wait, I am coming down."

Music he had never heard before played loud, lyrical folk-rock with a woman singer. Smiling, carefree, attractively dressed women and men gathered in the hallway of the flat. From every open door came animated, cheerful shouting and laughter; they were not talking English. Some gently swayed to the beat, not quite dancing.

Straight away Neil feared this was the wrong place for Irina and, especially, Liliana. They needed somewhere peaceful. He watched Liliana. She was subdued and withdrawn.

"Having a party?" he thought to ask.

Limor shot him a pitying glance. She led them towards a closed door at the back of the flat. "Another thing I remember about you! Stupid questions."

"I meant – celebrating something?"

As she turned to reply, at once she reached out with concern, taking Liliana's hand. She guided her carefully through the crowd. "Yes, tonight it's Rosh Hashanah," she called back, "Jewish New Year, you call it. Shana tova – a good year to you."

Only then did Neil notice that almost everyone was speaking Hebrew. A few conversations faltered as faces turned curiously to Limor's three strange new visitors, for Liliana and Irina still wore the assorted clothes he had taken from the van, together with some of his own. Suddenly he saw Liliana through their eyes, a pale, skeletal, blank-faced young woman.

"Shana tova," Neil said into Limor's ear. "So sorry to intrude."

"Why should it intrude?" she retorted. "You were right to come here."

They stepped into a small consulting suite. Limor switched on the lights, and Neil saw a couple of treatment rooms, quiet and empty, maybe for massage or yoga, painted and carpeted in pale, minimalist style. As soon as the door had shut behind them, the din of voices and music ceased abruptly. Limor faced the two women. "Who has done this to you?"

There was no answer. Instead, Neil explained that neither of them spoke much English.

"Well, *you* tell me. How did it happen to them? This young woman," she gestured towards Liliana, "is terribly sick. She is malnourished. Her muscles are wasting away."

"The other one speaks French. I can translate," he offered.

"That's OK, I know French," she said. "What else do they speak? What is their language?"

Haltingly, softly, still holding Liliana's hand, she addressed them in Russian. Irina answered and then Liliana. It seemed that she had simply asked their names. To Neil, Limor turned and said, "Leave us in privacy. Go join the party. Practice your Hebrew. Have a dance – there are a couple of nice English girls from the tango class. There's food, if you want. Try the honey cake; it's wonderful. I'll see you later."

"Look, Limor, I need to tell you something. This girl here," Neil gestured to Irina, "will say that I raped Liliana, but – "

Across Limor's astonished face, a troubled, questioning frown passed rapidly. She stopped him with both hands raised. "Don't say more. If someone accuses you, I will come for your explanation." She reached out and took his hand in a gesture somehow both formal and intimate. Her voice sincere, she said, "Thank you for bringing them to me – *haver*."

"*Havera*," he replied.

Neil closed the door behind him and went out into the noise. How would he ever find those girls from the tango class? He moved slowly through the crowd. The mood was exuberant and good-humoured. On Limor's dining table he found a colourful spread of salads in big glazed bowls, plates of cheeses, baskets of pitta bread, and falafels, shallow dishes of hummus, tahina, nuts, olives, dried fruits and cakes, unrecognisable juices and soft drinks, bottles of beer and Israeli wine. Few people, he noticed, were drinking – other than soft drinks. He wondered if they were all health freaks like Limor. He picked at the food, chewed on a mouthful of nuts, sipped white wine from the Golan, dipped a cracker into an unfamiliar red sauce. It was deliciously spicy.

This is nicer than trying to deal with bloody Moldovans!

One young woman stood alone, as perfect and unnoticed as a pearl fallen onto a busy pavement. Neil was always especially drawn to something overlooked. She seemed embarrassed by her shyness and solitude. He asked her, "Who's this singing?"

Unglamorous and unremarkable, she wore a long grey sweater, like a short dress, over black tights. The wool gently held the smooth curve of each breast.

"Don't you remember?" she answered. "It was in the Eurovision Song Contest. This was Israel's entry." She had light brown hair and the prettiest green eyes.

Neil shook his head, amused. "No, I never watch that. I'm Neil. What's your name?"

Even before he caught the answer, Limor came into view, moving hurriedly towards him. She grabbed his hand and led him away. "Neil, I have a couple of friends here, they are doctors too, who help me," she said. "It will be best if you leave Liliana and Irina with us. They need a lot of care. Liliana's problems are worse than I thought. We'll look after them for a while. They'll sleep in my relaxation room, each one in her own bed, and I'll stay in there with them."

"Thank you, thank you, very, very much."

"This is worse than anything I imagined. They told me their experience." Limor shook her head as if to rid herself of what she had heard, yet went on with dark indignation, "I want to know who did this. We must do something."

"We can talk about that."

"I think Liliana has an acute depression. We've given her a tranquillizer."

"And she needs medical treatment?"

"She will have treatment. And I'll help her with my therapy. I told you about it – music, dance, singing. I will hold her hand and bring her back to health."

"What about Irina?"

"Not so bad. Yes, you were right: Irina said you raped Liliana."

Neil listened grimly.

"You know, I told her what I think," Limor said, "rape is by force. But she said no, it is not always so; rape is if the woman will not consent. But what they told me was that Liliana did not refuse you. Because she could not. So this is like if we buy something in a shop. Jeans, trainers, tee-shirt. Or a pizza, or a bag of fruit. Do we know if it is made by people who are slaves? Does anyone know? Do you ask at the counter before paying? But maybe it is. So if it is, are you to blame? No, the people who raped Liliana are those who *made* her do this."

"You are good, Limor, to think of it like that. You don't hate me?"

"Hate you? Well, to be honest, I don't like," she combined a shrug with a look of disgust, "such activities. Maybe I'm surprised at you. But these are private things." She opened her eyes wide. "Is it true, also, what they told me, the fire, the gun?"

"Well, it depends what they told you."

"What kind of gun? Air gun?"

"Do you know about guns?"

"Of course."

"Beretta 9mm semi-automatic, model 92F." Neil repeated Winston's words.

"Wow! American military. I don't ask where you got it. Where did you train?"

He snorted with amusement. "I've never fired a single shot. Just waved it at them."

"You were lucky," she said. "I will teach you to use it."

"First tango, now firearms!"

She made a wry expression. "We'll talk soon. Now, I will spend Rosh Hashanah with Liliana and Irina. And it feels so," she searched her mind for a word but did not find it, saying only, "so much the right thing to do at such a time."

Neil looked around again for the girl with pretty green eyes, but she had gone. Maybe, unnoticed, she had slipped away.

* * *

Later, in cold, damp streets, Neil walked from Primrose Hill to Chalk Farm and up past the closed gates of Belsize Park tube station. A slight mist gave the night a melancholy tranquillity. Earlier in the evening, he had been exhausted. Now every cell in his brain seemed tingling and alert. He walked, and the air and the effort eased his mind.

Occasionally a solitary car passed at speed. He thought of Limor, at this moment setting out a mattress for herself between Liliana and Irina, while in other rooms her guests laughed and danced.

When Limor said *We must do something*, what did she mean? He had already done something. Bernard had said, *Do your bit, do what you can*, but hadn't he also said, *You can't help everyone*?

The fire, the taxi, even this morning's Ascot round, it all seemed like something he had read about or seen in a movie. Tomorrow, too, going to work, was unreal and impossible.

Hampstead's idling queue of traffic had vanished, the High Street still and quiet at last. The lights were out in the empty pubs and the clothes shops, and at Maison Blanc and the Coffee Cup, at Waterstones and Starbucks and Café Rouge. All the tables had been cleared away, leaving the pavement surprisingly wide.

At Whitestone Pond, traffic lights turned green, turned amber, turned red where no cars drove, stopping no one. The City's flag hung more limply now, in the humid atmosphere. The Heath smelled moist; he heard a bird cry in alarm. Down towards Golders Green he walked.

No, this was no film or fiction. At home a real gun was hidden, and a real fortune. The two women were really at Limor's. Something in him was contented, as if he had lived always waiting for this day. Another part of his mind regretted everything; today his life had changed, and he wished it had not, and was afraid.

He decided to walk by the burnt house, to see how it looked after the fire, although that seemed risky. The police might be keeping watch on the place. When he arrived, though, a few ribbons of blue and white tape – marked *Crime Scene Do Not Cross* – hung abandoned around the tall hedge and battered wooden gates. There was no one in sight.

Noticing that the gates of Osborne Park were still open, he cut across the dark space. London's low, distant sound of traffic had died away. The enveloping blackness thrilled him. He heard a motorcyclist passing on the A41, the whine fading into silence. In the heavens, beyond a net of silvery haze, the moon was nearly full, surrounded by a pale blue aurora. A handful of stars came faintly into view. Of all things, Neil most loved the feeling of having the world to himself. This day was his alone, and the night. Only a glimmering light behind the shutters at the café pierced the park's opaque stillness.

Nearly half-past three! Don't tell Bernard! He'd be furious if he knew the café and the park had not yet closed for the night.

And behind the café's shuttered doors and windows, the Bosnians have studied the CCTV footage, often pausing the recording for a closer look, and have remembered seeing this Englishman. The owner of the café has also spoken up: he recognises this man too. This man often passes through the park on a bicycle, he told the others. Never before was he in uniform. Yesterday he even stopped at the café for a drink. They are all puzzled by this. Yesterday? Yet he had never been there before? Surely then, he must have come to the café to spy on them? So, does this man know their movements? What exactly *is* the uniform he put on especially to carry out this attack? Obviously, no one would wear a uniform to do anything secret. Is it, then, some kind of militia? If it's a militia, then there is more going on in England than they realise.

The Bosnians phoned the Albanians who provide them with their girls. They did not mention that they suspected the Albanians might be involved somehow. They listened attentively to the Albanians' reaction to the news. No, the Albanians solemnly promised, this outrage was nothing to do with them. They even offered to help in any way they could.

Some of the girls, the Bosnians knew, had been purchased by the Albanians from suppliers. Others, they had taken after paying for a tip-off – single Moldovan girls with no ties. Either way, the Albanians might know where the girls would go if they ran away.

The Bosnians emailed some still frames from the CCTV film. The Albanians called back to say that they had spoken to their contacts in Paris and in Moldova, and forwarded them the images, but there was no immediate information. More phone calls were made. Other groups in Britain and Moldova, and families and friends around the country, said they will look for the girls, and the man. The Albanians called to offer the Bosnians a house to use in Camden.

The Bosnians thanked the Albanians. However, they suspected another trick. They did not trust Albanians, nor believe anything they said. The other groups, too, would surely only work against them. It might be better to find a new house without any help from anyone. Still, to remain on good terms with the Albanians, for a short while they would have to take up the Camden offer.

The Bosnians are right to be suspicious. High up in the Barbican, the Albanians wonder if the Bosnians are playing a trick on *them*. Nazim has told his boss that Osman and Zlatan tried to cheat him when he delivered a new girl. And, he said, the Bosnians wanted to sell used goods back to them, half price for something that was actually now worth nothing at all. Surely it could not be a coincidence that the two missing girls – if they really were missing – just happened to be the new one they had not yet paid for, and the one they wanted to sell. The boss had never trusted Bosnians. He decided to offer them a house that he could keep under close surveillance. He might as well post a search for the Englishman, just in case. After all, he didn't want to fall out with the Bosnians. They had been useful customers.

In Osborne Road and Blenheim Road and Kenilworth Road, and in the council estate behind, most residents were asleep in their beds. Perhaps a few were still awake, drinking cocoa or whisky, or watching late-night television, or making love. Bernard and Elizabeth lay beside one another under a duvet, dreaming their separate dreams. László Viktor and his wife did the same. So it was everywhere; in tiny apartments and great houses, men and women shared the night.

Rats and foxes and cats, though, were wide awake, slinking deftly through cracks and spaces between fences, sniffing gutters and darting along alleys.

And in the park café, the Bosnians banged the table in fury and shouted that they will stop at nothing to find this English gangster and the two stolen women. They will kill him, they will cut him to shreds. One slice at a time. They will feed the pieces to him, make him chew his own flesh. Set fire to their property, would he? Well, they would set fire to him, his hands, his feet, his genitals, before his very eyes. They will teach him such a lesson. He does not know who he is dealing with.

An Englishman, of all people! One of the pathetic, feeble, cowardly, naïve, weak, idle, good-for-nothing English! No, they will *not* kill him, yells another, better to keep him alive in a cage somewhere, *keep* him alive and make him *beg* to be killed. *Keep* him alive, like a dog on a chain. Skin him, blind him, chop out his tongue, but *keep* him alive.

The older woman says she regrets such savage talk. "*No* harm will come to him," she warns, "until he has led us to our girls. And our money."

There are times though, she reasoned, when strong measures do become justified. After all, a family must defend itself and its property. Her sons and nephews are not really violent men; at least, rarely cruel or vicious; but like their fathers they are not afraid of whatever becomes necessary, no matter how unpleasant. Truly, she admires the muscular directness of such men, the forthright vigour, their unsentimental determination. Their fathers would have been proud of them, she says.

What would her husband have advised? The answer is obvious. She and the boys must do as *he* would have wanted.

* * *

The night passed and morning came, the morning of Rosh Hashanah. After three restless hours on his bed, Neil drove Critchlow's van along the country lanes of Ascot and Sunningdale. No one in the yard noticed anything unusual about him. He listened to the nine o'clock news, and the world was just as before. More Islamist bombs had gone off in India. The House of Representatives disapproved of bailing-out American banks. The crew of a Ukrainian ship had shot some Somali pirates. It was almost as though his visit to Liliana, his insane burning of a house, had not really happened – except that his mind revisited the experiences constantly.

In Primrose Hill, Limor made breakfast for Liliana and Irina – cherry tomatoes, cottage cheese, rye bread, herb tea – and they were as surprised by it as Neil had been. Liliana was persuaded to eat a tiny amount. In the sitting room, cleared of every sign of the party, Limor talked to them about traditional Moldovan music and dance; but Liliana retorted that she preferred house music, europop and disco dancing (and gave the first smile Limor had seen, when she ventured that her favourite bands were Akcent and Animal X), while Irina said she would especially love to hear Dvořák's Cello Concerto in B minor. Limor downloaded several MP3 tracks for each of them.

Liliana listened thoughtfully and said she did not like those bands so much any more. "I think *those men* liked this music." Irina began to weep on hearing Dvořák. In the afternoon, Limor put on a DVD that filled her TV screen with an exquisitely musical, joyously foot-tapping country-style American hootenanny of brass and banjo like nothing they had ever heard, and she actually persuaded both of them to get up and dance.

In her treatment room they tried to follow Limor's sinuous steps. The room was as white as a sugar cube, light and empty, with plain walls and smooth wooden floor. Irina, then Liliana, danced alone, ever more freely, more abandoned, jumping wildly in time. And then, the disciplined steps of some more formal dance, in which Limor played the part of the man.

Each lingered in the bathroom, washing away every microscopic pollution by 'clients', and massaging herself with Limor's soothing skin creams, silky, luxurious Ahava moisturisers and lotions and purifying gels. From time to time Limor called to Liliana through the bathroom door, asking if all was well. She called back that she was fine.

In a bathroom drawer Liliana found some nail scissors. Slowly she parted the blades and looked at them. Her thumb moved slowly over one sharp point. She touched it onto her skin and paused, savoured the little area of pain, wondered if she would like to press it into the flesh, pierce the surface, score it across in red, red lines; but she held back, running it lightly above her breast, up to her throat, making barely a scratch. She liked the sensation. As the seconds passed she became more tempted to make the deeper cut. She told herself that with one quick decisive move she could do it.

When Limor knocked on the door and opened it a little to look in, Liliana hastily put down the scissors, ashamed. Limor cried out at the sight, rushed into the bathroom and held Liliana in her arms. She wrapped a warm towel around her.

"Let's dry your hair. Would you like me to brush it?" Limor asked. She took a hairbrush and slowly ran it through Liliana's thin golden-blonde hair.

Liliana sat lost in her anxieties, troubled by what she had almost done. "My mother," she said softly, "used to brush my hair like that."

"And perhaps you," said Limor, "will do it for your daughter."

The Kassin family, cheerfully dressed against the possibility of rain, made their way to shul. One of Bernard's highest joys was the walk on these festival days, all the family together, joining with the streams of others, converging at last on the synagogue. At such moments it was almost possible to experience the fleeting pleasure of being a mighty nation, visible and numerous, were it not for the security cameras and volunteer guards that protected them from the great world all around.

Friends found each other in the gathering crowd, exchanging

kisses and traditional greetings in Yiddish and Hebrew. It could have been a party, the prayer hall filled with talk before the start of the service. Many were dressed in the pale colours or traditional pure white of Rosh Hashanah, Elizabeth and Ruth among them.

Bernard adored the poetry and song of the High Holy Day services, the vast repeated themes, majestic and unhurried.

Avinu malkenu... and *Hashkiveinu...*

and, especially, *Adonai, adonai, el rahum ve hanun...*

Oh, how he loved that rousing melody, the drawn-out vowels! And *B'rosh Hashanah, yikatevun, u'v'yom tzom kippur yehatemun...*

At each of these moments the voices of the community rose as an ocean of sound and of emotion, the deep, slow Hebrew words turning like waves in his heart, a rousing chorus – of fellow Jews, men, women and children, here and around the world, today and in ages past.

Throughout all the prayers, Bernard did not feel any sense of God's existence. The idea of a Creator was meaningless to him, a contradiction in terms. Bernard believed in Man alone, and had a suspicion that the rabbis of old surely agreed with him. The natural world he saw only as a setting for human society. Absence of faith, or even of sincerity, did not bother him as he stood among his tribe praising its God, or asking the Lord of the Universe to forgive Man's failings. For he heard only the voice of a people, his own, which spoke aloud and heard itself.

The Torah is read from a weighty scroll, and the Haftarah from a book. The rabbi speaks about life, and the shofar is sounded and sounded again and again. One hundred times the shofar is blown on Rosh Hashanah, the community standing in silence while the primeval note peals from a polished coil of ram's horn. Each hearer seems rapt, caught in solitary thoughts. Bernard, as always, heard the plaintive blast like a banner across the whole sky: *Think! Remember! Repent! Survive!*

The service is long and the mind wanders. Bernard started to visualise lunch. Then the time came for the reading of the U-Netaneh Tokef and he paid attention once more. It was another of the landmarks which thrilled him.

    U-netaneh tokef... Let us now declare the power of this day
    You unfold the book of remembrance, and it reads itself,
    for every person is found therein.
    All living things pass before you,
    you determine how long each shall live, and its fate.
    On Rosh Hashanah it is written,
    on Yom Kippur it is sealed,
    How many shall pass away and how many shall be born;
    Who shall live and who shall die;
    Who shall complete his years and who shall not;
    Who shall die by fire and who by water;
    Who by strangling and who by stoning;
    Who shall be at ease and who shall be afflicted.

11

It seemed he had got clean away with it. Uneventful working days passed. Neil did wonder if efforts were being made to track him down. On Wednesday, he was sent out once more with Stan. Together they drove through the City's tangle of narrow lanes, along crooked streets sluggish with buses, beneath the hem of mighty buildings.

Stan could work for hours without a word, it seemed. As before, while the old man sat slumped behind the steering wheel, Neil hefted parcels up white stone steps, through glass doors into tall, cool atriums adorned with marble and polished steel, water features and floral displays.

Even when they stopped for lunch, Stan would be prepared to sip his tea, eat his cheesecake and read his Daily Mirror in silence.

Neil took the empty mugs back to the tea-stall, and Stan went for his 'Jimmy Riddle' at the Public Conveniences in Shoreditch High Street.

When he returned, Stan turned the key and the van juddered noisily into wakefulness. They edged slowly along Bishopsgate.

Neil felt a warm affection for the man. He viewed Stan's crankiness as a laconic, disappointed tenderness for humanity. He longed to speak to such a person, unburden himself and seek advice. Stan, though, had again become taciturn, meditatively gazing at the traffic in front of him.

"Stan, I want to ask you a question."

The lined, tired face showed wariness. "Go on then, son."

"You ever been in trouble?" he asked. That was as far as he could go.

"With the law?"

"With the law – or anyone?"

Stan raised one eyebrow. "Are you?"

"I know it's personal, but have you ever been to a..." he didn't know what word to use (a tart? a lady of the night? Sanina had said whore), "to a prostitute?"

"Not the kind of thing you ask someone." Stan's lips twisted with disdain.

"Well, this one wasn't a prostitute. She was like – one of these trafficked women. I wanted to help her, but..."

Stan blew a tired, contemptuous puff of smoke.

"Don't tell me about it, son. Tell the police and keep it to yourself. That's the way to do it."

It was impossible, of course, for Neil to tell the police now. Too much had happened. Nor could he explain that to Stan.

On Thursday, alone this time, Neil drove through the City as usual. As always his mind drifted longingly to the Maypole pub and its lunchtime striptease, but he resisted the temptation. He went to the steamy-windowed café opposite Stan's tea-stall for a proper cooked meal.

While he was eating, Limor phoned to say it would be better if Liliana and Irina moved somewhere else; it can be harmful for patients to become too close to the therapist. It was important to find a home for them, she told him, now they were past the first shock of being released. "Irina," she said, "cries a lot, but will be fine."

"Has she contacted anyone? Her family?"

"No. No one. She likes to sit and think quietly."

"That's OK, I suppose."

"Of course. And she went out for a walk by herself, into Camden."

Neil lowered his voice. The workmen and cab drivers at the other tables could overhear. "She should be careful. They must be looking for her. Maybe wear a wedding ring, I dunno. She could disguise herself a bit. Dark glasses, and a headscarf or something. Maybe dye her hair." He abandoned his plate of food and paid at the counter, leaving the café quickly to return to the privacy of his van.

"She recognised a man in Camden High Street," Limor told him. "She was scared."

"So am I. I don't like the sound of that."

"They can't stay always in the flat!" Limor replied. "It was only for half an hour. It's good to go out, you know, for her confidence. She is very anxious, and angry. But best for her, is get on with normal life. I suggested to phone her embassy for help, but she said no, she is afraid. She doesn't trust them."

"Not surprising."

"But she must! She has no papers! Do you know, Irina came to London only to be a tourist? That would be good for her. Maybe you can show her, you know, Buckingham Palace, Trafalgar Square."

Neil paused. "You forgot something," he replied. "Irina hates me. She thinks I'm a rapist. *You* take her."

"*I* don't know London!" she protested. "Take both of us! I would love to be shown round by a real Londoner!"

"What – by bike, I suppose?"

"Of course! Why not?"

"We'll see. And what about Liliana?" asked Neil.

Limor paused, the humour quickly gone. "Liliana is eating more regularly now, and in a better state of mind. But her case is much worse. Very frightened. She has panic attacks. There will be a lot of work to do with Liliana. And she has more serious problems. She has a meshugass about yids."

"A what about what?"

"How is that expression? A bee under the bonnet? About yids. Yids, yids, yids. *Judanii, judanii, judanii.* She thinks Jews are the cause of all her troubles. It's annoying. She spat at me when she found out. Now she said, she doesn't want my help."

"Found out what?" Then he understood. "Spat at you! No, you shouldn't have to put up with that!" He remembered the van driver's spittle, landing on his own face, how humiliating it was.

"And she steals my stuff. She takes my things and hides them under her bed. My underwear, do you believe? It's OK. I understand. Never mind. I will help her. But she can't stay here.

It's not good for her."

"I'll see if I can think of somewhere else, somewhere safe," said Neil, though nothing came to his mind. "Language is a problem. What about some of your Israeli friends? Do they speak Russian?"

"No, they don't want Liliana."

"Look, for the time being, if they're going out on their own, give them both a mobile phone. Make sure they've got your number. And mine. You know, a really cheap phone. Pay as you go."

* * *

The morning service proceeds at its brisk pace, and before the final *amens* Bernard hastily unwinds his tefillin, folds his tallit and with a quick, cheery "Good morning" is on his way to work.

On a crowded Northern Line train, he stands pressed close between passengers absorbed in headphones, putting on make-up or pushing a breakfast of confectionery into open mouths. Some read magazines or turn the pages of free newspapers. *The Paedophile at the Palace*, blares the front page of Metro. All along the carriage, they stare intently at screens and tap at tiny keypads.

He shifts himself away from an armpit and glances around briefly. Hundreds of strangers, a minestrone of nations, in which he is just another diced ingredient. And yet, and yet – which of these would not help the others, if disaster befell them now? Another 7/7.[1] He scans the faces more closely, but today no one looks as if he would like to blow this transient little community to heaven or hell.

Where are all the men? There are no men any more.

In his childhood, in his youth, the morning tube carriages, buses and streets were full of men. Men are unassuming and taciturn, physically spare, stony faced, dressed in grey or black. Men wear macs and smoke cigarettes and read big broadsheet

---

[1] 7 July 2005: 52 passengers killed in coordinated Islamist attacks.

newspapers with no colour. Among men, the greatest sin is self-pity. Each man goes modestly about his business, calmly resigned to the burden of unavoidable duty. Any who try to be different from the rest seem merely vain and foolish.

In fresh polycotton shirts and business suits, big-boned and big-mouthed, these flabby boors now pass for men.

Men. Tube carriages used to be dense with their cigarette smoke, and their cigarette butts were crammed into all the grooves of the wooden floors. The escalators too, were wooden, scattered with cigarette stubs. Dark woollen overcoats and oil-streaked hair were pungent with a cigarette odour. In drawing rooms and waiting rooms, on reception desks and in offices, at restaurants and cafes and pubs, in cinemas and theatres, the ashtrays were overflowing. Fingertips were yellow with nicotine.

And at the end of the day, booze; the unwinding, the unloosening glass. The smell of beer, the sound of masculine bellowing and roars of laughter, carpeted saloon bars and the bare wood of public bars. His father, a clever little Jew who liked opera, never went inside such places. As a child, Bernard saw goyim[1] dead-drunk in the street, men lying unconscious on the pavement, heard raucous fighting behind closed doors as men's tensions exploded in rage, and sometimes, women squealing.

Now he remembers: there were a few pretty young women among the dark commuting masses, bright-looking office girls, secretaries and assistants, career girls in prim, crisply smart jackets and skirts. He remembers hair lacquered into immovable rigidity, perms and shiny red lipstick that came off with every kiss. In other parts of town, he knew, women moved in a vast tide, morning and evening, between factories and housing estates, but this he had never seen: he never went to such places.

Women's lives meant monotony and tedium, interrupted by a wedding. He wondered though, where now are the hard-faced drudges of his childhood, the hard-labourers of housework,

---

[1] Non-Jews [Yiddish].

toiling in sculleries, washing clothes without a washing machine, shopping without a car or a supermarket, polishing furniture without aerosol sprays, cooking meat, potatoes, carrots and cabbage without ready-meals or microwaves nor even a potato peeler that worked? That said, Bernard had a soft spot for any woman in an apron, sleeves rolled up, hair tied back with a headscarf. And at the end of each day, she would put on make-up and a nice dress for the daily homecoming of her hardworking Englishman.

In those days, everyone on the tube was English. Everyone. Their roots went deep into the soil of Essex and Middlesex, Hertfordshire and Kent. No one wanted to intrude, nor be intruded upon. When sober, they were wonderfully phlegmatic. Most had thin lips and bitter, even brutal eyes. Everyone remained quiet. Any that talked had mastered a level of speech little above a whisper. Remarks were private. If you met anyone you knew, you could use jovial stock phrases. Or make comic, ironic comments. People laughed politely, sometimes cruelly.

Those English men and women could let their hair down, though, at the right moment, with a drink inside them! Dancing, singing, guffawing without restraint. Knees-up, singalong, have a good laugh! He supposed they had all been in the army, that generation, or stayed at home and seen the Blitz.

But of course, he reminded himself, not *everyone* was English. Just everyone *else*. His own parents had been foreign. They were not actually immigrants – both had been born in London. He feels a sad pride, thinking of them, relieved that he did not fall short of their hopes. His family had so loved England and the admirable, mysterious sang-froid of its natives.

This morning, no one standing near him is English. Bernard counts five passengers in the compartment wearing kippot. He wonders if they know each other. Perhaps they, like him, still have marks on their forearms made by this morning's tefillin. One of them, in jeans and trainers, speaks to another, in suit and tie and polished shoes. It's clear that these two, at least, have met before. He hears the word Yerushalayim – Jerusalem.

In a thousand years, when England and the English are no

more, and global caliphates have had their bloody triumph and died away again, Jewish men will still daven shaharit and lay tefillin[1] and talk about Jerusalem.

At the Temple Café he sat for a few moments with a coffee and pastry and turned the pages of the Daily Telegraph before walking to the office. *Savers Move Billions To Safety.* He scanned the headlines. *School Trips Deemed Too Risky.*

* * *

At about four o'clock Neil drove back into Critchlow's yard. In the locker rooms he washed his face and hands and changed out of his uniform. He clocked off and knocked at the door of the transport manager's office.

"Mr Sanina, sorry to disturb you."

The bastard Sanina looked up from some spreadsheets. "Yes, Mr Chapman?"

His gaze ran over Neil's upright physique, rested briefly on the blue of his eyes.

"It's something personal."

"Mr Chapman, that is not my job. Please, for personal matters, go to the medical centre, or the chaplain. Both are on the fifth floor. I deal only with transport."

"You remember that note, Mr Sanina? In Romanian?"

"I said I can't help you with that problem."

"I rescued two girls from captivity. They are in serious trouble. These girls, they speak Romanian. You are the only other person I know who speaks Romanian. They need somewhere to stay for a few days, or a week, say. While I sort things out for them."

Andrei Sanina examined the papers on his desk as if they were more interesting than anything Neil had to say.

This young man, he thought, is so unlike the others. Everything about him is enigmatic, concealed, restrained. One senses that nothing is as it seems. He is educated, yet he is

---

[1] Daven shaharit – say morning prayers [Hebrew]; Lay tefillin – put on tefillin (phylacteries) [English and Aramaic].

uneducated. He is defiant and unyielding, yet he is submissive and compliant. He says lightly *I rescued two girls from captivity*, without any hint of drama. How did he achieve this? His voice, his bearing, give nothing away. If anyone can keep a secret, it's him. "May I ask you to keep such personal matters to yourself? Don't mention this to me again, Mr Chapman," Sanina answered brusquely. "Good night."

"Good night, Mr Sanina."

For it was the custom at Critchlow's to say *good night* on finishing the day's work, even in the middle of the afternoon.

After a shower, still wrapped in a towel, Neil sat on the sofa and flicked through the free local newspaper. Again he studied the illustrated ads offering massage, happiness and relief, which had got him into this situation. He turned the pages, glancing through furniture supplements, paid-for restaurant reviews, reports of burglaries, muggings, assaults.

Suddenly, in front of his eyes, was a photograph of himself. Under the headline *Mystery Gunman in Blaze Drama*, the hazy, blown-up black-and-white picture, looking like an Andy Warhol artwork, showed a man apparently holding hands with a woman in a flimsy dress. The picture was too unclear to reveal much. According to the caption, witnesses identified the object in the man's right hand as a gun. Anxiously, Neil read on...

Four fire engines and twenty firefighters, called to a Golders Green blaze on Monday, were confronted by a gunman who ran from the scene accompanied by two women.

The fire badly damaged the ground floor and first floor of a substantial £1.5 million 7-bedroom family house which neighbours said they had believed was let to a Serbian tycoon. But witness to the fire, Mrs Eida Vidi, who used her mobile phone to take the dramatic photo above, said "I think they were squatters. He waved the gun right in my face and threatened to kill me."

Staff at the Golden Years Nursing Home next door said they and the elderly residents were all very deeply shaken and would take time to recover.

Student Nescio Denksero, studying Classical languages at

nearby Golders Green College, confirmed that East European squatters were living in the house. They had vanished by the time police arrived. A spokesman for West Hampstead Fire Station commented, "The cause of the blaze is now under investigation."

His panic subsided. It was clear no one knew anything. At least, no one at the local newspaper. Neil was curious. What *was* happening now at Liliana and Irina's former prison? Was anyone there? Perhaps it was business as usual. With a suddenness that surprised even himself, he stood up, determined to quickly ride over and see the place.

* * *

The suspected arson and firearms case was allocated to a detective constable. He considered it of negligible importance. After all, no one had died, been injured or made any kind of complaint to the police. Members of the public had taken pictures on mobile phones, but none was remotely good enough for a positive ID. And the mystery gunman... well, frankly, it had a slightly apocryphal ring.

Still, when he called West Hampstead Fire Brigade, he learned that the fire definitely had been the result of arson. He was told, too, about the half-dressed girls, the men at the gate.

"And your crew members who witnessed an armed individual, can I arrange to speak to them?" asked the DC.

"It's only the one feller," and the DC noted down a name. "He reported that he saw, like, some bloke shouting and waving a handgun, who's run out the house, into the street, and disappeared, just like that."

"Oh, yeah? Do you want to ask your crew man to call me on this number?"

"I'll pass that on."

"Is it safe to go into the premises?"

The detective constable drove to the house with a uniformed police constable. They ducked under streamers of blue and white police tape and explored the scarred, dishevelled garden. Both at once remarked on the security cameras.

"If we can get the disc off that, we'll prob'ly have all the evidence we want," said the PC.

Cautiously stepping inside the house, they gazed around at scorched remnants of a table and chairs in the hall. The walls and stairs were blackened. An unpleasant oily haze of smoke hung in the air, scratching painfully at their eyes and lungs.

"Smell of... what is it, petrol?" the DC wondered. "Gas? Lighter fluid?"

"There is a whiff of something," the PC concurred. "Telly and armchairs in the hall? That's funny. And look, more cameras," he pointed out.

"Cameras here, too," said the DC from the top of the stairs.

"All the downstairs is bedrooms," the PC called up.

"Up here same," replied the DC. "You know what this place was, doncha?"

"Yeah. That's what I was thinking. Knocking shop, innit?"

"You know what I reckon? This was all done by a punter who didn't get his money's worth."

The PC nodded. "That crossed my mind. What about the gun? Do you believe that?"

"Let's see what's on them security cameras."

Finding no film though, nor any computers, they returned empty-handed to the station to write their reports. In the afternoon, the DC did manage to speak to the fireman, who was unable to be sure whether the armed man was tall or short, even white or black. "I was busy, yeah?" he excused himself. "I was dealing with a ruddy fire, wasn't I? And people was at risk. I had a lot on my mind. But he *definitely* had a gun. That is certain. I saw that clear enough."

No CCTV film, no victims, no proper witnesses. Nothing useful at all.

* * *

Would it be risky to ride over to the house? He'd be careful, of course. Neil reached for the holster, then changed his mind.

No, I really can't go everywhere carrying a gun. That would be paranoid. Everything will be fine. I'll just have a quick look and ride home again.

He freewheeled down to the park entrance at the bottom of Blenheim Road.

It was a pleasant evening. Birds sang and flew from tree to tree. Neil was reminded that life can be good. In the distance, traffic hummed on Finchley Road and Hendon Way. He pedalled gently through Osborne Park. Shaven-headed East European boys played football with enthusiastic shouts. At the café's outdoor tables, a few men and women – perhaps the children's parents – wrapped in their coats, smoked cigarettes and chatted over coffee or Coca-Cola. One of them, smiling or laughing at something, casually looked up as Neil passed. He caught Neil's eye. There was a puzzling moment of recognition.

It took Neil a moment to recall where he had seen the fellow before, but the man had already kicked back his chair, was moving towards him like a train and calling to someone inside the café. Then Neil remembered: the two giant gatekeepers in the garden after the fire. He began to pedal desperately, yet it seemed that this man could run as fast as he could cycle.

Neil rode furiously away from the café, across the grass, making for a footpath on the other side of the park. The man behind was still running but losing ground, one hand pressing a mobile phone against his ear. He urged the footballing boys to give chase too. Some at once leapt onto their own bicycles and, excitedly calling out in their own language, vigorously pursued him like a ferocious little swarm of wasps.

Now he heard a different sound behind him and glanced back to see a smart grey Mercedes box van, its wheels tearing at the earth and grass as it quickly drew closer. It managed to follow him along the footpath, audibly scraping bushes and fences to either side.

Reaching the road, Neil raced towards Hendon Way past unmoving lines of rush-hour traffic. His pursuer tried to force a way through, but cars edged out to stop this pushy van overtaking. The boys gave up their fun and stood watching with something like admiration as Neil rode straight through a red traffic light without a pause.

At last the van did overtake the waiting lines, ignoring the other drivers' indignant horns. He swerved hard in the direction Neil had taken, but naturally the van had to drive on the left of the divided highway. He could see Neil in the distance, riding fast on a sidewalk, unreachable on the other side of the road beyond a crash barrier and high mesh fence.

Neil pushed forward hard, glancing at the grey van which kept pace on the far side of the highway. The driver, gazing back, was on his phone.

Suddenly pursuer and pursued lost sight of each other. For Neil was pedalling feverishly onto the network of concrete pathways that lead pedestrians safely across the North Circular Road into Brent Cross shopping centre.

Above the North Circular Road and below the Brent Cross Flyover, suspended between the two, a busy roundabout hangs in a tangled web of grey concrete bridges, underpasses, on-ramps, off-ramps and slip roads. The van driver circled the roundabout, not once but twice, intently scanning every direction for a sight of the vanished bike. And suddenly he saw it, but could not follow, for Neil was moving rapidly along a slender footbridge.

Neil dared not guess whether he had shaken the van off. He rode quickly towards the shopping centre. Surely he would be safe in there. Double glass doors swung open automatically to let him inside.

Suddenly the traffic was all forgotten. For here was soft music, and all the innocent world gathered in peaceful communion, ten thousand people moving at their ease in broad aisles, beneath majestic domes and high curved ceilings. Most walked slowly between big window displays and bright familiar shops, as happy as if soma were seeping into the atmosphere. Some plate-glass corners were sprayed white in mock winter frost, and the first Christmas decorations had already appeared.

Young couples black and white sauntered hand in hand; women chattered about refreshments and toted a great burden of sturdy carrier bags; frail elders nodded amiably in their slower progress; whole families drifted sedately forward like galleons. Hasids in their hats and Sikhs in turbans brushed against one another amicably, Hindu women in saris and Muslim women in hijab, side by side, pushed pushchairs in which each gurgling toddler clasped a McDonald's red balloon. More troubled wanderers could sometimes be glimpsed, a lonely man or woman who has come not to buy, but to seek the companionship of the public.

The peaceful air was a little disturbed only by tribes of rowdy teens who, in the rival colours of their school uniforms, roamed the centre's wide spaces or clustered outside open-fronted fast-food eateries. Yet these young consumers were benignly tolerated.

Nervously Neil glanced all around, but no one seemed to notice him at all. At last he leaned the bike against a bench and sat down. Here he would rest and consider his situation. He wiped sweat from his head and face. The breath came in big sighs as he recovered himself. If he went back outside he might be recognised and pursued, especially if he went anywhere near his home. Yet he could not hide in here forever. For a moment, he rested his head in his hands. There would be no end to it, he realised; he could not live like this. He must find a solution.

Neil was mistaken in thinking he had not been noticed. On a bank of screens in the control room, every person in Brent Cross is being watched. Scores of unobtrusive cameras are swivelling, tracking individuals, focusing.

Security guards, some in blue-grey uniforms with epaulettes and metal buttons, others in plain dark suits with ID strapped to their sleeves, others in jeans and trainers and identifiable only by a spiral of wire heading to a single discreet earpiece, scrutinise the crowd like prison guards. There are plain-clothes police here too, mingling with contented shoppers, and uniformed police officers in pairs. There is more surveillance inside Brent Cross Shopping Centre than in any High Street.

Neil had already caught the attention of the Control Room. His offences were two-fold: he had brought a bicycle into the shopping centre, and he was an unkempt young man on his own. Now a mobile phone in the Control Room received a text, with a picture attachment: *U potrazi za ovog momka. Zovi me.* – Looking for this guy. Call me.

A security officer pressed Reply: *Zdravo. Da, ja sam ga vec vidim. Gde si?* – Hello. Yes, I see him already. Where are you?

He could simply have requested this young man to take the bike outside. But as a favour to a compatriot, he was happy to detain him.

The man was one of those in plain clothes. For a few seconds he stared fixedly at Neil, then walked rapidly towards him. "Excuse me, sir." He seized Neil's upper arm and raised him forcefully to a standing position as if to lead him away. "Security," he announced, holding out his badge for inspection.

"Hey!" protested Neil. "What is it? What's wrong?" he asked, perplexed – for this fellow, surely, had nothing to do with Liliana and Irina or the men. Neil did not recognise the security officer. Just another big East European.

"No bicycles allowed inside the centre, sir." He could not resist mentioning that.

Neil smiled with relief. "OK, OK – I'll take it out."

Yet the man did not release his grip. "And there have been complaints about you. We need to talk to you in private."

"Complaints? About *me*?" Neil half laughed, incredulous. "What kind of complaints?"

"Better not to discuss here." Still holding Neil's arm firmly, he spoke into a small microphone, rather too quietly, in Bosnian.

Neil did not understand the words, but he understood what was happening. It *was* something to do with Liliana and Irina.

He jabbed a knuckled finger sharply into the man's eye. As the hold on his arm loosened, Neil was on the bike and away, riding quickly through the mall.

Cameras swivelled and security guards, in uniform or plain clothes, began to run. Their earpieces buzzed, "Guy riding a bike on the Upper Mall. Assaulted security staff. Block all exits and detain him." Neil made a turn into the North Court and Food

Gallery, but saw guards ahead. He swerved back, past Boots on the right.

A roar of screams and yells was rising though Brent Cross. Hands and arms were thrust forward as helpful citizens eagerly tried to share in the drama, grabbing at Neil as he approached. His speed and reckless determination scattered them in the last moments, and he rode headlong through the wide entrance of John Lewis.

Inside the department store, Neil at once inhaled the heady air of Perfumery, where heavily made-up young women stood aside, amazed, to let him pass; he raced by glass cases in glittering Jewellery, past Haberdashery's rainbow-bright racks of coloured knitting wools, and among *petites* and *fuller figures* in Womenswear. A team of security staff danced in front, closing in, ready to seize him.

Suddenly Neil took a wild chance and pedalled onto the escalator, juddering down the moving metal steps. He emerged abruptly in the midst of fragile Chinaware, swerved between teacups and cruet dishes and dinner services to reach hot, brilliant Lighting. Clear pathways of white lino were laid from Electrical Appliances to Furnishing Fabrics, from Bedlinen to Bathroom Accessories. Just as suddenly, he was emerging again from John Lewis, cycling fast through the Lower Mall. Here no security men were deployed, since every one of them had rushed to the Upper Mall. Now all their earpieces rattled, "He's on the *Lower* Mall, *Lower* Mall, block all exits on the *Lower* Mall."

Neil spun around lifts and escalators outside Marks & Spencer, saw that the exit to the North Car Park was blocked. At Starbucks a score of coffee drinkers rose to their feet to watch excitedly. Some laughed, some screamed; some cheered and clapped. Through a wide open entrance into Fenwicks, Neil passed quickly through Cosmetics, into Handbags, looking frantically for a way out.

Ahead lay Kitchenware. Beyond the kettles and woks and espresso machines he glimpsed an unguarded glass door; manual, not automatic. Even as he approached, someone unwittingly held it open for him. Through it he rode straight from the shop into the liberating air, and towards the North Circular Road.

Osman sits in his van, high in a Brent Cross car park, listening intently to his phone. Now he learns that Neil has left the shopping centre. Quickly he spirals down the ramps through the car park hoping to intercept him. Indeed Neil is clearly within view, hurtling onto the North Circular Road, heading east. Once again, though, Neil is on the far side of the divided highway, moving against the stream of dense traffic. Osman tries to keep track of him.

"Zlatan," he yells into his phone, *"where are you? Come from Golders Green Road by North Circular. He is cycling straight towards you. Remember, don't kill him. Don't use your gun. OK? We don't want trouble."*

And so it is. Zlatan's Ford turns into the North Circular Road. Despite Osman's warning, on the passenger seat his handgun lies ready – just in case things go wrong. But everything is just as Osman said. A few hundred metres ahead, the Englishman rides towards him, staying close to the kerb. A few cars and trucks sound their horns and swerve, but the bike keeps coming. Zlatan laughs at the sight. Easy to simply knock him off his bike! Zlatan too keeps close to the kerb, ready to bump Neil's bicycle.

Neil notices the Ford in good time, though. To avoid it he suddenly swerves into the middle lane and passes it on the driver's side, slipping between the lines of oncoming traffic. A shouted conversation takes place in Bosnian.

Fuck! Did you see that. I nearly had him. The guy's a lunatic.

Zlatan, you idiot. He's passed you!

Where the fuck has he gone?

I'm beside him now – but on the wrong side of the road.

Do a U-turn at Golders Green Road, come back in this direction.

I can't get there quick enough, it's moving too slow here. But remember we want him alive. No shooting, OK?

He won't survive long anyway, riding a bike in this traffic.

Shit, the bastard's turning! Quick, Zlatan – go next left, and left again. Catch him at the junction.

Zlatan spins the Ford to the left and doubles back along a horribly shabby litter-strewn road. Osman is correct: after a few moments Zlatan sees the Englishman. He's pedalling crazily, sometimes on the pavement, sometimes weaving between decrepit vehicles large enough to transport a family with five or six children. To either side the houses are ill-kept, their paved frontages a mess of weeds, overflowing bins and abandoned supermarket trolleys. Zlatan follows hard behind.

Dowdy women, wearing unconvincing sheitels and tired dresses of pilled black fabric, stand chatting in the street with double buggies. Little boys with long peyess and tzitzis[1] play cheerfully alongside. They all stop and look up entranced as a cyclist races by, closely followed by a fast car. At first amused by the sight, they quickly grasp that it is not comic. But then, sometimes it seems that the whole world outside their own community is peopled by madmen, wild and raving.

In the distance ahead, glimpsed between two streets, the raised bowl and slender leaning arc of Wembley Stadium cuts across the sky.

When Neil reaches Golders Green Road, rush-hour jams wait beside Torah Treasures, Menachem's Butchers, Kosher Kingdom and others, in parades of small shops busy with hasidim. He cycles recklessly past the idling lines of cars.

For a few seconds, Zlatan fears he has lost the Englishman, stares about furiously, then catches sight of his quarry fleeing into a side road.

He puts his foot down hard, gaining on the bike, racing now through calm streets of well-kept detached and semi-detached houses. Large bow-fronted brick frontages stand a little above street level, looking onto handsome little rockeries and patches of lawn, each one a dignified distance from the next. Some are adorned with Ionic columns or plaster lions and cameos and cartouches, some too with black railings rising to gilded points.

---

[1] Sheitels [Yiddish]: wigs worn by observant Orthodox Jewish women. Peyess/peyot and tzitzis/tzitzit [Yiddish/Hebrew]: sidelocks and fringed smock worn by Orthodox Jewish men and boys.

Zlatan reaches out to touch his gun, pulls it closer. Here, he decides, no witnesses would interfere, though sometimes he passes little groups of Orthodox boys and young men who gawp at the chase in wonder. Older frummers[1] shake their heads and mutter dismissively, *These goyim, the things they get up to!*

Zlatan doesn't look at them, focusing only on his target. He doesn't even notice a little footpath between two houses. Down it, like a fish turning in water, with silvery ease the cyclist darts away and is gone.

Zlatan brakes sharply and gazes in disbelief. Yes, sure enough, the Englishman has completely vanished. Zlatan looks beyond the sign, *No Cycling*, to a metal barrier which blocks the path to vehicles.

On his phone, he sees his precise position as a small blue arrow on a Google map; he can even make out the alleyway itself. It's no more than a short path which leads directly to Finchley Road at Temple Fortune. What he does not know, and Google cannot tell him, is which way the Englishman will turn next.

Osman? He gave me the slip. He cut through to Finchley Road. Drive south, to Golders Green, I'll drive towards you, and together we'll have him.

But Osman is too far away. And Neil has already crossed Finchley Road, heading now towards the Heath, looking for somewhere that no one can follow.

Kenwood House is a fine and imposing mansion, designed by Robert Adam in the eighteenth century. With palatial elegance, and an immaculate cream façade, it stands above a rolling estate of park, lawns, woods and meadows abutting Hampstead Heath. Its picture galleries and original furnishings attract refined sightseers, and its tea rooms a more common crowd, many fresh from a walk on the Heath. The landscaped banks of its lake provide the setting for picnic concerts on summer evenings.

At sunset, all visitors must leave Kenwood; the gates to its

---

[1] Observant Orthodox Jews [Yiddish].

grounds are locked and the estate becomes eerily deserted, silent but for the movement of animals and the evening cry of gathering crows. Hidden in its woods, as daylight seeps away, Neil walks nervously, wheeling his bike between holly, sycamore, rowan and oak, glossy evergreen laurel and dark fir, the earth underfoot soft with decaying leaves. Here, surely, he cannot be found.

He pushes at last into a big field. He has no thought, nor any emotion. The space, the dusk and the distance are like a sort of medication, something to soothe the mind and the nerves. Crows swirl in hundreds around him, screaming, screaming like a whole orchestra on saxophone. They settle in every tree top, the branches interwoven like lace, fly up in dispute and ceaseless cacophony, swarming black shapes scattering and regrouping. He walks among them, crossing the field to a bench at the far end, well away from footpaths.

Neil would have liked to write the music of the crows' raw, cantankerous song, if he only knew how.

As he waited on the bench, night gradually hid the view. The big birds settled into restless, irascible slumber in their high colonies. There were other, obscure noises now, curious movements and unseen rustling, creatures that flew in the dark. Sometimes a sound like a bark could be heard, and always, the low, distant murmur of London's unceasing energy.

How much noisier than crows are human beings. Nowhere can we get away from our din, either near or far.

Eventually Neil knows that he must risk returning home. He's cold, hungry and tired. In darkness, Neil hoists his bike over the Kenwood fence and scrambles over, dropping down into the Heath. He pushes the cycle awkwardly forward on rough ground, unable to see the paths and tracks. Reaching Spaniards Road, he crosses quickly, and makes his way through Sandy Heath towards the lights of North End. The Bull and Bush pub is closing as he passes, the last drinkers and diners leaving with cheerful laughter. Avoiding them, he returns to the dark, following a bridleway across the West Heath, mud underfoot and overhung with branches. Then at last he must cycle again in the streets and to Blenheim Road.

Mrs Viktor looks out of her door as he arrives.

"A'right?" he asks casually. He leans his bike against the wall.

She nods. "Those young ladies – everything is good now?"

He smiles, says everything is fine with them now, shuts the door. Fearful of turning on the light, he creeps around in the dark. He eats a slice of bread, a piece of cheese, drinks milk from a carton. He collects together a few things, his passport, a razor and toothbrush, in case he has to make a quick escape. The rucksack full of money must be within reach. He walks around the flat gathering all that might identify him, payslips, statements, bills. These too he puts in the rucksack. He can't watch television tonight. He must remain alert and attentive. He lies down on his bed. He will stay dressed. And keep the gun beside him. He waits for something to happen, not knowing what it might be.

After an hour of tense, expectant silence, the sudden shriek of the phone almost throws him into the air with shock. But it's only Bernard calling.

* * *

Having taken the two previous days off for Rosh Hashanah, Bernard worked until late in the evening. He finished the day as exhausted as a boxer. As fellow citizens walked cheerfully through the area dressed for dinner or the theatre, Bernard strolled from the office in cool, refreshing air along the Strand, finally descending the steps of Charing Cross station.

At least there was no difficulty getting a seat at this hour. He picked up an abandoned Evening Standard and flicked through stories that no doubt would appear again in tomorrow's Telegraph. Too tired to continue, he let it fall to his lap. The lurching train rocked him into a slumber, from which he emerged at every station. As the train left the tunnel and stopped at Golders Green, with an uncomfortable start again he awoke, and wearily made his way down the station steps.

There in the entrance hall, something odd caught his eye.

Suddenly he was more alert. A notice, a simple sheet of A4 paper, had been taped to a tiled wall. The other passengers passed it with hardly a glance, or not even a glance. A few allowed their eyes to rest just a trifle longer on the words and picture.

While Bernard studied the poster, another man studied Bernard. When Bernard removed the poster from the wall and folded it into his pocket, the watcher turned the ignition key of a pizza delivery scooter and made ready to follow wherever Bernard might lead.

"Hello, ah, Neil." Bernard spoke the name as if no longer sure that it was correct. "Sorry to call at this hour."

"Hi Bernard, what's up?"

"Too late to phone?"

"No, no." Neil looked at the clock: eleven forty-three. In fact it was surprisingly late for a phone call from Bernard.

"Mm – well, I'm at Golders Green station. I've seen something *very* strange. A little *poster*. I've got it with me. Can I come round and show it to you?"

"What, you mean now? I'm just going to bed." A poster! The last thing Neil wanted tonight was to get drawn into Bernard's preoccupations; a planning application perhaps, the park café, litter, the wrongdoings of officialdom and the rest.

Bernard said, "It's got your picture on it."

Neil struggled to understand. "*My* picture? Really? That *is* weird." He told Bernard he didn't have the energy to deal with anything more today. "I'll look at it tomorrow," he said calmly. "G'night, Bernard – and thanks."

In all conscience, Bernard felt he could not leave it until tomorrow. He went home and kissed Elizabeth. He told her of his long, tiring day, and she told him of hers. Outside, the whine of a pizza delivery went unnoticed. They sat together for a little longer, and then, before going to bed, he announced, "I think I need a little walk, Liz, to help me relax." She approved.

He went only as far as 2 Blenheim Road, and on the way back home sent Neil a message: *I've put the poster through your door.*

Neil went straight downstairs and found the sheet of paper lying on the hall floor.

Across the top, in the centre, were the words **MISSING PERSON**. Below it was a large photograph of a man's face. The man was himself. Under the photograph were a few lines of text:

Our good friend and brother **Oleg Zhavoronkov** disappeared. We are **very worried** about him. We believe he is in **Golders Green area**. He suffer from **anxiety bipolar depression**. He need **medication and help** urgent. He speaks **very good English**, maybe **using English name** and maybe say he is English. If you seen him or know where to find, please To Call His Friends **In Confidence** and we pray you to let us know he is OK! Thank you with all our heart. God Bless You!

There's a mobile phone number. In the photograph, Neil sees, he's wearing Critchlow's uniform. He looks more closely. The picture was taken while he was waiting to see Liliana, on the second visit. He looks a bit of an idiot. And the more he thinks about it, that's what he has been.

12

Neil reached out to silence the alarm, astonished and abashed to awake fully dressed with a handgun weighing heavily on the duvet beside him. He covered it with a pillow. The rucksack, he pushed sheepishly under the bed. His vivid fears during this restless night were vanishing like mirages. Already they seemed absurd.

The only thing true and real was that he had to get ready for work. Yesterday's crazy ride inside Brent Cross; a race for his life along the North Circular; hiding in the dark at Kenwood! Was any of *that* real? In the bathroom he splashed cool water on his face. If those things actually did happen, he would *never* be able to go shopping at Brent Cross again! That thought made him smile. But then he remembered the two women sleeping in Limor's flat – he could not quite picture them. They too would soon awake to this real and unreal day. And the others, other women locked in other rooms, whom he did not know, invisible – yet they were horribly real for all that.

He quickly pulled on his clothes, glanced in the mirror, stepped into the living room. The *Missing Person* poster still lay on his dining table. For a moment he studied the picture of himself. The truth is, he assured himself breezily, no one would have noticed it. People have better things to think about. Most people. Anyway, Bernard has taken the poster down now. So, no problem.

Yet, suppose someone *had* seen it? One of his neighbours arriving at Golders Green station would have noticed it straight away. The people who do stop to look at a thing like this, are, of course, those who recognise the man in the picture. After all, Bernard stopped to look at it.

No, surely this will all blow over. Nothing will happen. Life will go on. Won't it?

He wheeled the bike into the street.

Before riding, Neil turned both ways, cautious, wondering who might be watching. Cold, damp air touched his face and moistened the pavements. A couple of squabbling magpies glided easily from branch to branch along Blenheim Road's curve of trees. It struck him that they, the birds, were at home here; they knew the neighbourhood, they courted and mated and reared their young in this insignificant London street. An odd, poignant emotion stirred, an awareness that he too called this place his home.

Still, better not go to Brent Cross again for a while.

As usual on a Friday, Neil was not on a regular round. Instead, today, he was given a small mahogany cabinet to take to a customer in the town of Deal, on the Kent coast.

Glad to be sent somewhere new, and happy to go to the seaside, he pictured girls in bikinis, sunbathers, skirts flipping in sea breezes. That was plain silly, he rebuked himself: the holiday season was long past. As he loaded the cabinet into the van, his phone rang.

"Mm – Neil, have you looked at that flyer yet?" he heard Bernard asking.

"Oh, that poster thing? Yeah, I saw it."

"Well, what's it about? Is it some kind of joke?"

That possible explanation had not occurred to Neil. "Yeah, I dunno. They got their pictures mixed up."

"What do you mean, *their* pictures? Who? What pictures?"

"Look, Bernard," Neil replied, "it's not important. What can I say? Their poster is rubbish. Sorry, I can't talk now, I'm loading the van."

"It sounds like you actually *know* who made this flyer," Bernard persisted.

"Why is it so important, Bernard? Best forget all about it. Anyway, I really *can't* talk now."

He crossed the river on Vauxhall Bridge, drove through

Kennington and Camberwell. As he passed Denmark Hill, he cast a thought to Joy-Bell. The last time he had passed this way, she was sitting in the passenger seat wearing a pretty Fifties-style dress. How simple all that life seemed, now. This time, he continued through New Cross, onto the A2 and then the M2, speeding across lush Kentish farm country. He turned at last for Deal on a route of lanes and fields and hedges down towards the sea.

He had already delivered the mahogany cabinet when the phone rang again. This had been one of the most enjoyable days for weeks. Deal's streets were narrow and on a charming small scale, but the town's waterfront stretched vastly wide and empty. He parked the van and walked to the pier. Waves pulled idly onto the beach, rattled across the pebbles and sank away. In summer this must be a respectable seaside resort, one of those good old British places that Stan Forrest would like. Today, though, there were no tourists at all, not an ice-cream cone nor a sunbather in sight. Something of a ghostly nautical spirit seemed re-awakened in the chilly air, as if long memories of seafaring could not be erased.

* * *

Afternoon sunshine through a closed window warmed the room pleasantly. The very air seemed sedated. A few microscopic dust particles, suddenly visible, floated slowly in bright beams, looking to Limor's eye like stars in a dazzling night, galaxies turning in a miniature universe. She sat idly at her desk, contemplative, a mint tea beside her laptop. Pale, vanishing wisps of steam, illuminated and silvery, curled from her glass. She scrolled through her email.

Limor savoured such tranquil moments. Yet she was troubled. Liliana's case was worse than she had first thought. Physically she was much recovered, and although an acute depression seemed to be passing, there were signs now of more entrenched problems. Perhaps they predated her bad experiences. But how could such a patient – an illegal immigrant without any ID – be referred for psychotherapy?

Whatever else happened, the girls must move out of her flat soon and stay somewhere else. Somewhere safe, where they would be cared-for. She could continue their therapy better that way. The relationship here was too intense. It encouraged fantasies.

Liliana's remarks about Jews were increasingly savage and irrational. Oddly, the more she recovered, the worse they became. There had been a rash of rages, accusations and delusions. Irina anxiously reported all Liliana's hissed theories: that Limor was one of the Jews behind the kidnappers, that she had secret, malign influence, that she was a parasite sapping their strength, that she was using them, wanted to drain their blood, steal their organs, poison them, was just in it for the money. Liliana had even told Irina that their only escape would be to kill Limor before she killed them.

Limor mused and wondered. Had Liliana *really* said those things? Well, why not? It was starting to look as if Liliana must always have been a very stupid and troubled girl. Which certainly did not mean one should not help her. Anyway, Liliana's fantasies were little different from those of respectable British politicians and journalists, actresses and academics, who accused her – Dr Limor Shalit or Sergeant Limor Shalit or any other Israeli – of the most bestial crimes a fervid mind can imagine. The press, the internet, were full of such ravings.

At the moment, Liliana was in the bedroom, asleep again. Irina rested in the sitting room, listening to Mozart's *Requiem*, which was, as Limor had proved, beneficial to mental well-being.

There was no email of interest. Limor opened her Twitter account. She clicked @Mentions, to see if anyone had addressed a tweet to her personally. She noted that she now had 457 followers. She pondered what clever thing she could say that might push it up to 460. However, all the clever observations by others seemed vain and ridiculous. She clicked to see who her new follower was, but it turned out to be someone trying to sell medical technology. In a way, she felt, it was cheating to count such people as followers. She ought to block them. She wondered how many *real* followers she had – people who *wanted* to hear her thoughts and comments. Followers! She hated the fascist word even more than Leaders.

Scrolling down, she noticed a re-tweet with the hashtag *#missing*, and it prompted her to wonder – had Liliana or Irina ever been reported missing? It was certainly possible, even likely.

Liliana, after all, had presumably vanished one day, one afternoon, months ago, and never again contacted any of her friends or family. She had once mentioned a boyfriend, she had mentioned a brother, and her mother. Yet she had never phoned any of them. Irina, too, had shied away from the subject of friends and family, and had not phoned home. "I am not ready," she explained, "either to tell anyone what happened, nor to say nothing about it."

Limor urgently wanted to do more than help these two Moldovans. It was intolerable that the people who had inflicted such damage on them were still at liberty, no doubt harming other women. The entire problem must be confronted, she raged inwardly.

Yet it was too large to contemplate. Limor visualised all the nations of the world as she had seen them on a globe at school, blurring and merging as she spun the sphere quickly round with her fingertips. In every European country, every African country, every Asian country, in the Americas and indeed in every single country on earth, there are women like these; and men.

Limor clicked *#missing*. Some tweets, she saw, were #missing the old days. Some, #missing u, #missing sex or #missing my kids. Some were about pets that had gone #missing. It surprised her though, that dozens, scores, of tweets mentioned #missing people.

Limor wondered about these people who disappear from view. They move away, beyond the limits of the circle, and lose touch altogether with their world. They must pass, she supposed, into some other world, a parallel existence with new friends, new neighbours. Some of the tweets had links, to pictures and websites. *Pray for our #missing brother* linked to a Facebook page.

She exclaimed aloud when she saw it. She leaned forward for a closer look. *Please 'like' this page, and help us find our missing friend and brother.*

More than seventy people had already clicked that they 'like' the page.

For several moments she wondered if something was wrong, if it mattered, and what to do.

Neil had just reached the café at the end of the pier on Deal beach. The wind made it hard to hear her clearly. He pressed the phone close.

Limor seemed to be saying she was uneasy about the girls. He missed a few words. That they must stay somewhere else. That he must not visit. He asked her to speak up.

"You won't believe what I saw," he heard.

"Not you as well!" he replied. "A poster?"

"A what? Poster? No. On Twitter." She did not sound happy about it.

"On Twitter?" He thought he must have misheard.

"A link to Facebook. A page about a missing brother. With *your* picture, Neil. The name is wrong. They ask everyone to pray for you and find you. Never mind the name. They look for *you.*"

When the call finished, Neil gazed from the end of the pier towards the bright seafront promenade, where his parked van looked like a miniature blue toy. At this distance from London, he could picture starting a fresh new life, here by the cold swell of the English Channel.

From men with guns there may be an escape. But from Facebook and Twitter, how could he get away? Straight away when he got home tonight he would delete his own Facebook. Click *Deactivate* and he would be no more. If only it were that easy! He looked into the swirling waves below.

He reflected that even a charming town like Deal – once a great military port, dirty and clamouring with fighting men and men from ships – must always have had prostitutes. Where he had hoped to see laughing bikini girls, there ragged daughters once offered themselves by the hour at a fair price. Today, they wait for calls in flats and rooms and whitewashed houses with sea views. *Escorts* and *masseuses*. Some – who knows? – may be prisoners.

He had heard people use the phrase, being a slave to one's desires. Sometimes he felt that way about himself. These girls are slaves to something even harder to escape: other people's desire. For money.

The capital's limits were crossed almost unnoticed, the first houses masquerading that they were in Kentish towns and villages. Beyond the hard shoulder of the A2, a few streets reached into pleasant fields and paddocks like threads of fungus fingering fine timber. Sometimes a row of bright suburban red tile roofs rose incongruously above country hedgerows and autumn foliage.

Neil did not notice the names, mere words quickly passed: Darenth, Wilmington, Foots Cray, Bexley. The closer he got to London, the more his mood darkened. The highway continued unswervingly into deeper, denser housing estates and urban neighbourhoods. Blackheath seemed an oasis of space and light, its church spire under a shifting clouded sky and a line of handsome Georgian houses small across the green, as if in a painting by a Turner or Constable.

That bastard Sanina met him as he pulled into the yard. "Mr Chapman, see me in my office," he instructed.

Probably all set to give me the sack for talking out of turn yesterday. Or it's a query about those missing clothes for the Ascot school. Or someone saw me driving with a passenger. Or somewhere off my round. Whatever, he's looking to get rid of me.

Strangely, Sanina stood politely to open the door to Neil, and shut it behind him. "Please sit down," he said with sombre considerateness.

It reminded Neil of the indulgences, the favourite last meal, offered to a man about to be executed. He waited warily for whatever criticism may come.

"Your request yesterday," continued Sanina.

"I apologise for that," said Neil.

"Well, I am willing to take these young women, if they don't mind." He lowered his voice so that it was barely audible. "I have plenty of space. But I have to discuss something personal with you. There are some things you need to know about me. In confidence, yes? The most strict confidence."

Now at last Neil learned the hold that the nasty little crook Darren had over Sanina. Yet Sanina's fearful shame seemed needless. If what he had told Neil was the whole story, Sanina was doing nothing illegal. It was hard to see why he was so scared of anyone finding out.

* * *

Elizabeth liked the atmosphere in Golders Green and Temple Fortune on a Friday afternoon, as the world prepared for Shabbat. Some might leave it late, and for all she knew there might be a Shabbat rush hour as the daylight began to dwindle. She preferred to leave the office early and have everything ready in good time.

The weekly pilgrimage to Isaac's for challah she especially savoured, finding a sort of joy even in parking the car, walking to the shop and waiting in line with other women. Always she met friends, people that she knew from shul. She liked the quick, comfortable greetings, a smile, sometimes a hasty kiss.

"How are *you?*"

"I'm *good!* How are *you?*"

"Busy, busy! Have a good yomtov?"

"*Lovely!* You?"

"*Yes!* Lovely!"

"Kids well?"

"Everyone's *fine!* You all OK?"

"We're all *fine!*"

"Well, shana tova! Good Shabbes!"
"Shana tova! Good Shabbes!"

Tonight she would bake sea bream in a savoury Provençal sauce of her own invention. There was a nice white wine to go with it, and a tarte Tatin for dessert, one of Bernard's favourites.

Poor Bernard was so bogged down with things. As well as his work, he was always trying to help other people. Yet where did it get him? He was so determined to do something for Hilda King.

Of course, the very first time they met she had seen his heart of gold shining. After spending hours preparing Hilda's case, Bernard would probably end up paying for her car repairs himself. That's just the kind of man he was.

As Elizabeth walked back to the car, the plaited loaves of challah warm in a carrier bag, she could not help feeling that, actually, all *was* well with the world. Her world, at least. Except, of course, for the things that were annoying Bernard. But even then, really... if one counted one's blessings.

* * *

Neil texted Limor at once. "Found somewhere for L and I. Call asap." Hardly a moment later his phone rang.

"How soon?" she asked.

"How soon can they get to Waterloo station?"

"A nice place? Someone good and kind, I hope, who will look after them?"

"Yes. Well, I... I don't know. I hope so. People who speak Romanian, anyway."

"Good. They need someone they can talk to. I'd like to meet them, obviously, to make sure it will all be OK."

Rush hour was at its impatient, irascible peak. As agreed, Neil bought tickets and waited by the escalators. Sanina quickly arrived, and the two men stood together awkwardly, perhaps father and son, the one in lumpish grey suit and Clarks' leather casuals, the other in black jeans, hooded sweatshirt and Converse plimsolls. They said nothing to each other. Neil found it quite unnerving even to see his hated manager outside work. This evening, each man knew he would discover something of the other's real life, and reveal something of his own.

There was a difficult question in the air: would they continue with Critchlow's rules of politeness and formality? For all his size and muscle, the bastard seemed a smaller, more pathetic creature than Neil had expected. And less of a bastard.

Huge departure boards beside them clattered constantly, the names of places on Critchlow's rounds flickering one after the other. Weybridge, Woking, Sunningdale, Surbiton, Guildford, Twickenham, Wimbledon. Announcements continued without pause as if in a bizarre bingo game, loudspeakers calling numbers above the din. Eighteen twelve, platform one, eighteen thirteen, platform fifteen, eighteen fifteen, platform thirteen, eighteen fifteen, platform sixteen, eighteen eighteen, platform eighteen.

Eventually Neil felt obliged to speak. "Uh, I'm wondering what made you change your mind."

"Yes, I did not want to do it," Sanina nodded, "but when I mentioned it at home…"

He left the sentence unfinished and Neil looked away. He tried to scan the passengers' faces rising up ceaselessly on the escalator from underground, merging into the mass already seething through Waterloo's vast, echoing concourse. Soon, among them would be Limor, Liliana and Irina. How could Liliana cope with such noise and confusion?

Not that it was truly a confusion. He admired the masterful order that hastened the crowds away, out of the city, funnelled each of these workers, every one clasping precious laptops and handbags and briefcases or bearing a smart little backpack, towards his or her platform, where punctual trains waited ready to depart, heavily laden, for London's satellite towns.

Suddenly Limor approached from the opposite direction. She had not brought the two Moldovans by tube after all. She arrived by taxi and led them a short distance through the station to their meeting place. Liliana seemed marvellously changed, still very thin, but healthier, stronger and walking properly, though she touched Irina's sleeve a little anxiously. Her expression, too, looked quite normal. Irina, also slightly nervous though she affected poise and confidence, remained close to Limor.

It was good to see that they were both wearing modest, sensible clothes of their own, everything the right size and attractive – jeans and light jackets, Liliana in a fitted V-neck sweater, Irina in a smart tee-shirt and cardigan, and low-heeled shoes. They even had inexpensive bracelets and necklaces and handbags. Both of them pulled little suitcases on wheels.

It was wonderful what Limor had done for them, and probably no one even knew the effort and expense it had cost her. He would offer to pay for all these things, and she, of course, would refuse to accept.

They look for all the world like ordinary young women.

And indeed that is exactly what they were.

Except, that they were unusually good-looking. A beautiful blonde and beautiful brunette side by side. God help him, he even experienced a certain physical pleasure in having them close to him.

He shook their hands rather formally. They appeared taken aback to meet him again.

For a moment, Irina did not release his hand. "Merci," she said.

Liliana, reserved and uncomfortable, answered in English with a cool "Hello."

They were even more cautious with Andrei Sanina, who followed Neil's example, shaking hands and greeting all three women politely in Romanian with a "Bună seara." He said a few more brief words to them, stiffly told them his name, and added that he knew about their troubles.

Neil murmured to Limor: "They are frightened."

"Liliana is fragile. Not suicidal. That phase has passed, I hope," she answered quietly. "I told them, I won't leave them with anyone until I am sure it will be all right."

"Good."

"But Liliana doesn't believe me. She doesn't trust me."

Suddenly Neil noticed the CCTV cameras everywhere. Who was watching? Who were they contacting?

"I'm not sure," Limor said now, "about leaving them with a man. Let's see how they are this evening."

Sanina led them towards the platform, his steps hastening towards a waiting train. Neil noticed that Liliana in particular eyed his manager with suspicion. It was understandable, he told himself.

On board, they forced a way through a warm crush of passengers who already occupied all seats and standing room. The train pulled out of Waterloo between brick walls bright with elaborate spray-painted tags, the logos of graffiti artists. The streetlights of busy South London high roads and terraced backstreets and estates of tower blocks gave way to the dark spaces of parks and commons, then black fields broken up with industrial estates and tracts of large detached houses.

As daylight faded, the train windows showed only reflections, the passengers inside the carriage dozing with arms folded, reading novels and free newspapers, many listening to headphones, some intent on crosswords and puzzles, or tapping out text messages. Every few minutes dozens of them stood and pushed to the doors as the train halted at small stations beside big, brightly lit car parks.

The two Moldovans, though, did not relax. Liliana's eyes darted around as if she feared whom she might see among the crowd. Her jaw was clenched tight. Neil wondered if anyone had explained that they would arrive in less than half an hour. If not, the train's gentle rattling on the rails might bring to mind real journeys to real places far away.

Irina reached out and touched Neil's arm. She came closer and murmured, "Qu'est-ce que je fais ici – What am I doing here? How did it happen?"

"Do you still call me a rapist?" he asked quietly.

"You also freed me from rapists, and I am grateful. But it was to satisfy you and men like you that I was captured."

He looked around to see if anyone could hear and understand them. "I only wanted a willing partner. This is not the place to talk."

"You know," she said sadly, "I thought I wanted to get back to normal life. I wanted to forget what happened. Now I feel normal life is gone forever. I will never get back to it. I just have to carry on like this."

Sanina's partner, Niki, waited to meet them, and the little group assembled by a ticket barrier for more introductions and handshakes. Niki greeted everyone with sincere politeness and heartfelt sympathy and kindness. For Liliana and Irina there was a special, tender understanding.

Niki was quite extraordinarily pretty, an artwork on whom they all gazed fascinated, a perfect human object.

No one could be blonder, with vanilla-pale skin and a bob of fine, smooth alabaster-white hair. A short fringe was angled artfully, a few dainty strands drifting across sculpted, smiling, boyish features, the teeth straight and white, the lips a pale rose-pink as delicate as petals, eyes snowy blue and eyelashes like tiny threads of silver.

A closely fitting red-check shirt of cotton poplin, with a pair of tight pale blue jeans, emphasised a body sleekly slender, shapely and sinuous, every movement exquisitely demure.

Niki was so effeminate that Neil feared for him living in this world. The bulky masculine ferocity of Sanina was calmed by the presence of this charming, androgynous young Russian. As Neil's glance caught his, in the brusque transport manager's face he found a mixture of embarrassment and glowing pride, as if to say, on the one hand, "Well – now you know all about me," and on the other, "Everything else may be yours, but this precious, beautiful thing is mine."

Neil wondered who did what to whom in their relationship. They appeared monstrously incompatible, a gorgeous moth partnered with a grotesque mastiff. Did the Romanian fuck the Russian, or the other way around? Or did they fuck each other? Or were they just good friends? Niki drove the three women, while Neil followed alone with Sanina. They cruised along pleasant, anonymous streets, well-lit and orderly, lined with trees and grass verges and driveways.

"I still don't understand about Darren," Neil said quietly. "Why keep it all a secret? Why are you struggling with this? Who cares what Darren knows? Bring it all out in the open. It's no crime to be gay."

"No? When I left Romania," Sanina replied softly, "it was a crime. I think they changed the law now. You are naïve. You ask these questions as if they need no answer," he said. "Here is the answer. If Darren shows anyone his photos, I will be ruined. It will destroy me. At work the men would not respect me. There will be no more promotion. I can never advance. I might lose the job because there is no respect."

"Or, you might be promoted *because* you're gay. Gay people help each other, don't they?"

"You think so?" Sanina pursed his lips and shook his head. "Gay is one thing. What's in these pictures is another. These are not nice photos. Neighbours will want me to move. Much worse, if anyone in my family finds out – my parents, my grandparents, my brothers and sisters, nephews and nieces, cousins – *none* of them will speak to me again. I will be reviled, an outcast, and perhaps even would be murdered."

Neil considered this for some minutes, unwilling to disagree. "Are they in Romania," he asked. "your family?"

"No, all in Germany and Austria and England. My brother and uncle are in Manchester."

"Can I ask, what did you do in Romania? Were you a transport manager?"

Sanina half smiled at the idea. "Farm," he replied simply. "Family farm."

"You were a farmer! Who's working on the farm now? Or did you sell it?"

Sanina gave a low, short laugh. "Sell it? Who to? No one has money and no one wants a farm. It is tiny, remote. And now we are in the European Union, it's not allowed to use a horse and cart on the public road, so – " To Neil's disbelieving expression he nodded, "Yes, it's true. Animal welfare laws from Europe. My parents, they could not afford a truck. The farm is abandoned now. Yes, like many Romanian farms."

The darkness seemed to make it possible to admit things, to talk intimately and make confessions. "I don't see how that guy Darren got these photos in the first place."

"I don't want to explain everything. You can work it out. I paid Darren and his friends for sex. I didn't know, but he took pictures. He sent me copies. Then he threatened me, first that I must find him a job at Critchlow's. I had no choice. And now, I have to let him run his little business of stealing."

"Wow! So, are you saying... no... that Darren is a rent boy? I can't believe it."

Sanina frowned. "Rent boy? That is a good expression. Yes, and Niki, too, he was like this when I found him. A boy for rent. I rented him by the hour, then by the day, then I bought him to keep. But he will not stay forever. He likes too much to go out and have fun."

They were driving through an ordinary modern estate. Neil peered out at small detached houses, geometrically arranged in identical patterns, each set back behind unfenced lawns, everything clean and comfortable, tidy and neatly-clipped, the lights on in front rooms and bedrooms.

"Christ! Well, Mr Sanina, you better go to the police. Blackmail, that's major, it's serious."

"What, and have it in the papers? What I do, what I like? For everyone to read?"

Sanina turned the car slowly into a drive and pulled up behind Niki. He looked across at his passenger. "A little English house with a little English garden in a little English town is the nearest any of us will ever get to paradise. There is nothing more to life than this. I don't want to lose it. I don't want to gamble anything. That is why I did not want the girls here. Yes, I feel sorry for them, but it is a risk for me. Anyway, it is done. It was Niki who said we must not refuse to help them. And he is right."

"Obviously I can't advise you, Mr Sanina, but all this secrecy and fear. In paradise? There are no secrets in heaven."

"It's OK, you can call me Andrei."

"OK."

"When we are back at work on Monday, we will act as before, and pretend this has not happened."

"I can deal with Darren for you," said Neil.

Sanina shook his head. "No, you can't. He is protected by the other men. They get money by selling to him. They need him to stay at Critchlow's. He needs me to be transport manager."

"Yes, I see. So it's impossible to remove Darren from the scene. Why not remove yourself? You could change your job."

"No, Darren would still have the images. It would be worth his while to find me and keep using them."

"I see, yeah." Neil shook his head. It appeared that Sanina's problem had no solution.

"Why am I telling you this? It is no one's business except mine. I want to ask you for something, very seriously," Sanina said. "Promise me to never discuss this, my home, my life, Niki, anything with anyone."

Neil remembered Pamela's angry voice on the day she threw him out. *You're not capable of keeping a promise, are you, Neil?*

"Don't worry," he said, "I won't talk about you at all. And, um, Mr Sanina, could you not tell anyone about me."

Niki excitedly insisted that they all drink a toast at once, to freedom and happiness, in tots of Moldovan brandy. Limor put her doubts aside and took a careful sip, while the others threw a whole glass of the scorching liquid into their mouths two or three times. Soon Andrei and Niki were in jocular mood, laughing and talking loudly.

On the dining table Niki began to place a feast of fried meats, ghiveci stew and polenta-like mămăligă, sour cream, salads and soft, salty bryndza cheese. Liliana and Irina laughed and clapped and embraced in their delight. Neil said to Limor, "Maybe food, too, is a therapy?" Liliana's happiness reached the point of tears, while Andrei Sanina announced "By the way, Niki is a professional chef," and filled wine glasses to the brim.

* * *

Neil and Limor travelled back together, by train and tube. Limor was pensive. Neil commented, "She seemed pretty happy there, didn't she?" That he meant Liliana was understood.

"Well, we'll see. Of course, I will visit them often. I did say, I will bring her back to health. So I must keep seeing her."

"I guess it's not ideal," he conceded.

"And what will they do all day?" Limor wondered aloud, "Watch television? Eat cholesterol and carbohydrates and drink alcohol? I fear Liliana can move quickly from starving to overeating."

"At least Niki and Sanina aren't interested in women."

"We need a better solution," she said. "We'll keep looking." At Chalk Farm station, she quickly touched Neil's lips with hers and said goodnight. "Call me tomorrow."

Neil continued to Golders Green, reluctant to arrive for fear of any new problems at home. It had been a pleasant day and an extraordinary evening.

To his horror, even before he reached the exit barrier he could see that the MISSING PERSON poster on the station wall had reappeared. As he approached he saw that the picture was not of himself. It was Liliana.

He walked quickly and stared with heart pounding. The picture was a better likeness than the one he had been shown in the house. You could see how emaciated she had become. Again and again he read the words, trying to make sense of them.

MISSING PERSON

Name **Liliana Petreanu**, 20 years, female. Height 1m 67cm. **Live-in domestic worker** of Moldova nationality. She does not speak English and has become separated from her employer. Her employer is very concerned about her safety and for her to avoid any breach of UK immigration regulations. Substantial **reward** for information to reunite her with her employer. To claim reward, Please send information to her employer.

There's no contact name, no phone number, not even a mobile, only a Hotmail address. He grabbed at the paper, ripping it down, and walked briskly from the station with the poster in his hand. A pizza delivery man, watching, turned the ignition and moved away, keeping his distance.

* * *

Fine rain was blowing in gusts as a grey Mercedes box van without lights cruised slowly up Blenheim Road in the early hours of the morning. It paused briefly, the door sliding open to let out a man in jeans, dark sweatshirt and black trainers. He carried a sledgehammer. At the end of the road, the van turned right, and right again into the Kilnmeadows Estate. It slowed beside a row of lock-up garages. Two more men jumped out. One carried some empty plastic beer crates. He ran to a wall and, standing on the crates, peered over. He took a torch from his jacket and scanned the poky gardens and back walls of terraced houses. Speaking quietly to the other, he shone the light quickly along brickwork, windows, shabby little rear extensions, small greenhouses, fences, toolsheds.

Neil wasted a moment wondering what had happened and what time it was. He lay in the darkness and tried to think. Ceiling collapsed? A bomb? Two in the morning? Three? In one instant more he understood.

The house door had been smashed open, and now, with an immense crash, the door of his own flat was giving way to a hammer blow.

Already fully dressed, in frantic haste he leapt up, grabbed the pistol which lay beside him on the bed, pushed the bedroom window open and climbed out. He jumped onto the flat roof of the kitchen extension below.

Damn! Forgot the rucksack! They'll find the money and ID.

Almost every house in Blenheim Road has a single-storey rear extension like this. It is easy to run along them, from one flat roof to the next. That's what Neil expected to do, and so escape to safety. Instead, a dazzling security light on the back of the house, turned on automatically by his presence, shone down on him like a spotlight. It illuminated the falling rain like a shimmering curtain, and the edges of its silvery brightness reached across the back garden. There he saw, among the roses and hydrangeas, a man raising a handgun, taking aim – at him.

In fear Neil ran fast onto the neighbour's rear extension, jumped onto a shed roof and down into a muddy flower bed, concealed by bushes and a low garden fence.

He heard a voice from the house and looked back. The security light showed a man climbing out of the bedroom window from which he himself had just climbed. He too held a handgun, and now stood uncertainly on the roof of the extension, gazing intently.

Neil recognised the patterned hair and the tattoo on his face. This was one of the half-dressed brutes he had glimpsed through an open door, assaulting a woman. In memory he saw again, even clearer than before, the forced pleasure in her frightened eyes.

He must wait no longer. He stood among the flowers with his feet parted exactly as Winston had shown him, grasped the pistol with both hands and aimed carefully with arms held straight ahead. His right index finger gently touched the metal trigger and slowly pressed, feeling its resistance. At first he pulled not quite hard enough, then, after a second of panic, felt the trigger begin its movement.

With astonishing abruptness the act was done. The sudden volume of noise and smack of recoil shocked him. He had not realised it would be like that. Neil's first bullet had left his gun and passed straight through the sweet and tender red flesh of a young man, splashing its dark moisture to either side.

Gratified that he had managed to hit his target, Neil watched entranced as the man's mouth opened to release a cry of horror that reminded him of Liliana's own horrible, unrestrained shriek a few nights ago. Some lights went on in nearby houses. Close by, a dog began to bark furiously.

The man staggered to the edge of the flat roof as if struggling with an impossible burden, and flapped his arms in agony like an ungainly, injured bird, dropping his gun.

He tumbled forward into the unsupporting night air, descending fast, the arms and legs oddly purposeless. The strange sound as his head and body landed on the ground, an inanimate cracking thud, came as another shock to Neil.

The bigger shock was that he did not find it revolting. Until this moment Neil had considered himself squeamish. Winston had been right, but wrong. Yes, as Winston had warned, all in a single instant Neil did feel a torrent of nauseous pity for this fellow human creature, his wife, his children and his parents in a foreign land, and for the tragedy of life's awful emptiness. Into his mind darted a sharp awareness of the wretched, pointless journey from some God-forsaken place in the Balkans to this degraded, violent end in a London suburb. He did not know whether the man was hurt slightly, badly or mortally, or was already quite dead, yet Neil was surprised to feel a wrench of sorrow for all the hopes of childhood that reach their sad, disappointing maturity.

In the same instant – *I must tell Winston* – Neil felt a great, smiling happiness sweep through him. He had dealt as harshly as he truly wished with one of these men. By giving this bully a slap, a proper slap that knocked him for six, or to Kingdom Come, something was fulfilled, correct and concluded.

In the very next instant came the sudden clap of a second shot, painfully loud. He felt the air move as something skimmed past his head and shattered the slats of the fence behind. He could not calculate where it had come from. Then a ghostly figure could be seen half-hidden at the end of the garden, moving among black foliage, a gun held up. Neil slowly raised his pistol, aimed and pulled the trigger. The same stinging sound sang out, at once followed by a strange gasp and a guttural exclamation. Neil saw that this time he had hit only the edge of the moving figure – an arm, a shoulder, an elbow, he could not tell – and had given his position away. The figure began to move in his direction. Further away, other dogs joined the barking.

Now another shot was fired, louder than before and from quite a different direction. Neil first crouched down among the bushes and shrubs, now knelt, now lay flat on the wet soil, staring around, trying to see more clearly among the shadows and shafts of light. It seemed another gunman was in the garden. Yet surely it was the ghostly figure – whose arm he had clipped, who was moving towards him – who cried out now and seemed to lean suddenly sideways, toppling to the ground.

Confused, Neil raised himself and gazed around. Had two of the men shot each other? In the beam of the security lights, surrounded by its deep well of rain and darkness, he could not understand what was happening.

There was movement at the far end of the garden, someone running, breaking twigs underfoot.

And now a fifth shot – from the house, it seemed – reverberated. A man's voice yelled, there were sounds among the bushes, crashing through plants, breaking glass, indistinct shouts, before complete silence fell again. After a few moments of stillness, the security lights clicked off. Neil could not discern anything, and waited, crouching, in his flower bed.

From the house a voice called "Neil!" into the darkness.

Neil paused, uncertain, making no reply. How did they know his name?

"Are you all right, Neil?" called the voice this time. That sounded like his landlord, his neighbour, László Viktor.

"Mr Viktor?" he called, afraid of giving his position away.

"Is this your Russians?"

"Yes."

"We have them all, I think."

"Was that you? Did you shoot them?"

"Come out. It's safe now."

László Viktor, wearing nothing more than immaculate striped cotton pyjamas and soft bedroom slippers, stood at the back door casually holding a long, heavy rifle, its scarred wooden stock marked with strange insignia and badges. He seemed quite untroubled by what he had done. "And you, young man," he said cheerfully, "you took one out. Good work. Very good. That one, by the lawn, is yours. He is finished. Pah! Bandits! Rapists! Russian gangsters! Cowards! This gun has shot so many of them," he added, with bitter satisfaction.

"That your gun?"

"Yes, my M44! A trusty comrade! But I didn't know *you* had a gun. That is a big surprise."

"Should we take a look at these guys? Try to help them?" Neil suggested.

"No, no, we should not touch them," warned Mr Viktor. "Anyway, you must leave here immediately, straight away now at once. That is the most urgent. Neil, very seriously, say nothing to anyone about this." Turning, he called into the kitchen in English. "Zsuzsanna! Call 999! Ask for police and ambulance. Tell them I have shot some armed burglars who broke into the house. Tell them I have the licence for the gun. Tell them we are all OK but the burglars are hurt bad. And this time," he grinned, "I think the police will come."

"Oh, my God, yes – the police! What have I done? And my bag!" Neil remembered. "Can I get my rucksack?"

"Yes, yes, but be quick," said Mr Viktor, "and take off your shoes first! Hurry!"

"Mr Viktor, don't tell anyone my name. Say you don't know me. Or say I'm a foreign student. Say my name is... say it's Oleg Zhavoronkov."

Of course, several neighbours had called the police already. A whole orchestra of sirens could be heard approaching through the Golders Green night.

13

Elizabeth stared confused into the darkness of the room. "What *time* is it? Don't go down, Bernard," she cautioned, "look out of the window, see who it is."

He lifted one edge of the curtain. The roadway and front gardens of Kenilworth Road, softly lit by yellow streetlights, were silent and at peace. Thin rain fell from dark, quickly moving clouds. He saw no one. Nevertheless, someone had certainly rung the bell. He wrapped his dressing gown around and went downstairs.

Elizabeth listened as the front door opened and closed, and low, male voices spoke urgently in the hall. At last, curiosity forced her to leave the bed and peer down from the top of the stairs. "Bernard?" she called quietly.

"It's that chap Neil," Bernard called up.

She was outraged. "Now what?" she exclaimed.

"Problem," he answered.

* * *

"Can I come in? I must explain about that poster."

"No, I'm sorry, it'll have to wait, Neil. You do realise you woke us up? You look dreadful. Have you been fighting, or something? You've got mud on you. Are you drunk?"

"It's a matter of life and death. I'm really not kidding."

"No," repeated Bernard flatly, "it's the middle of the night. I'm really not – "

"Sorry, no, I – "

"And look, Neil, it's Shabbat! I think I did ask that people please not disturb us on Shabbat." Bernard knew that he had definitely mentioned this to Neil. "Just go home, go to bed, sleep it off. Call me tomorrow night. Or some other day."

"Sorry, I forgot about Shabbat. What does your religion say about helping someone who's being kept a prisoner? A slave? Or is Shabbat more important?"

Until that moment, it had been a lovely evening. Elizabeth had lit the candles, Ruth standing beside her to recite the words. Ruth could be so sweet sometimes. And she had that clever, dark, vivacious look Bernard so admired, full of eager intelligence. Friday night had passed with its familiar blessings, for challah and wine, for his child and his wife. Amen!

A good wife who can find![1] Strangely, or so Bernard suspected, most men do manage to find one. *And nothing shall he lack.* Bless and be blessed. It helped that the sea bream in Provençal sauce was succulent and the tarte Tatin richly sweet and tasty.

At the Shabbat table he resolutely put criminals and criminal trials, witness statements and judges' comments quite out of his mind. Nor could any residents' forums, or meetings of KOBRA or the Federation of Residents, or council planning committees come between him and his family. Instead he enjoyed the simple delight of eating and singing together and an ineffable *shalom bayit* – peace in the home.

When they left the table, it's true, the world did return a little into their thoughts. There could be no television, of course (although Ruth slipped away to watch it in her room). Bernard liked above everything – especially on a Friday night – just to be with his own dear Liz, within the walls of their own home.

Bernard asked him in. Neil took off his wet hoodie and his shoes and sank exhausted into the sofa. He put the rucksack on the floor beside him and ran an anxious hand over his face and head. He noticed dirty leaves on his jeans, but dared not brush them onto Bernard's pristine upholstery.

Bernard pulled a chair close and the two men spoke quietly

---

[1] From *Eshet Chayil* (A Woman of Worth, Proverbs 31:10-31).

together. Astonished, Bernard listened intently to Neil's story. The girl, her note, the men, the shootings. He felt the familiar sensations, at the top of his chest, across his stomach, warning that he must remain calm. He feared he was becoming flushed. Soon he had to wipe beads of sweat from his temples.

Grimly he responded, "Obviously you can't stay here, Neil. Think about it. I have a daughter, a wife. You're putting them at risk. I implore you to go to the police. It's the wisest course. Tell them about these people. I'll go with you if you like."

"No, that wouldn't help." Neil smiled faintly and shook his head at such a foolish suggestion. "They'd think I was some kind of nut. And even supposing they believed me, they couldn't do anything about it. These guys would still be after me. Did you hear the shooting? Must've woken everyone in Golders Green."

"No, I didn't hear a thing," answered Bernard honestly. "Who would have thought it? Gunshots in Golders Green!" Then, "You must need a cup of tea or something."

"Love a whisky, if you've got any."

Bernard went to a cabinet and poured whisky into two glasses, one with twice as much as the other. He handed the larger of the two to Neil but emptied his own glass in one gulp and began to pace around the room. "At least you could have shown the police Liliana's note. Then your conscience would be clear."

Neil blew out a deep sigh. He explained once again – "Though I'm sure you know this, Bernard, being as you're a solicitor" – that he would immediately have been charged with the crime of paying for sex with a trafficked woman.

Bernard stopped moving and stared at him. "Neil, you prize idiot! Are you talking about the Policing and Crime Bill? That hasn't become law yet! Sorry, my poor, dear chap," Bernard declared with exasperation and pity, "but you've been a complete fool! You've got yourself into the most terrible trouble for absolutely nothing. And now me too, possibly. Even when it does become law," he added darkly, "you surely don't think paying for sex will be considered as serious as the other crimes you've just committed?"

Neil sipped his drink and looked a little shamefaced. "What other crimes?"

"Well, now," Bernard began, raising his eyes to heaven, "there's the unauthorised possession of a firearm, possession of a firearm with intent to endanger life, grievous bodily harm, attempted murder, maybe even murder! I'd try and get that reduced to manslaughter, if I were you. And – oh, God! – it wasn't you, was it, who started that fire in Finchley Road? Are you the mystery gunman arsonist they're looking for?"

Neil took a long deep breath and made a pained expression. After a moment he said only, "You know the most incredible thing about the whole experience, for me? It's Mr Viktor. Will he be charged with something?"

"Certainly he will. No doubt he's in custody already. Want to know the most incredible thing for *me*? It's *you*, Neil. I would never have guessed what a total bloody lunatic you are. Though I suppose it's even *more* incredible that women were being imprisoned and tortured right around the corner from my own house. That really is, well, staggering."

"Actually, I'm not quite the idiot you think," Neil said, "because listen: at the moment, no one knows I committed any offences. No one knows anything about me at all. No one knows my name. Hopefully they never will. But if I'd gone to the police, well, obviously they *would* know about me. I'd be in the nick by now, accused of paying forty quid to get laid."

Bernard squirmed with distaste and gestured that they should keep their voices down. "Look, I keep telling you," he said, "paying for sex isn't an offence – yet."

"Anyway, there's an even better reason not to tell them." Neil recounted his fears of what would happen to Liliana at the hands of the authorities.

"Mm – well, I'm sorry to say you're right," Bernard admitted. "The Home Office probably *would* keep her in some ghastly detention centre, then deport her back to Moldova. The police might well charge her with some offence. Or, quite possibly, leave her at the mercy of her captors."

Elizabeth could be heard coming downstairs. "Don't tell her

all the gory details," Bernard murmured. She appeared at the sitting room door in her dressing gown. "What on earth's going on?"

Bernard led her away, into the kitchen. Neil was left alone, but in the quiet of the night could hear their whispered exchange.

"Mm – well, ah, Neil has been involved in a very serious incident."

"What kind of incident?"

"Mm – well, a *violent* incident. Police have been called to his house."

"I said he was trouble. Didn't I, Bernard? Didn't I say he was trouble? Are you all right? You don't look well."

"He's *not* trouble," Neil heard Bernard say, "he's *in* trouble – that's different. It's not his fault. He tried to do the right thing, to help some people, and it turned nasty. It's a long story, but he's afraid to go home."

"And I still say he's trouble. I don't want him staying in the house. What if the police come *here*? This is exactly what you don't need. Hasn't he got friends he can go to?"

"Yes, but not round here. How could he get to them at this hour?"

"So give him the money for a taxi!"

"Go back to bed, Liz. I'll be up soon."

Returning alone to the sitting room, Bernard said, "My God, it's nearly morning."

The quiet was disturbed by a helicopter. Soon the air was thumping as it hovered closely overhead.

"I expect they're looking for someone," Bernard said thoughtfully.

"Yeah."

"You need to get cleaned up. We'll put your clothes in the machine. I expect my son has something you could wear. And, ah... Liz and Ruth and I will be going to synagogue in the morning." He was thinking that he must do everything as normal.

"All right." Neil's fatigue was becoming too much for him. He longed to lie down and rest.

"After lunch," said Bernard, "we'll try to find somewhere for you. By the way, the Jewish religion has plenty to say about hostages and captives. In fact, Judaism's all about freedom from slavery. That's our story."

"Oh, yeah?"

"Yup. All captives must be redeemed. That means, buy them back. Did you think about paying for Liliana's freedom? Buying her from the kidnappers, if necessary?"

Neil snorted. "What, on my wages? Anyway, there were at least six other women in there, Bernard. Whose job is it to pay for *their* freedom? Each one prob'ly cost thousands. Anyway, I doubt if they're for sale. In any case, the idea is horrible."

"Yah, I s'pose."

"Bernard, for such a bright guy, you're so naïve. Everyone knows nice-looking women are bought and sold and shipped around the world like truck-loads of furniture or cheap clothes or something. Women like this aren't just captives – they're livestock. They're an industry. Buying them all would be impossible. And it would make matters worse. You'd become another customer."

"Well, yuh, mm – I do take your point," Bernard nodded, "though 'livestock' may be slightly exaggerated. As always," he muttered peevishly, "what was needed was some attempt to enforce *existing* laws. But Neil," he queried, "aren't *you* the naïve one? A punter who didn't realise what he was buying?"

Neil shrugged indifferently. "OK, that's true. But how *could* I know? I'm tired, and I don't know what to do next. Can you help me?"

"Mm – so, ah, where is this, ah, this gun of yours, now? Did you hide it somewhere safe?"

Wearily Neil nodded towards the bag at his feet.

"You brought it *into our house?*" Bernard stared in horror. "God, she's right, you *are* trouble."

* * *

László Viktor was indeed in custody, snoring as he slept soundly on a built-in wooden bench, his head a couple of inches from a soiled metal toilet. The case was investigated by a detective sergeant, who asked a police constable to do the leg-work.

The PC already had most of the facts. He had been in the first police car to make its noisy arrival outside 2 Blenheim Road in the middle of the night. Mr Viktor was standing by the front door in pyjamas, dressing gown and slippers.

As officers leapt from the car, he greeted them with an amiable wave and a knowing smile. "Ah, so if we want police to come, we have to shoot someone first! Ha ha!"

An officer replied with a shout: "Put the gun down, sir, put the gun down!"

"Here," László shrugged, holding out the rifle harmlessly "you can take it."

"No, sir!" shouted the constable, "Drop it and step back."

László at once obeyed, and several police officers approached warily.

"Three of them are shot," László told them cheerfully, "you'll find them in the garden. But a fourth one ran off. He's armed with a pistol. I think he is hiding in neighbours' gardens."

A helicopter was scrambled to look for the fourth man. More police cars screamed along Finchley Road and turned into Blenheim Road, pursued by ambulances.

Soon the narrow street of little terraced houses was illuminated by throbbing blue lights like a nightclub dance-floor, and faces peered fascinated from every window. They saw László Viktor being put in a police car and driven away at speed.

* * *

After the Kassin family left for synagogue, Neil spent a while in their bathroom. He felt that the waters of a hot shower somehow purified him. Afterwards he rested in the unused bedroom of the grown-up son, Gideon.

Wrapped in a thick white towel, he sat on the side of Gideon's bed without any clear thought. There were tattered posters of folk-rock bands on the walls and an acoustic guitar leaning in one corner. On a desk stood a sleek black computer monitor. Shelves in the alcoves were crammed with Jewish religious books, books about Israel's history and Middle East politics.

The Hebrew lettering reminded him of Limor. She alone understood how he felt about helping Liliana and Irina. She probably knew, too, what it was to fire a bullet into another human being.

He picked up his phone and texted her. Whom else in the whole world could he tell?

He borrowed a clean white shirt and dark trousers from Gideon's wardrobe, then lay back on the bedcover and stared at the plain white ceiling. Like a screen it showed vivid rememberings as if the events of the night had taken place under arc lights. His eyes itched with sleeplessness.

Voices tugged him back from dreams. The Kassins were arriving home from synagogue. Neil sat up and saw that he had received a text from Limor.

On the door came a gentle tap. Bernard looked in with a wry smile. Neil could tell he was forcing himself to be friendly. There must have been a difficult conversation between Bernard and Elizabeth, and, even more so, Ruth, about their unexpected guest.

"Want any lunch? You'll have to put up with us making blessings."

Neil said he would rather rest, if no one minded. "Was it a nice service?" he asked awkwardly. "Is there, like, a sermon, prayers, singing, reading the Bible and stuff?"

"Yup," Bernard nodded. "And after the service, I got chatting to someone. A couple of friends, neighbours. Simon and Penny. I told them, ah, about your plight. Your situation."

"Why? Why did you mention it? I wish you hadn't."

Bernard closed the door and lowered his voice. "Don't worry, I didn't tell them the whole story. In fact, I didn't tell them anything. I only said you needed to lie low for a while."

Neil could not see where Bernard was heading. "You didn't tell them why?"

"Mm – ah, I only said you had landed yourself in some very hot water."

"But they must have asked you a bit more about it?"

Bernard bit his lip. "No. Well, yes they did – but I sort of – I told them you'd fallen out with a rather unpleasant chap about his girlfriend and he's after your blood."

Neil stared at him silently for a moment. "That's it?"

"Yes. That's it. I told them a little fib. Well, I lied to them. And I lied to my wife. And my daughter. Of course, I couldn't tell them the truth of it, could I? Look, Neil, I'm not condemning you for seeing a prostitute. It's the sort of stupid mistake anyone could make, but –"

"Have you, ever?"

"No, I haven't. Didn't you feel that you might be doing wrong, going to a prostitute?"

"'Prostitute' *sounds* wrong, doesn't it? But I've never thought of women who do that as in any way *prostituted*. For me they were like – just willing girls, basically. Willing to do it for money."

"Well, I couldn't possibly go to one," Bernard said. "Not that I would have the need; I am very happily married, thank God. Even if I weren't, frankly I can't even imagine it. I *always* felt, the important thing is not to do anything that would make my community or my parents ashamed of me."

"Community! Community isn't my thing. I haven't got a 'community'. No one round here knows me. And my father is dead, my mother has mental problems."

"Still, I'd never do that, no matter how frustrated I became. I would feel sullied by it."

"Don't say what you would or wouldn't do, until you've been in that situation. Walk a mile in another man's shoes."

A sceptical eyebrow showed what Bernard thought of such airy phrases. "As I said, I'm not condemning you for it. Anyway, Penny suggested – well, the thing is, they have a place in France. Needs a lot of work doing, modernising and all that. Are you a

270   *Andrew Sanger*

practical type? How's your French?"

Now Neil saw clearly.

"Penny and Simon would like to meet you to talk about it," added Bernard. "Which could be tricky. Just leaving this house could be risky."

Neil shook his head sharply. "Nice idea, Bernard, and it's very kind of them. But it's Liliana and Irina who need help, not me. And they can't go anywhere. For a start, they have no papers. I'm not going to run off while they're still in trouble."

"Of course!" Bernard's disappointment was plain. "How stupid of me! Never mind. Have to think of something else."

"But if you know anywhere to get false papers..."

Bernard smiled nervously and held up a warning hand. "No, no, no. I wouldn't even consider it. It's a serious crime! Please don't ask. I'm already putting my whole career at risk, my livelihood."

"Already? I don't see that. What have *you* done wrong?" quizzed Neil.

"Are you kidding? Section 1 of the Firearms Act. And I'm an accessory to everything you've told me. I shouldn't even be talking to you." He grimaced painfully and took a deep breath, "I don't think breaking the law is the best way forward – for either of us."

"Don't you? Seriously, they need new ID," Neil insisted. "There's no alternative."

Bernard laughed. Perhaps he really thought Neil was joking. "Shall I get you up for tea, later?"

* * *

During the afternoon, the police constable reported to the detective sergeant, and the two men frowned in puzzlement and uncertainty.

On the desk in front of them lay the *Missing Person* poster found in the upstairs flat. This, they considered, could be important.

"So, someone called Oleg Zhavoronkov is missing. He is

wanted. So what? Might be irrelevant."

"Suspect confirms the picture is his upstairs tenant. Neighbours agree."

"You called the number. And?"

"Number not in service," answered the PC.

The DS pressed his lips together. "Not burglars, are they? Looks like a gang thing. Or drugs."

"Nah, doubt it," the PC shook his head emphatically. "Our suspect Viktor is very respectable, law-abiding. He's a pensioner. In his seventies. He's fully ID'd. Car, TV licence, council tax, all correct. Popular with neighbours. Distinguished war record."

"Distinguished war record! That's all what we bloody need." The DS gritted his teeth and thought things over. He tutted with irritation. "Respectable pensioner with a firearm? I doubt it."

"Sarge, suspect's got a licence for the rifle," revealed the PC. "Keeps it in a gun safe. It's pre-War, covered by the Act. All totally legit."

"What does he say went on? Self-defence?"

"He says, crashing noises wakes him and his wife, and he hears voices in the house. So he's grabbed his gun."

"How could he grab the gun if it's in a gun safe?"

"Safe's by the bed, Sarge. He keeps the key under his mattress. Next thing is, he says, there's two armed men coming through the door. So he's gone out and confronted them, gave chase after 'em, and they've smashed their way upstairs and jumped out the window."

"Why didn't they go back out the front door, like normal people?"

"I don't know, Sarge. The suspect says he was trying to effect a citizen's arrest."

"That's a good one," the DS smiled. "I can't see this old feller running up a flight of stairs. Any evidence?"

"Well, we did get two sets of shoe prints off the windowsill."

"He didn't have no need to shoot them, then, did he? If they was running away? *That's* not self-defence."

"No, you see what's happened, Sarge, he's run back

downstairs and he's gone to confront them in the back garden. But he says they started shooting at him. The neighbours all agree, the first shots came from the garden. Looks like shots was fired at the suspect and he's just returned fire."

"So you saying the old gent has seriously wounded three fit young blokes all armed with pistols? But somehow he gets out of it without a scratch, while still wearing his pyjamas?"

"Well, yes, that *is* how it looks. Except," said the PC, "it *wasn't* the suspect shot all of 'em. What it looks like, is one of the gang has shot one of the others, and he's cleared off. And that fits with the Viktor's account, see? He says there was four intruders, two in the house, two in the garden, and one of them has ran off. Ballistics verify there was at least four men, all with different weapons. One's took a lethal hit."

"What about the two in hospital? What's their angle on it?"

"One of 'em's unconscious and in a bad way. The other one won't talk, Sarge," answered the PC. "Not a single word. No ID, won't give no name. Tried 'im with Russian, Albanian, Serbian, Romanian, Polish, you name it. No response."

The DS persisted, "What about the upstairs tenant? Oleg. Has he turned up?"

"No. Our Mr Viktor says the tenant ain't called Oleg. He's English, young feller, comes and goes as he pleases. It's just an informal thing, like. No tenancy agreement or nothing. Pays cash. Viktor only knows his first name, which is Ollie. He says he's a student. Only no one's seen him for quite a while. Neighbours say he rides a bike, but they don't know nothing else about him. We gave the upstairs a spin, but apart from a bit of cannabis, nothing at all. Dusted all the prints, nothing known. Absolutely nothing to ID him. No paperwork. Apart from that, typical single man's place. Story hangs together and it rings true, Sarge. And Viktor's missus backs him up on everything."

"So what's this poster?"

"I've got a theory, if you want to hear it."

"I've got a theory too. This tenant guy Ollie isn't English at all. He's really called Oleg. He's fallen out big time with some pals from his own country. He's seen this notice on a wall somewhere and he's split before things come on top. He's gone in search of pastures new, and he won't be back. In the meantime, the people he's fallen out with have come looking for him. Unfortunately, they didn't bargain on meeting a sharp-shooting retired war hero."

"That's my own theory in a nutshell, Sarge. What's happened here is nothing to do with our Mr Viktor."

"All the same, there's *something* iffy about it, isn't there? Last Monday afternoon, we had the knocking-shop arsonist just round the corner, the so-called mystery gunman. And now this. Two firearms incidents in one week, in the same quiet neighbourhood. There *must* be a connection. Mustn't there?"

The PC shook his head. "If there is, I don't think it's down to this Viktor bloke. We can still book 'im for something. It's GBH at the very least, isn't it?"

"Nah," the DS pursed his lips doubtfully, "we'd never get a conviction on what we've got. CPS[1] won't touch him, with the public mood like it is."

"'Police arrest pensioner for fighting off armed burglars.'"

"Exactly." The DS drummed his fingers on the desk. "Looks like all we can do is bail him with some strict reporting conditions. I'll call the Inspector."

"What about the rifle?"

The DS said he thought they should hang on to it for a while. "And by the way," he asked, "has this chap Viktor got an alibi for last Monday afternoon?"

"Yes, Sarge. He was at the Hungarian Cultural Centre."

"Oh, yeah?" The DS glanced up sceptically. "Enjoying some Brahms and Liszt, was he? Any witnesses?"

"About a hundred."

"A *hundred*?"

"Mr Viktor was singing Hungarian Folk Songs to the Hungarian Veterans Association."

* * *

[1] Crown Prosecution Service

"The colours! So soft and beautiful! It's like an old Flemish tapestry. Look how some trees are covered in gold, while others are still so green. And so many flowers still in bloom! In October! What a glorious day!" cried Bernard. The others agreed. "The last of the roses!" he exclaimed. He stopped to plunge his nose into one. "Wonderful!" Despite his smiles, the voice gave away worry and concern.

Slowly through Golders Hill Park the three of them walked together, Limor, Bernard and Neil. There were pleasantries. Limor and Bernard were curious about each other. Bernard was always thrilled to meet a sabra – a native-born Israeli – be she as secular as Limor. For her part, Limor remained intrigued by these well-rooted diaspora Jews.

"Bernard Kassin? So you are Syrian?" she asked.

Bernard chuckled merrily, delighted by the question. "You think I even *could* be Syrian?"

"So why Kassin? A Syrian name?"

"You want the whole megillah," offered Bernard, "or the short version?"

"How short can you make it?" asked Limor with a wry, amiable smile.

"You think the family should have kept the name Katzenberger?"

"Why not change to Katz?"

Bernard shrugged with mock sadness and opened his hands as if to say *don't ask*. "Since when is Katz a good English name?"

"And 'Kassin' is English?"

Bernard laughed. "At least we don't sound German. Ach! Never mind. Have you seen the little zoo here?"

And the three of them began to stroll over the mown grass, sprinkled with brown and yellow leaves, towards the park's animal enclosure.

As Neil walked on ahead, Bernard asked Limor if she would be fasting on Yom Kippur, in a few days' time. "Of course!" she exclaimed. "Why not?"

"Why fast, if you don't pray?"

"Is it written that we must pray?"

"You think Yom Kippur is only about *fasting?*"

"Yom Kippur is about atonement, no? Atonement is not a bad thing. More people should do it. Nations should try it. Every nation, even."

"No, it's really not about atonement," argued Bernard, "it's about community."

"Ach!" Limor dismissed the subject. "You know" she reminded him gently, "there is something more important to discuss."

"Yes," Bernard nodded, "these women."

"Yes, these women. What must we do for them?"

"These two of Neil's, or all of them?"

"All," Limor answered, "all women like this. But starting with two." She stopped walking and abruptly turned towards him, grabbing his arm to make her point clear, "And did Neil tell you, one of his Moldovans is a nasty little antisemite? OK," she acknowledged, "she is suffering. But it's not easy to help someone who hates you."

They looked up as wild screeches came from bird cages not far ahead, where Neil stood gazing. He beckoned them to come and look.

"No, not easy," Bernard sympathised. "Makes you think. If someone needs help, do I *have* to help them?" he said. "Shame, really, that we can't only help nice people."

"So, these two?"

"Mm, well, truth is, I don't know how to help them. You've already done a very great deal," Bernard said, "Let's talk tachlis.[1] What do they need? Money? Legal advice? Counselling?"

"Yes, yes. But what they need is to get away from here. Go somewhere safe."

Startled by a curious, deep, guttural sound from the deer enclosure, they stopped talking and moved to watch a rutting male, head heavy with great antlers, moving wild-eyed among his skittish females. His throat seemed enlarged to the width of a tree-trunk, the "Adam's apple" of this sinless creature projecting sharply close to his chest.

---

[1] tachlis = details, practicalities, facts [Yiddish].

From the sheath of his long, twitching penis hung a huge tuft of fur. None of them mentioned this conspicuous feature. Limor said only, "Wow, look at him!" to which Bernard responded, "An impressive creature." Neil wondered silently if rutting male deer feel the same as horny male humans.

They passed a watery aviary where a flock of white egret screamed and skated through the air; they stood a few moments at the cages of coatis and lemurs and kookaburras.

Bernard turned and spoke quietly. "All right – listen. I've made a decision. We can get ID for them, but I mustn't be personally involved. If anyone connects me to this, I'm finished. I'll put you in touch with a client. My name mustn't be mentioned. He'll do a highly professional, flawless job. It can all be ready in a few days if the money's right. I'm talking about a thousand pounds each. Who's paying? I'll chip in."

Neil was taken aback. Now that the offer was made, he regretted driving Bernard to such a point. Surely every principle had just been abandoned by this highly principled man.

"No, it's all right," he answered, "I can pay for it. Can I tell Liliana and Irina?"

Bernard nodded. "We need passport pictures of them. Neil, you do understand, this is tricky for me, and I'm not sure it's the right thing to do." He paused. "In fact, I'm sure it's not."

"No, it *is* the right thing, Bernard," Neil argued gently, as if to allay his own concerns

Bernard snorted and shook his head. "A solicitor breaching client confidentiality, that's already bad enough. Doing so to conspire with another person – a person already wanted by the police – to commit a crime?"

Limor stepped forward to take Bernard's arm tenderly. "A thing is not always either right or wrong," she said softly, "but still it's a mitzvah,[1] for the saving of life."

"Try telling the Law Society it's for the saving of life!" Bernard retorted with bitter humour. He kept his voice low, as if he feared that animals and birds in their enclosures might

---

[1] A commandment; saving a life being the greatest of them [Hebrew].

overhear.

At which, Limor kissed him on the cheek. "You are a good man. You have a good heart. You are a mensh."[1]

"Mm – well. After Neil's heroic acts, and yours, I feel I must do something."

"No, you are the real hero, with all that you do for everyone round here," Neil argued.

Bernard waved the comment away, and as they turned and walked back uphill he observed in a melancholy tone, "I s'pose we'd all be heroes, but for our flaws."

* * *

Neil woke up in Limor's bed. She was still sleeping. Quietly he slipped away from the big white duvet, hurriedly dressed and left the flat without breakfast.

The air was cool and fine, as pleasant an autumn day as one can ever hope for in London.

At Critchlow's, 'that bastard' Sanina greeted him stone-faced, just as always. "Morning, Mr Chapman. You'll go out with Mr Forrest this morning."

"What about Ascot, Mr Sanina?"

"You'll be on the City today."

With Stan at the wheel, Neil beside him, the two men set off together on their familiar route into the City of London. "Had a good weekend?" Neil asked.

"Nothing special. Peaceful. You?"

"Yeah, not bad," said Neil.

Stan lit a cigarette. He offered one to Neil, who as usual held up a hand in polite refusal.

The morning had fulfilled its promise. Balmy air, warm for this time of year, moved through the heart of London. The traffic inched forward slower than walking speed. Partly because of the cigarette smoke, Neil opened his window and gazed at people passing on the pavement. His eyes followed the office

---

[1] A good human being [Yiddish usage].

girls making their way to sandwich bars. Most wore dark pencil skirts or closely fitted trousers, and tight, buttoned shirts.

Look at that! Talk about visible panty line! You can even see the pattern on hers!

They stopped at Stan's favourite tea stall off Shoreditch High Street. "You know this bloke Darren, in the Ring?" Neil asked.

"I know him," Stan muttered.

"What do you reckon?"

"Me, meself – what *I* reckon? Listen, son, I know all the dodges. I don't need no help from blokes like him."

"What dodges?"

Stan's tight lips nearly smiled. "When yer bin 'ere fifty years, you'll know 'em. And I'll tell you what – none of 'em en't worth the trouble. Why take a chance with a good job? Doing things on the sly, hoping not to be found out. No way to live, is it?"

Neil said, "You told me to go to the police about that girl. Why don't you tell them about Darren?"

Stan's lips pulled away from his teeth in an expression of distaste. "That's different. Police need evidence. It's up to Critchlow's security to do something about that, if they want to."

"Why don't they, then?"

"'Cause they're on the bleedin' fiddle an' all. They're all on the take. An' I know that for a fact, 'cause my nephew's one of 'em."

"Really! Can you introduce me to him?"

"Why?" asked Stan, surprised. But he already understood. He assented with the barest sign. "Here," he handed Neil the Daily Mirror, "want to read the paper?"

Neil flicked through it. A Ripper-style killer had been sentenced to thirty years for murdering two young women. A footballer was jailed for seven years for knocking down and killing two children. A police chief had killed himself in remorse for having an affair.

Neil's mobile sounded. There was a short text from Irina.

Lili disappeared.

14

I am Liliana Petreanu! A new identity, I would love, if it is a different past, a different family, a different destiny, different memories. But my name, I must keep.

The mad Englishman had handed her a Romanian Carte de Identitate. According to him, Romanian ID would be more useful than a Moldovan card. You can go anywhere in Europe with it, he said, no questions asked. No questions asked! Why should *she* be afraid to answer questions? What had *she* done wrong?

As she walked, she looked at it again in the fading light: ROUMANIE at the top, a real picture of herself, but a *Nume*, *Prenume* and *Prenume Parinti* that had nothing to do with her. Doina Grigorescu! She was not Doina Grigorescu!

Liliana Petreanu is my name, and I have nothing else left of my own. Those men made me use a different name, too. Well, I am free of them now, and I want my own proper ID card, and my own life.

Better a fine, fresh evening than pouring rain, she supposed. Somehow, though, weather did not matter any more. She didn't know or care if it was hot or cold, wet or dry, or if she was happy or not. Most of the time, she just thought about what had happened to her, daydreaming vivid scenes of nauseating, degrading, painful things done to her. Sometimes she almost felt the physical sensations again. Why exactly, she seethed furiously, do so many men want to push as hard as they can into a woman's anus? Why do they want to press themselves onto a woman's face? Why do they get viciously excited by spreading come over her eyes and mouth and hair? Is there a reason?

To either side were strange houses and gardens. Every single one had its lush patch of land which could be properly cultivated, but which was turned over to grass and flowers and parking spaces. Stupid rich foreigners!

The Englishman said he had put some money aside for her, but she didn't know where he was, or how to get hold of it. Besides, it wasn't even his money. He stole it! During the fire, she watched as he crammed the bundles into his bag. In her opinion, every cent belonged to the girls in the house. Not to Irina, though, because she was only in the house for one single day.

She, Liliana, had more right to it! Instead, she had been left with nothing. She had filched an English note of twenty pounds from the pocket of that disgusting Russian homo. She did not know how much it came to in Moldovan leu.

Anyway, Moldova is nothing to me now. I must forget it. I will never go back there. It has disowned me, and I disown it. I have no country any more. All that is meaningless now. Everything true has become false. Even my name is fake.

Without that, she neither knew nor cared what might happen next. This very day she would start a new life. Her own life didn't belong to her any more.

Again and again she heard Sergiu's words as clearly as if she were having the conversation at this very moment. At last she had put the phone down, knowing it was probably the last time she would ever speak to him.

What's wrong? Irina asked, and she had told her. *It was Sergiu. It was my own brother all along.* Irina cried like a baby and tried to give her a hug. Sobbing, useless sympathy. But she didn't want that, Liliana told herself, not from people like her. Not from anybody.

She could survive here, or anywhere. After all, she had learned a few English words and had IT skills. Something would turn up. So long as she could get away from everything, every one of those people, and have nothing more to do with her treacherous family, or anyone.

Breathe deeply, breathe the cool, damp air of England. Get used to it. Bad times are over.

Yet try as she might, she kept thinking something would go wrong. She batted away frightening visions of the men, Sergiu among them. She told herself like a mantra, *Nothing more will go wrong*, but then other thoughts intruded again.

In a way it was a good feeling, like a feather floating in air, unconcerned which way it may be blown, or where it will land.

To be treated like that by your own family! Pure evil! It's too much! Unbelievable. And why? They said I made no contribution, and never came to see them! So what? They wanted some profit from the job of bringing me up. Is that the attitude a mother and father should have?

She had always hated them. Ignorant peasants. Uncouth pigs. Brutes. That horrible sly, crooked brother of hers. They had always objected to her having her own apartment in Chişinău. She was too good for them and they knew it.

She would show them, show everyone. And if she failed, and died in the attempt, then let it be on their rotten, stinking consciences, if such sick un-Christian bastards had consciences.

It might have been better not to phone home at all. Irina made a call to her parents and afterwards she said, go on Lili, you call home too.

Irina's call was a big fucking lie, because she didn't even tell her folks what had happened. She told them everything was going well and she was staying with a friend in London. According to Irina, it didn't matter if what you said was true. She said the main thing was to get back to normal. She said, *At least let your family know all is well. They must be so worried.*

So she had tapped out the numbers and waited, heart pounding as she heard the Moldovan ringing tone. With painful excitement she visualised the old family house, the yard with pigs and chickens. She would not tell them everything, of course. It would upset them. Anyway it was impossible to describe what she had been through.

As he answered the phone, his words, his voice, thrilled her. To hear again the sound of her brother Sergiu, and the good accents of the childhood home! She could have cried with relief.

But how... Lili? Where are you? Do they know you are making this call?

I am coming back, Serg. I am all right, I am in England, I have given up the work and I will soon be on my way to Moldova. Are you happy to hear from me! Did you wonder where I was? How are mother and father? How is everyone? Can I speak to them?

Liliana, think! What will happen to mother and father if you come back? It's selfish of you. Has anyone said you can come back? There is an agreement. If you come to Moldova, they would take you back to England. I had no choice. You must understand. Because otherwise, we have to return the money. And how can we? It's all spent. Try to see our side of it, Lili. We used the money to improve the house for mother and father, and buy a tractor. We'd be glad to see you, but don't you see the position we are in? You're making it difficult for the family. Go back to work.

But you don't know what work I did, Serg... or, you did know? Surely, mother and father don't know?

What's the matter with you? We don't think of it like that! We don't discuss it. I don't want to hear the details. Everyone has to do something in life, and they don't always enjoy it, Lili. It was a commercial arrangement. Look at it this way: finally you helped your family.

And Pavel? Did he know?

Who?

Pavel. My Pavel.

Oh, that Noua Dreaptă guy. I told him you left Moldova and wouldn't be back. In all honesty, he wasn't bothered. He said he had expected it of you. Forget about him, Lili. He's no good. Anyway, he's with someone else now. Liliana, stay where you are. It's not such a bad life for you, really. Better than here.

To the station was much further than she remembered. She arrived exhausted. There were shops, people walking fast, electronic barriers onto crowded platforms. Trains rushed past without stopping. It was not obvious how to make them stop. Nor could she see where to buy a ticket. Everywhere were English words, and she understood nothing.

Then, like a gift from God, she heard Romanian voices. She knew the type, tough, strong, hard-working lads. In one way, they seemed pretty decent, but she knew well enough what rough brutes they could be. Scores of such men had used her and abused her. She was wary of the way they were looking at her. One nudged another and pointed her out with a lustful grin. It would be safe though, surely, to ask them which platform she needed. There was only one English place whose name she knew – London.

But they knew as little as her, simply gesturing what they believed to be the direction of London. They were not going there. At last a train stopped and she boarded it without a ticket. There were plenty of soft, comfortable seats this time. The rocking movement sent her into a dreamy doze. When an inspector woke her, she did not understand what he was saying. She gave him her English banknote; he gave her some coins and a piece of paper – a receipt or a ticket, she supposed. It was impossible to know how much he had kept for himself.

She got off at a terminus, but it was not the one she remembered. A city as big as London, she reasoned, probably had more than one train station. She walked uncertainly into a busy street. None of the road signs made sense to her.

Where were these people going, in the dark? She felt unique and estranged and utterly different from them. Because they did not know about captivity, and would be incapable of imagining what she had experienced. These were normal women and normal men with normal lives, and normal innocence. That was all lost to her now.

It didn't matter. The nightmare which began on the day she left Chişinău with Sergiu had finally come to an end. She had freed herself from the men, and from Moldova and from her family. Today, tonight, she was once more herself, in control of her own destiny.

She felt the first pangs of appetite. There was the question too, of where to sleep. She was not stupid enough to spend all her coins in a café. There were odd little shops everywhere, still open. She would buy a bread roll, some yoghurt, a tomato. When that was gone, clearly there might be a problem. She was not above stealing something if she had to. As for the night, she was resigned to sleeping anywhere, out of doors if necessary, alone and free.

* * *

Bernard left work early that day. Several of the staff came out of the office all together, walking smartly along the Aldwych before parting at Waterloo Bridge, breezily wishing each other "good yomtov" and "well over the fast." Some, he supposed, would indeed feel perfectly well over the fast. Bernard knew that he would not. He continued along the Strand to Charing Cross tube station, with something of a sense that he was steeling himself for a trial. Bernard's stomach did not enjoy being given dinner at tea-time, and nor did it anticipate with any pleasure the coming deprivation. His dread had been increasing for some days already.

For this was the evening of Kol Nidrei, the evening which starts the long, difficult day of Yom Kippur, the day of atonement. This year, the Kol Nidrei service started at 6pm.

Even more than on Rosh Hashanah, the broad streams of Jews making their way along each street in Golders Green stirred strange emotions of excitement, hope and fear. Generations walked together, teenagers beside grandparents. To Bernard's eye it seemed that the pavements thronged, as well, with others unpresent; that the streets were haunted by those who had lived, those who had died, and those who had been denied life.

Security patrols and policemen scrutinised every corner and every pathway to protect this most reviled of peoples, his very own, as they made their way to prayer. At shul before the service began, the crowd pressed close, greeting one another in a curiously intense, upbeat mood, chatting, smiling.

Because, of course, Kol Nidrei is not so bad. After all, you're hardly fasting at all if you've just eaten a meal. The mood grows sombre later as the congregation disperse. The return home, with its expectation of a cup of cocoa in front of the television perhaps, maybe with a biscuit, is when the trial gently begins.

At a loose end, Bernard, Elizabeth and Ruth sat in the sitting room. There will be no television, and no bedtime snack. They could not listen to music, and it seemed inappropriate to read. "Well, I think I'll retire," said Bernard, and he went upstairs to bed without taking his usual glass of water.

* * *

She was thirsty, but did not know where to find water. She might have gone to a public toilet to drink from a washbasin tap, but there was a charge to go into the toilet. In the end, she paid even more to buy a small bottle of spring water. Annoyingly, she had not realised it was carbonated. She used some of it to rinse her hands and face. It was cold, and she had nothing to dry herself.

Bread, yogurt and a tomato, eaten at the narrow plastic bench in a bus shelter, made a refreshing, simple, tasty and nourishing meal. Having no table, Liliana deftly held the yoghurt and tomato in one hand, and having no spoon, she scooped the yoghurt with pieces of bread. That was quite successful. Then she ate the tomato, biting into it like an apple, alternating with mouthfuls of bread.

The meal did not sustain her as she had hoped. In a matter of hours, as the crowds thinned and the cars and taxis became less frequent, and as the air became chill and damp, already she felt renewed pangs of hunger. She would have to ignore them. Defy them. She walked looking for a quiet sheltered corner in which to sit or lie down. She crossed a canal and walked aimlessly between brick warehouses and blocks of flats.

She wondered about hostels, about waiting rooms, about late-night stores and gas stations and fast-food eateries where she might rest indoors. Not enough remained from her twenty English pounds even to buy a cup of coffee, let alone a bed for the night. She urgently needed another twenty-pound note to keep her going. Perhaps she could steal one. Longingly she pictured the fitted carpets and central heating in the home of those two horrible perverts, where even now, as she imagined, Irina might be naked in the bathroom preparing for a night of dreams in a clean, warm bed. Liliana even began to wonder if she had been better off in that squalid room where the men kept her to be raped. At least she had had food, and a bed to lie on for her rest.

Railway viaducts on brick arches, dripping and dank, spanned unlived-in roads of locked-up yards and warehouses. Here Liliana paused, hoping to spy some out-of-the-way hiding place, but it was far too noisy with echoing voices, and then the long screeching rumble of a goods train.

Ahead of her, some indecently dressed young women, all of them skinny and blonde, were clustered together, talking loudly. She wondered what could have brought them to this grim setting. As Liliana approached, some started to shout at her with uncouth Russian voices, and she heard *blyat* [whore] and *pizda* [cunt] and *chertovskaya schlukha* [fucking whore] and *otyebis!* [fuck off] and *poshel na huy* [fuck you]. Did they think she was a prostitute? Did she look like one? They laughed, and one called something in English. She understood nothing, except at the end, the word *darling.*

She walked on hurriedly, anxious that they might attack her, turned a corner, tired and afraid. A car drove past with raucous yells and thumping music that shook the ground. She crossed the street to avoid a shabby bar with a hand-painted sign, and came to a bleak, broad junction of wide roads. A group of black teenage boys were standing there, boisterous, drunk and excited. One thrust his pelvis towards her, making the others laugh, and again she heard the word *darling*.

There was a roundabout with a flyover above. She did not know which way to go, and longed to sleep. Her thoughts became confused, as she struggled to remember who she was, and where. A few saloon cars passed, slowing as drivers noticed a pretty, well-shaped blonde alone at the roadside.

Some of these men, Liliana realised, would give a twenty-pound note for a few minutes of her time.

* * *

Bernard wakes terribly thirsty, but may not drink. His movements soon rouse Elizabeth. It is well past the time they would normally get up, so in this way, at least, he tells himself, Yom Kippur has its compensations.

The lack of breakfast should perhaps be reckoned too trivial to be called a hardship. In the streets, all who are not Jewish go about their business unaware that this is no ordinary day. For Bernard, it is hardly a day at all, but a slice of time excised from the diary. Again the atmosphere at shul is strangely convivial, though soon a weary sobriety has set in.

Acquaintances not seen for a full year are greeted amiably, but by twelve o'clock Bernard's Yom Kippur headache is well under way and he is not in the mood for conversation. He is ardently looking forward to lunch, which he knows he will not have. The next landmark, after that, would be tea-time, a difficult moment some hours away. He calculates what proportion of the day has already passed.

Those who lead the service, skilfully guiding the community through hundreds of pages of chanted text, those who give readings and sermons, seem untiring. Yet even his own flagging spirits are buoyed by waves of uplifting song, and a liturgy whose sentiment, repeated again and again, is that if we only undertake to be better in future, then our past and present failings must inevitably be forgiven. Because life has to continue.

And repeated, in pleasing chant, is the list of our sins, *ul het shehatanu*... for the sin that we have sinned...

A catalogue of wrongdoing, from "gossiping", "brazenness", "a begrudging eye" and "foolish speech", to "immorality" and "the evil inclination" and "a session of vice" and "the sins for which we incur the death penalty".

It pains him – more and more, as the hours pass – to consider that in the midst of these very Days of Awe, during which we shall supposedly be judged, he has actually facilitated not only sin, but crime! In flagrant contradiction of his profession as an upholder of law, and his avowed belief that the law of the land should be respected and enforced.

Which sin has he committed? As he scans the list, he looks out for his own contribution to it. Has he caused wickedness, sinned wilfully, given evil counsel and been deceitful? Arguably he has. Has he encouraged others to lie and cheat? Certainly he has. And he himself, he has cheated and he has lied, even to his own good, dear Liz, who deserves nothing but the best from him.

On the other hand, well, one shouldn't make excuses, but you do know all the circumstances, Lord, don't you? The evidence must be properly examined. We must be permitted to put our defence, and our mitigation. Limor has told me to point out that it was all done for the saving of life. I hope you'll be willing to accept that. With respect, my Lord, bear in mind that no one suffered as a consequence. No one. And nor did I profit by it.

And it's hardly my fault, is it, what terrible crimes Neil has committed? Anyway, he's not even Jewish, so does any of this apply to him? Surely he is outside our jurisdiction?

Voices all around begin to rise in song.

V'al kulam... For all of these, forgive us.

And his mind eases, contentedly, into the chant of *ashamnu*, poetic, insouciant alphabet of our misdemeanours, repeated ten times during Yom Kippur.

Ashamnu... we are guilty...

Ashamnu, Bagadnu, Gazalnu... each one ending in *–nu*. Which means, we, us, our.

For this confession is not for *I* nor *me* nor *mine*, but for the wrongs of all.

Uttering each of them, *–nu, –nu, –nu*, he slaps a contrite fist to his own chest as if in shared responsibility. That's what it is, Bernard tells himself, to be a community, a people, a nation.

Outside the synagogue window, at last the light is angled low, and Bernard longs for the end. His head throbs. He tries to see a pattern in the throbbing. He cannot fight the pain; he goes with the flow of it, passing through it slowly to the other side. In the final aching hours of constant standing, all thoughts of food and water have been left behind, with only a desire to sit.

Finally the community reaches the rousing last kaddish of the long day, *Oseh shalom bimromav, hu yasay shalom* almost shouted as much as sung.

The sudden silence which follows is broken by a single trumpet blast of the shofar.

The penance was over. Brightly febrile on being released, Bernard, Elizabeth and Ruth shook hands eagerly with friends, wished them a good year, and made their way cheerfully to the home of Simon and Penny Silver to break the fast together. They jested as always about the speed with which people return to their everyday sinning.

The Silvers' table was spread with sweet, tasty treats, babka and kokosh, and plain sponge cake, and delicate little sandwiches. The longed-for cups of tea were served at last, and glasses of water.

Later, heartier dishes were brought out, and a bottle of wine opened. There was laughter and happiness, the aches and pains of the day soon cured, and all seemed to have been worthwhile, even enjoyable.

The doorbell rang and Simon left the room to answer it. He reappeared to beckon Bernard into the hall. To Bernard's great surprise, Neil was standing there. Tall, muscular, unsmiling, he looked very goyish, Bernard thought. The eyes were so very blue this evening: it was unnerving.

"Sorry to disturb you. I'd have come earlier," explained Neil, "but I didn't want to intrude. I knew it was Yom Kippur."

"Not at all," replied Simon. "You're very, very welcome. Come in. Have something."

"Excellent food!" confirmed Bernard.

Neil was puzzled. "Are you having a party, then? I thought it was, like, a solemn thing. I thought you were fasting."

"Oh, it *is* solemn, if that's the word for it," Simon answered, "but it's finished now."

"Yup, that's it for another year," interjected Bernard.

"I've come to tell you: it was my last day at work. And my last day in London."

There were amazed exclamations.

"Why leave on a Thursday? Why not at the end of the week?" queried Simon.

Neil shook his head as if he did not have an answer. "My plan for tomorrow," he said, "is to take Irina back to her flat in Paris, and then" – he nodded to Simon – "head down to your place."

"Well, I hope Critchlow's gave you a nice parting gift, or something," Bernard joked.

Neil chuckled at the thought. "No, nothing. Just 'Goodbye and good riddance'."

The sharp features of Simon Silver's face, behind narrow metal-framed glasses, looked on with penetrating, sceptical curiosity. "Sudden decision," he commented quizzically.

After all, it was only a few days since Neil had first asked them about the house in France. He had stood in this very hallway and told Simon and Penny he was just curious about the place, that was all; that he had no particular dates in mind; and anyway he might not be able to go there. It depended on a lot of things, he had said. Above all, he wanted a bolthole where he could be confident of being left completely undisturbed.

Talking with Neil like that, Penny had wondered at herself for finding his presence almost thrilling. No doubt he is quite attractive, in his way, she admitted. Oh, not physically, of course – she dismissed that idea. It's only because he is enigmatic, and looks like a man of action. And complex. And so very calm. Yet unpredictable. In this man are undercurrents invisible to the eye, that might tow you far out to sea. He has quite a flair for languages; a linguist herself, she respected that in a man. As her friend Lisa had put it, she 'liked the guy'.

After that first visit, Simon told Penny he had doubts about Neil and his request. If he stayed in their house, it would – apparently – have to be kept a deathly secret. Bernard had been at pains to emphasise that. They were not to mention it to anyone. But why? Bernard and Neil had been cagey about the reason. Some unconvincing story about falling out with someone.

"There seems to be far more to this than we've been told,"

Simon said. "Honestly, Penny, I think we'd better say No. Tell them it won't work after all."

Penny strongly disagreed. Her feeling was that Neil could stay in her house as long as he wanted. They must do whatever they could to help him. If he needed to keep it quiet, that was fine by her. Besides, as he had said, it would probably come to nothing.

Yet now here he was in their hall again already, dropping in unannounced, this inscrutable young man, suddenly ready to leave at once! Simon found himself explaining to Neil how to get to the village, and how to find the house. "I'll let Marianne know – that's our neighbour who keeps an eye on the place. She's very nice, very helpful. She'll make sure everything is ready for you. Here..." he moved away for a moment to look in a bureau, and returned with a large old-fashioned iron key.

"How splendid!" declared Bernard. "Looks like it would open a cathedral or a castle!"

Simon smiled. "Every house in the village has a key like this." And to Neil: "Got your tickets?"

Neil nodded and said everything was booked.

"Do you know Paris? I've got a little tip for you. When you arrive," Simon suggested, "walk out of the station and across the road to the Brasserie du Nord for something to eat. Phone to reserve a table. That's a lovely way to arrive in France."

Simon shook Neil's hand warmly before returning to his meal and his guests. Bernard pulled Neil gently aside. "Any word about Liliana?"

"Nothing. Her phone's always switched off. Not sure what to think."

"Could she have been kidnapped? You know, recaptured?"

"From Sanina's house? That seems unlikely," said Neil, "but, well, it is possible."

"Mm – look, give me her number, I'll see if I can trace it. There are ways. I'll help her somehow."

"That's good, Bernard. Thank you. How d'you feel after a fast? Bloody hungry, I suppose?" Neil smiled with a faint sympathy.

"Happy to have survived intact. And sad that our list of sins never gets any shorter. People have been trying to be better for thousands of years. So far, they haven't managed."

"But you don't *really* expect humanity to become different, Bernard?" responded Neil quite amiably. "I mean, do cats change, do dogs change? Cats in Roman times were the same as today, right? So were the human beings."

It was Bernard's turn to laugh. "The difference is, old chap, that cats haven't been *trying* to change. Well, now," and he took Neil's hand affectionately, "look after yourself."

Neil held on to Bernard's hand, reluctant to part. "Maybe," he said, "that's what makes us human. That we keep on trying."

* * *

Liliana has not slept well on the concrete under the flyover. She has been awake through many of the night hours. There were bad dreams, and when she awoke, bad memories. She wished she could free her mind of everything. As the first pale streaks of morning crept into the eastern sky she was disturbed by a smiling man. She did not trust such smiles. He would look after her, he said kindly, and he had a room for her, where she would be safe. He would buy her some breakfast.

But she could not understand the words, and ran from him as fast as she could, almost into the path of a truck. It braked suddenly and, through the windscreen, she saw only that the driver looked old, his head bald with a fringe of grey – and for a confused moment almost imagined that it was her grandfather. She could make out the movement of his hand beckoning to her. The passenger door opened and she climbed up. Inside, the cab was as warm and comfortable as a sitting room.

Liliana slammed the heavy door and the driver pulled back into the traffic, glancing at her curiously every few moments. She saw now that he did not resemble her grandfather, and was not even especially old. He said something, the voice raw and deep. She tried her two languages, Romanian and Russian, and her few mispronounced words of English. It soon became obvious that they did not have any language in common.

She did feel hungry; but the mood was on her again, telling her that she must refuse to indulge herself. Life would be simpler and she would need less money. Holding on to not-eating was a rock of determination on which she could stand firm. Then she would need nothing from anyone.

Half-hidden by a loose curtain behind the seats, Liliana noticed the driver's narrow overnight bunk. On it were a rumpled, soiled blanket and a grubby pillow. She mimed sleeping, leaning her head against the palm of her hand. The driver understood, and nodded. Liliana scrambled into his bunk and lay down.

Taped to the wall beside the pillow were full-page photographs torn from magazines, brightly coloured pictures of young blonde women like herself, except that these, smiling and voluptuous, were posing naked with their legs stretched far apart, tugging their labia wide open. Behind the pillow was fixed a gold-painted wooden crucifix, and to either side of it, framed snapshots of a handsome woman in a cheap summer frock and some neatly dressed children.

In a Golders Green bedroom, Bernard's eyelids flicker gently. He remembers that it is Friday; so he does not go to shaharit this morning. Yet he feels uneasy. There is something of a malaise, almost a headache, a grasping around his chest. Is he ill? At first he cannot understand, until he realises that it is a mental distress, nothing more than profound shame at getting involved in Neil's law-breaking schemes.

He runs a hand over Elizabeth's hip; adored curve. He snuggles closer to her. If she only knew that he has placed his whole career in jeopardy to help these two unknown women! What madness!

On any view, he has committed an absolute offence. He ought simply to have advised the police that he suspected the women had been trafficked. As a solicitor, he might have had a better response than Neil. Of course – his heart sinks horribly as he thinks of it – they would then have asked him what he knew about the women and how they escaped, and he would not have been able to answer.

If all this were ever to be traced back to him, as somehow it might! As he lies there, another realisation comes into his mind. Bernard's heart and veins seem turned to ice, yet a prickly heat of sweat creeps across his scalp. What worries him now is that his client, a professional deceiver and forger, will easily figure out for himself who sent Neil to his door. If he does figure it out, he will have a hold over Bernard to use in whatever way he can.

Bernard leans forward and kisses Elizabeth's head without disturbing her. He must leave the bed now, for as on every other day, there is work to do.

* * *

For the briefest instant, as she approached, he could not restrain an admiring eye. She wore the same jeans and low-heeled shoes as the last time he'd seen her, a creamy silk shirt, and a dark brown jacket that matched her hair.

They greeted each other rather stiffly at the platform barrier. Neil felt Irina's reserve, her reservations, and was determined not to trespass. Nevertheless he had planned some surprises that he hoped would make her happier.

"Heard from Liliana?" he asked straight away.

"I text, I phone. Nothing. I am worried they found her again."

Neil nodded briefly. "That could happen. Bernard's trying to trace her number. You OK?"

She sighed and shook her head. "Tonight I will be at home. I will sleep in my own bed. That's all."

"We have some time before we leave," he said. "Come and see the river."

"La Tamise?"

"The Thames."

From Waterloo Station, Neil led Irina to the foot of the London Eye. He wore his rucksack, she pulled her small case on wheels. Again he experienced a thrill of pride at having such an attractive woman at his side. If there was a woman he *never* wanted to sleep with, though, it was Irina. She had insulted him, accused him of raping Liliana and said she hated him, and besides, she really deserved to be left in peace.

They leaned against a grey stone parapet and gazed at the flowing water. A police launch passed at speed, and some heavily laden barges, and a sightseeing cruise.

"Did you remember your new passport?" he asked.

"Bien sûr." She took it from her handbag. While Liliana had been given a Romanian identity card, Bernard's contact recommended that for Irina, since she was planning to live in France, it would be best to have a British identity. Her poor English would not be a problem, he said.

Neil fingered the pages, studied the photo, examined the watermark. "Yes, it's the real thing all right. Funny though, you have the same name."

"Non, regardez. I am still Irina, but the nom de famille is a little different. My real name is Inescu, but look, it says Ionesco. *Attention,* don't drop it in the river!" Anxiously she took the passport and slipped it into her handbag.

She tutted with frustration. "Et enfin – and after all that, I never visited London! I'm not sure, now, if I..." she looked for the words, "ever will."

"Come on, then, visit London now!" said Neil. He looked at his phone to check the time. "We have one hour. And, voilà", as like a magician he conjured them from his pocket, "I have tickets for the London Eye!"

This first surprise was met with utter, gaping astonishment. He liked that.

As their glass capsule rose, Irina exclaimed at the rapidly expanding vista. Soon the broad, stately curve of the sparkling Thames could be seen sweeping through the metropolis. Neil pointed out the slender Post Office Tower like a spindle, the dome of St Paul's Cathedral defiantly elegant among the menagerie of City skyscrapers, the overbearing mass of Canary Wharf and, directly beneath them as the wheel turned higher, the waterside Palace of Westminster like an exquisite balsawood model resting on a table.

"Impressionant!"

He pointed to Hampstead Heath and, beside it, little Primrose Hill. "Next to Limor's flat, remember?"

Irina slowly scanned London in every direction. The city's edges reached to a distant rim of low, misty hills. She stared down at the thousands of streets beneath her, each one as tiny as a line on a map. "Is Liliana down there, somewhere?" she wondered. "Where is she at this moment? What is she doing?"

"Try her again. Phone her."

"Not now. Later."

Neil lowered his voice. "Irina, I need to know more about Liliana. What did she tell you about herself?" he asked, "Where exactly is she from? And this brother of hers, what did she say about him?"

She shook her head sharply. "Not now. Not with all these people." For they shared the capsule with a group of excited Italian tourists.

He hurried her over Westminster Bridge and into Parliament Square, where 'protestors' sat in groups playing music and drinking from cans. Gingerly they stepped through the encampment's overlapping tent ropes, its garbage, banners and placards. When Big Ben struck, Irina listened, rapt, staring at the huge clock face, her hands pressed together as if in prayer.

Along Whitehall they jogged quickly. He gestured, "These are monuments to Britain's empire. And all these," he waved his arm, "are Government offices. And this here, is called the Cenotaph. It's the monument for British soldiers killed in the World Wars."

"And that one?" she stopped to look at a dark sculpture of women's uniforms and bags and hats hanging from a block in the middle of the road.

"That's a memorial for the women of World War Two. Good, isn't it? And this," as for a moment they joined a coach party peering through black metal railings, "is Downing Street." He pointed to number 10 and had to insist, against her incredulity, that it truly was the Prime Minister's official residence. "But it is a normal house!" she objected.

"No, it isn't. Not inside."

Neil felt rather proud of London, and of himself, and of doing something to please Irina; proud of his knowledge of the city, most of which he had recently gained from Stan.

At the Horse Guards they stopped to stare at a flamboyantly crested guardsman, clothed in a blood-red tunic, adorned with glittering silver and wearing polished thigh-high leather boots. He sat astride a great horse and held a shining sword. Irina watched horrified as tourists made fun of the man, touching him, stroking his leg, leaning against him, posing comically, while friends shrieked and took pictures.

"He must use the sword!" she cried. "He must cut off their head! Why does he allow them to mock? They mock Sa Majesté la Reine!" But the guardsman remained perfectly unmoved. When a young woman lifted her skirt, trying to force a response from the man, Irina turned to march away in disgust.

Neil took her across Horse Guards Parade to the Mall for a glimpse of Buckingham Palace, at the far end of the pink roadway. Crowds of plane trees, their bony branches visible through autumn leaves, densely lined the route as if hopeful of a royal procession. The Royal Standard could just be made out. "And that," as Neil explained, "means the Queen is in residence."

Irina grinned. "She is drinking tea, avec du lait, à l'anglaise, with her dames-d'honneur."

"Probably meeting boring politicians."

Through the majestic curve of Admiralty Arch they entered Trafalgar Square, Irina staring greedily at the sights, the views, the statuary, as they paced rapidly across the paving. He hurried her to the National Gallery, on the other side of the square. "You did say, didn't you, that you love Cézanne? And Van Gogh?" He glanced at his phone, urging her up the steps. "We only have time for two or three pictures. To Room 45 – quick!"

Leaving the gallery, they ran to catch a bus. Irina was thrilled. She considered sitting on a bright red double-decker the very essence of London. However, they were soon idling in the traffic of Charing Cross Road. Neil worried that he had cut things too fine. Their hour was already over. "We could get to the station in five minutes by bike!" he muttered. "We have to get off," he told Irina, "and try to find a cab."

At St Pancras station, there were not two minutes left before check-in closed. Irina became scared as they ran towards the ticket-reading machines, inserting their tickets just in time.

"You think they will believe my passport?" she asked in a low voice, hoarse with nervousness.

"I have an idea," Neil proposed mischievously. "Let's swap passports. See if anyone notices."

"Non! Idiot!" As they passed through the barrier, she lowered her voice. "And your gun, where is it?"

"Don't worry," was all he said. He did not want her to show any particular concern while his bag was X-rayed, nor when they asked him to remove his belt – for his belt, his shoes and his bag were all partly made of the dismantled gun parts. He simply hoped that there were no dogs sniffing for explosives, if that's what bullets contained.

He need not have worried. A couple of officers, a man and a woman, fresh-faced and amiable, cheerfully waved all passengers through security without a glance at their luggage or passports. There were no dogs.

The subdued, warm and intimate lighting in Eurostar's 'premier' class brought the word 'boudoir' to Neil's thoughts. He flirted with the hostess. It was quiet, too, the quietest place he had been for weeks or months. Or years. The train murmured, making a pleasant, powerful hum as it sped along the track.

Irina seemed in bliss, occasionally smiling. "It's true, then?" she said, "I am free again? I am myself?"

Outside the glass, the green countryside of Kent and Picardy – the two separated by a brief, tranquil interlude in the tunnel – turned to a watercolour blur, far-away objects briefly recognisable, a village, a house, a tree.

Neil, too, so he believed for a little while, was free again. Perhaps now all would be well. He was travelling at speed from the dangerous men who pursued him. Away from the noisy vans and the little world of Critchlow's.

* * *

That very morning, Critchlow's & Sons' security guards, together with police officers, had come into the yard like invading commandos. Men were singled out and questioned. After opening Darren's locker, they drove him away in a police van, together with a plastic bag of evidence.

Down in the Ring, pickers and packers and drivers eagerly swapped titbits of hearsay and information.

"Who would grass up Darren? It don't make sense!" some protested.

"Will they come arter us now, when they find out what's gone missin'?"

"Nah! They got Darren. They'll leave it at that. They can't prove nuffink. Or can they?"

"What was in 'is locker? Anyfin' we should know about?"

"Yeah, they've took a list of names."

"Oh, fuck."

"And they've found this bloody great glossy book in there, abaht jazz, with a set of CDs. Bleedin' docket was tucked inside it, 'n all – got 'im bang to rights on that one. God knows what it was doin' in there. They come lookin' specially, like they already knew where to find it. Security bloke said it was nicked off the City round a few weeks ago."

"Then they must o' planted it! Darren never kep' nuffink in his locker more'n a few hours. That's what he told me."

"City round? 'E must've 'ad the book off Neil."

"Makes ya wonder, why did Neil leave so sudden? Not 'cause o' that, surely?" someone asked. "Or was he in on it? Yesterday Neil leaves, today Darren is nicked. Did he set it up?"

One of the men offered an explanation. "Nah! Neil left 'cause that bastard Sanina was always on 'is fuckin' back. These last few days, Sanina kep' callin' Neil into the office. You notice that?" They had all noticed it.

Stan calmly put them right, saying what Neil had asked him to say. "No, it's nothin' like that. Neil was an educated bloke. He told me he's found something better. He was always goin' on that he wanted an office job. He wanted to be a manager, not a driver."

Conversation stopped abruptly as the transport manager himself appeared in the Ring. "Gentlemen, please," he gestured to the men, "that's enough talk. We have work to do, I think?" Andrei Sanina seemed strangely contented this morning. He even smiled.

* * *

When he awoke, Irina was staring at him. Miles of flat countryside lay outside the window, a high Gothic spire rising in the distance under a sheet of dark grey sky.

"Where are we?" he asked.

"I don't know. Everywhere is the same. Nowhere. Anywhere."

She seemed to have had a change of mood. He pressed his lips together thoughtfully. "What's wrong? What's the matter?" he asked. "Is something the matter? Are you OK?"

"My text to Liliana," she said dully.

"Yeah?"

"She sent an answer." Irina raised her eyebrows enigmatically.

"Wow! That's great!" Puzzled by her reticence, he shook his head questioningly.

She read to him from the tiny screen on her phone, awkwardly translating from Romanian into English. *He has my money. Need it urgently. Don't look for me.*

"All right, but *where* is she?" Neil asked. "Bernard has some cash for her. How can he give it to her if she won't say where she is?"

Irina tapped out a reply: *Collect money or want it delivered?*

A trolley was pushed through the carriage and they asked for cups of coffee.

It seemed Liliana had no quick answer. As time passed, Neil

tried to imagine where she could be, what she was doing. At last Irina's phone buzzed again. She read the screen twice silently, then aloud with wavering voice. "It's not good," she warned. *"Neil is a thief. He took all our money. I need it, very urgent. Can you leave it somewhere. But don't come looking for me."*

Neil winced. "God, she's in a mess. Explain to her that we want to help."

"You don't understand. 'Help' really means nothing to her," Irina shrugged helplessly. "She doesn't care about that."

"But if she wants money, she must let Bernard or Limor know where she is."

Irina tapped the keys and clicked *Send*. "Maybe she will do it."

The train slowed sharply and began to slide carefully through a jungle of high-rise blocks and concrete-slab embankments painted with graffiti. It was getting dark. The ghostly white Byzantine domes of the Sacré Coeur, lit by bright lights, came startlingly, briefly, into view, like something transported from Moscow or Istanbul – or Moldova; and then, far away, Neil made out a tall illuminated shape that could be the Eiffel Tower.

The platform was crowded and cold, and loud with confusing, indistinct announcements. Irina seemed tired and disoriented. "Alors, to my apartment?"

"What about dinner, first?" Neil revealed now that he had booked a table at the Brasserie du Nord. Even if this second surprise fell flat, and even if she were not in the mood to eat, at least she would realise that he had tried to please her. "It's smart, very good, just over the road," he said casually, as though he were a regular visitor to the place.

Irina made a slight gasp of astonishment. Her eyes opened wide. She assured him that she would love to go there.

A waiter in a full-length white apron, his expression utterly indifferent, led them unceremoniously between gilded woodwork and polished mirrors, padded banquettes and gleaming Art Nouveau lamps, to a table cloaked with heavy white damask. He handed them a couple of large embossed menus tied with gold thread.

"I didn't think you would want to do this, with things as they are," Neil told her frankly.

"We will help Liliana, of course," Irina declared, "but we will eat and drink and laugh. We must remember to live our own lives, n'est-ce pas?"

It struck Neil as a little heartless, but he accepted that she was right. "Bernard said something like that. He said, don't agonise about everyone who has problems. Just help those you can help. He said to me, *Do your bit.*"

"You have done it, Neil. Vraiment."

"I don't know. I think Bernard meant, 'doing your bit' never stops. Liliana is in trouble, and I promised to help her. And the others, if I can," he said.

"Promised? You didn't promise her anything."

"No, myself. I promised myself."

Setting down the plates with deft efficiency, the waiter curtly wished them 'bon appetit'. To each other they raised their glasses and did not know what to toast to make. Neil simply said, "Well," and sighed deeply. Irina said she wanted to celebrate her freedom. She proposed, "Liberté," and they drank to that.

"Ah! I am back in Paris! I feel good now," Irina declared. She told Neil that, after their meal, there would be no need for him to take her all the way to her door. She urged him instead to take the Métro straight to Gare de Lyon for his train south. She would happily go back to the apartment on her own. Her doorkeys had gone, of course, but the concierge would let her in and everything would be fine.

He said, "No, really, I'll take you. I'd like to." The truth was that he felt obligated, somehow, to see it through to the end.

"And where exactly are you going, afterwards?" she asked.

"It's a small village, near Montpellier. It's called Puilhac." He said the name as Simon had told him.

"'Puyac'," she repeated. "What will you do when you get there?"

"Make myself useful. See what work there is. What about you?

What will you do tomorrow, and the next day, and the day after?"

"I don't know, to be honest. I will rest."

"And when your sabbatical's over, you'll go back to your job in Moldova? When will that be?"

"Next summer," she nodded thoughtfully.

"And your family still don't know what has happened?"

"There's no need for them to know. They are respectable people. What can I tell them? They would not recover from the shock, never."

"Do they love you? Imagine if it were *your* daughter; would you want to know about something like this, and care for her?"

She shook her head as if she did not know the answer. "I am not a child," she said. "I don't run to my parents."

"What is your father's business?"

She laughed slightly. "I don't know. He owns some franchises for international companies. He has Government contracts. And my mother is a director at the National Academy of Music. She was an opera singer."

As Neil ate, sometimes Irina observed him curiously, making his way steadily through the courses, his soupe à l'oignon, his flambéed veal kidneys, tearing pieces of bread to wipe sauce from the plate, refilling his glass from the pichet of red wine, eating and drinking without restraint.

From time to time he declared that it was all "Excellent!"

She admired his robust enjoyment. The way he focused, concentrating like a cat on what he was doing, intrigued her.

His uprightness, his muscularity, his quickness; she found him fascinating to watch. The eyes made her think of something, high mountains, snow, the chill of dawn, she did not know what. She remembered one clear, still winter morning, far below freezing, dangerously cold. In reality, she suspected – she told herself that it must be so, although she was not quite sure – Neil was not quite the cool customer he seemed.

"I see something interesting about Neil Chapman," she declared. "The dinner pleases him, everything pleases him, yet he is not a happy man, never content."

"What the heck are you talking about?"

She smiled indulgently. "I am not criticising."

This remark irritated him even more than the first. He carried on eating.

"And I see something sad," said Irina, "a little froideur in the heart, n'est-ce pas?"

"Rubbish! Not at all!" he replied. Into his mind came the image of a man, a brute, his moist red flesh torn through, falling ungainly from the roof. Coldness in the heart? The sight had actually pleased him. She was right, of course; he was disturbed by his own coldness.

"You do not like tenderness, you do not long for love," she said.

A slight pain struck home. He held back an unexpected emotion, warded it away before he had clear sight of it.

He supposed she was making free with these last moments to mock him before they finally said goodbye.

He topped up her glass and said, "You're spoiling a good dinner!"

"Neil, I want to say something. To say a kind of sorry."

"What for?"

"You are not a rapist. That was cruel. You made a terrible mistake. I know now, you are good."

"No, I'm not good. Don't worry about it."

"I see what you are," she said, "you are a man of appetites."

He shook his head. "Juste un mec." Just a guy.

"Juste un mec bien." Just a nice guy.

The nearest Métro was Saint-Placide. Irina pulled her case on wheels, and Neil carried his rucksack, as she led the way from the station along a busy Boulevard Raspail. In the hectic, confusing darkness of a city evening, he gained no impression of the neighbourhood.

He followed her into a narrow street, a dark sliver between five- and six-storey apartment buildings. Windows were too high to look into (and in any case, were all covered by grey metal shutters). Large plain doors opened straight onto a thread of sidewalk hemmed in by parked cars and vans, and heavily soiled by dogs.

He spoke in French. "This your street?"

"Yes. I love it here. I was lucky to find it," she said. "There's a little restaurant down the road, and a fantastic boulangerie round the corner. And good bookshops. The Jardin du Luxembourg is two minutes away. I go there all the time to sit alone and think."

"Great! And you live here... by yourself?"

"Yes. That is how I like to be," she admitted.

"Sounds lovely."

He mused at the improbability of this beautiful young woman being left unnoticed and in peace as she sat all on her own in the park. "No boyfriend?"

She answered with a slight laugh: "Boyfriend? No!" she shrugged as if it was of little consequence. "That might have been a nice idea – once. Now, the thought makes me," and her expression changed to disgust, "God no, no thank you. I did not meet anyone special."

They said goodbye across the street from her apartment building. He held out his hand to shake hers rather formally, and she did take it. As they were parting, she leaned forward quickly to touch her lips against his cheek.

"Au revoir, Neil. What can I say? I can't say anything, except 'thank you'. And that is not enough. Well, we won't," she shook her head with emotion, embarrassed as tears started, "we won't discuss everything now. It's as though I dreamed a nightmare. I have not quite woken up." She brushed wet eyelashes with her fingers.

Neil looked into her eyes and attempted good cheer, "Goodbye, Irina. And good luck. And always remember, if you need help, ever in your life, call on me. I mean it." Their hands separated.

Neil walked a few paces, then turned to watch as she rang the bell. The door was answered by a middle-aged woman. It was the concierge, he supposed. But Irina did not go in. She seemed in intense discussion with the concierge. Both women began to gesticulate rather oddly. Irina gripped her head with her hands and turned, looking around wildly. She saw Neil, half hidden by a parked van, and quickly ran towards him.

15

"**M**en came looking for me, she said, very frightening men. Now, my apartment, she rented it to someone else." The metro was too noisy and too crowded for them to talk. Besides, they were intent now only on reaching the Gare de Lyon. On the way, Neil phoned to change his booking to *deux personnes*.

Not until they were in their seats and the TGV began to hum quickly through the southern edges of the city did Irina repeat in hushed voice all that the terrified concierge had told her.

"So," she concluded bitterly, "I am not to use my own name, and now, not to live in my own home," she covered her eyes with one hand, "because of these – men. Who are they?"

Neil turned away; he did not know the answer. These were not the men who met at a café in Osborne Park. These were not the men who had chased him on the North Circular Road. These were not the men who imprisoned women at a house in Finchley Road. These were some different men. Obvious, really, that it all extends beyond the borders of Golders Green.

He looked blankly at the train window, his eyes following the streetlamps of unknown towns and villages passed in the blackness outside.

"What did she do with your stuff?"

"In the basement. And it's so wet down there – damp! Everything will be ruined, like the rest of my life." Exasperated tears began to flow, and two elderly ladies across the aisle looked at her curiously and then with concern. Neil smiled painfully at them, with a reassuring "Ça va, ça va."

Irina continued in a hissing, resentful whisper. "*Why* did this happen to me? Am I being punished? Someone makes evil magic against me? Somewhere there is a little Irina doll, and they stick needles in it?"

His instinct was to comfort her, to give her a sympathetic hand, but he held back. Nothing seemed appropriate. He remembered, and wondered if she had forgotten, that she had already declared *him* to blame for her plight, and men like him. Eventually he said, "Not evil spells. Just evil people. We can deal with them. You'll stay in Simon and Penny's house till we work out what to do."

"Stay there? With only you?" she frowned.

"Not if that's a problem. I'll find somewhere safe for you."

She gave a doubtful nod of consent.

"If they're still looking for you," he murmured to himself, "then they're still looking for Liliana. And if she's wandering around, we don't know where, they might find her." He stopped to think. "Better take the SIM card out of your phone," he said, "throw it away. We'll get you a new one."

Again she nodded, and handed him her phone. "But if Lili needs to call me?"

"No," he answered, "she can call Bernard or Limor. Not us."

"Neil, I am scared."

He nodded pensively. "Me too."

The carriage became subdued. Every conversation gave way to dozing or reading or listening to headphones. Some passengers studied crosswords or flicked through magazines, at last pushing even these aside. The two elderly women now played chess on a small travelling chess set. Neil put in his earphones. Outside the windows there was seemingly nothing at all, except an occasional swarm of cold lights passing low near the horizon.

Irina nudged him. "What are you listening to?"

Neil took out one earpiece, wiped it fastidiously and handed to her. "Have a listen."

She pressed the tiny speaker into her ear.

A tenor saxophone was playing slow and easy, long, mellow notes. Trumpet notes moved as quick and fluid as mercury. Behind them someone was brushing drums gently.

"C'est fabuleux, Neil. Does Limor know about this? Maybe she can use it to cure people. Who is it?"

"Dizzy Gillespie and James Moody."

"I heard of Dizzy Gillespie. I never heard of James Moody. Can you teach me about this?"

"About jazz, you mean? OK," he nodded, "if you teach me some Russian."

"Russian! You want to learn Russian? Why?"

"Because," he replied quietly, "if they're still after you, I'm still after them."

She frowned. "What more can you do? I don't understand."

"I know what I'm going to do."

* * *

Neil turned the long iron key in a huge lock and creaked the door open. Like its neighbours, Simon and Penny's house was built of sandstone in big, rough-cut weather-eaten blocks. Thick, curved, terracotta tiles made a shallow roof. French windows were flanked by wooden shutters, their faded blue paint peeling. A large barn-style door, rotting at the base and fastened by a padlock, closed a ground floor storage area. Stone steps on the outside wall of the house, edged with geraniums in pots, climbed to the front door.

Puilhac lies at the inland edge of Languedoc's coastal plain. South and west of the village, the dry land is criss-crossed with a neat geometry of vineyards, the grape bushes in rows as parallel as the teeth of a comb. The grape vines are not trained on wires, but grow as separate bushes, low to the ground, covering the pale earth with a grid of coloured dots. North and east of the village, limestone ridges and slopes rise up on ancient terraces like a flight of stairs, now all abandoned to the dense vegetation of the garrigue.

The day had started in separate Montpellier hotel rooms. After breakfast, Neil and Irina treated themselves to half an hour in the balmy air, walking along narrow streets and lanes in the Old Quarter, on busier Rue de la Loge and down to the great marble-paved space of Place de la Comédie. For Irina it was a joy, a gentle intrusion of light into her dark preoccupations. Most of the shops were still closed at this hour, but as some unlocked their doors she stepped in to buy toiletries, a notebook and pen, some liquid for hand-washing laundry and, in a bright, friendly patisserie aerated with appetising freshness, she selected little pastries "to eat on the way".

For Neil too, the morning stroll was an enjoyable distraction, though he was never at ease. In his room he had already assembled the pistol again, and wore it now under his shirt, unwilling to trust that he and Irina would be safe even between here and Puilhac. He signed for a hire car at an office by the station and they left the city on a wide, fast highway. Neil offered her the wheel, but Irina said, "I am not ready."

The road climbed among slopes scattered with rock and heath. Then, on a wide curve, the immense view opened, of hills falling away to a sandy plain – covered as far as the horizon with fields of grapevines. Small, perfectly white clouds moved across a sky of flawless blue. In the distance, a slender trace of pale mist followed the line of a river.

Irina said, "I love the shadows of clouds. I would like to paint that."

"Oh, do you paint?" Neil asked, and she said, "Yes, yes, I paint and draw. My pictures are being spoiled, in a wet basement in Paris."

"I'll go and get them for you," he promised, "soon."

As they descended into the plain, in places the roadside vineyards appeared ravaged, grape bushes bare of all fruit, their big green-and-crimson leaves wildly dishevelled and torn. Other fields were undisturbed, gaudy with vivid foliage seeming splashed with red wine, and the spindly branches weighed heavy with bunches of ripe, violet grapes.

In yet others, gangs of labourers worked, bent double or squatting, men and women, young and old. Wearing heavy boots and loose, colourful clothes and oddly assorted hats and cotton scarves, they progressed along the rows of bushes, clipping the bunches and tossing them into buckets. Among the cutters ambled strong youths who upturned the buckets into larger containers, which they hauled to waiting tractors and trailers.

"Oh, I've done that work," exclaimed Irina, "the grape harvest! On grandfather's farm. We used to go to the country and help him. Moldova made the best wine in the Soviet Union."

"Just tell everyone you're British, right?" said Neil. "Never even mention Moldova."

He pushed the door wide and they stepped inside a large room. The floor was of red quarry tiles, unglazed, and the walls, oddly misshapen and uneven, were pure white. On a table stood a bottle of red wine without a label, beside a baguette and a hand-written note. *Bienvenue. Je vais passer plus tard pour voir si tout va bien. Marianne.*[1]

It pleased Neil that there were no soft fabrics anywhere, no curtains and no rug. Every surface was hard and clean. There was a simple oak dresser, upright chairs, a heavy old dial telephone. Bookshelves filled with English and French guidebooks, novels and maps leaned against one wall.

A door standing open led into a kitchen, where a mistreated sideboard now served as an all-purpose storage cupboard. Irina gazed intrigued at a tiny, shallow stone sink, built into the wall, wondering at the toil of the centuries of women who had stood here, perhaps eking out water from a jug. There were no worktops at all, only a battered table on which to prepare food.

A blue metal canister of cooking gas stood beside a curious hybrid cooker with both gas and electric rings. Inside a bulky old fridge she found a wedge of freshly-cut Cantal cheese, a cube of butter, a litre of milk and four large eggs in a paper bag.

While Neil tried to turn on the gas, Irina explored upstairs and found two bedrooms, both with white walls and a floor of patterned tiles. The larger was filled with sunlight; against one wall stood a double bed made up and covered with a white embroidered eiderdown; a tall window looked down onto the

---

[1] Welcome. I will stop by later to see if everything is all right. [French].

alleyway outside. The smaller room had no window; she switched on its light and saw a single bed with no bedding.

Hopefully it would be Neil, rather than herself, who would take the single bed. She really would prefer the pretty, larger front bedroom, and already knew that Neil would grant her that favour, or any other that she cared to ask.

She passed through the small bedroom into a third room. Here, the floor was tiled, yet the walls were bare unplastered stone. Overhead was no ceiling, just the rough underside of roof tiles on timber rafters. A large window-opening was covered with wooden shutters. Daylight shone in from iron-framed skylights. Through one of them, Irina meditatively watched a small white cloud pass across the blue sky.

It was a room, but not for living in; more like an attic. This was space enough to divide into two, even three new bedrooms; and the smaller bedroom with no window should become an upstairs landing. Perhaps that's what Neil meant when he said they must do some work on the house. She stood and pictured how it could be; a corridor here, skylights, sun shining onto white walls, embroideries.

In one corner, a modern shower cubicle had been installed, and a washbasin, and a mirror fixed to the wall. It struck her that this was the only bathroom, and at the moment the only way to it was through the small bedroom. In the past, she supposed, there had been no bathroom at all.

"It's a lovely house," she reported to Neil. "And best of all, no one knows I am here. No one but us."

By midday, though, of course Marianne also knew. She dropped in as promised and discovered that Neil had not arrived on his own. She informed Simon and Penny at once. Simon told Bernard, who naturally mentioned it to Elizabeth. But all these were resolved to help Irina – she called herself Irène again – to disappear into the obscurity of a village in the South.

By evening, Marianne's husband knew too (and was made to swear an oath of secrecy), and then one or two of his closest companions at the Bar des Sportifs in Place de la Libération were let into the confidence.

Marianne knocked on the front door and ventured inside, calling out *Bonjour!* Onto the table, beside the wine and the bread, she casually set down a freshly baked sponge cake encircled with almonds. She also handed Neil a plastic bag bursting with leafy celery from her garden.

Short and dark, more than a little plump, laughingly cheerful, Marianne Salasc had been born and brought up in Puilhac. Her speech rang with the local accent, ends-of-words resounding like a bell. No older than about thirty, mother of a little girl and wife of a builder, she already had the air of a warm-hearted country matron. She knew everyone in the village, it seemed, and everything.

Astonished and impressed by Neil and Irina's French, within ten minutes of her arrival, Marianne had taught them about the brisk *Vent du Nord* bringing crystal-clear weather "for three days or six" – she called it *lou Terrau*, not *le Mistral* – and the *Marine* wind blowing miserable, moist days from the sea, the tempestuous *Grec* sweeping across the Rhône, and the breezy, unpredictable *Tramontane* from the north-west, with its blue skies and fluffy white clouds and occasional brief showers, which was blowing merrily today.

They learned about roadside herbs – thyme, fennel, catmint – that saturate the air with scent, and that the market in Clermont l'Hérault was on Wednesdays, where to get hold of a *mobylette* – a moped – and how to buy a *bidon* of cheap wine direct from the Cave Co-opérative. Marianne even knew a shop in Montpellier that sold pastels, watercolours and paper for Irina.

Neil said, "Marianne, most of all, we want to find work and earn some money."

She clasped her hands together in joy. "Parfait!" she said, because her uncle Pascal urgently needed another cutter and porter to help with the vendanges, the grape harvest. "And you, Monsieur, would make an excellent porter." Her uncle's harvest started about ten days ago, she told them, and would continue for another twelve days. If they wanted to, she said, they could start work tomorrow.

When asked if they had ever harvested grapes before, Irina began with a smiling "Oui", but catching Neil's warning glare, went on to say she thought it must have been on a childhood holiday somewhere.

And after the harvest? Did Marianne know of any jobs? Neil said he had always worked as a driver, but would turn his hand to anything. Again, she had a suggestion: her husband Jean-Claude could ask Olivier Roussel, the cousin of a friend of a friend who ran a transport company in St André, not far away.

Marianne made this observation: in the months to come, it could prove useful to have worked for Pascal Salasc, if they pulled their weight. People would respect and accept them. Because during the vendanges, she said, anyone who can, lends a hand; even the post office will be closed if the clerks are needed in the fields. Irina longed to interject, *Yes, it used to be like that in Moldova, too!* But she kept quiet.

Because helping with the vendanges, explained Marianne, shows you are sérieux – serious and willing to work hard. It's a quick way of becoming part of the community.

What community? Neil asked, puzzled.

Our village, Marianne said – Puilhac.

* * *

"Look, Hilda!" As he drove into the car park of the County Court, Bernard paused and with indignant satisfaction pointed a finger at a row of metal garbage bins assembled behind the court building. "Look, wheels not locked. We can show the judge. Then he'll know it's true."

Hilda looked but made no reply. She felt that nothing of *that* sort would make any difference. The judge would know in his bones, she believed, that ordinary citizens cannot be allowed to win against their borough council.

Bernard believed the opposite. The judge, if he be an Englishman, would surely look favourably on a citizen bringing a plea for justice against the might of the local authority. There is something about it, he thought, of the renowned case of *David vs. Goliath*. Besides, that was the whole spirit of the Small Claims procedure.

They sat in the waiting area among others whose cases were listed on the board, the cheaply dressed public awaiting trials and hearings. Hilda's slight frame in its simple skirt, blouse and cardigan remained as still and quiet as that of a frightened bird. On the noticeboard in front of them was pinned: *Hilda King v. London Borough of Barnet.* "It makes me feel quite sick, seeing it written like that," said Hilda.

Bernard leaned back and read the Daily Telegraph. To distract her, he showed Hilda the front page picture. Just the day before, Barack Obama had been elected president of the United States. The new president was shown embracing his wife, under the stirring headline, *The Dream Comes True.*

"Very moving! Very exciting!" he commented, quite sincerely. "Whatever one may think of his policies. A momentous day," he said. "America's first black president! I do hope he can make a success of it."

Hilda glanced sceptically. "They all come into office like that, don't they? Full of promises and dreams. The shine will wear off soon enough, black or white."

This was so obviously true that Bernard dared not try to deny it. They were interrupted by the approach of a smart, smiling young man. "Hilda King?" he said amiably, and held out his hand to her. "Hi, I'm Felix, Felix Cheshire."

For an instant, Bernard took him to be a court official, and then, a friend of Hilda's, or, more likely, the son of a friend.

"Could I clarify about your hearing?" asked the young man. "Suppose you tell me what it's all about? Something about a council lorry hitting your car, isn't it?"

Then Bernard grasped that this was no friend at all. He stood and held out his hand, "Morning," he said, "I'm here as Mrs King's advisor. I'm sorry, who are you?"

"Oh, hi," replied the smiling man, warmly shaking Bernard's hand. "Representing the council in this case. Lovely to meet you.

"Haven't you read the papers in the case?"

"No, actually – I've been given the brief this very minute. I know nothing about it at all."

"Well, can I suggest you have a quick read-through?" replied Bernard tartly, determined not to give this grinning counsel for the council any advantage. But Hilda, before he could stop her, was already starting to give Mr Cheshire all the details, and Mr Cheshire – to her gratification – listened most sympathetically and attentively.

Mr Cheshire ignored Bernard and spoke only to Hilda, "May I ask, why didn't you just claim on your car insurance, if it was a car accident?

"Car accident! It wasn't a car accident!" she exclaimed. "I'm telling you – it was the council's bin rolling into my car and denting it!"

"Don't say any more," Bernard advised her.

"How do you *know* it was the bin which caused the damage?" asked Mr Cheshire. "You can't be sure, can you?"

"But I saw it!" Hilda replied, becoming annoyed. "With my own eyes! We've been over that a hundred times!"

"No, but not to me," replied Mr Cheshire, gently apologetic. "Is there any evidence? I'm not suggesting anything, but I mean, did anyone else actually see it happen?"

"Hilda, please," warned Bernard, as she gasped with indignation. "Remember he's against you. He shouldn't be speaking to you at all. It's not allowed. He's not *your* barrister. He's acting for the council."

"No, no, not at all," smiled Mr Cheshire, "we're all friends here. Just trying to get a handle on what the case is actually about."

Inside the courtroom, Hilda and Bernard sat together at a long table. Further along it sat Mr Cheshire. The table faced a platform, on which rested a fine oak desk where the judge would be seated in judgement. To one side sat a dark-suited clerk.

From his bag, Mr Cheshire took the brief sent to him by Huxters, untied the red tape, and with a frown, began to scan the pages, turning them rapidly and highlighting important points with a yellow felt pen. Thus Bernard saw that it was true, counsel for the council, hired at a fee greater than the whole of Hilda's claim, had walked into the courtroom without ever once reading the papers in the case.

Bernard's own briefcase was full of the signed affidavits and witness statements he had gathered, the scale diagrams and photographs on which he had worked, the questions and answers between himself and Huxters, that left no doubt at all that the council's bin men routinely leave the wheels of large metal bins unlocked, that these sometimes move and cause damage, and that this particular bin had rolled into Hilda's car and dented it. The council's defence consisted only of denials.

Everyone in the room stood to honour Deputy District Judge Sir Pheenote Barr, who entered from a side door and took his seat rather grandly. Sir Pheenote and Mr Cheshire were devoid of wigs or gowns or anything that might hint at the majesty of the law. However, its majesty was evident enough, and Hilda trembled with anxiety to the point of speechlessness. Bernard was glad he had offered to help her.

The judge, too, noticed Hilda's nervousness, and addressed her with courtesy and kindness. The embarrassing muddle in which Mr Cheshire floundered went in her favour at once.

Bernard presented his various sworn statements from witnesses and from workers at the Blenheim Road offices. He cross-examined the council's rubbish collectors; the three men appeared in turn, each one in clean, casual clothes and with a dignified, unassuming bearing. They confessed with perfect frankness that their supervisor had dictated identical statements to them, and that in truth they could not remember what they had written nor the date in question.

Bernard questioned the men's supervisor, and it was freely established that neither the supervisor nor anyone else ever checked whether the rubbish collectors' work was of good standard, or even if it had been done at all.

Thus the whole scene, of a large metal container more heavily laden that usual, rolling down a forecourt and crashing into Hilda's car, came so vividly to life that Bernard thought the judge must almost hear the bang.

And so it was. In giving his judgement, Deputy District Judge Sir Pheenote Barr declared he had no doubt whatsoever that the council's bin had rolled into Mrs King's car and damaged it, he didn't believe for one moment that the bins were always locked, and furthermore he found the council's treatment of Mrs King utterly deplorable.

However, he was minded to find against her. He could not be convinced, he said, that some third party, some individual unconnected with either the council or the Blenheim Road offices, possibly a visitor, or a mischievous passer-by, might not have unlocked the wheels of the bin, or given it a shove, intentionally or unintentionally.

Useless at this stage to explain why this would have been impossible, too late for any reply at all, as now the judgement was already being spoken: "I order that the claim be dismissed."

Bernard stood aghast, more disappointed than he had been by any courtroom disaster for one of his ordinary clients.

"Does it mean I lost?" asked Hilda.

Bernard pulled an agonised face. "I'm afraid so," he said.

"I'm not surprised," she said wryly. "I said all along."

"Thank you, sir," said Felix Cheshire, and Bernard wondered if perhaps gentle Sir Pheenote Barr had felt a certain tender wish to assist this very junior member of the very junior bar to make a good start in life by letting him win this trifling case.

"However, I would like to add," said the judge, speaking to Bernard and to Hilda, "though it is not my place to advise you, and I may not do so, and I am not doing so, I say only this: if the council had treated *me* as they have treated *you*, ignoring your letters and phone calls and eventually creating a situation where one had little alternative but to issue legal proceedings, the cost of which would fall upon the public purse, I would certainly bring a complaint of maladministration to the Local Government Ombudsman."

"Thank you, sir," said Bernard.

Bernard did not wish to make a complaint to the Ombudsman. The Ombudsman could advise and admonish, but had no statutory powers over local councils. Bernard wished only to take Hilda back to Blenheim Road, give her the money to repair her car (he could tell her that KOBRA members had already had a whip-round), and sit down quietly somewhere to nurse his wounds.

This he did, driving her home with little talk on the way, other than to say, "Ah, well! We had to try." Of course, he must put a brave face on things and carry on with life. He had now to go to work and do what good he could with the rest of the day.

What with one thing and another, armed criminals in his own neighbourhood, and even forced prostitution, no less; and the police not giving a tuppenny damn about anything, not to mention letting selfish bastards park on the pavement; litter everywhere, idleness, dishonesty and incompetence all around; crooks being allowed to pay for retrospective planning permission; and rotten, wicked, thieving MPs at the helm of it all; and the shame that weighed on him for himself stepping into the putrid mire of this quotidian lawlessness; and now this – this humiliation of a poor innocent like Hilda; it was all too much for him.

Bernard walked slowly to Golders Green station in the deepest despondency. He turned on his phone to scroll through the morning's texts, voicemails and missed calls.

There he found something even worse. As soon as he saw a message from the police, he guessed it would be about Liliana.

* * *

Neil drove a 7.5-tonne refrigerated truck. Inside, it smelt of cheese and sour milk. Each morning, his alarm clock went off at ten minutes to seven. He cycled five kilometers on the straight, narrow road from Puilhac to Roussel's depot in St André, moving fast and silently. To either side, November's plane trees shed sheets of pale bark and huge yellow leaves, crisp and dry.

Three days a week, he did the 'cheese round'. With the van's windows open to clear the air, it took him along lanes winding between vineyards, and through a fragrant, hilly wilderness at the edge of the plain.

On those days he delivered not just whole cheeses – Gruyère, St Paulin, Cantal, Roquefort – but hams, big rounds of butter and crates of fresh milk in plastic bottles, to ancient villages, dried by sun and wind, forgotten in the garrigue. The houses were made all of unfaced stone. Some, uncared for and now abandoned, were collapsing, gradually becoming just piles of rock in a rocky landscape.

When he turned off the engine, the silence was complete. Even a child playing somewhere, or a dog's bark of surprise, or the murmurs of two old men standing against a stone wall, would intensify the stillness of the air.

His own village, Puilhac, was on the cheese round too. Everyone there knew him. He had to drive down an alley barely wider than the van. There was a bend at the narrowest point, which happened to be next to the patisserie. If he pushed in the wing mirrors to make more room, he could not see how close he was to the walls. A number of customers would be trapped in the patisserie doorway waiting for him to get by. He appeared calm as he crept past them, but was concentrating intently lest he should disgrace himself by scraping the wall or breaking a wing mirror. It would have been all over the village by the time he came home from work.

During the rest of the week he was sent further afield, to towns and cities in every part of Languedoc. On those days he had to start at five in the morning. By the time dawn broke he would be in the van, on the road somewhere, and at a roadside bar would trade two litres of his *patron*'s fresh milk for a croissant and a large café crème.

It was at the end of a cheese round that Neil heard the news about Liliana. He cycled back to Puilhac after work and stopped as usual in Place de la Libération at the Bar des Sportifs. He often paused there for a drink or a coffee with friends and neighbours, men of the village. Just like most men Neil had known, they talked too much about sport and television. These, though, accepted without demur that he was more interested in jazz and film, and after all, at least he shared their interest in the finer points of lunch and dinner.

Whether at indoor tables or under the trees, much fiery discussion centred on the forthcoming pétanque championship, the election of a black man as president of the United States (announced on the news that very day), and the many building applications by the mayor's cronies, which must be vigorously challenged by the leader of the opposition and *his* cronies. For Neil had discovered that Puilhac was in the pocket of its mayor, who viewed the village as one of his business interests and had nearly absolute power over local development. Bernard, he thought, would say that Puilhac is not as different from Golders Green as one might think; and nor, perhaps, is anywhere.

Often Irina joined Neil at the Bar des Sportifs for a glass of *panaché* during the apéritif hour while he sipped his cold *pression* or his *pastis*. For Neil and Irina – or rather, Irène – were known in Puilhac as a fond couple. She was his *femme*, and he her *mari*, whether married or not. In order to remain inconspicuous and make the village their home, it was better like that.

Indeed, since their first night in the village, it really was so. Neither had intended it. Marianne, of course, had assumed the two of them lived as men and women normally do. It seemed unwise to disabuse her; less likely to invite comment. Neil and Irina did not want comment.

They passed a strange, tense evening of planning together, eating together, walking together around the village, then sitting quietly together in the front room. From Neil's point of view, the situation was as delicate as glass, as relaxing as the dentist's chair.

When it came time for bed, on that first night in the house, without discussion Neil avoided going upstairs at the same time as Irina. He listened as her footsteps passed through the little room to the makeshift bathroom, then returned. He heard her bedroom door close.

A full ten minutes later, he made his way up to the smaller

room. He could see a light behind her closed door. He imagined her under the covers, and at once forced the enticing picture out of his mind. She must be reading, or pondering her captivity, or missing her flat in Paris, or thinking about this strange day.

Stepping into his own room, gratefully Neil saw that someone – Irina, obviously – had made up the bed for him. His bag was neatly placed on a chair. He checked that the pistol and holster and the cartridges were still there, where he had put them. In a single movement he pulled his shirt over his head without unbuttoning it and dropped it onto the chair. He sat on the side of the bed and pulled off his shoes. He stood and undid the top button of his jeans.

Through the wall he now heard her moving about. There was a knock and Irina put her head round the door. "Oh! So sorry! May I use the bathroom again?"

She was still fully dressed, but had loosened her hair and untucked the pale silk shirt from her jeans. This slight déshabille made her intensely alluring. In one hand she held her little bag of toiletries.

"Go ahead. I thought you were already in bed."

"No, I was writing in my notebook. I'd like to have a shower now. I'll be quick. If it will be a nuisance, I can leave it 'til tomorrow."

"No, it's OK. There won't be time in the morning," he replied, and she walked through his room to the other door, locking it behind her.

She must be undressing. He heard her bare feet on the tiles, some Romanian words muttered to herself, the sound of the shower cubicle closing. The water-heater made a low roar. He imagined her arms and shoulders, her wet legs. Reveries of the woman standing there, her nakedness, the water running over her back, grew quickly into gaudier visions and more lustful hallucinations.

It might have been best, he thought, if he had gone back downstairs. Now was too late; these images would not leave him. When there came an urge to peek at her if he could, he suddenly resolved that he must not remain in the house with her at all. This arrangement with the rooms, the bathroom, would not work.

When Irina emerged from the shower, modestly encased in a damp towel, he announced brusquely that he would sleep in the rented car. Her washed hair, dripping, straggled over her shoulders. The jeans and silk shirt and underwear were held discreetly under one arm.

"No, why?" she exclaimed, incredulous. The note of bitterness in his voice puzzled her. Had she annoyed him somehow? "You won't sleep well. We have hard work tomorrow."

He shook his head. He could not discuss the reason. The soft towelling reached to the mid-point of her thighs. The shape beneath was concealed, yet revealed, by the fabric tightly wrapped and tucked into place.

"You are angry." She reached out a conciliatory hand towards his, but he refused it. "What have I done?"

"Not angry. Not at all," he replied. The blue eyes glared at her.

She was reminded of that argument, in the first hour at his flat, after he had brought her away from the nightmare house. His eyes had been so exactly like this.

After all that had happened, his impulsive decision to rescue her, and to bring her here, and everything he had done to help her and Liliana, she felt keenly that he should not be repaid with some unkindness of hers.

"Is it the bed?" she asked. "I will have the small bed, you can have the bigger one!"

The suggestion was ridiculous to him.

She pleaded, "Neil, tell me what is wrong."

"I'm fine."

"No," she told him, "you will not sleep in the car. You will not." She tossed her bundle of clothes onto the floor and scrutinised him as if exasperated, or mystified, or trying to understand. But as she studied his face, she began to accept a difficult idea. She sensed what the problem was.

Besides, she was afraid of being alone in the house at night.

"Please, Neil, will you stay if we –" she paused before uttering the words, "share the big bed?"

It seemed to Irina that somehow his mask became transparent. She glimpsed a whole mosaic beneath.

"No," he shook his head, "I'm not asking for that. I won't ever ask you for that."

She reached up and touched his face for a moment. He did not respond.

"It's all right," she said quietly.

"Irina, you don't need to. It would change everything," he warned.

"I know you are not asking, but Neil, I want to say, if we do –" now her hand moved to his, and this time, he took it. Just to hold hands breached all the unspoken rules they had set themselves.

"What?" he said quietly.

"If we do," she repeated softly, "then, that is, do you mind – we must take each step – very slowly?"

"That's right."

"We must be sure the ground is safe, for both of us. Otherwise, no: we will go back."

"Step by step," he agreed.

She gave him her other hand. "Like learning a dance."

She liked the cautious smile, that she had not seen before.

On this day, though, when Irina came to meet him at the bar, it was not for her glass of *panaché*. She walked fast, and strangely, with fists held close to her body. As Neil sat with his *pastis*, one of his companions said "Eh, Neil, ta femme arrive." Hey, Neil, your wife is coming; and, he added, she looks upset about something.

It was true. Neil left the table and moved quickly towards her. She was distraught.

"Very bad news." Without even a greeting, she said the words.

"Is it the men? Are they here?" he asked quietly.

"No," she reassured him.

"The police?" he asked.

"No, no," she shook her head. "Phone message from Bernard."

As if in a spasm of agony Irina now gripped Neil's shoulders. Without warning, she began to cry, to sob, in Place de la

Libération, in front of the Bar des Sportifs. Every face turned towards them as Neil wrapped his arms around her.

She held on to him desperately, leaned her head forward against his chest, banged her head against his chest in fury.

"Because of all those bastards, *all* of you."

"Who, Irina, who? What's happened? Tell me!"

"Lili is dead."

* * *

In a sitting room in Golders Green, Penny Silver and Lisa Shaw discuss the forthcoming Annual General Meeting of the Kenilworth, Osborne and Blenheim Roads Residents' Association. Lisa reclines rather seductively on the sofa, her legs tucked beneath a brightly tie-dyed long skirt. Penny, in smart grey suit, sheer nylon and elegant patent-leather, sits more primly in the armchair on the other side of the room.

The two women are rather dismayed. Bernard has intimated to the KOBRA committee that at the AGM he will stand down as chairman. He has had enough, he said. He urged the committee to think about a replacement.

Their concern is that no one else can possibly do the task quite so well. Is anyone on the present committee capable of taking on the chairman's role? Would someone new like to try it? Penny shakes her head doubtfully. Like other local committees throughout the land, KOBRA thirsts always for 'new blood'.

"I think we can persuade him to change his mind," says Lisa. "I've been calling his number all day, but he's not at work, and not at home, and didn't answer my message."

"He's at a funeral."

"Oh! Whose?"

"No one close. I think it's a friend of that chap Neil. D'you remember him? 2 Blenheim Road."

"Oh, yes. He didn't stay long, did he? What became of him?"

Penny, of course, never tells anyone – not even her friend Lisa – that Neil is staying in her very own house in France. She says only, "He's gone abroad somewhere," and assures herself that the remark is no lie.

"No wonder he left Blenhein Road," says Lisa, "after what happened at his flat! László shooting people!" She laughs throatily at the thought. "I expect he hopped straight on his bike and rode at top speed into the sunset. Good-looking chap, wasn't he? Fit."

Penny smiles. "Someone should have told him, Golders Green isn't usually like that."

* * *

When the police were called one November night to deal with a dead female – white, early twenties – lying in a shop doorway, they had the body delivered to the local mortuary and informed the coroner's office. It might have been a matter of simple routine for the coroner to establish whether she had been the victim of a crime, of some other misadventure or was a poor homeless wretch who had died of natural causes. This case turned out to be a little more complicated. Although the cause of death appeared to be starvation and exposure, there were signs of a violent struggle and sexual assault, and of drug-taking. On the upper thigh were recent parallel slashes, scored into the flesh with a razor or sharp knife, that appeared to be self-inflicted.

The coroner also needed to establish her true identity and contact her next of kin. That proved impossible.

In the woman's pocket was a Romanian ID card, but the Romanian Embassy had no record of anyone of that name living in the United Kingdom. An official suggested the woman might have been using an identity stolen from someone already dead, someone in Romania. She was not registered with a British doctor, nor with social services, had no criminal record and was not on the DNA database.

She had a phone, though, and about four pounds in cash. The phone had rarely been used, but the battery was flat. It had received text messages from only one number, nearly a month ago. In Contacts were listed just two other numbers. Both had been called only a couple of times; that too, was weeks ago.

Naturally, the police called all three numbers. One turned out to be no longer in service. The second was answered by a doctor at a women's clinic, but on realising she was talking to the police she said at once that she had never heard the name before. They phoned the third number and left a voicemail.

Bernard called back as he walked gloomily to Golders Green station after Hilda's unsuccessful court hearing.

"What was the name again?" he asked.

The officer sounded the syllables with difficulty. "Looks like Doina Grigorescu. Not sure if I'm saying it quite right. Something like that."

"Mm, well. Might be someone who came to my office for help," said Bernard cautiously. "Doesn't ring a bell. I get a lot of, you know – illegal immigrants knocking on the door. Can't usually do anything for them. You say she might have been Romanian. You've asked the Romanian community here in London?"

"Yeah, we tried that. Couldn't help. Well, if nothing turns up, it's a Person Unknown, basically."

"Mm – yuh. Who organises the funeral in a case like this?" asked Bernard.

"Oh, the council deal with it," the officer explained. "Public health burial, sir, you know, multiple grave. Taxpayer picks up the bill."

Bernard tutted. "How awful! How very sad! If it *was* someone I turned away, you know, I'd like to make a small contribution," he said, "a donation. To make sure she has the right kind of funeral, Eastern Orthodox or whatever. There's a church near my office that does services in Romanian. Maybe they could see to it."

The officer tried gently to discourage him. "She's just one of hundreds, sir. Literally hundreds. And you can't tell by looking what religion they are. As she's got false identification papers, we don't even know this young lady is Romanian. She might not be Orthodox. She might be Catholic. Could be a Moslem. She might even be Jewish or something like that. No way of knowing. She might just as well have a C. of E. funeral. Makes no odds now, does it?"

* * *

You'd never know what went on there. Neil travelled straight from the airport to Golders Green Crematorium. As his taxi passed the corner of Finchley Road and Heath Avenue, he turned to look. The house had been repaired and repainted. The hedge had been cut back and the scorched shutters removed from the windows. There was a proper garden gate. He guessed it was lived-in now, just an ordinary house on an ordinary London road.

There were twenty minutes to wait before Liliana's funeral. He looked inside a small waiting room, but chose instead to stand in the cold, breezy driveway. Soon Bernard arrived, and the two men shook hands awkwardly. Bernard remarked that Neil had become quite tanned. Neil nodded.

Bernard asked about the new job and about work on the house, but Neil's careless "Yeah, that's all fine," seemed to answer for both.

"Mm, Neil, you still in touch with Limor?"

"All the time." Had she been invited to the funeral? She didn't want to come, Neil told him.

It seemed to Bernard that, since going to France, Neil had become even more taciturn. Somehow he looked taller and stronger, too.

"What happened about having an Orthodox funeral?"

Neil said the Orthodox priest had not returned his call, and an email had bounced back.

Bernard mentioned that he didn't like cremation. Neil insisted that cremation was cheaper, and anyway, if Liliana had a proper grave, there would be no one to tend it. "There's nothing sadder than that," he said.

And yet somehow, sadder still for Bernard was that the body of a human being should be rendered into smoke and ash, into mere substances. Something of the girl would rise from the chimney and be blown across north London.

"D'you know, a lot of famous people had their funerals at this place?" ventured Bernard after a pause. Neil made no reply, so he elaborated, "Yup, writers and, you know, actors, entertainers. And politicians. And some great musicians. Tubby Hayes, he was cremated here. And Tony Crombie, Phil Seamen, Ray Ellington, Ronnie Scott, I can't think who else. Dozens of them."

This awakened Neil's interest and he asked tersely if the ashes had been scattered there, if there were plaques or memorials.

"Yes, I think there are," said Bernard, and together they walked through a brick archway into the tranquil Garden of Remembrance. On a long arcaded walkway at the back of the crematorium, the brickwork was densely covered with small plaques, and in flowerbeds and rose gardens, nameplates showed that each bush and tree had been planted in honour of a dear friend or lost relative. On the paving, floral displays large and small were laid out from recent funerals, the flowers sometimes spelling out names, or Mum or Dad or Grandma or Darling. Others had but a single flower, or none at all.

An icy wind blew through the archways from the car park. They stared at the plaques and read silently. In a small enclosed yard were still more. "Look," said Bernard, as he pointed out memorials to Marc Bolan, Larry Adler, Bernie Winters, Bud Flanagan, "and there's Ronnie Scott! 'OBE, jazz musician, raconteur and wit'," he read aloud.

It was time to go back. Outside the chapel, they were joined by an Anglican priest, draped in his black cassock, who quietly asked if either of them were related to the deceased. He asked what they knew of her, and they had to reply – nothing. "We're only neighbours." He invited them to go inside and wait for him there.

As soon as the door swung shut, all the sounds of the world were hushed. Within were bare brick walls and a few wooden pews either side of an aisle. Near the front, Liliana's coffin rested on a simple stand. Neil approached it with an anguished expression. He groaned audibly. It seemed to Bernard that Neil could not have been more upset had he in fact been a relative.

This story is about three people: Neil Chapman, Bernard Kassin and Liliana Petreanu. They are together now for the first time.

If it had been an Eastern Orthodox funeral, Bernard pointed out, the coffin would be open. "We'd be able to see her face."

"You want to know what she looks like?" From his pocket, Neil carefullly unfolded a picture of Liliana. It was cut from the tube station *Missing Person* poster.

"You can tell she was beautiful once," Bernard said awkwardly.

"I only wish..." Neil began, then stopped. He said instead, "She was terribly thin by this time. She looks awfully sad, doesn't she? That's not really a fair picture. She was prettier than that. She was good-looking." He tutted. "And if she hadn't been, maybe she'd still..."

He rested the photo on the coffin and left it there. To the young woman herself, nailed inside the wooden box, he whispered softly, and Bernard turned away, embarrassed to overhear the words. "I'm sorry, I'm sorry Liliana, I'm so sorry. I wanted to help, to set you free. This is the result. I'm sorry, I'm sorry for it all. But I can still do something for you, I promise."

Neil was painfully conscious that her ears heard nothing, and he spoke only to himself.

During the brief service, Bernard opened the prayer book respectfully but did not read from the alien text. Neil held only Liliana's note in his hand, the scrawl in Romanian on a torn scrap. The minister addressed the whole church and its congregation of two. He told them that although none present knew this young woman, there were people on this earth who had known her and loved her. She had once had friends and colleagues and, somewhere, a family, a loving mother and father, and neighbours. And of course, she was known best of all to a compassionate God, who knew the sad secret of what had brought her here today, and who was still watching over her, and to whose tender love she was now returning.

The Holocaust came horribly into Bernard's mind as the coffin rattled over the rollers towards the open hatch. The human body is a poor vessel for the greatness of the human mind, he thought. The coffin disappeared into the hidden furnace.

The hatch clicked back into place and it was all over.

By this miserable, unwarranted, lonely, youthful death Bernard found himself moved nearly to tears. He noticed that Neil, too, bowed his head in abject misery.

"Would you like to come for a walk?" Bernard proposed afterwards. They had shaken the minister's hand and stepped into the cold air.

Exchanging few words, Bernard and Neil strolled slowly on a footpath through the Heath Extension, the younger man tall, upright and vigorous, the older short and overweight.

"Did you get to know her a bit, in the end?" Bernard asked. "Were you fond of her?"

Neil shook his head. "I didn't know her at all. Altogether I spent a couple of hours with her. She didn't speak much English; we didn't ever talk."

"So what is it you feel, then?"

"Nothing," replied Neil. "I feel nothing." Thin clouds blew fast overhead. The daylight was subdued and grey, the wind biting. At last he said, "I don't know what I feel."

Neil remained pensive. He was bitter about Liliana's fate. Again and again he wondered if her death was any responsibility of his.

Bernard stared blankly at the path ahead. It troubled him, unknown victim, unknown crime. Almost a murder, he thought. The whole book of crimes. He half-heard the endless charge sheet being read out, half-saw a ghostly dock crowded with the accused, among them ordinary men and women, MPs, police, neighbours.

The two men made their way towards Golders Hill Park. At the ice cream counter, the shutter was closed, and no one sat at the café terrace. They paced across the grass and chose a bench with a view across rooftops to Hendon in the distance. Moist, wintry gusts blew sharply. An occasional walker in waterproofs passed with a dog tugging at a leash. To one side of them rose the deserted bandstand where, in summer, amateur musicians had played to sunbathing crowds. In the other direction, neatly clipped lawn curved down pleasantly towards the park's flower garden, now almost bare, its earthy beds carefully dug and weeded in preparation for spring planting.

"And what do *you* feel?" Neil thought to ask.

The reply was hesitant. Bernard frowned. "What upsets me *most* about it," he said, "is the ones you didn't rescue. Where are they? What happened to them?"

Neil nodded. "And it's not just them."

"Oh, this country! It was good, once." Bernard shook his head. "And our civilised little neighbourhood. Ah, yes, it's all over now for England. The battle is lost. There's no way back. Our efforts have come to nothing. Everything will go down the pan. It can't be saved."

"Hey," Neil cajoled him gently, "come on, Bernard! Last time we were here, you said how beautiful everything was. Well, take a look around! It's still beautiful." This was true: the autumn colours had reached their crescendo, and the grass was speckled with fallen leaves scattering in the wind.

"No, I mean it," Bernard declared in despair. "We're in the last days. All that we have built, of justice, of learning, of government, everything good will be destroyed. Greed and ignorance are triumphant. Politicians and officials clamouring for swill from the trough. The whole shebang is beyond repair. Rottenness has penetrated the heart of things."

Neil patted his companion's arm sympathetically as he dismissed such garish terrors. "It must be the funeral that's upset you. Think about the good stuff that's happening. Women's equality! Human rights! America's first black president! That's progress, isn't it?"

"No, no, no," Bernard shook his head vigorously. "That's a flash in the pan. Barbarians are on the rise around the globe," he said bluntly. "Those who treat women as chattels. Slavery is on the up and up. Stoning people is all the rage. Beheading. Cutting off hands. Piracy. Savagery. Brutality. New forms of tyranny. And an inhuman piety that goes with it."

Neil hardly knew how to calm his friend. "Don't talk like that, Bernard," he urged him. "You're not saying things were better in the past? Tell me a century you'd rather have lived in. You don't think everybody was honest and kind, once upon a time?"

"Mm – no," Bernard ruefully agreed, "I'm not saying that."

"And you think people didn't used to do vile things, in the past?"

Bernard shrugged. "Obviously that's *not* what I mean."

"And haven't there *always* been good men, a few decent nutcases – like you – who tried to do the right thing? A few daft idiots? And isn't it really them who keep the world in orbit and life worth living?"

Bernard almost smiled, "Well, *that* isn't me!"

"Yes it is!" declared Neil, "So, pull yourself together! We need you. All that 'don't stand idly by' and 'do your bit' – you've been my inspiration!"

They watched as scores of dry leaves flew suddenly from the grass, spiralling and circling like wild dancers in the swirling air.

"Have I?" said Bernard.

"Yes, you bloody well have."

* * *

Pascal Salasc, bending over one leafless grape bush, feels the soothing balm of the sun as soon as it emerges from behind the dark blue shadow of the hills. Straight away the air is filled with brilliance and warmth. He takes note that although the wind is coming from the north, it is not especially strong nor cool. Indeed there is something of summer in the wind this morning.

He has come out to examine the flower clusters appearing among the new buds on the cropped wood of his vines. The quality of next autumn's vintage depends a good deal on these spring flowers. He stands and unzips his heavy jacket, eases a stiff back and breathes deeply. For a moment he gazes idly as the sunlight spreads rapidly across his neighbours' fields and illuminates all the pale earth of the plain.

Standing among the landscape of vines are the familiar landmarks of his little land, the high spire of Notre-Dame-de-la-Garrigue, at Lagamas, and the green glazed tiles of the roofs at St Jean-de-Fos, and the serpentine line of trees following the shallow valley of the Hérault.

Small in the distance, a white van can be seen on the road, moving towards the Pont du Diable. Pascal recognises it at once as the van of the Englishman. Where has he been, so early in the day? Coming back, perhaps, from one of his working trips to Paris or Eastern Europe. He's a strange one, this Englishman; there's something about him, as if he has a secret. Well, maybe he does have a secret, and maybe it's no one's concern. He and his wife are decent enough, work hard and have made Puilhac their home – not a 'second home'. Marianne told him they're looking for a place of their own, and in just a few months the fellow has even started his own little transport business. Good luck to him! The wife is a wonderful artist. They speak good French and enjoy French food, and helped him during the vendanges. What else is there? No one objects to them, even though they are foreigners.

The white van descends into the valley and disappears from view, then reappears as it climbs again on the Puilhac road. Close enough now to read the words on the side, *Est-Ouest Express,* Pascal jerks his head in laconic greeting to the driver and raises a friendly hand.

Neil gives a little toot and an answering wave. Beside the road, almond trees are pink with new blossom. The dry morning air is already exquisite, and a cool, silky breeze sweeps through the open window. John Coltrane's *Ascension* is playing loud, an insane liberty of sound and emotion. The majestic cacophony reminds him of voices at a huge party, each and every note trying to be heard.

Soon he will arrive at the village and park in the Place. The music will stop abruptly and there will be silence. He'll walk slowly along Puilhac's lanes, between stone houses, beneath balconies hung with laundry. Irina will come to meet him. "How was it?" she will ask. He'll say it's all going according to plan, and she will ask nothing more.

Someone who has betrayed their own sister will betray anyone, until they too are betrayed. Liliana's brother Sergiu, he discovered, would do anything at all for money. Now those he had betrayed had taken their revenge on him.

* * *

Bernard pulled the chairs into tidy rows and turned on the heating. He hated this bleak, modern hall where KOBRA held its public meetings. It had been his routine always to arrive half-an-hour early, to make sure everything was ready.

He moved along the rows of chairs, putting a copy of the agenda and treasurer's report on each one. In ones and two, early arrivals drifted into the hall, respectable, mostly elderly couples pleased to see one another; greeting him, too, with friendly words and smiles. There's nothing so charmless, thought Bernard, as members of the British public in their shabby winter jackets. Still, that's people for you. He had to concede that it was too cold in this hall to take off one's coat. At the same time, it was an uplifting sight, and an inspiration, that people came out on such an evening to discuss local issues. Someone helped him drag a table into place, to make a kind of podium for the committee members and chairman.

The committee – and Elizabeth – had persuaded him to stand again as chair. Of course, he was unopposed. That would be the day, when someone else took on this task! Still, he didn't blame people. There was no reward for the job, just harassment and frustration and aggravation, and the stress of speaking at meetings. He hoped it wasn't an immodest thought, but most of them just could not do it. Thank goodness *somebody* could.

Despite a heavy heart, Bernard opened KOBRA's Annual General Meeting with smiles, welcomes and apologies and jocular remarks, followed by a brief summary of the year. He was able to tell the members that the little neighbourhood of

Blenheim, Osborne and Kenilworth Roads, unnoticed amidst the great sea of similar roads, all knitted as one into other London neighbourhoods, had passed a year just like other years.

Residents had struggled to preserve decent, quiet family life in their street, against the destructive tide of crime, commerce and council planners. There had been successes: all the streetlights were now working properly. There had been failures: the Planning Inspectorate had given retrospective permission for the illegal development at 18 Osborne Road. There were continuing problems from the squalid offices in Blenheim Road.

Then, of course, Bernard must also mention the dramatic events of last October. "I think we all know Mr Viktor. But it seems there were some rather vicious burglars who did *not* know him. Well, they know now." Laughter and spontaneous applause, and even cheers, showed what residents thought of László's actions. There was an awful, fearful, admiration for this amiable hero who was known to have done desperate things, once, in some foreign revolution. It was generally held that László Viktor had now done what householders throughout England would like to do, if they only had the courage, and a gun – shoot a burglar.

Three rows from the front, László himself sat beside his wife. She prodded him and urged him to stand. He did so reluctantly, as faces turned with big smiles, sitting again as quickly as he could.

* * *

Neil races ahead along a thread of lane. To either side, low, sandy vines give way to dunes and scattered grasses, and tall reeds moving in the dry air.

He stops to wait for her. A few small birds chatter quietly against the great silence of the land. At last Irina appears, pedalling without haste.

They push their bikes to a low crest, where the whole horizon of the glittering Mediterranean comes into view, a dark blue line with blue above, blue below. A broad band of yellow extends from their wheels to the water's edge.

Neil and Irina have not yet seen the summer crowds that will gather here, but for now the sunlit beach is empty, and the water sharply cold. Unclothed, they abandon themselves to it, swimming hard or idly, or floating freely in the movement of the sea.

Briskly drying and dressing on the shore, Neil takes Irina in his arms. He savours the moment, as joyous and carefree as any he has ever lived.

Far away, a church bell sends out its note faintly, the sound rising and falling in the breeze.

"Reminds me of my childhood," she says.

They listen.

"The bell?" he suggests.

"The sense of peace."

In her eyes he sees some disturbing thought passing. These strange, brief moments, he notices, come less often now. Neil and Irina do not discuss each other's secret. She knows that he pictures a young woman dying in a shop doorway. She knows that he feels compelled to act against a wrong in which he himself played a part. She knows that in the end he expects to make little difference to it.

And he knows her secret burden, of sounds and images hard to bear, a locked cage inside a van, men's voices, men's furies and men's desires, and her own smouldering anger, and a scar of shame.

"Happy?" he asks gently.

"Happy."

The distant chime comes to an end, or can no longer be heard; there is only the north wind, and the endless, soothing breath of the waves.

– the end –

Afterword – the true story

This story is fiction, but it is based on many true stories.
The experiences of "Liliana Petreanu" are drawn from
those of real women held captive for sex in London.

The online Afterword gives facts and arguments from the real
world about trafficking, prostitution and the law as they affect
the imaginary people and events in this book.

www.andrewsanger.com/the-slave/afterword

9069864R00192

Printed in Great Britain
by Amazon.co.uk, Ltd.,
Marston Gate.